Uprooting the Kingdom

the

— *A Novel* —

THOMAS WINN

WESTBOW
PRESS®
A DIVISION OF THOMAS NELSON
& ZONDERVAN

The Scripture quotations contained herein are from the New Revised Standard
Version Bible, copyright © 1989, Division of Christian Education of the National
Council of Churches of Christ in the U.S.A. Used by permission.
All rights reserved.

Images: The cover photograph was taken by Perry Zipoy,
and is being used with his gracious permission.
The map was created using Adobe Illustrator software by Perry Zipoy
from a more primitive drawing by the author. Used with permission.
The author photograph was taken by DeAnne Winn,
and is being used with her kind permission.

WestBow Press books may be ordered through booksellers or by contacting:

WestBow Press
A Division of Thomas Nelson & Zondervan
1663 Liberty Drive
Bloomington, IN 47403
www.westbowpress.com
1 (866) 928-1240

Because of the dynamic nature of the Internet, any web addresses or
links contained in this book may have changed since publication and
may no longer be valid. The views expressed in this work are solely those
of the author and do not necessarily reflect the views of the publisher,
and the publisher hereby disclaims any responsibility for them.

ISBN: 978-1-5127-1065-6 (sc)
ISBN: 978-1-5127-1064-9 (hc)
ISBN: 978-1-5127-1063-2 (e)

Library of Congress Control Number: 2015914131

Print information available on the last page.

WestBow Press rev. date: 09/08/2015

For my lovely wife, DeAnne,
who encouraged me to write this book

Selected Cities in the Province of Judaea in the First Century

Sidon
Damascus
Tyre
Caesarea Philippi
Jamnith
Sepph Biri
Acco
Kfar Nahum
Bethsaida
Magdala
Tiberias
Tzipori
Hammat
Natzerat
Caesarea Maritima
Beit Shean
Samaria
Gerasa
Shechem
Antipatris
Joppa
Gophna
Philadelphia
Ephraim
Lydda
Yeriko
Jamnia
Yerushalayim
Bethabara
Emmaus
Qumran
Bet Lehem
Machaerus
Hebron
Gaza
Beer Sheba

0   20 mi.
0   20 km.

PROLOGUE

The beginning of this story takes place during the fifteenth year of the reign of Tiberius Caesar, in the northern part of the land that is sacred to the Jewish people. Later generations would more readily identify this period as 28 CE. To the dismay of most Jews, Judaea has been controlled by Roman occupation forces for the past ninety-one years. Roman historians proudly boast that it already has been 692 glorious years since the city of Rome was founded by Romulus, but most of the people of Judaea would be happy if the Romans returned to their great city and gave this occupied land back to its own people.

CHAPTER 1

Eliezer awakens to a pleasant summer morning, near the Hill of Moreh and the town of Nain. The sky above the mountains to the east is shining with a golden glow that heralds the sun's rising. The air smells like rich soil, dry straw, and of faraway wildflowers. He says a quick prayer of thanks for this new day, for the health and safety of his family, and for himself. He plans to recite the complete morning benedictions a little bit later. But right now, he has to take care of some other responsibilities first.

He knows that he still is about fifteen miles from Beit Shean, that is the last stop of his seasonal trading journey through southern Galilee, but he also is aware that he still is thirty-five miles from his home and his family in Hammat.

He performs a quick check of his goods and his two donkeys, Amit and Marit, and verifies that everything is as it is supposed to be. Next he relieves himself by emptying his bladder of its nighttime accumulation before washing his hands. Then he finishes his morning prayer routine, hastily eats a couple of pieces of bread, and drinks a few sips of water. He thinks, *If I succeed in finishing my business at Beit Shean today, and if I can get started early tomorrow, I should make it to my home by midafternoon tomorrow . . . just in time for Shabbat.*

Eliezer still has a few luscious melons, as well as some cucumbers, onions, and beans left to sell. He had grown this produce himself in the terraced garden that is adjacent to his hillside home in Hammat. He also is looking forward to buying some wheat, and some fine linen fabrics that Beit Shean is well-known for producing.

Eliezer is just under forty years of age. Besides being a farmer and a traveling merchant, he is a widower, and the father of a twenty-year-old daughter named Miriam, and an eleven-year old son named Yaaqov. He is a devout member of the Pharisees. Eliezer appreciates the Pharisees' progressive, practical approach toward keeping the Jewish law.

The Pharisees have a well-deserved reputation for scrupulously observing the requirements of the ancient law, both written Torah as well as certain oral traditions, but they are willing to make a few reasonable adjustments to accommodate present needs and circumstances. The Pharisees' practices are based on strict adherence to Scripture-centered principles and interpretations that have been handed-down by certain sages.

All Pharisees are somewhat exclusive in their dealings with other people, but this varies from person to person. Some of them avoid all contacts with persons who aren't faithful Pharisees just like themselves; while other Pharisees are less restrictive. As a traveling merchant, it is inevitable for Eliezer to encounter many different kinds of people, but he does try to avoid interactions with pagans, known sinners, and Samaritans. But, following a saying of Joshua ben Perachya, Eliezer always tries to "give everybody the benefit of a doubt," especially his customers.

At the edge of Mount Gilboa, Beit Shean has been an important Canaanite city since before the time of Joshua, and it didn't become an Israelite city until it was conquered by King David. The current population of Beit Shean is a mixture of descendants of Canaanites, Egyptians, Philistines, Greeks, Romans, and Jews. Since the Seleucid period, Beit Shean also has been called Scythopolis. It is the largest city of the Decapolis, and a Roman administrative center. Beit Shean is home to more than ten thousand residents.

Being familiar with Beit Shean/Scythopolis, Eliezer is wary of its cosmopolitan influences, but the abundance of its market is too good to miss. So Eliezer prepares Amit and Marit for the half-day journey to Beit Shean, carefully attaching his bags and baskets of goods to them. Then he leads his donkeys to the road, and they begin walking together.

About four and one-half hours later, Eliezer and his donkeys pass through the freestanding western gateway to the new Roman city of Scythopolis, with its beautiful, gleaming white marble buildings, and colonnaded, stone-paved streets. Eliezer can see the amphitheater on his right, near the southwest corner of the city. The acropolis and temple of the old city of Beit Shean are visible at the top of the *tel*, that is northeast of the more recently constructed buildings in the valley.

He continues down the main street, past the fountain, the new temple, and the bathhouse, until he arrives at the commercial agora, the marketplace. The agora is ringed by buildings containing shops, and the enclosed plaza is filled with many displays of goods that are being offered for sale by merchants.

Because it is midday, Eliezer notices that most of the traders and shoppers are already engaged in lively bargaining. He sees his friend, and fellow merchant, Peleg. Peleg lives in the sparsely populated, but fertile, Yizreel (Jezreel) Valley. Eliezer leads his donkeys over to where Peleg set up his wares to sell.

As soon as Peleg notices Eliezer, he waves his arms invitingly to his friend. When Eliezer arrives at Peleg's stall in the agora, the men embrace each other warmly, and Peleg says, "Eliezer, you are welcome to sell your produce with me here. As you can see, I am selling wheat and figs. What did you bring to sell?"

Eliezer replies, "Thank you for your generous invitation, my friend. Today I will be selling vegetables and melons, so we won't be competing directly with each other."

Eliezer removes his cloak, spreads it out on the pavement, and arranges his melons, cucumbers, onions, and beans on top. Soon customers come to Peleg's and Eliezer's displays, and begin bargaining for produce.

During lapses in their business, Eliezer and Peleg visit with each other about their family members, their speculations concerning the rains that they hoped would come to Galilee after three more months, and their religious ideas. Peleg also is a Pharisee.

Peleg says, "I have heard about an exciting, new prophetic preacher named Yohanan who has begun attracting followers about forty-five miles to the south, next to the Nehar haYarden (River Jordan). This man is calling people to repent of their sinfulness, and to the unusual act of submitting themselves to baptism in the Yarden, just as if they are pagans who are newly converted to the Jewish covenant. What do you think about that?"

"Well, I don't know what to think about that. This is the first time that I have heard about this Yohanan. But I do like the idea of people starting over again, and the symbolic act of washing in the Nehar ha Yarden seems like an appropriate way to begin."

"We have been hoping that the Maschiah will be revealed soon, and that the Maschiah will expel the Roman pagans from our Holy Land, and restore Israel to its former greatness. Do you think that this new prophet might be the Maschiah, or perhaps have something to do with the revealing of the Maschiah?"

Eliezer responds, "Peleg, many of us have been eagerly looking forward to the appearing of the Maschiah, but I feel that I should remind you that, during the past ninety years, several would-be Maschiahs, among them Judas ben Hezekiah, Simon of Peraea, Athronges and his brothers, and Judas the Galilean, all were executed as rebels by the repressive Romans. There hasn't been a successful rebellion in the Land of Israel since the Maccabees, that was about one hundred years before the Romans arrived. To be successful today, a Maschiah would have to lead an army more powerful than the Romans have, and that seems highly improbable."

Peleg nods his head, and shrugs his shoulders in response.

After a few hours, both merchants had sold most of the produce that they had brought. Peleg says, "Eliezer, I think that I am ready to close up business and return to my home, but you are welcome to continue selling your vegetables here after I leave."

Eliezer replies, "No, Peleg, I am ready to close, too. But, before you go, I want to buy an ephah of wheat from you." Eliezer hands Peleg some coins whose total value equals the price that Peleg had been asking for his wheat, and Peleg gives the container of grain to Eliezer in exchange for the currency.

Then Eliezer gives Peleg all of his remaining vegetables, saying, "I want you to have these vegetables, in gratitude for allowing me to share your business space today."

Peleg and Eliezer embrace each other and Eliezer says to him, "I hope that we will meet here again in two months, after the early olive harvest."

And Peleg replies, "Shalom, Eliezer. You are always welcome to share this stall with me. I will expect to see you again in two months."

Before leaving the commercial agora, Eliezer visits a few of the stalls that are selling large pieces of linen fabric, and he purchases several of them for use by his own family. He also buys a very nice pottery jar, which by its decoration appears to have been imported from one of the Greek islands. Eliezer thinks that the vessel will be a good surprise gift for his daughter, Miriam. Then Eliezer fastens his personal gear and his purchases to Amit, and he leads both of his donkeys out of the southeast gateway of the newer part of Scythopolis. He proceeds toward the Yarden River.

Less than an hour after leaving Beit Shean, Eliezer is on the north-south road along the west side of the Yarden. He travels northward for a while, until he finds a suitable place to spend the night. He estimates that he only has about seventeen miles to go before arriving at his home in Hammat.

[Eliezer is able to keep track of the distances he travels on his marketing journeys because of the inscribed milestones that the Roman soldiers have placed at regular intervals alongside many of the important roads in Judaea. A Roman mile is the distance that a contingent of Roman soldiers can cover in one thousand two-step paces (approximately 1.5 kilometers). The word "mile" is a shortened form of the Latin words, "mille passus", which means "one thousand paces". The Romans consider a well organized network of well-maintained roadways to be essential for public administration.]

During the past five days, Eliezer has traveled fifty miles and sold his produce in markets at five Galilean cities. He has earned the equivalent of almost four weeks' worth of a laborer's wages, but very often during his journey he found himself thinking about his family. Later, during his evening prayers, he mentions how much he still misses his beloved wife, Ahuva, who died ten years ago. And he expresses thanks for his very capable daughter, Miri, who so effectively manages the operations of their household, especially during the past five years, as well as his winsome young son, Yaaqov, who he expects will continue the business after him.

He is still thinking about his family when he drifts off to sleep.

CHAPTER 2

Early the next morning, Eliezer is heading northward, toward his home. After about three hours, he comes to the southern tip of Lake Kinneret and he passes by Beit Yerah. At this point, he knows that he only has about four miles left before arriving at Hammat. Even Amit and Marit seem to know that they are close to their home, as they are walking a little faster now, and they seem to be anticipating the familiar sights, sounds, and smells of their village. Hammat is an ancient settlement whose history goes back at least until the time of Pharoah Rameses II. Unlike many other Israelite cities that were destroyed or abandoned during the Assyrian conquest, the Exile in Babylon, or the Persian period, Hammat has been continuously occupied since its beginning. Hammat's well-watered and fertile land adjacent to Lake Kinneret is especially well suited to agricultural use.

Eliezer and his donkeys walk though the southern gate of Hammat just after midday and, as he passes by the synagogue, he sees Yitzhak the rabbi sitting outside, and Eliezer calls-out a greeting to him. He passes by the house of his brother, Reuel, and his sister-in-law, Serah. Reuel operates an olive press in Hammat. Then Eliezer comes to a bathhouse that was built over one of Hammat's famous therapeutic hot springs and, just past it, he turns left on an uphill street that leads to his own home.

As he draws closer to his house, he sees Yaaqov playing outside with the chickens, and he also sees Miri sprinkling some water on the vegetable plants in the garden. He shouts to them, "Hello, my children!" and they come running to him excitedly. To Eliezer, the best part of each trip is his homecoming. Miriam helps him unload the baskets and bags that were on Amit. And Yaaqov leads Amit and Marit over to their pen, where he waters them and puts fresh food in their trough. The house itself is constructed of stones, and includes three roofed rooms and a partly-covered central courtyard. Two of the interior rooms are used for sleeping, and the larger, third one is used as an inside, shared-use area, and also as a storeroom. The interior walls of the house are finished with plaster, and include benches and storage shelves that are built into the walls. Some of the walls also have windows to the outside, that are located high on the walls and with shutters that can be opened or closed. The small number of high windows helps to ventilate the home, while also providing privacy and security for the occupants. The donkeys' pen is attached to one of the home's exterior walls, and it includes a covered shelter in one of its corners. Eliezer's garden is located in a terraced area that is adjacent to the house, and also next to a cool spring that flows into a cistern that Eliezer built.

After washing their hands, Eliezer, Miriam, and Yaaqov gather around their small family table, seated on stools. Eliezer says the mealtime blessing, "Blessed art Thou, Lord, our God, King of the Universe, who bringest forth food from the earth. Amen." Then they eat their midday meal of bread, wine, olives, and salt.

After they have supped, Eliezer shows his children the things that he had purchased during his trip. He shows them the pomegranates that he bought in Tzipori (Sepphoris), the olive oil from Natzerat (Nazareth), and the linen cloths from Beit Shean (Scythopolis). Then he gives Miri the beautiful pottery jar from the Greek Islands, and his gift delights her very much. Eliezer can see that Yaaqov seems to be a little disappointed that Eliezer hadn't brought anything for him. Eliezer tells Yaaqov that he will take him to Tiberias' market on the first day of the week, and that perhaps they will find something for him there. This pleases Yaaqov greatly, because he always wanted to accompany his father on his market excursions, but never before had he been permitted to do so. Then Eliezer rests from his travels, and Miriam cleans the house and makes other necessary preparations for their observance of Shabbat.

While Eliezer sleeps, Miriam prepares a stew containing vegetables and chicken meat, she mashes some beans that she had cooked into a smooth paste, and she bakes several loaves of bread. The family will eat this food during Shabbat, between sundown today until the same time tomorrow evening. Everything has to be prepared beforehand, because no work may be done during Shabbat, including cooking and tending a fire. And observant Jews also limit their travels during Shabbat to just 2000 cubits (*about 1000 yards*).

Miriam is happy with her life. As the woman of the house, her responsibilities include doing almost all of the cooking, baking, housecleaning, spinning, weaving, sewing, and laundering. Unlike the experieince of most of her female friends, Miriam's father taught both of his children to read, and he shares his Torah studies with her. She understands that her father loves her very much, and she also knows that her young brother looks up to her. However, she wonders what life is like beyond the familiar towns on the west side of Lake Kinneret, where she has lived all of her life, with additional trips to Yerushalayim for pilgrim festivals. Most of the young women that she grew up with are already married. The usual age for Jewish women to marry is about eighteen years or less, and Miri is already twenty. Several times during the past five or six years, her father told her that men had spoken to him about wanting to marry her, but that each time he had declined their marriage proposals. He told her that that the reason he turned down the offers was partly because of her wishes, and partly because he relies on her so much. But she knows that the real reason that he keeps rejecting the offers of marriage is that he doesn't consider any of the unmarried men that he knows to be good enough for her. And it worries her just a little bit that she agrees with him. In a culture where young women generally have no say in the matter, she wonders if she has been too picky: *Perhaps she would never marry -- now that would really be scandalous!*

Later, Miriam sets the table with two oil lamps, a cup of wine, two of the bread loaves that she had baked, a bowl of water, a towel, and the family's best stone plates and wooden eating implements. She covers the loaves of bread with a linen covering. Just as the sun is setting, Eliezer and Yaaqov join her at the table. They all cover their heads, and then Miri lights the two oil lamps, that represent the two commandments to remember and to observe the Sabbath. She waves her hands over the lit lamps, welcoming in the Sabbath. Then she covers her eyes, and recites the blessing, "Blessed art Thou, Lord, our God, King of the universe, who has sanctified us with His commandments and commanded us to light the lights of Shabbat.

Amen." Then she removes her hands from her eyes, and she looks at the flickering light of the oil lamps.

Then Eliezer picks up the cup of wine and says, "And there was evening and there was morning, the sixth day. The heavens and the earth were finished, and all their multitude. And on the seventh day God finished the work that He had done, and He rested on the seventh day from all the work that He had done. So God blessed the seventh day and sanctified it because in it God rested from all the work that He had done in creation. Blessed art Thou, Lord, our God, King of the universe, Who creates the fruit of the vine. Amen." Eliezer puts the cup back on the table. Then he raises his hands and says, "Blessed art Thou, Lord, our God, King of the universe, who sanctifies us with His commandments, and has been pleased with us. You have lovingly and willingly given us Your holy Shabbat as an inheritance in memory of creation, because it is the first day of our holy assemblies in memory of our exodus from Egypt, because You have chosen us and made us holy from all peoples and have willingly and lovingly given us Your holy Shabbat for an inheritance. Blessed art Thou, who sanctifies Shabbat. Amen."

Then, one at a time, Eliezer, Miriam, and Yaaqov put their hands into the bowl of water, and then dry them with the towel. As each one washes their hands, they say the blessing, "Blessed art Thou, Lord, our God, King of the universe, who has sanctified us with His commandments and commanded us concerning washing of hands." After all of them had washed their hands, Eliezer removes the linen covering from the two loaves of bread, that represent the dual portion of manna that the Lord provided to the Israelites for their Sabbath during the time when they were in the desert. Then he lifts up the loaves in his two hands and says, "Blessed art Thou, Lord, our God, King of the universe, who brings forth bread from the earth. Amen." Then he breaks one of the loaves into pieces, and he shares them with Miri and Yaaqov. They eat some of the bread, and they share the cup of wine, and then Miri puts some of the stew and bean paste on the table for their joyous family meal.

After dinner, Eliezer recites the grace after meals, and they sing some of their favorite portions of Tehillim [Psalms] together, ending with this portion:

> "But the steadfast love of the LORD is from everlasting to everlasting on those who fear Him, and His righteousness to children's children, to those who keep His covenant and remember to do His commandments.
> The LORD has established His throne in the heavens, and His kingdom rules over all.
> Bless the LORD, all His hosts, His ministers that do His will.
> Bless the LORD, all His works, in all places of His dominion.
> Bless the LORD, O my soul."
> [Psalm 103:17-22, New Revised Standard Version]

After the singing, the family spends about an hour happily talking and listening to each other, before blowing out all but the two special Shabbat oil lamps and going to their own beds for sleep.

The next morning, after sharing a light breakfast of bread and pomegranates together, the family spends some time discussing portions of the Torah together, remembering the Creation of the heavens and the earth, God's loving provision of a covenant for His chosen people, and the exodus from slavery in Egypt to freedom.

At midday, the family shares some more of the same festive meal that they had eaten during the previous evening, and including some of the same blessings.

And after dinner, they take naps, and afterwards they go for a short walk together, and enjoy a brief visit with Reuel and Serah and their children.

During late afternoon, Eliezer and his family eat a light meal, and then after sunset they share another brief ritual to conclude their observance of Shabbat.

They all feel that this Shabbat has been a relaxing time of rest and enrichment together, a holiday from their ordinary daily routine -- as it was intended to be.

CHAPTER 3

On the morning of the first day of the week, Eliezer did not have to remind Yaaqov that on this day they would take a short walk together to Tiberias, to visit some of the markets in that city. Yaaqov was ready to go whenever his father decided to leave. Eliezer remembered that, during his visit to Tiberias during the preceding week, one of his customers asked him to bring some lentils and garlic with him to sell the next time he came to Tiberias, so Eliezer harvested and cleaned some fresh lentils and garlic from his garden, for them to take along. When Eliezer was ready to go, he found Yaaqov and the two of them started walking northward. Tiberias was only about two miles from their home at Hammat, so it didn't take long for them to travel to the main market agora in Tiberias.

Tiberias is a new city that was founded by Herod Antipas about ten years ago; he named it in honor of the emperor Tiberius. Herod Antipas moved his administrative center of Galilee from Tzipori (also known as Sepphoris) to Tiberias. Tiberias was constructed a short distance south of the ruins of Raqat that like Hammat had been one of the important ancient Israelite settlements in the tribal territory of Naphtali. Tiberias is at a strategically important location because it is close to the Via Maris, the main route that connects Egypt and Syria, and also because roads lead from Tiberias to Gadara, to Beit Shean and Jericho, to Tzipori, and to Samaria. Besides being a governmental center, Tiberias also has become an important city for fishing, agriculture, and international trade. It is administered by an archon, and a council of ten magistrates who also are called profoi. But, next to Antipas himself, the most powerful person in Tiberias is the agoranomos Nicanor, who manages Tiberias' multiple markets, each of which specializes in selling different types of goods.

Eliezer and Yaaqov arrive at the main market at which fruits and vegetables are sold, and Eliezer notices that Zibrah is there. She is the woman who wanted to buy some lentils and garlic from him last week, so he goes to her and opens the cloth bag that he has been carrying, that contain the lentils and garlic bulbs that he had brought for her. Eliezer tells Zibrah his asking price for the vegetables. She tries to haggle with him about the price, but he remains firm concerning his valuation of the lentils and garlic. Zibrah knows that Eliezer's vegetables are of excellent quality, and that his price is fair, so it doesn't take too long for her to pay his asking price.

That business being settled, Zibrah asks Eliezer if his daughter Miriam is married yet. She says that she believes that Assurbani, who now is one of the ten profoi of Tiberias, might still be interested in her. He is one of the intended suitors for Miriam who previously was rejected by Eliezer, but this was before Assurbani became an important magistrate. However, Eliezer doesn't like Assurbani for reasons that are very important to him. First of all, Assurbani isn't an observant Jew; in fact, he might not even be Jewish at all. Usually, Assurbani wears Greek-style clothing. There is a rumor that Assurbani came from Amman, a large city beyond the Yarden River. Eliezer has been hoping to find a very good Pharisee that she might be willing to marry. And secondly, Eliezer thinks that, as an ambitious and corrupt political opportunist, Assurbani exemplifies the very worst kind of Herodian.

The Herodians are political partisans of Herod Antipas, who frequently exploit advantages that proceed from their friendship with the Roman authorities, to the detriment of ordinary religious people. In contrast, devout Jews care more about serving God and other people than in promoting their own personal benefits. Many Herodians are known to take bribes, and Eliezer has heard stories about Herodians making threats of violence against people who oppose them. But whatever one believes about those stories, most Pharisees avoid all politicians, following advice that was handed down by both Rabbi Shemaiah and Rabbi Abtalion. Eliezer doesn't think that he needs to explain himself to Zibrah, so he politely leaves her and heads toward the craftsmen's market with Yaaqov.

As Eliezer is walking away, Zibrah looks at him with admiration. Clearly, he is a careful father to his children, and he seems to have strong convictions about justice. She thinks, *A righteous man such as this might be a good companion for me.* Zibrah is a widow.

At the market where the craftsmen sell their wares, Yaaqov finds a small, carved, wooden horse that reminds him of the animals that he had seen some of the Roman soldiers riding upon. However, Eliezer doesn't want to bring this kind of a carved object into his house, so he tries to interest Yaaqov in looking for something else instead. So Yaaqov finds a round, hard ball that is made of leather; the ball is a little bit larger than Yaaqov's hand -- that is just the right size for a toy. Eliezer knows that Yaaqov enjoys playing various ball games with his friends, so he buys the ball for Yaaqov. As they start to leave the market, Eliezer notices that Assurbani is walking directly towards them. Eliezer cannot think of a polite way to avoid Assurbani, so he allows him to approach himself and Yaaqov.

Assurbani greets Eliezer, "Good day, Eliezer. How are things in Hammat, and who is this young man that is with you?"

Eliezer responds, "Life in Hammat continues to be very good, and this is my son, Yaaqov."

Then, looking at Yaaqov, Assurbani says, "I am pleased to meet you, Yaaqov. Did your beautiful sister, Miriam, also come with you and your father to Tiberias today?"

Eliezer doesn't wait for Yaaqov to answer Assurbani. He says to Assurbani, "Miriam is not in Tiberias with us. She is at home, working."

Then Assurbani asks Eliezer directly, "Is Miriam married yet?"

And Eliezer responds, "Miriam is not yet married, but that should not be of any concern to you. There are many fine Jewish men who are interested in her. And now, Yaaqov and I must be on our way home. We have our own work to do. Good bye."

As Eliezer and Yaaqov are leaving, Assurbani follows them with his eyes and thinks, *What an arrogant Jew! He shouldn't have spoken to me in that manner. Doesn't he know how important I am? Perhaps I should visit Hammat myself soon, to tell the people there about our recent improvements in Tiberias.*

CHAPTER 4

Eliezer and Yaaqov are on their way home from Tiberias. As they are walking along the road that connects Tiberias and Hammat, Yaaqov is playing with his new toy, tossing the ball from one hand to the other and occasionally dropping it and gently kicking it up into the air, where he either catches it with his hands or, failing that, retrieves it from the ground. All the while, he keeps chattering to Eliezer about the bright, whitewashed buildings of Tiberias, and the abundance of goods being sold in the two markets they had visited.

As they are walking, Eliezer is quietly thinking about his daughter, Miri, and wondering if he should be pressuring her to identify a person that she thinks might be suitable for her to marry. But he doesn't really want to rush her, and he also can't think of anyone he knows that he likes well enough to accept as his son-in-law. It troubles him that someone like Assurbani expresses interest in Miriam. Perhaps that wouldn't happen if Miri were already married . . . but then Eliezer reminds himself that unscrupulous people aren't always respectful of social boundaries. It bothers Eliezer that the Lord permits people like Assurbani to become leaders in His Holy Land. It just doesn't seem right.

Then Eliezer remembers that Rabbi Yitzhak had said that the Maschiah would ensure that only worthy overseers will govern the chosen people. Eliezer reminds himself that righteous people should persist in doing right things themselves and continue to trust in the Lord, even when facing injustice. At just the right time, the Lord will put things right. Eliezer reminds himself that he should stop worrying about matters beyond his own ability to control. He prays, "Blessed are you, O Lord, the shield of Abraham and the redeemer of Israel. Amen."

At the same time, Assurbani also is thinking about Eliezer's daughter, Miriam. He remembers her as being both beautiful and innocent, and this memory evokes lustful feelings within him. He likes the idea of violating pretty women who also are pure, and of making them abase themselves with him. The main reason why he previously had proposed marrying Miriam was because he also was seeking the respectability that would come with marrying the daughter of such a greatly-admired man as Eliezer. But Eliezer had rejected Assurbani's proposal before, and he also had spurned Assurbani again today. Assurbani thought that since he now is one of the governing leaders of Tiberias, that should have improved his standing with Eliezer, but somehow that didn't seem to make any difference with Eliezer. Assurbani will try to figure out a way for him to indulge his lust for Miriam, and maybe also to hurt Eliezer.

Miriam decides to use some of the linen fabric that Eliezer had bought in Beit Shean by sewing it into a new tunic for her father to wear. She knows that his old one is becoming quite worn, and it needs to be replaced. It has been repaired so many times with patches, that she is embarrassed whenever he wears it. She will use some blue-dyed thread to join two of the rectangular pieces of cloth, and also to add a decorative pattern around the holes where the head and arms go through. As she sews, she thinks about her father: *Who will take care of him, after she leaves this home to live somewhere else?* She decides to use a piece of the new linen cloth herself, as a covering for her long hair. It is customary for women to wrap their hair in a piece of cloth whenever they go into public places, and Miri likes the way the linen feels against her face. But she also wants to add some decoration to her new hair covering.

At about this same time, Yohanan is in the Nehar haYarden (River Jordan) southeast of Yeriko (Jericho), baptizing a man from Natzerat (Nazareth) named Yeshuah. Afterwards, Yohanan identifies Yeshuah as the "Lamb of God" to two of his followers, and they become Yeshuah's first disciples.

CHAPTER 5

Two months later, the baptizer Yohanan was beheaded in prison by order of Herod Antipas. Throughout that period, and for many months afterward, the ministry and reputation of Yeshuah grows steadily throughout many of the cities and towns of the Upper and Lower Galilee, the Yizreel Valley, and the region of Gaulanitis. Presently, Yeshuah and his closest followers spend much of their time in the vicinity of Kfar Nahum (Capernaum) that is only about eleven miles north of Hammat, and less than three miles from the Yarden River.

Sometimes Yeshuah and his followers travel back and forth across the Yarden which separates the region of Galilee that is ruled by Herod Antipas, and Gaulanitis that is in the territory of Antipas' estranged half-brother Philip, who is the Tetrarch of Iturea. Besides Antipas' political ambition, another reason for the enmity between Antipas and Philip is that Antipas persuaded Herodias, who was his own niece and Philip's wife, to leave her husband and to marry him instead. Prior to his arrest, Yohanan had publicly denounced Antipas' marriage to Herodias, and this humiliation probably is what led to Yohanan's execution. Moreover, Yeshuah's close association with Yohanan could also make him more susceptible to attack by Antipas. So Yeshuah avoids Antipas' home city of Tiberias, and he also sometimes seeks safety from Antipas' reach by crossing over into Philip's territory, temporarily visiting Bethsaida, Caesarea Philippi, the Golan wilderness, and also some of the nearby independent Decapolis cities. Kfar Nahum is less than ten miles from Tiberias. Safety must be an important consideration during this early phase of Yeshuah's ministry.

Around the middle of the month of Elul, Eliezer makes his customary six-day, late-summer marketing journey through markets in five Galilean cities, selling some more of the produce that he had raised, and also buying some goods that he wants. His friend Peleg is very disturbed by the news that Yohanan was executed, and Peleg wonders aloud what will happen next, and how the Lord will establish the kingdom of the long-awaited, next king of Israel, and sweep away every obstacle, including the Romans. To Eliezer, Peleg's assertions seem ludicrous.

As usual, autumn begins with the first rains that occur in the region since the preceding spring. The rain comes during the important holy days of the month of Tishri: Rosh Hashanah, Yom Kippur, and the seven-day pilgrim festival of Sukkot that is a commemoration of the time when the Israelites lived in thatched huts after their exodus from Egypt. Sukkot also marks the last harvest before the onset of winter.

Eliezer and his children observe the first day of Tishri at their home with a day of holy rest and the sounding of the shofar. On the tenth day of that month, in observance of Yom Kippur, they abstain from eating food, drinking, all forms of frivolity, personal washing, and even the wearing of sandals -- knowing that solemn rituals are being carried out at the Temple in Yerushalayim (Jerusalem) for the expiation of the people's sins.

The day after the solemnities of Yom Kippur, Eliezer and his children leave Hammat for a five-day journey to Yerushalayim, to participate in the joyous observances of Sukkot. They don't arrive in Yerushalayim until the second day of the festival, but each day of the festival includes ceremonies, libations, and sacrifices at the Temple, as well as Eliezer and Yaaqov dwelling joyfully in a booth that they share outdoors, while Miriam, her aunt and female cousins stay in a house with relatives who live in the holy city. Even though this week-long festival always happens during the season of occasional early rains, everyone has an enjoyable time. And they also know how important the rains are for their agricultural productivity.

Two weeks after they return to Hammat, Eliezer completes the midautumn harvesting of his late olives and winter figs. Next he plows his moist garden and fields, with the hard pulling done by Amit and Marit, but also with some help from Yaaqov; and then Eliezer plants the wheat that he hopes he will be harvesting next spring. As he is working in his garden and fields, Eliezer thinks, *How often the Lord uproots His people's lives in order to make possible a later harvest of changes that always prove to be beneficial. Going through this process is never easy, but it always produces good results, eventually.* Eliezer prays, "Blessed are you, O Lord, for uprooting and humbling the arrogant enemies of your Divine Will, and for causing salvation to flourish. Amen."

Sometimes Miriam or Yaaqov accompany Eliezer on short marketing excursions to Tiberias, Magdala, and Kfar Nahum. While visiting the markets, Eliezer, Miriam, and Yaaqov all hear firsthand reports regarding Yeshuah's teaching and healing ministry. People tell them that, unlike most other rabbis, Yeshuah's teaching is refreshingly direct and engaging, and the miraculous healings that he performs are sensational. It is said that practitioners of the healing arts have produced some remarkable results in Alexandria, Rome, and in a few other important cities, but in the Holy Land of Israel there generally is no cure for persons suffering from serious illnesses or injuries. Therefore, Yeshuah attracts many excited people who are desperate to receive relief from their illnesses and injuries. And Yeshuah's reputation keeps growing. Eliezer, however, receives these miracle stories about Yeshuah with a mixture of skepticism and caution. Although Eliezer certainly believes that the Lord is capable of performing supernatural acts, Eliezer's own experiences have shown him that such events are exceptionally rare, and he doubts that the Lord would act through someone like Yeshuah, who interacts so freely with everyone, including known sinners. And Eliezer is concerned that Yeshuah's growing popularity is distracting many people from the pathway of covenant faithfulness; he thinks, *They are seeking quick solutions for their problems, instead of waiting for the Lord to act according to His timing, and also according to their own dutifulness.*

Nevertheless, Eliezer and his family are curious about Yeshuah. On one occasion, while Eliezer was selling some fruits in Kfar Nahum, someone directed his attention to an ordinary-looking man standing nearby, and told him that this man was Yeshuah. Eliezer wondered, *What would it mean if even some of the stories being told about this man are true?*

The following day, in the Mediterranean seaport city of Caesarea Maritima, that is located about fifty miles to the southwest, a group of Roman soldiers debark from the transport ship that brought them from Alexandria to Judaea. Carrying their gear, the soldiers proceed directly to the Roman military headquarters of the Italian Cohort in

Caesarea, to receive their assignments. One of them, a junior officer named Marius Octavius Syrianus, is assigned as tesserarius to the small detachment that is garrisoned at Capernaum. He is advised against traveling alone on the highway to Capernaum, and he is invited to ride along in a wagon carrying supplies to the military garrison at Capernaum. Like most other soldiers in Judaea, Marius is a non-citizen member of Rome's auxiliary military forces. Although he was raised in Syria, he is an ambitious professional soldier with five years of military experience serving with the Roman army in Aegyptus. And now, Marius is beginning his journey to Capernaum on the Via Maris.

The Roman Legions only admit volunteers who are Roman citizens. At this time, the nearest legions in Judaea are stationed in Syria, but they can be moved quickly to Judaea, if it became necessary either to snuff out a rebellion or to make war. Auxiliary soldiers are usually stationed in Roman provinces other than the province from which they were recruited. Besides some Italians, most of the Roman soldiers serving in Judaea are Syrians, Arabians, Cappadocians, Aegyptians, or Greek-speaking non-citizens. At this time, more than half of the Roman army's regular land forces are comprised of non-citizen auxiliary regiments, that serve in support of, and sometimes alongside, their legionary counterparts. Almost all of the Roman army's cavalry, light cavalry, archers, and slingers are auxiliaries. Auxiliary recruits are mostly volunteers. An important enlistment incentive is that, after serving twenty-five years as an auxiliary soldier, a retiree and all of his children are awarded Roman citizenship.

One morning early in the late-autumn month of Chislev, Eliezer returns to the market in Kfar Nahum to sell his produce. Yaaqov accompanies him on this trip, and Miriam sent along a meal of bread and broiled fish for them to share. On their way to Kfar Nahum, and only about two miles from that city, Yaaqov notices a grassy field containing several palm trees, and with seven springs flowing freely from that place into Lake Kinneret. The "place of seven springs" is called Ein Sheva in Hebrew, because that is the meaning of that name. Eliezer mentions to Yaaqov that the springs are a good source of drinking water.

Kfar Nahum is a city of about 1,000 residents; it contains a great number of rectangular groupings of small houses made out of stone, and roofed with dried mud and straw. The synagogue, that is made of basalt stone blocks, and the market agora are located in the northern part of the city, and the fishermen live in the southern part of the city, adjacent to the shoreline of Lake Kinneret. Some shops are interspersed amongst the homes. Access to the whole city is provided by narrow streets that are arrayed in an orderly north-to-south and east-to-west pattern. The Roman military garrison at Capernaum is on the east side of the town. The tax station is located at the northern edge of the town, next to the road that goes eastward toward Philip's territory on the other side of the Yarden River.

Eliezer and Yaaqov set up their produce display in the marketplace, and Eliezer begins visiting with customers. Yaaqov wanders around the agora, looking for some other children his own age to play with. Not finding any, Yaaqov comes back to where Eliezer is trying to sell his vegetables and fruits. After a couple of hours of dealing with Yaaqov's restlessness, Eliezer regrets having brought him along with him to Kfar Nahum. Then Yaaqov remembers the grassy field with the springs outside of town, and he asks his father if he could go there for a little while. So Eliezer gives Yaaqov his water container, and asks him to bring him back some water. Eliezer also gives Yaaqov the cloth bag containing the meal that Miriam had prepared, telling him to eat from it when he becomes hungry.

Several hours later, Eliezer realizes that Yaaqov had not returned, and so he decides to close his business and to look for Yaaqov. He suspects that Yaaqov had found some new friends, had become distracted while playing, and somehow lost track of the time. Eliezer goes to the house of his brother-in-law, Aharon, just in case Yaaqov was visiting there; but Aharon says that he hasn't seen Yaaqov. So Eliezer walks to the lakeshore, and looks around there briefly for his son. Then Eliezer walks along the shoreline in a southwesterly directon and toward Ein Sheva. As he is walking, he notices very large number of people walking eastward along the road, and heading back toward Kfar Nahum. And looking across the lake towards Magdala, he can see another crowd heading southward from Ein Sheva. He goes over to the road, and asks the people if they had seen an eleven year old boy carrying a water container, and with a small bag containing some food. They smile and point him toward the grassy plain that is just ahead.

When Eliezer arrives at the spot, he sees that most of the people had gone, except for several people with baskets who are gathering up scraps of food, and his son Yaaqov, who is filling his water container from one of the springs. Eliezer is relieved to have found Yaaqov, but he also is angry that his son had not returned to the marketplace as he had been instructed. Just as Eliezer was about to rebuke Yaaqov, a man with a basket of food approaches Eliezer to speak with him. The man introduces himself as one of Yeshuah's disciples, and then he says, "I know that you are angry with your son, but please do not deal with him harshly. He was here for a Divine purpose, in order that a great multitude might experience the Glory of the Lord."

When the man said that, Eliezer became confused. He grabs his son by the hand, and immediately starts walking with him toward Hammat, that is still eight miles to the south. Eliezer knows that they won't arrive at their home until after dark. As they walk homeward, Yaaqov enthusiastically tells his father what he remembers from Yeshuah's teaching, and especially about Yeshuah feeding a very, very large number of people with just the five loaves of bread and two broiled fish that Miriam had packed that day for Eliezer and Yaaqov to eat. Eliezer asked Yaaqov some questions about his description of what had happened, but Yaaqov's explanation didn't make any sense to him.

CHAPTER 6

The next day, Assurbani overhears some people talking in a Tiberias market about the miraculous feeding of a multitude at Ein Sheva during the preceding day. Assurbani is curious about this news, and he notices that a person who seems to have firsthand information about the event is someone that he knows, Zibrah. So Assurbani asks Zibrah to tell him what had happened. She happily describes how Yeshuah was able to use the small meal that Eliezer's son had brought with him to feed thousands of people near the seven springs. Assurbani cannot understand how anyone could multiply a small amount of food into a huge feast, but if Yeshuah somehow possessed that magical ability, then perhaps Yeshuah is planning to use it to increase his political power. Assurbani believes that Herod Antipas would be interested in finding out about any potential political rivals, especially concerning someone who also had been connected with Yohanan the Baptizer. Therefore, Assurbani decides to increase his own influence by gathering more information about Yeshuah and giving it to Antipas.

Eliezer and his family are enjoying their midday meal together at their home in Hammat. After Eliezer says the blessing for bread, Yaaqov is disappointed that the quantity of their bread did not increase, as he had seen happen yesterday, after Yeshuah had said the same blessing. Eliezer notices Yaaqov's thoughful hesitation before eating, and he realized that Yaaqov probably was thinking about what was supposed to have happened at Ein Sheva.

But then Yaaqov asks his father, "Abba, who do you think Yeshuah is?"

Eliezer thinks for a moment, and then says, "I was told that Yeshuah is a builder's son from Natzerat who wants to become a rabbi."

Yaaqov responds, "Yeshuah already is a great rabbi, and probably more than just a rabbi. I think that he should be our king."

Then Eliezer says, "We already have enough rabbis. We don't need another one. Furthermore, Israel hasn't had a king since Herod died thirty-two years ago, and Caesar doesn't seem very eager to let us have another one."

Miriam says, "I have never seen Yeshuah, but from the things that I have heard about him, he must be wonderful!"

Then Eliezer says, "But can we be sure that the stories we have heard are true? Things aren't always what they seem to be."

Miriam replies, "Don't you believe what your own son has told us about Yeshuah?"

As Eliezer is geting up from the table to leave, he says, "I think that Yaaqov believes that what he saw was true. My problem is that I cannot explain what appears to have happened, and I don't believe in magic."

As the tesserarius of the Capernaum garrison, Marius serves as the supervisor of the soldiers who guard the camp and at other posts that require a sentry, and he is third in command of the detachment, behind the centurion and his optio, or deputy commander. As tesserarius, Marius receives one and one-half times the pay that is received by lower-ranking infantrymen, and he is exempted from performing hard labor, such as road building. Like many other Roman soldiers from Syria, Marius is a skilled horseman and archer, but his present assignment does not normally involve using either a horse or a bow. When he was serving in Aegyptus, Marius was learning to operate field catapults and ballista, but artillery equipment is almost never used in Judaea. Here in Capernaum (also called Kfar Nahum by the locals), Marius' equipment includes a metal helmet, chain mail armor, a gladius (sword) and scabbard, pugio (dagger) and sheath, a javelin (spear), and an elliptical shield. He also wears a tunica, caligae (heavy sandals), balteus (a plate-covered belt including an apron of leather strips), and a cloak.

The centurion at Capernaum is Gaius Cornelius Crescens, a Roman citizen from Italy with nineteen years of service in the Roman army, the last six years of which have been spent leading auxiliary units in Judaea. During his military career, Gaius worked his way up through the ranks to his present position; he accomplished this entirely by merit, and not as a result of any political connections. He presently commands about eighty soldiers. While most Roman soldiers are unfriendly toward the Jews, Gaius is often sympathetic toward them. It is said that Gaius even donated a substantial amount of money to pay for making some improvements to the Capernaum synagogue. However, Gaius never allows his feelings for the local population to interfere with carrying out his orders.

Gaius' deputy commander is Titus Aelius Magnus, who also is a Roman citizen from Italy, having spent sixteen years in the Roman army, and serving alongside Gaius for the past ten years. Titus is a very stern disciplinarian, whose military specialty is the physical training of all of the men in his unit, including himself. The two senior military officers at Capernaum are uniformed and equipped similarly to Marius, but with more decoration on their helmets, armor on their shoulders and chest, greaves covering the front of their lower legs, more ornate swords and daggers, and finer quality tunics and cloaks.

Marius is marching with his soldiers around the circuit of sentry posts in Capernaum, relieving the outgoing watch and posting the incoming watch of soldiers, post-by-post. One of the posts was the tax station. When he arrives there, he overhears one tax collector talking with another one about leaving his job to join with a traveling preacher. That certainly seems odd, since tax collectors generally have a dependable source of income, while most other people don't. Marius reminds himself to notify the centurion about this development after he completes this circuit. And in a few hours, Marius will make another unaccompanied circuit of the sentry posts, as a part of his continuing responsibility to inspect all of the sentries, and to query them about their orders.

CHAPTER 7

The following day, Eliezer is at Hammat's synagogue, engaged in a spirited discussion with his brother Reuel, and with Rabbi Yitzhak and some other men about what they believe to be the most important principles contained in the Torah, and how they apply to the repayment of debts.

Reuben cites the law concerning the year of jubilee in Devarim xv [Deuteronomy 15], which provides for the cancellation of debts after six years. He knows of several instances in which the period of indebtedness extended well into the seventh year, and even beyond that.

He asks, "Shouldn't those debts have been cancelled?"

Kenan says that he believes there are good reasons why the sabbatical year regarding indebtedness is not practiced uniformly. He asks, "Why was this idea instituted in the first place?"

Rabbi Yitzhak explains that this compassionate provision of allowing debts to lapse in their seventh year was intended to ensure that poor people would not become hopelessly entrapped in their poverty.

Then Kenan mentions the importance of preserving social justice also by protecting both creditors and debtors from losses. He says that this is the reason that the seventh year remission of debts is widely ignored by most creditors, because doing so actually protects needy persons from being refused loans of money for fear of loss. Kenan points out that lenders would be less likely to make loans if they believed that those loans weren't going to be repaid.

But Reuben says that he believes that Jews shouldn't decide for themselves which provisions of the Law should be observed, and which should be excluded.

Eliezer responds by asserting that compassion is required of the whole community, and not just of wealthy persons.

Rabbi Yitzhak agrees, and he quotes the sage Hillel who said, "What is hateful to thee, do not unto thy fellow man: this is the whole Law; the rest is mere commentary." Yitzhak explains that the Torah teaches the community to function as a family of brothers and sisters, generously and ungrudgingly sharing both their abundance and their burdens with one another in fulfillment of righteousness, and always remembering that at one time they too were slaves. This foundational precept of brotherly love is derived from a scriptural text in Vaiyikra xix [Leviticus 19:18b]. Therefore, the rabbi says that debtors should pay their obligations just as soon as they are able to do so, and lenders should be forgiving toward those debtors for whom repayment is extremely difficult -- in this way Hillel's fundamental principle of the Jewish moral Law would be honored.

As Pharisees, Reuben, Kenan, Reuel, and Eliezer would prefer having clear rules to resolve every problematic situation, but Rabbi Yitzhak urges them instead to accommodate themselves to the inherent ambiguity of applying fundamental principles of their Jewish teaching, and not just to rely on the following of rules. He says, "A righteous person has a duty to make righteous choices."

Their study meeting together ends with that comment.

As Eliezer, Reuel, Reuben, Kenan, and the other men are leaving the synagogue, Reuel asks Eliezer about what had happened at Ein Sheva two days before.

Eliezer replies, "I really don't know what happened at Ein Sheva. I wasn't there at the time."

Then Reuel says, "But I heard that my nephew Yaaqov was involved somehow. Do you think that it is a good idea for any of us to be seen with Yeshuah? I hear that Yeshuah has been very critical of Pharisees, and that he has been stirring up the people."

Eliezer responds, "Perhaps the people *should* be stirred up. In any case, my son is free to explore the different facets of our tradition for himself, including the teachings of this preacher from Natzerat."

Reuel says, "Well, how can you explain that people are saying Yeshuah fed a large crowd of people with your son's small meal? If this is true, then some people will say that you endorse this sorcerer, or at the very least, they will hold you responsible for Yaaqov's involvement in Yeshuah's misleading of the people."

Eliezer replies, "Since Yaaqov is only eleven years of age, I know that I am responsible for him. However, I do not know whether or not it is true that Yeshuah is able to multiply a small number of bread loaves and fish so that they become sufficient to feed a great number of people. My son says that it happened, but I am unable to explain it."

Reuel asks, "Well, if it is true, then what does it mean? And who is this Yeshuah, that he is able to heal people, and also to do other wondrous things?"

Eliezer says, "Yes, Reuel, you have touched on what is surely the most important issue of this situation. I have spent many hours trying to figure out *how* Yeshuah could have multiplied the food. But I have come to believe that if this story is true, then we may never fully understand *how* it actually was accomplished. So it seems to me that the more important question is, what is the source of Yeshuah's power? Of course, nothing is too difficult for the Lord to do, but would the Lord work through anyone who interacts so readily with sinners, the way Yeshuah is said to do? On the other hand, if Yeshuah's power does not come from the Lord, then its source would be from Satan, the ruler of demons, which is frighteningly dangerous. You asked, 'What does it mean?' Well, since I cannot identify the source of Yeshuah's power, then it would be wrong for me to speculate about its meaning."

Then Reuel says, "I am wondering, could this Yeshuah be the Maschiah? Isn't the appearance of the Maschiah supposed to be accompanied by wondrous deeds?"

Eliezer answers, "I thought about that too. I suppose that it is possible that Yeshuah could be descended from David. But so far as we know, he has not been anointed to be our king, and he hasn't done any of the important things that the Maschiah is supposed to do. To cite just a few of them: Yeshuah has shown little interest in our Temple practices, in driving the pagans out of our Holy Land, or in obtaining Israel's independence from foreign powers. Furthermore, he doesn't have an army behind him, and he doesn't seem to have a lot of money. So how can he be the Maschiah?"

Reuel replies, "Maybe you are right, Eliezer. Nevertheless, we should keep an eye on this Yeshuah. After all, Rabbi Yitzhak has taught us, 'A righteous person has a duty to make righteous choices.'"

Meanwhile, in Capernaum, Marius overhears some people talking excitedly about the miraculous feeding of a very large number of people by someone named Yeshuah, in a grassy field by the place of seven springs located two miles west of the city. Marius reports this occurrence to his commanding officer, and then Centurion Gaius tells him that this Jesus, or Yeshuah as the locals called him, is a good man who has performed many miraculous acts during the several preceding weeks. In fact, Gaius tellls Marius that Jesus had healed Gaius' own servant from a grave illness, just by commanding that it be done, and without the servant even being present at the time. As Centurion Gaius is telling the story to Marius about Jesus healing his servant, Marius observes that Gaius' explanation plainly reflects his own respect and admiration for Jesus.

While Eliezer leaves the synagogue in Hammat, Miriam and Yaaqov are visiting an herb and spice shop that is in a building adjacent to the main market agora in Tiberias. Miriam is shopping for some fresh cloves and cinnamon for household use in the family's besamim box, and also for some honey. The owner of the spice shop recognizes Yaaqov as the boy who provided the bread loaves and fish for the miracle at Ein Sheva, and he asks Yaaqov about Yeshuah. As Yaaqov is telling the man about the rabbi from Natzerat, the profoi Assurbani enters the shop, listens to Yaaqov's statements, and then greets the shopkeeper, Miriam, and Yaaqov.

Then Assurbani says to Yaaqov, "I am very interested in Yeshuah myself. I would like to talk with you some more about him. Would you mind coming with me to a place where we can have a visit?"

Miriam interjects, "No, Yaaqov! Abba would not want you to go with this man, unless he could accompany you himself."

Then Assurbani tells Miriam, "Miriam, if you want to, you also may come along. I have some sweet pastries that we all can share."

Yaaqov is excited about getting to eat some sweet cakes -- perhaps these will be his favorites, the kind that are dripping with honey, and covered with chopped nuts. So, with some hesitation, Miriam completes her transaction with the shopkeeper, she puts the spices and the container of honey that she purchased into her cloth bag, and then she and Yaaqov follow Assurbani across the agora, and into another small building. As the group enters the building, Miriam sees that one of Herod's soldiers is there. His name is Mibzar, and he is one of

Antipas' protective bodyguards who also functions as a policeman in Tiberias. When Miriam realizes that this probably was not going to be the friendly visit that Assurbani had described, she tries to leave the building with Yaaqov, but Mibzar prevents them from doing that.

Assurbani says, "I don't want you to leave until after we have had our visit. You haven't even eaten any of my pastries yet."

Then Miriam responds, "Assurbani, I insist that you let us go. My father would not agree to this meeting."

Assurbani replies, "Well, if you insist on leaving, then you may go. But Yaaqov must remain with me here. Please tell your father that Yaaqov has been detained in Tiberias for questioning."

Miriam says, "Please, Assurbani. Let him go. Yaaqov hasn't done anything wrong."

Assurbani smiles and says, "Herod Antipas needs to learn all about Yeshuah, and Yaaqov may be able to help us with that. But if you must go, I do hope that you will come back yourself soon, so that you and I also can finish our visit."

Miriam is filled with fear, anger, and disgust as she leaves the place. And she knows that her father will be upset, too. She runs all the way back to her home in Hammat.

Eliezer is sitting in his courtyard, thinking about the conversation that he had with Reuel about Yeshuah, when Miriam arrives, gasping for breath and visibly upset. He says, "What is the matter, Miri? Why are you in distress?"

She replies, "Assurbani has taken Yaaqov! Yaaqov and I were shopping in Tiberias, and Assurbani detained him for questioning about Yeshuah."

Eliezer asks, "Why did you let him take Yaaqov? What happened?"

Miriam responds, "Assurbani tricked us. He said that he was interested in Yeshuah, and that he wanted to find out what Yaaqov might know about him."

Eliezer says, "But Yaaqov doesn't know anything about Yeshuah, except for what he believes to have happened at Ein Sheva. Come, let us return to Tiberias, to see if we can get Yaaqov released."

So, after giving Miriam enough time to put away her purchases and to get herself a drink of water, Eliezer and Miriam start walking to Tiberias.

When Eliezer and Miriam arrive in Tiberias, they go directly to the administrative building where Nicanor, the agoranomos in Tiberias, has his office. Eliezer remembers this important official from some previous dealings that he had with him, and he believes that perhaps Nicanor might be able to expedite Yaaqov's release. He finds Nicanor at his office and he explains what Miriam had told him about Yaaqov's arrest. Nicanor replied that he hasn't heard about anyone being interrogated concerning Yeshuah, and he also said that it seemed highly irregular to detain a child for that purpose. Nevertheless, he said that he would make some inquiries about this matter himself, and that he would contact Eliezer about it whenever he either had retrieved the child, or had discovered something to report.

Then Miriam led Eliezer to the building next to the main market, where Assurbani had brought her and Yaaqov, but no one was there. So they went back to the government building and asked if someone could direct them to where the profoi Assurbani was, or where the military policeman that Miriam described could be found. No one seemed to have any idea about where to find Assurbani, but there was a suggestion that the policeman might be in the vicinity of the northern entrance to the city. They went and looked all around the northern entrance, but they weren't able to find Mibzar there. Then Eliezer remembered having seen Assurbani previously at the craftsmen's market, so they went there too, but to no avail. Eliezer and Miriam were disappointed, and very worried, but there didn't seem to be anything else that they could do about it today. Reluctantly, they decided to return to their home in Hammat, but to return to Tiberias tomorrow.

As they are walking home, Eliezer and Miriam are praying, "Blessed are you, O Lord, for you hear the prayers of your people with mercy and compassion. Have pity on us, and bless your servants with safety and protection. Please help, shield, and save Yaaqov. We put our trust in you. Blessed are you, O Lord, who answers our prayers. Amen."

CHAPTER 8

Early the next day, Eliezer and Miriam return to Tiberias. They are so anxious and concerned about recovering Yaaqov, that they don't even notice when they are passing through the city gates while on their way. They walk quickly to Nicanor's office in the administrative building, and see that Nicanor is there. But before Eliezer even speaks a word to him, Nicanor tells them that he had spoken with Assurbani about Yaaqov. Assurbani had admitted to Nicanor that he had been questioning the boy, but that Yaaqov hadn't provided Assurbani with much useful information about Yeshuah. So Nicanor asked Assurbani to release the boy, and Assurbani had assured him that he would do so, but only to Miriam. Nicanor told Eliezer and Miriam that Assurbani could be found at the same place near the main market agora, where Yaaqov had been taken from Miriam.

So Eliezer and Miriam go to the place by the main market agora, and they did find Assurbani there, just as Nicanor had said. And Mibzar, the same military policeman that Miriam had seen with Assurbani yesterday, also is there. Eliezer tells Assurbani, "We're here to get Yaaqov back. Where are you keeping him?"

Assurbani replies, "He is nearby. But before I will release him, I want to speak to Miriam alone."

Eliezer is enraged by Assurbani's demand, but Miriam says to Eliezer, "Abba, I will talk with Assurbani. Yaaqov was with me when Assurbani took him, so I will see to it that my brother is returned to us. And since there also is a policeman here, I won't have to be alone with Assurbani."

With concern, Eliezer goes outside to wait in the commercial agora, leaving Miriam with Assurbani and the policeman.

As Assurbani steps closer to Miriam, she asks him, "What do you have to say to me, Assurbani? Please say it quickly, so that we can get this over with, and then you will set Yaaqov free."

Assurbani is standing so close to her, that she can feel his warm breath on her face. He says, "What would you be willing to do, in order to have Yaaqov released?"

She replies, "I will not do anything for you, Assurbani. You have no justification for detaining Yaaqov at all. He didn't do anything wrong, and he doesn't possess any information about Yeshuah that is useful for you. Set Yaaqov free and let me, and my family, return to our home in peace."

Then Assurbani reaches up with both of his hands and he grabs Miriam's arms roughly. She tries to wiggle out of his painful grasp, but is unable to do so. She looks toward Mibzar pleadingly, but all he does is grin.

While still squeezing Miriam's arms, Assurbani says, "Who are you to talk to me in this way? I am an important official in this city, and you are a person of no consequence to anyone besides your father. You have no husband and no suitors. There was a time in which I would have been willing to marry you myself, but all I want from you is to have my pleasure with you. I intend to do that when I decide that the time is right, and there is nothing that you will be able to do to prevent that from happening."

Assurbani lets go of her, and pushes her away from himself. Then he goes through a back doorway, and he returns a couple of moments later with Yaaqov. "Here, take him and go. Miriam, we will continue our conversation someday soon."

Miriam anxiously hugs Yaaqov, then takes him by the hand and quickly leads him through the front doorway to where Eliezer is waiting outside. Eliezer is greatly relieved to have his family back together again, but he asks her, "Miri, what did Assurbani say to you, when you were with him inside?"

Miriam tells her father, "Abba, don't trouble yourself about Assurbani. He isn't worth it." And then she starts walking ahead of them towards Hammat, and their home."

Eliezer and Yaaqov catch up to her, and they all continue walking homeward together.

On the way, Eliezer offers a prayer of thanksgiving for Yaaqov's return: "Blessed are you, O Lord, for answering our prayers and supplications, and for not turning us away from your presence empty-handed. We bless and thank you for your mercy and your loving kindnes which never cease. Amen."

Then Eliezer queries Yaaqov about what had happened to him while he was detained. As they are walking, Yaaqov chatters happily about the pastries that Assurbani had given him to eat, but Miriam is unusually quiet. She doesn't say anything about it, but Miriam feels that someone is watching them as they are walking home, and it makes her uncomfortable.

CHAPTER 9

On the first day of the week, Assurbani is summoned to the palace of Herod Antipas, that is located high on a mountain overlooking the city of Tiberias.

Antipas asks Assurbani, "I heard that you detained a boy from Hammat for a couple of days without the consent of his family. Why did you do such a thing? Nasty rumors have been circulating about this inappropriate encounter."

Assurbani answers, "Your Excellency, I assure you that the boy was not harmed in any way while he was with me. The reason why I took him into my custody is because of a report that I received concerning the boy's connection with the teacher Yeshuah from Natzerat, who is now living in Kfar Nahum. We have heard that Yeshuah has been performing miraculous deeds and, because of his reputed magical powers, he has been attracting many enthusiastic and hopeful followers. It also is said that Yeshuah was associated with Yohanan the Baptizer, who was so disrespectful toward your Excellency. I have heard some people talk about Yeshuah in terms of his own possible political aspirations, and I know that your Excellency wants to be kept informed about any potential rivals. So I was questioning the boy from Hammat, to find out what he might know about Yeshuah's intentions. But I determined that the boy does not possess any special information about Yeshuah's future plans, so I released him. I regret that my actions may have unintentionally created a controversy, but I believed that I was acting on your behalf."

Antipas responds, "I have heard about this Yeshuah, and I am concerned about him. Do you think that he could be Yohanan the Baptizer, returned from the dead to torment me?"

Assurbani replies, "I don't believe in Jewish superstitions, so I truly doubt that Yeshuah could be one of their prophets raised from the dead."

Antipas says, "Nevertheless, I do want to learn all about Yeshuah, and I would like to see him myself. So, I agree with you that we all need to pay close attention to this teacher. I am pleased to learn that you believed that your inquiry was carried out in support of my interests. But I expect you to be more careful to avoid creating any scandal that might reflect badly upon us Herodians. Do you understand me?"

Assurbani replies, "Yes, your Excellency. I will strive to be both vigilant and more discreet."

After being dismissed by Antipas, Assurbani thinks, *I am pleased that my initiative was noticed by Antipas, but I will have to act more cautiously in the future, especially regarding Miriam.*

With the arrival of the first rains and, at higher elevations, the snows of winter, Zibrah is thinking about how good it would be to have a man in her life again, to keep her warm and especially to provide her with companionship. She wonders what Eliezer is doing. He is such a good man.

Zibrah is the owner of two fishing boats at Tiberias, which are manned by some local fishermen, and which provide her with good seasonal income from her share of the profits, but with the onset of winter the boats don"t go out onto Yam Kinneret (Lake Kinneret) as often. The name, Kinneret, comes from the Hebrew word for harp, kinnor, because the shape of the lake resembles a harp. It is about thirteen miles long (north to south), and about seven miles wide (west to east) at its widest point. Other names for this body of water are Lake Gennesaret, the Sea of Galilee, and the Sea of Tiberias. This freshwater lake is fed from the north by the Yarden River, whose source is melted snow from Mount Hermon, as well as from springs located at Panias (Caesarea Philippi), Dan, and elsewhere. The River Yarden also flows out of Yam Kinneret at its south end, and continues to flow southward until it terminates in the Dead Sea.

Lake Kinneret contains an abundance of more than eighteen species of fish, which are caught either by line or by net. A type of tilapia and some sardines are especially popular fish. Fishermen are licensed by the government, and fishing boats are customarily met by tax collectors upon their return to the docks. Sometimes the tax is almost 50 percent of the value of the catch. Most of the caught fish are dried and salted for later consumption, but some fresh fish are sold, cooked, and eaten right away. A major facility for processing fish is only three miles north of Tiberias, at Magdala (also is known as Migdal, and Taricheae). Even with the heavy taxation, fishing still is a profitable business. Zibrah's husband had been a fisherman, and he acquired their two boats and equipment.

Since Zibrah and her husband didn't have any children, she took over her husband's business after he died. The reason Zibrah and her husband didn't have children wasn't because they hadn't tried -- they frequently had enjoyed sexual intercourse together, especially when they were young, but for His own reasons the Lord had never blessed their marriage with children. And now, at thirty-seven years of age, Zibrah believes that, although many men might not consider her as physically attractive as some younger women, she still knows how to satisfy a man's desires, and she also is still interested in fulfilling her own urges with a suitable companion. Presently, however, her circumstances and propriety afford her no opportunity, but she still thinks about it from time to time.

Meanwhile, Eliezer and Miriam are on their way to Kfar Nahum, to visit his deceased wife's brother and sister-in-law. Aharon farms some land that he owns north of Kfar Nahum, and he is a prominent Pharisee at the Kfar Nahum synagogue. Aharon's wife, Bilhah, knows almost everyone in that city. Eliezer is hoping that maybe they will be able to recommend a suitable spouse for his daughter. They walk along the waterfront at the southern part of Kfar Nahum, and then turn northward on a street that goes toward Aharon's home. As they are passing by an entrance to the Roman garrison, they notice the changing-of-the-guard procedure, as it is carried-out under the direction of the tesserarius. Miriam thinks that the guards' supervisor seems to be interested in her, even as he is performing his duties. But, like her father, she avoids contact with gentiles.

As Eliezer and Miriam arrive at Aharon's and Bilhah's house, Eliezer calls-out, "Aharon? Bilhah? We are Eliezer and Miriam, your brother-in-law and niece, from Hammat."

In response, Aharon comes to the doorway and says, "Welcome, brother! Welcome, niece! Please, come in."

Eliezer and Miriam each show due respect to the mezuzah box attached to the doorpost of the house, and then they cross the threshold of the house.

Inside the house, Aharon and Eliezer hug each other warmly, and each one kisses the other on the cheek in greeting. Bilhah stands from a bench in her courtyard and she and Miriam greet each other in the same way. Then Eliezer says "Shalom" to Bilhah, and Miriam also says "Shalom" to Aharon.

Aharon invites Eliezer and Miriam to sit on the benches at a table in his courtyard, and Bilhah goes to prepare some refreshments to share with their guests.

As Bilhah is entering the main part of the house, Aharon says to Eliezer, "The last time that you visited Kfar Nahum, we remember that you were looking for Yaaqov. Later, we heard that you had found him at Ein Sheva, and we were relieved to learn that he was safe."

Eliezer responds, "Yes, that was a worrisome experience for me. Everything did turn-out well. But you know how exasperating children can be sometimes."

Aharon says, "Yes I do, Eliezer. It is no wonder that you and I both have grey hairs on our heads! We heard that Yaaqov was there when Yeshuah was teaching, and when he fed a large multitude with only a small amount of food. What do you think about that?"

Eliezer takes a deep breath, and then he replies, "Aharon, I don't know what to think about Yeshuah. Apparently, this event really happened, and yet there doesn't seem to be any rational explanation for it. I have heard that Yeshuah has been staying in this city for most of the last few months. So, what do you think about him?"

Aharon says, "Well, Yeshuah's teaching seems to be consistent with the Torah, but he and his closest followers openly associate with gentiles and known sinners, and they also have been lax in observing some of our Pharisee practices about washing before eating, and even about our observance of Shabbat. Sometimes his remarks about us Pharisees have been quite critical. So, as much as possible, we have been carefully monitoring almost everything he does. But, as for myself personally, I like him."

Eliezer asks, "What do you think the source of Yeshuah's power is?"

"We believe that Yeshuah's power comes from the Lord."

"But why would the Lord manifest his power through someone who interacts so readily with sinners, the way Yeshuah does? Shouldn't he strive to keep himself pure from potentially contaminating influences, as we do?"

Aharon replies, "Maybe the Lord is telling us that He loves *all* of His children, and not just those who strive to please Him by meticulously keeping the covenant."

"So, what does Yeshuah have against us Pharisees? I think that a righteous preacher should favor a group of people like the Pharisees, who vigorously promote faithfulness to the covenant."

"I didn't understand Yeshuah's criticism of the Pharisees either, until I realized that Yeshuah is challenging the hypocrisy and pretentiousness of many Pharisees, and not just our practices. I agree with him that many Pharisees focus too much on rules-keeping, and not enough on promoting justice and mercy."

Just then, Bilhah returns to the table with cups of fruit juice mixed with water, and also with some dates.

Eliezer says, "But how can anyone separate covenant faithfulness from attentiveness to details? It seems to me that disregarding the observance of certain details, just because someone decides they aren't important, is only partial faithfulness, at best."

Aharon replies, "Eliezer, you have to admit that many of our practices actually go beyond the Torah's requirements. Our insistence that people follow our expanded guidelines imposes an unnecessary burden upon people who find themselves unable to do so, and too frequently it also leads to pride, arrogance, and immodesty among those who think that they can."

"From what you have said, it sounds like you have given up being a Pharisee yourself."

"No, I still follow our religious practices as a Pharisee. But I have stopped expecting everyone else to follow the same rules that we observe. And I have become more tolerant, and less judgemental, of others."

Eliezer asks, "What happened to bring about this transformation in you?"

"It happened when I invited Yeshuah to come to my house for dinner. I wanted to find out for myself about this man, and to question him about his beliefs. Actually, I was hoping that he would do something miraculous, to show us his power. But when Yeshuah came, he didn't perform any miracles, but he did show me how prideful and condescending I had been, not only towards him, but also towards other people who aren't just like you and me. He showed me that I am not better than other people, and that God cares about all of us."

"Yeshuah must have really dealt harshly with you."

Aharon says, "No, Yeshuah actually was quite gentle when he talked with me, but he was direct."

Eliezer asks, "So, are you one of Yeshuah's followers now?"

"I am not part of Yeshuah's traveling group, but I am one of his admirers. And I have learned to look at our religious practices with much more discernment and thought than before."

During a pause in the men's conversation about Yeshuah, and while Aharon and Eliezer are sipping their drinks, Bilhah asks Miriam, "So, how have you been doing, Miriam? Are you engaged to be married yet?"

Miriam replies, "No, Aunt Bilhah, I am not engaged, and that seems to be of some concern to several people. I haven't met anyone that I like well enough to marry, and my father hasn't found anyone that he regards as suitable for me, either. So, that is why we came here today. My father is hoping that either you or Uncle Aharon will recommend a fine, single man that you might know for our consideration."

Aharon and Bilhah both seem surprised, but they are honored to have been consulted for such a responsibility as brokering a betrothal. Aharon shrugs his shoulders, and Bilhah thinks for a moment. Finally, Bilhah says, "Right now, no one comes readily to our minds, but let us think about it some more, and make a few inquiries on your behalf. We will let you know when we find an excellent man to recommend for you."

Eliezer says, "Thank you very much for helping us with this matter. This is one of those times when I especially miss Ahuva. I think that she would know what to do."

Aharon responds, "Yes, I miss my sister too."

Later that day, as Eliezer and Miriam are again passing by the entrance to the Roman garrison at Kfar Nahum, Miriam notices the same soldier that she had seen earlier, the one who was the supervisor of the guards. He smiles at Miriam, and he gives her a friendly wave of his hand. Eliezer sees the communication, but he keeps walking past the gate and he doesn't say anything. Miriam returns his smile, but she keeps walking with her father.

Marius thinks, *What a pretty young woman! She seems too young to be that man's wife or his girlfriend, so she probably is his unmarried daughter. I like Judaea more and more, all of the time!*

CHAPTER 10

Around midmorning on the next day, Yaaqov is outside of his home, playing with his ball, when he sees Rabbi Yitzhak walking towards his family's house. So Yaaqov goes to the doorway of the courtyard and calls to his father.

Rabbi Yitzhak arrives just as Eliezer is coming out. Rabbi Yitzhak touches the mezuzah box on the doorpost with his hand, kisses his fingers, and then says, "Peace be to this house! Good day, Eliezer and Yaaqov."

Eliezer says, "Rabbi, what a nice surprise for me, to welcome you to my home. Have I done something wrong?"

Yitzhak replies, "Of course not, Eliezer! However, I have noticed that, recently, you have appeared to be somewhat troubled about something, and I thought that it might be helpful for you to talk things over with someone. So here I am, willing to listen to you."

"Thank you, Rabbi. I *have* been experiencing some distress lately. I was upset when Yaaqov was detained for questioning in Tiberias, during part of last week. I was upset when Miriam had to deal with an inappropriate advance by a corrupt politician, in order to secure Yaaqov's release. I have been upset ever since I realized that I have failed to identify an acceptable husband for my twenty year-old daughter. And I have been upset because I haven't been able to figure out why the Lord would choose to bless the ministry of a teacher with a reputation for being lax in spiritual practices."

"Well, Eliezer, Yaaqov has been returned to your home. Miriam still has her good reputation. You have always been a good father for both of your children. Personally, I can't think of any young men that I regard as worthy of marrying Miriam, either. And, finally, the Lord is free to work through anyone he chooses, including Yeshuah from Natzerat. I have listened to some of Yeshuah's teaching, myself. He certainly does communicate that the kingdom of God is available for everyone! In my opinion, Yeshuah is a very good teacher."

"Don't you agree that we already have enough rabbis, without Yeshuah?"

"No, Eliezer, we need teachers like Yeshuah. He reaches people who don't actively participate in synagogues, and he gives the people hope."

"But Yeshuah associates freely with all kinds of people, including sinners and gentiles! Shouldn't he keep himself separate from persons who are different from us?"

"Eliezer, not all Jews are as strict as those Pharisees who insist on separating themselves completely from outsiders. We should remember that the Torah teaches us to show hospitality to the strangers and sojourners that are in our midst. That has always been part of our tradition."

"But what about keeping ourselves holy?"

Yitzhak replies, "Certainly, we should strive to live differently from some others, but not to completely isolate ourselves from them. And we cannot be a light to the gentiles while acting as if they do not exist."

It rained throughout the following day, so there didn't seem to be a good enough reason for most people to do anything but to stay inside. Of course, Yaaqov is restless. He keeps looking outside and wondering aloud when the rain will stop.

Eliezer smiles, and reminds his son that the winter rains are needed to ensure that they will have an abundant crop later in the year. He understands that, in nature, changes are happening, even when they aren't visibly obvious to anyone.

Miriam knows that her father is thinking about the cycle of seasons, and about plowing, planting, watering, weeding, and harvesting. She asks him, "Abba, since Imah died, have you ever considered marrying another woman? Wouldn't it be helpful if you had another companion to help you to deal with the changes in your life?"

Eliezer thinks about this briefly, and then replies, "Miri, I have thought about that sometimes, but I don't think that anyone else should take the place that your mother has in my heart, and I think that I would feel disloyal if I ever tried to do that."

Miriam responds, "Abba, the relationship that you and Imah shared will always be special. No one else could ever change that. But perhaps you should open yourself to the possibility of experiencing a new relationship with another woman that will carry you into your future in a similar, but different way, than your past was with Imah. Continuing to deprive yourself of the joy of intimacy does not honor the memory of your deceased wife; instead, it denies the importance of intimacy itself. I believe that Imah would want you to be happy. There is no disloyalty in that."

Eliezer becomes quiet and he thinks about what Miriam said. Finally, he says, "Thank you for caring enough to speak to me in this way. I will think about what you have said. Changes are all around us, and each of us should be open to the future that the Lord is preparing for us. But for now, even though it is raining, I'm going to take myself for a walk."

Miriam says, "Try to stay as dry as you can. We do need you to stay healthy."

Yaaqov says, "Abba, can I go walking with you?"

Eliezer replies, "Yes. But first, bundle yourself up."

About half-an-hour later, Eliezer and Yaaqov return home from their walk, and they discover someone, who looks like Assurbani, is lurking outside of their home. When the person sees them coming, he leaves in a hurry. Eliezer goes inside to make sure that Miriam is alright, and she says that she didn't realize that anyone else had been nearby, evidently watching her. Eliezer is relieved to find that his daughter is safe, but he also is angry. He goes back outside, to see if he could pursue the prowler that he had seen, but he is too late. He didn't find anyone else outside on the rainy streets of Hammat.

Eliezer realizes that he needs to be more careful about leaving Miriam alone. He expects to be traveling again after Purim, around the end of winter, following the harvest of his citrus fruit. He decides to make arrangements with Reuel and Serah to watch over Miriam during at least some of his future marketing trips.

Chapter 11

Six weeks later, Eliezer and his family decide to visit Aharon and Bilhah in Kfar Nahum, and to stop at the market in Tiberias on their way. They leave their home early in the morning, just after saying their morning prayers and eating their breakfast of bread and olives. As they are walking, Yaaqov notices that some of the almond trees are just starting to show their white blossoms.

Eliezer explains that the almond trees are the first of the fruit trees to awaken in winter, and that their blossoms appear even before the almond trees put forth their leaves. He says that the almond blossoms are a reminder of the Lord's eagerness to fulfill His promises to His people.

They arrive at Tiberias' main market just as the spice shop is opening-up for business. Miriam feels a slight shudder as she remembers the last time she had entered that shop, and encountered Assurbani there. This time, however, she is comforted by having her father along with her. She tells the shopkeeper that she wants to purchase some more honey and some saffron. And Eliezer adds that they also want to buy some cinnamon, to give to Aharon and Bilhah. The shopkeeper is delighted to measure the agreed-upon amounts of each item for his customers, and to receive payment for them from Eliezer.

Just after Eliezer and his family leave the spice shop, they encounter Zibrah in the main market agora. She comes right up to Eliezer and says, "Shalom, Eliezer. It has been quite a while since I last saw you. How are you faring?"

Eliezer replies, "Shalom, Zibrah. I am very well, thank you. I have been enjoying the mild winter we have been having, and especially the relaxing interlude from my normal work that it brings."

Then Zibrah says, "Well, since you won't have much work to do for another month or so, please come visit me sometime. My house is farther down this street, adjacent to the dock." As she said this, she points down by the lakeshore.

Eliezer is surprised by Zibrah's boldness, but he responds, "Thank you for the invitation, but my children and I are currently on our way to visit with some of our relatives in Kfar Nahum."

Zibrah replies, "I hope that you will have an enjoyable visit in Kfar Nahum. Will you be available to come to my house for dinner two or three days from now?"

Eliezer could see that Miriam is amused by Zibrah's boldness, but she looks at Eliezer and nods encouragement to her father at Zibrah's invitation to dinner.

Eliezer hesitates a moment, but then he looks at Zibrah and says to her, "Yes, thank you. I could come for a visit to your home in three days."

Zibrah smiles and says, "Wonderful! I am looking forward to welcoming you to my home. I will prepare a delicious meal for us to enjoy together."

Then Eliezer says, "But, who else will be there? Many rabbis have promoted the idea that it should be forbidden for an unmarried man and woman to be alone together in a private place."

Zibrah replies, "Well, since you are concerned about propriety, then why don't you bring your children with you to the dinner at my home. Their presence should safeguard both of our reputations. And I will prepare enough food for all of us."

Eliezer responds, "Thank you. My family and I are looking forward to having dinner at your house three days from today. Until then, goodbye Zibrah."

As Eliezer, Yaaqov, and Miriam are leaving the market agora of Tiberias, to continue on their way for their visit to Kfar Nahum, Yaaqov thinks, *I don't understand why we have to eat a dinner at someone else's home, in another town.*

On the other hand, Miriam does understand, and she thinks, *It is interesting that my brother and I will be serving as chaperones for our father! Perhaps this Zibrah is something like an almond blossom in the winter of my father's life.*

At that same time, Zibrah is thinking, *How can I make the most of my upcoming opportunity to entertain Eliezer, especially with his children being present.*

After three hours of walking northward from Tiberias, the family enters Kfar Nahum at midday. As they pass by the entrance to the Roman garrison, a soldier approaches them and says, in Aramaic, to Eliezer, "Excuse me, sir, but I have been watching you and some of the other travelers on the road. Do you realize that man appears to be following you?"

Eliezer is surprised to find that the soldier is pointing toward Assurbani, who is about thirty paces behind them, and who seems to be trying hard not to draw attention to himself. When Miriam sees that Assurbani is nearby, she feels uneasy and her face becomes pale.

Eliezer is grateful that the soldier had noticed Assurbani's strange behavior, and had spoken to them about his observation. Ordinarily, Eliezer would avoid conversing with any Roman soldier, but this circumstance seemed different, because Assurbani had been threatening his family.

So Eliezer says, "Thank you for wanting to protect my family from that man. He has been causing trouble for me and my children. We live in Hammat, which is just south of Tiberias."

Marius replies, "I will speak to him, and I will try to convince him to stop pestering you."

Then Eliezer and Miriam continue on their way for their visit with Aharon and Bilhah, while Marius confronts Assurbani. As Eliezer walks away from the helpful soldier and Assurbani, he hears Assurbani protesting that he hadn't done anything unlawful and that, since he is a profoi of Tiberias, he should not be harrassed as if he were a wrongdoer.

Marius tells Assurbani, "This is Capernaum, not Tiberias. If you want to be treated differently, then you should go back to Tiberias. But, regardless of where you go, you must stop bothering that man and his family. Do you understand what I am telling you?"

Eliezer didn't hear Assurbani's reply to the soldier, but he is delighted to discover that at least one Roman soldier could be open-minded, fair, and protective toward people who are different from himself. And he is surprised that the soldier was able to speak to him using an Aramaic dialect that is similar enough to his own, so that Eliezer was able to understand him perfectly.

As Eliezer and Miriam arrive at Aharon's house, Eliezer calls out, "Aharon! Bilhah! We are Eliezer and Miriam, from Hammat."

In response, Aharon and Bilhah come to the doorway and say, "Welcome, brother! Welcome, niece! Please, come in."

Eliezer and Miriam take turns giving proper reverence to the mezuzah box before entering Aharon's and Bilhah's house.

As before, Aharon and Eliezer hug each other, and each one kisses the other on the cheek in greeting. And Bilhah and Miriam also greet each other by exchanging hugs and kisses. Then Eliezer and Bilhah, and Miriam and Aharon exchange verbal greeetings.

After they all sat down together inside, Eliezer asks Aharon and Bilhah if they had found a possible suitor for Miriam.

Bilhah replies, "During the past six weeks, we have made some inquiries on your behalf, but so far we haven't found any potential matches for her that are close to her own age. However, we did find two older widowers, in case one of them might be acceptable."

Eliezer noticed that Miriam grimaced a bit at this suggestion, and he understands that she would prefer marrying someone whose age would be no more than ten years older than her, so he mentions that desirable qualification to Bilhah and Aharon.

Aharon and Bilhah shake their heads, and then Aharon says that they would continue seeking to find a good man who might be right for Miriam. Then the four of them share a conversation about the winter weather that they had been experiencing, and about their prospects for getting a good crop in the spring.

Later that afternoon, Eliezer and Miriam return to their home in Hammat, carefully taking a different route through the city of Tiberias.

CHAPTER 12

Three days later, Eliezer and his family go to Zibrah's home at the lakeshore in Tiberias for dinner. Yaaqov brings some apples in a sack, and Miriam has a shoulder bag containing a beautiful, braided challah bread that she baked for the occasion. Eliezer calls-out Zibrah's name from the doorway. Zibrah comes to the entrance, she looks deeply into Eliezer's eyes, she smiles at him and his children, and then she invites her guests to come inside, and to follow her to the house's central courtyard. When they enter the rectangular courtyard, they see a table that has been set with four places, and a platter of broiled fish, a bowl of saffron-flavored cooked rice, and a pitcher of pomegranate wine are already on the table. Miriam takes the challah from her bag, and she presents it to Zibrah.

Zibrah exclaims, "What a lovely challah! Thank you, Miriam, for making this for all of us to share."

Miriam replies, "You are very welcome, Zibrah. I enjoyed making it."

Eliezer beams with pride, on account of his talented daughter. Since everything is ready for their dinner, Zibrah sits at her customary place at the table, and she asks Eliezer and his family to join her. But first, Eliezer and his children wash their hands, and then they join Zibrah at the table. Zibrah asks Eliezer to offer the blessing before eating.

Eliezer lifts his hands and says, "Blessed art Thou, Lord, our God, King of the universe, who brings forth food from the earth. Amen."

Zibrah invites Eliezer to take some of each of the foods on the table, before passing them to the other persons. Then, beginning with Eliezer, each person takes turns taking their helpings of the broiled fish, rice, bread, and wine.

After tasting each of the foods, Eliezer turns to Zibrah and says, "Zibrah, the food that you prepared is delicious! Thank you for inviting us to share this meal with you."

Zibrah looks at Eliezer, and she says, "I am glad that you are pleased with my cooking. I have been thinking about inviting you to my home for quite a while. It seems to me that both of us could benefit from spending more time together."

Once again, Eliezer is stunned by Zibrah's directness, and he can't think of anything to say in reply. Miriam was paying attention to this exchange, and she can't remember any occasion when she had seen her father become this flustered before.

After a brief, awkward silence, Miriam giggles a little, and this breaks the tension between her father and Zibrah. Soon they all are laughing together, although Yaaqov doesn't understand what is so funny. Eliezer remembers when he and Miriam had talked about the possibility of him enjoying a woman's companionship again. But he still doesn't think that he is ready for another intimate relationship, even though it has been almost eleven years since his wife, Ahuva, had died.

Sensing his confusion, Zibrah turns toward Eliezer and whispers to him, "Eliezer, I am sorry if you find my behavior too brazen. I want you to know that I really am interested in you. If I have made you feel uncomfortable, then we can slow things down a little."

Eliezer takes a deep breath, nods, and says, "Thank you, Zibrah. I am flattered by your frankness. Let us wait and see where our feelings might lead us."

Zibrah smiles and says, "Eliezer, you are a very special man. You will always be welcome here in my house."

Eliezer responds, "I appreciate receiving your invitation, Zibrah. But perhaps our next encounter could be in Hammat, at my house. Of course, as a protection to both of our reputations, I would see to it that someone else would also be present."

Zibrah smiles, and whispers to Eliezer, "Yes, I would expect you to make those arrangements. However, I do think that both you and I could enjoy being together by ourselves someday."

Neither Miriam nor Yaaqov heard what Zibrah said to their father, but they did observe that, once again, Eliezer did not reply to Zibrah, and that he was blushing.

However, the meal did continue to a cheerful conclusion, and all of its participants had a good time together.

Later that evening, as Eliezer and his children are walking through Tiberias, on their way towards Hammat, Miriam notices that they are being watched by the same military policeman that had been with Assurbani when he had accosted her. Seeing Mibzar made her feel very uncomfortable, and she wonders how long he has been watching them. She tells her father that they are being watched and then, as soon as she had said it, she notices that the man is gone. Miriam is very alert as the family walks the rest of the way to their home, but she doesn't notice anything else that seems unusual.

Marius had heard about the bathhouse at Hammat, which makes use of a hot spring that is reputed to have therapeutic properties. And he knows that Hammat is only about eleven miles from Capernaum that should take him less than three hours to walk to on his day-off. The bathhouse is a favorite location of a few of his fellow soldiers, and Marius wants to see some of the local scenery beyond Capernaum. So, on the first day of the following week, Marius put on a simple tunic and some non-military sandals and, leaving his uniform at the Capernaum garrison, he sets out for Hammat. He walks past Magdala and through Tiberias, and after a little more than two and one-half hours, he arrives at the bathhouse in Hammat.

In the Roman world, bathhouses are typically places in which people from every social strata share the experience of bathing together in warm water -- men, women, wealthy, poor, ordinary, and influential. Some of these bathhouses include elaborate facilities with multiple chambers and complicated engineering, but the Hammat bathhouse is smaller and simpler; it has a changing room, a latrine, a hot water pool called a caldarium, a cold water pool called a frigidarium, and a pool called a tepidarium that contains water whose temperature is in-between. And there are benches by the walls for relaxing between immersions. Marius observes that a few of the Hammat bathers are wearing special bathing garments, but most of them are nude like him. And none of them seem to give much of their attention to the other bathers, especially to those whose bodies are fully exposed. Conversations between bathers are quiet and respectful. Marius finds his bathing experience to be both pleasant and invigorating.

After drying his body and putting his clothes back on, Marius gives the bathhouse attendant two coins and then he leaves the bathhouse.

It is about two o'clock in the afternoon. Looking around outside, he thinks, *What a nice village this is! The physical setting is beautiful, and the people that I have encountered here seem to be very agreeable.* And just then, as he is looking farther up the hill, he notices someone that he thinks that he recognizes. Her appearance is like the beautiful young woman that he had seen before in Capernaum, the one whose family had been stalked by that weasel from Tiberias. Marius remembers that the girl's father had said that they lived in Hammat. So Marius walks up the street towards the girl. But by the time he arrives at the house, he sees that she had already gone inside. He calls out, "Hello!" And then Eliezer opens the outer door from inside the courtyard.

Eliezer asks, "Do I know you?"

Marius responds, "Good day, Sir. My name is Marius Octavius Syrianus. I am the tesserarius at the garrison in Capernaum. I have seen you and your family in Capernaum several times. Perhaps you may remember when I stopped that unpleasant man from Tiberias from following you, several days ago?"

Of course, Eliezer remembers that incident. And now he recognizes this man as the helpful Roman soldier that had spoken to him, although he looks differently without his uniform. Eliezer replies, "Yes, now I do recognize you! But why are you here, at my home?"

Marius says, "Sir, let me assure you that I am not here because of any problem involving you or your family. Today I am just visiting your village and enjoying the bathhouse. I remember when you told me that you and your family live in Hammat, and I was wondering if it might be possible for me to share some of your time. I have been away from the land where I grew up for a long time, and I get lonely sometimes, having no one to talk with except other soldiers. Most of the people in your country seem to hate soldiers like me, but most of us are really not very different from any of you. In a little while, I will have to go back to my military duties. But, until then, would you mind letting me spend just a little bit of time with you, talking about ordinary, non-military things?"

Eliezer had never been a soldier himself, and he never really talked with one before this, but he knew what it was like to feel all alone among people who regarded him as being different from them. And he remembered what Rabbi Yitzhak had said about the obligation of showing hospitality to strangers and sojourners. So, despite the fact that this gentile is an unwelcome intruder in this Holy Land, Eliezer surprises himself by impulsively deciding to invite the man into his own home. Taking a step back from his doorway and waving his arm invitingly, Eliezer says, "My name is Eliezer. Welcome to my home. Please come in."

Marius is genuinely relieved to have an opportunity to make his first friend in Judaea. He steps into Eliezer's courtyard with both gratitude and humility, and Eliezer shows him to a place at the family's table.

Then Eliezer calls to his children, "Miriam! Yaaqov! Come and meet our new friend, Marius." Miriam and Yaaqov come out to the courtyard and shyly greet Marius. Then Miriam fetches some bread and some cups containing fruit juice for all of them to share.

Marius is hungry; he hadn't eaten anything since his breakfast in Capernaum. But he doesn't want to appear inconsiderate in the eyes of this hospitable family so, restraining himself, he just nibbles on a small amount of the bread and drinks the cup of fruit juice that was provided to him.

They spend a couple of hours visiting together. Eliezer explains that his beloved wife had died almost eleven years ago, and that their small family works together to take care of the family's farm and home. Yaaqov and Miriam each tell Marius about their normal family duties. Then Eliezer asks Marius about his background, and Marius tells Eliezer that he grew up in a small village near Halab, in northern Syria. Marius is the youngest of three brothers, and his family's olive and pistachio farm is not large enough to be divided between the brothers, so Marius decided to enlist in the Roman army as an auxiliary soldier. He received his initial military training in Asia Minor, and after that, he served for almost five years in Aegyptus as an archer and an artilleryman, before being transferred to Judaea. Life in the Roman army is not easy, but it provides him with food, clothing, a place to sleep, interesting places to experience, the satisfaction of helping to promote peace and unity throughout the empire, and hope for his own future. Marius tells them that less than twenty years from now, he expects to be able to retire with a small stipend, and as a Roman citizen.

Eliezer mentions that most of the inhabitants of this territory that Roman soldiers had conquered do not view the soldiers as bringers of peace and unity, but as unwanted oppressors.

Marius understands what Eliezer is saying, since his own country of Syria also had been conquered by the Romans, so his own feelings toward the Roman Empire are somewhat complicated. But Marius also remembers that Centurion Gaius told him that more than ninety years ago the Jewish leaders had actually invited the Romans into their country, to rescue them from the corruption of their own rulers. When Marius mentioned this historical detail to Eliezer, Eliezer didn't want to hear it, but he didn't dispute its accuracy.

Eliezer tells Marius about the Jewish belief in one God, the Lord who created everything, and who had established an unbreakable covenant with their ancestor Abraham, and who had given His laws to Moses, and that covenant faithfulness has been passed down from each generation of Jews to its successors for thousands of years.

As Eliezer is talking about his beliefs, Marius could see both pleasure and confidence on the faces of each family member. Marius listens respectfully. Then Eliezer asks Marius about his own religious heritage.

Marius explains that his parents believe in several gods, including a few Greek deities, but they especially believe in the goddess who is said to control fertility in nature. Marius observed that sometimes worshiping that goddess seemed to work, but most of the time it didn't seem to have any effect. The Romans claim to be inclusive of the gods of every people in the empire, but they also keep adding many of their own former emperors to their list of deities. Marius says that he recognizes the social value of having people throughout the Roman Empire professing some common beliefs, but that he is personally skeptical about the underlying truth behind civic religion. Then Marius mentions that he had listened to Jesus' teaching about the kingdom of heaven a couple of times, and he said that he found that teaching to be quite appealing.

When Marius said that, Yaaqov and Miriam smiled, but Eliezer's facial expression remained the same. Then Eliezer commented that there are many good teachers among the people of Israel, including the one you know as Jesus, but that things that are said about them should be evaluated very carefully. Marius agrees with this remark by Eliezer, and he says so.

Then Marius stands up from the table and says, "Thank you all for your hospitality toward me this afternoon. Most of all, I am grateful for the generous way in which you have shared your time with me, and for receiving this stranger into your home. But now, I must return to my post in Capernaum. I hope that we will be able to visit together again sometime soon. Please let me know if there is anything that I can do that might be helpful for any of you. Goodbye, Eliezer, Miriam, and Yaaqov."

Eliezer walks with Marius to the doorway, and pats him on the shoulder as he is leaving, saying "Please come here again the next time you are near Hammat. I am looking forward to our next conversation. May the Lord be with you, Marius."

And Marius replies, "Thank you, Eliezer. I really enjoyed my visit with you. Perhaps I could help you with your harvest in the spring." Then he walks briskly all the way back to his garrison at Capernaum, thinking about his fine, new friends.

After Marius leaves, Eliezer, Miriam, and Yaaqov talk together about their visit with Marius, and they agree that in spite of the differences that exist between them and Marius in upbringing and religion, nevertheless, they all like Marius. He seems to be a decent young man. Eliezer knew what his friends would think about him befriending a gentile, but he decides that it doesn't matter. After all, didn't he have a religious duty to give everyone the benefit of a doubt?

When Marius arrives back at his barracks in Capernaum, he is confronted by his deputy commander, Optio Titus Aelius Magnus, who says to him, "Marius, I received a report that a few days ago you were disrespectful to a man from Tiberias, who happens to be one of Herod's aides. Don't you understand that the local people don't like us anyway, so don't make things worse for us by harrassing one of their magistrates!"

Marius replies, "Sir, the man that you mentioned was bothering some people who had done nothing wrong. I was just trying to help them."

Optio Titus responds, "Well, soldier, you offended the wrong person. Don't do that again. Keep out of situations that aren't of concern to this garrison, or you will be demoted."

Marius says, "Thank you, Sir. I will be more careful in the future."

Then Titus adds, "And don't forget that besides being here to take care of Rome's interests in this far-flung part of our Empire, we also are expected to prop up the local ruler and his subordinates."

Marius replies, "I won't forget that, Sir."

CHAPTER 13

Ten days later, Eliezer and his family harvest citrus fruit from the etrog trees in their garden, and celebrate the festival of Purim by reading their scroll of the Book of Esther, that describes how the Jews of Persia were saved from destruction by the intervention of Esther and her uncle Mordecai. The scroll of Esther, known as the Megillah, is read in the synagogue twice during Purim, first in the evening and again on the next morning. Members of the congregation participate in the reading by repeating certain verses after they are read, and by making noise whenever the name of the villain Haman is mentioned. During Purim, there is a light-hearted religious obligation for everyone to have fun, and Eliezer's family did that. Eliezer drank much wine, his children participated in humorous skits, and they all sang special songs

After Purim, Eliezer reminds his brother Reuel that he is planning another of his seasonal marketing journeys through some of the Galilean towns, and he asks Reuel to look after Miriam and Yaaqov while he is gone. Reuel readily agrees to do so. It has been six months since Eliezer's last six-day marketing journey, and he is eager to be traveling again in the Galilee.

On the sixteenth day of Adar, two days after Purim and the second day of the week, Eliezer loads Amit and Marit with etrogs (citrons), winter figs, onions, and dried dates, kisses his children, and heads north toward his first stop, that is the main market in Tiberias, where fruits and vegetables are sold. When he arrives at the market, he unloads his produce and begins making sales. One of the last customers to visit his display is Zibrah.

She says, "Good morning, Eliezer. How nice to see you again! When can I come to your house in Hammat for that dinner that we talked about a couple of weeks ago?"

Eliezer replies, "And good morning also to you, Zibrah. It probably would be best if we waited until around the end of next month. After I leave here, I will be visiting the markets in Kfar Nahum, Magdala, Tzipori, Natzerat, and Beit Shean, and then, shortly after that, my family and I will be traveling to Yerushalayim for Pesach (Passover). Let's wait until after the barley harvest is completed, at the very end of next month."

Zibrah says cheerfully, "Eliezer, would you like to stay at my house tonight, before traveling on to those other cities? You have to sleep somewhere, and it might as well be at my place."

Embarassed again by her boldness, Eliezer responds, "No, Zibrah. I am planning to stay with my relatives in Kfar Nahum tonight."

Zibrah winks at him and says, "That is your loss, Eliezer. Perhaps you will accept my invitation on another day. You won't regret it if you do."

Shyly and without speaking, Eliezer begins putting his fruits and vegetables back into their respective containers, as he is preparing to leave. Then Zibrah says, "Eliezer, I hope that I haven't frightened you away. Before you go, why don't you sell me some of those figs?"

After Eliezer sells Zibrah the figs, he loads up his donkeys again, and then he leads them on to Kfar Nahum.

When Eliezer is passing a guard station in Kfar Nahum, he remembers his new friend Marius. Eliezer sees another Roman soldier at his post, but he doesn't see Marius, so he walks on to the marketplace. It is midafternoon, and there will be just enough time for him to sell some of his produce before the end of the day.

At the marketplace in Kfar Nahum, Eliezer unloads his produce from Amit and Marit, and opens his bags, so that customers can see the fruits and vegetables that he is selling. A few customers stop-by and make some purchases from him. And Eliezer buys some newly-made leather sandals for himself from a merchant that is in the vicinity. Then, just as he turns to leave the leather-worker's display, he is surprised to see that Marius is standing nearby, with a smile on his face, and waiting to speak with him.

Marius says, "Shalom, Eliezer! What an unexpected pleasure to see you again so soon!" Marius extends his right arm toward Eliezer, in the Roman gesture of friendship.

57

Eliezer puts his own right hand out and touches Marius' hand, while saying, "And Shalom to you, too, my friend. I have been thinking about you."

Marius replies, "I hope that they have been good thoughts! How are you?"

"I am very well. Last week, my family celebrated the deliverance of our people from destruction in Persia, and today I am selling some of my fruits and vegetables here in this city where you are stationed. What has been happening here?"

"Well, for me, life is pretty much the same every day, as I and my fellow-soldiers try to keep things peaceful around here. But I keep hearing about your countryman, Jesus, who has been traveling around teaching the people, and healing the sick. Last week, I overheard someone say that Jesus was visiting a house here in Capernaum, and there were so many people listening to him, both inside and outside of the house, that a man with paralysis that was being carried by his friends to see Jesus was unable to get through the crowd. So the friends carried the paralytic up onto the roof, and then they lowered him through an opening in the roof to Jesus, who was below. Apparently, Jesus was so impressed by the faith of these people that he told the man with paralysis that his sins were forgiven. When Jesus said that, some of the religious leaders who were there said that Jesus had gone too far in telling the man that his sins were forgiven. But Jesus rebuked his critics, and then he demonstrated his authority by immediately healing the man of his paralysis, which astounded the critics."

Eliezer asks, "Marius, do you believe this story?"

"Yes, I do believe it. The person who told the story said that he was there, and he also said that he wasn't the only one who was astonished at what happened."

Eliezer says, "I can understand the witnesses' bewilderment. According to the Torah, obtaining forgiveness for one's sins comes through making prescribed sacrifices at the Temple in Yerushalayim, and not by some preacher's declaration."

Then Marius says, "But maybe the authority of this preacher with healing powers is greater than that of the Temple officials and the other religious leaders."

"Marius, I really don't know how to interpret this story about Yeshuah. But it certainly has given me something more to think about."

Meanwhile, back in Hammat, Reuel goes to his brother's house, to check-up on Miriam and Yaaqov while Eliezer is away on business, and Reuel discovers Assurbani outside of the house, and straining to look through one of the high windows. Reuel challenges the intruder, "Get away from there, you rat! If I ever see you at my brother's house again, I will beat you mercilessly."

Assurbani backs away from the house, and also from Reuel, saying: "Leave me alone. I am not a wrongdoer. In fact, I have been trying to put things right. You see, Miriam and I used to be lovers, and I have been trying to re-establish our relationship on a more legitimate basis, but her father doesn't know about any of his daughter's love affairs. And I wasn't her first lover, either."

Reuel is dumbstruck by what Assurbani said. He thinks, *If what Assurbani said is true, then perhaps Miriam's tarnished reputation is the reason why Eliezer hasn't been able to find a respectable husband for her.*

Then Reuel tells Assurbani, "Go away from here! If you want to spend any time with Miriam in the future, then you must first become acceptable to Eliezer. If you come back here before then, I promise that you will regret it." So Assurbani goes away.

Miriam and Yaaqov are inside their home, and they heard the commotion outside. Miriam heard what Assurbani told her uncle, and she is confused, hurt, and angered by what he had said. What Assurbani said isn't true, of course, but Miriam is worried that her uncle might not know that. For a moment, she wonders what her father will think when Reuel gives his report. Her father should know that what Assurbani said was a lie, but maybe he wouldn't. Why would Assurbani have said those things, anyway? Then she burst into tears.

As Assurbani was on his way back to Tiberias, he thinks, *Well, I was hoping for a different kind of confrontation, but if I wasn't able to enjoy Miriam's delights today, then ruining her reputation might be a second-best outcome. I wish I could be there when Reuel tells his brother the news that his precious daughter has been promiscuous.*

Reuel goes into the house, to make sure that Miriam and Yaaqov are unharmed, and he sees that Miriam is crying. He thinks, *Perhaps she is upset because Assurbani revealed her secret indiscretions. That would make sense.*

Miriam says, "Uncle Reuel, I heard what Assurbani said to you outside. He was lying! I am a virgin!"

Reuel replies, "Don't cry, Miriam. I am sure that your father will make the right decision when he returns."

CHAPTER 14

While Eliezer is returning to his home from his circuit of Galilean towns, he is eager to see his family again, but he also is thinking about all of them traveling together to Yerushalayim in just a few few days for Pesach. He knows that they don't have much time to prepare for their journey. Amit will need a few days to recover from the marketing trip, before he will be ready to carry the family's personal articles to Yerushalayim. They will travel as part of a group of their friends and relatives, which is a good idea because of robbers along the Yarden valley road, who sometimes prey upon vulnerable pilgrims. They need to arrive in Yerushalayim a full week before the festival, in order to purify themselves and to make necessary arrangements concerning the purchase and slaughter of a suitable sacrificial animal, that will be shared with other members of their extended family. The family will have to pack clean garments to wear during the festival. Not everyone travels to Yerushalayim for the festivals, but most rigorously observant Jews do. But just as Eliezer is thinking about these things, he arrives at Hammat.

When Reuel sees Eliezer walking by, he goes to greet him. "Shalom, Eliezer! Was your trip successful?"

Eliezer replies, "Thank you, Reuel. I sold all of the produce that I brought with me, but I really didn't have too much to sell. I received only a little more than what a laborer would receive as his wages for two weeks of work. Is everything well here?"

Reuel answers, "While you were away, I found that politician from Tiberias lurking outside of your house. He told me that he wants to have a proper relationship with Miriam, instead of the illicit sexual relationship that he had with her previously. I was surprised when he said that, because I thought that both you and Miriam would have had higher expectations for her than someone like Assurbani. Surely, you don't approve of him, do you?"

Irritated by his brother's report, Eliezer says, "No, of course not. Now, I must hurry home. Thank you for looking after my family for me, and for telling me what happened."

Then Reuel adds, "I am sorry to have to tell you this, but Assurbani also said that he wasn't the only one to have fornicated with your daughter. He said that there had been someone else before him."

Eliezer responds, "What? If that is true, then my family is dishonored and no respectable man will ever marry Miriam. Pardon me, but now I really must hurry home. Goodbye, Reuel."

When Eliezer enters his home, he is distraught. Miriam and Yaaqov run to him, and embrace him joyfully, but Eliezer is too upset to enjoy this homecoming. He sends Yaaqov outside to take care of the donkeys, and he asks Miriam to sit down at the table with him for a talk. Sensing that something is wrong, Miriam asks her father, "Abba, what is the matter?"

Eliezer responds, "As I was on my way home, Reuel told me about his conversation with Assurbani. Is it true that you have committed fornication with Assurbani, and also with others?"

Miriam replies, "No, what Assurbani said to Uncle Reuel is a lie. I assure you that I have never been intimate with anyone, and I certainly would never do so with Assurbani. Assurbani has been making inappropriate advances toward me, but I have consistently rejected him."

"But if what he said is untrue, then why would he have said it? How could saying that be of any benefit to him?"

Miriam replies, "I have spent much time thinking about it, and I think that Assurbani wants to shame me in retaliation for our rejection of him. But I am worried that he may tell lies about me to others, and that some people might believe him."

Eliezer tells his daughter, "Miri, I believe you. However, we cannot control what other people may say, and we should not overreact when what they say seems unfavorable to us. We must keep speaking only truth ourselves, and continue behaving in the best way."

Miriam says, "I know, Abba. And thank you for believing me."

CHAPTER 15

A few days later, on the fourth day of Nisan, Eliezer, and his family leave Hammat for Yerushalayim. They are traveling as part of a group of twenty neighbors and friends. A light rain is falling, but this doesn't dampen the enthusiasm of the pilgrims. They talk and laugh and sing songs as they walk south, on the slightly downhill road that leads to the ancient city of Yeriko (Jericho). After a few hours of walking, the group decides to take a short break by the side of the road. Reuel goes over to where Eliezer is resting and he sits down beside him.

Reuel says, "Did you talk with Miriam about what Assurbani said?"

Eliezer replies, "Yes, I did. Miriam told me that Assurbani was lying, and I believe her."

"I believe her too. But what will you do if he tells this story to other people? Gossip like that could ruin Miriam's reputation, as well as your own."

Eliezer responds, "Reuel, I don't indulge in gossip myself, and I try not to concern myself about those who do. I hope that people who know me and my family will disregard Assurbani's lies."

The environment in the Yarden River Valley changes steadily from shady, moist, green vegetation to sparse vegetation, and dry, reddish, tan-colored soil. On the afternoon of the fourth day of their journey, they enter Yeriko. The group of pilgrims had spent the last three nights near the side of the road or by the river, sleeping together under makeshift shelters, with the men each taking turns guarding the camps from possible bandits. But here in Yeriko, Eliezer and some of the others had previously been able to stay overnight in an inn that caters to religious pilgrims on their way to, or from, Yerushalayim. Since it isn't too late in the day, and also since most pilgrims won't be arriving in Yeriko for another few days, then perhaps at least some of their company might be able to obtain lodging at the inn, so they go to find out if any of them could be accommodated. The innkeeper tells Eliezer that another large group had just left for Yerushalayim a couple of hours ago, and that Eliezer's group could occupy the same space that the others had vacated. While the men carried in the belongings, the women went to a nearby spring to draw some fresh water, and also to visit the local marketplace.

The present town of Yeriko is located near the ancient mound that might have been the site of one of the world's earliest cities, and that had been destroyed or abandoned several times during its long history. Yeriko is famous for its tropical climate, and also for its date palms, balsam, and myrrh. The oily liquid extract from balsam trees is regarded throughout the Roman world as the best perfume. At the market, Miriam purchases two loaves of bread, some dates and a small jar of fragrant balsam essence. Then she returns to the inn.

Early the next morning, the group of Hammat pilgrims begins hiking the fifteen-mile, mostly uphill road from Yeriko to Yerusahalayim, over mountainous terrain through the Judean desert wilderness. *[The elevation of Yeriko is about 800 feet below sea level, and the elevation of Yerushalayim is about 2,500 feet above sea level, so besides traversing the fifteen miles, they also have to climb the 3,300 feet change in elevation.]* This tiresome walk takes most of that day, and their legs become quite sore. However, when they finally are close enough to Yerushalayim so that they are able to see the white-marble of the Temple gleaming in the late-afternoon sun, they are encouraged, and they sing together:

> "I was glad when they said to me, 'Let us go to the house of the LORD!'
> Our feet are standing within your gates, O Jerusalem.
> Jerusalem -- built as a city that is bound firmly together.
> To it the tribes go up, the tribes of the LORD, as was decreed for Israel, to give thanks to the name of the LORD.
> For there the thrones for judgment were set up, the thrones of the house of David.

Pray for the peace of Jerusalem: 'May they prosper
who love you.
Peace be within your walls, and security within your
towers.'
For the sake of my relatives and friends I will say,
'Peace be within you.'
For the sake of the house of the LORD our God, I
will seek your good."

[Psalm 122:1-7 NRSV]

This is only the eighth day of Nisan. Pesach is still a week away, but the joyous anticipation of participating in the climactic Jewish celebration of redemption, along with a vast multitude of Jews gathered from throughout the world is already evident in the city. All of the people they encounter in the crowded city seem to be happy, friendly, and considerate. It might be different at other times of the year but, during this season, the feeling of brotherhood binds all Jews together. The resident population of Yerushalayim is about 50,000 persons, but during Pesach the number of inhabitants swells to more than three times that number, but nobody seems too inconvenienced by the crowded conditions. Most of the local residents welcome pilgrims into their homes and courtyards.

Some of the pilgrims from Hammat, like Eliezer and Reuel, are able to stay with their relatives in Yerushalayim, while the others had already made arrangements for their lodgings in a rented storeroom belonging to a local grain merchant. All of the Hammat pilgrims had previously agreed to partake of their Pesach meal together in the storeroom on the evening of the fifteenth of Nisan. Many of the residences in Yerushalayim have miqvaot attached to them for ritual bathing, including Eliezer's relatives as well as the grain merchant who owned the storeroom. And the large bathing pool of Beth Hesda (which means "house of mercy"), that is located north of the Temple area, also serves as a miqveh for large numbers of people. After leaving their belongings at their lodgings, each of the Hammat pilgrims visits a miqveh to purify themselves for the festival with a ritual immersion. As the pilgrims walk around the city, they notice that special clay ovens are already installed throughout the city, for roasting large numbers of sacrificial sheep or goats on the fourteenth of Nisan. And they also notice that some out-of-town pilgrims are staying in tents that are set-up outside of the walls on the plain to the west of the city.

CHAPTER 16

The Pesach meal is shared either by a large family (containing at least ten persons), or by a fellowship group called a chaburah (that could include as many as twenty persons). On the afternoon of the tenth day of Nisan, Eliezer and Rabbi Yitzhak, representing the chaburah of pilgrims from Hammat, go to the marketplace in the Court of the Gentiles at the Temple to purchase a one-year old unblemished male lamb as the designated sacrificial animal for their chaburah. They could have brought a suitable lamb with them from Hammat, but it might not pass the priests' rigorous inspection, and all of the lambs that are being sold in the Temple court marketplace are raised in Bethlehem for sacrificial purposes and have been precertified by the priests.

While they are examining the lambs, they overhear a merchant telling another person about a disruption that had occurred in the Temple marketplace earlier that day. The merchant said that Yeshuah had entered the Temple court that morning and violently chased out the moneychangers and the persons who were selling sacrificial animals. Yeshuah said that the Temple had become a den for bandits. But after Yeshuah left, the people who had been doing business there returned and set everything back up the way it was before the disruption.

After Eliezer and Yitzhak selected a large lamb and determined its price, they exchanged their normal currency for the Tyrian money that is used at the Temple, they bought the lamb, and then they brought it back to the place where Eliezer's family is staying. Eliezer places the lamb in Yaaqov's arms and tells him to take special care of it for the next four days, being particularly careful that it not become injured in any way, that would make it unfit for sacrifice. Yaaqov proudly accepts that responsibility.

On the evening of the thirteenth day of Nisan, all of the Hammat pilgrims gather together at the storeroom where they are planning to partake of the Pesach meal on the following night. By the light of an oil lamp, Eliezer leads the members of the chaburah on a cheerful search of every corner of the premises for any hametz (leaven). Because the owner of the storeroom had already removed all of the yeast and leavened grain from his storeroom, they didn't find any hametz, but this was a necessary part of their observance of Pesach. If they had found any, they would have burned it, and afterwards scattered the ashes in the wind.

With the exception of the roasting of the sacrificial lamb, most of the preparation of food for the Pesach meal is performed during the morning of the fourteenth day of Nisan. These preparations included wine, matzah (unleavened bread), maror (bitter herbs -- horseradish and lettuce), karpas (green vegetables -- parsley and celery), bowls for dipping (containing salt water or vinegar), charoseth (a spiced puree of fruit and nuts), and some cooked vegetables.

That afternoon, Eliezer and Reuel bathed themselves, put on clean garments, and then brought their lamb to the Temple, joining the crowd of celebrants in the outer court. The people taking part in the sacrifice were divided into three groups. At the ninth hour of the day (three o'clock in the afternoon), the gates to the inner courtyard are opened, and the first group is permitted to enter with their offerings. Then the priests close the gates behind them, and the celebrants see a large number of priests standing in several lines between the altar and the court. Each priest in the lines holds either a silver or gold vessel for catching blood from the sacrifices. And at the end of each line, a group of priests are waiting to help with the sacrificial process. On the platform, an ensemble of Levite trumpet- and shofar-players play a loud sustained note, and then the Levite choir leads the assembly in singing the Hallel Psalms [Psalms 113-118].

While the Hallel Psalms are sung continuously, each offerer in turn brings his lamb to one of the stations, where he is required to tell the priest the purpose for which the lamb had been brought. For Pesach, the expected response is "Korban Pesach" (sacrifice of Passover). The actual killing of the Pesach sacrificial lamb can be performed either by the offerer or by a priest, by cutting its throat in a single stroke. Then a priest catches the blood in a vessel, and passes the container of blood to the next priest in the line, and receives from him another empty vessel. The full vessel is passed along the line until it reaches the last priest in the line, who pours the blood on the base of the Temple altar. As each priest in the line receives a full container, he hands his empty container to the priest who had handed him the full vessel. After the lamb is killed, it is hung on special hooks on the Temple court's walls and pillars and is skinned; then the animal's abdomen is cut open, the fatty portions are removed and offered on the altar by a priest, and the entrails are removed and washed.

When their turn comes, Reuel holds the lamb while Eliezer kills it, and then the priests at their slaughtering station take care of the other details, and after only a very few minutes, return the slaughtered animal and its intestines to Eliezer and Reuel.

After all of the lambs in the first group are sacrificed, the gates are opened, and the first group of celebrants leave with their slaughtered lambs, and are replaced by the second group while the priests wash-down the inner court. And after the second group offers their sacrifices in the same manner, then the third group also does so. The slaughtering of the sacrificial animals is well-organized and is carried out efficiently by teams of priests working together at the stations to perform the various tasks. In this way, more than 15,000 animals are sacrificed in less than three hours.

Eliezer and Reuel return to the storeroom-sleeping-and-dining hall with their lamb. They skewer it on a stick of pomegranate wood, rub it with olive oil and seasonings, and bring it to the nearest public clay oven. Since they were in the first group of celebrants at the Temple, they didn't have to wait while someone else used the oven before them. They add some wood to the oven, make sure that it is hot enough, and they start roasting the lamb and its intestines, taking care that no part of the lamb touches the inside of the oven. After each hour of roasting, they baste the meat with some wine, and they add more wood to the fire.

While the lamb is roasting, Eliezer thinks about the lamb's blood that was spilled on the base of the altar, *That blood is a reminder of the redemptive blood that marked the doorposts of our ancestors' homes in Egypt, and which made possible their deliverance from Egyptian oppression. But the blood also reminds me about the messianic promise of our future redemption. I wonder when, and how, that will happen?*

After just under four hours of roasting, the lamb is done cooking. It was only about one and one-half hours past sundown, that marks the beginning of the fifteenth Day of Nisan, the Feast of Matsot (Unleavened Bread). Eliezer and Reuel carefully carry the roasted lamb back to the storeroom where their chaburah of Hammat pilgrims is waiting to begin the festivities. All of the waiting pilgrims had bathed and put on clean garments beforehand. They are ready!

CHAPTER 17

The interior of the storeroom-dining hall is now dominated by the presence of a large table whose top surface is only about one cubit above the floor, and which extends around most of the room, with an opening at one end. Most of the chaburah of twenty Hammat pilgrims are reclining on pillows around the outside of the table, starting with Eliezer as the designated head of the chaburah at one end of the table, and continuing around the table from the oldest to the youngest at the other end.

Miriam and Yaaqov volunteered to serve as attendants for the Pesach dinner. After everyone else has reclined, Miriam and Yaaqov pour the first cup of wine for each pilgrim. Then, Miriam brings out a bowl of water, and Yaaqov a towel. Starting at the head of the table, and then going around the table, one at a time, each pilgrim puts their hands into the bowl of water that Miriam is holding, and then they dry them with the towel in Yaaqov's hands. As each person washes their own hands, they say the blessing, "Blessed art Thou, Lord, our God, King of the universe, who has sanctified us with His commandments and commanded us concerning washing of hands."

After all of them had washed their hands, Eliezer picks up his cup of wine and says the blessing. "Blessed are you, O Lord our God, King of the universe, who has created the fruit of the vine, and brought us out from under the yoke of the Egyptians. And you, O Lord our God have given us festival days for joy, this feast of unleavened bread, the time of our deliverance in remembrance of the departure from Egypt. Blessed are you, O Lord our God, who has kept us alive, sustained us, and enabled us to enjoy this season." Then everyone says, "Amen," and drinks their first cup of wine.

Next, Miriam and Yaaqov serve lettuce along with some bowls containing salt water or vinegar. Each participant in turn, starting with

Eliezer, takes a piece of the lettuce, dips it into a bowl and eats it. After everyone has eaten the maror, the attendants bring out most of the other foods to be eaten: unleavened bread, more lettuce, horseradish, parsley, celery, spiced fruit puree, and the roasted sacrificial lamb. After everyone eats some more of the bowl-dipped lettuce, Miriam and Yaaqov remove the food from the table, and then they pour a second cup of wine for each pilgrim.

Then the youngest boy at the table is coached by his father to speak the following: "Why is this night different from all other nights? On all other nights we eat leavened or unleavened bread, but this night only unleavened bread. On all other nights we eat all kinds of herbs, but this night only bitter herbs. And why do we dip the herbs? On all other nights we eat meat that is roasted, stewed, or boiled, but on this night why do we eat only roasted meat?"

In response to the questions, Eliezer then explains the significance of the unleavened bread, the bitter herbs, and the roasted lamb, by retelling the history of Israel's deliverance from slavery as recorded at Shemot xii [Exodus 12] in the Torah. Eliezer reminds his friends that their observance of Passover is a memorial of the first Passover when the Egyptian first-born were killed, while "our" homes were passed-over. Everyone understands that, in this context, whenever Eliezer uses the terms "our" and "we", instead of "their" and "they", he is identifying their chaburah as a people who also had been delivered from slavery. And when he comes to the end of his explanation concerning the Passover meal, Eliezer says that it also is a celebration of hope for their future redemption when the Messiah will be revealed. Then the chaburah joyfully sing the first portion of the Hallel Psalms together:

> "Praise the LORD! Praise, O servants of the LORD;
>   praise the name of the LORD.
> Blessed be the name of the LORD
>   from this time on and forevermore.
> From the rising of the sun to its setting
>   the name of the LORD is to be praised.
> The LORD is high above all nations,
>   and his glory above the heavens.

Who is like the LORD our God, who is seated on high,
  who looks far down on the heavens and the earth?
He raises the poor from the dust,
  and lifts the needy from the ash heap,
to make them sit with princes, with the princes of
his people.
He gives the barren woman a home,
  making her the joyous mother of children.
Praise the LORD!"
"When Israel went out from Egypt,
  the house of Jacob from a people of strange language,
Judah became God's sanctuary, Israel his dominion.
The sea looked and fled; and the Jordan turned back.
The mountains skipped like rams, the hills like lambs.
Why is it, O sea, that you flee? O Jordan, that you
turn back?
O mountains, that you skip like rams? O hills, like lambs?
Tremble, O earth, at the presence of the LORD,
  at the presence of the God of Jacob,
who turns the rock into a pool of water,
  and the hard rock into a spring of water."
                              [Psalms 113-114 NRSV]

Then Eliezer picks up his second cup of wine, and says, "Blessed are you, O Lord our God, king of the universe, who has created the fruit of the vine, and delivered us from bondage." Then everyone says, "Amen," and drinks their second cup of wine.

Then, Miriam brings out a bowl of water, and Yaaqov a towel for the second hand-washing. Starting at the head of the table, and then going around the table, one at a time, each pilgrim again puts his or her hands into the bowl of water that Miriam was holding, and then they dry them with the towel in Yaaqov's hands, while saying the same blessing as before.

After all of them had washed their hands the second time, Miriam and Yaaqov return to the table with all of the foods to be eaten in the meal: unleavened bread, lettuce, horseradish, parsley, celery, spiced fruit puree, cooked vegetables, the roasted sacrificial lamb, and cut pieces of the lamb's cooked intestines that had been pressed in salt.

Eliezer picks up a matzah and says the blessing. "Blessed are you, O Lord our God, king of the universe, who brings forth bread from the earth. Blessed are you, O Lord our God, king of the universe, who has sanctified us with your commandments, and commanded us to eat unleavened bread." Then everyone says, "Amen," and each in turn breaks their bread, dips it into the horseradish and spiced fruit puree, and eats it. After each of the pilgrims has eaten some of the unleavened bread, the second cup of wine is drunk, and the rest of the meal is eaten.

Eventually, all of the roasted lamb is consumed, with each person eating a piece of the meat that must be at least the size of an olive.

After the meal, the third cup of wine is poured. Then all of the participants say the after-meal grace together, and the prayer of blessing for the wine: "The name of the Lord be blessed from now until eternity. Blessed be our God of whose gifts we have partaken, and by whose goodness we exist. Blessed are you, O Lord our God, king of the universe, who has created the fruit of the vine."

Then Eliezer adds, "The Lord has redeemed us with an outstretched arm and with great judgements."

Then everyone says, "Amen," and drinks the third cup of wine. The fourth cup of wine is poured, and blessed by all of the participants speaking together, "Blessed are you, O Lord our God, king of the universe, who has created the fruit of the vine." To which Eliezer adds, "The Lord has taken us as his own people, and he will be our God, and we shall know that he is the Lord our God, who brought us out from under the burdens of the Egyptians." Then all of the participants say, "Amen," and drink the fourth cup of wine.

Even though all of the wine had been diluted with water, by this time everyone felt at least a little bit light-headed, and several of the children had become sleepy; but everyone was enjoying their special evening. After drinking the wine, the chaburah sings the last portion of the Hallel Psalms together:

> "Not to us, O LORD, not to us, but to your name
> give glory, for the sake of your steadfast love and your
> faithfulness.

Why should the nations say, "Where is their God?"
Our God is in the heavens; he does whatever he pleases.
Their idols are silver and gold, the work of human hands.
They have mouths, but do not speak; eyes, but do not see.
They have ears, but do not hear; noses, but do not smell.
They have hands, but do not feel; feet, but do not walk;
    they make no sound in their throats.
Those who make them are like them;
    so are all who trust in them.
O Israel, trust in the LORD! He is their help and their shield.
O house of Aaron, trust in the LORD!
He is their help and their shield.
You who fear the LORD, trust in the LORD!
He is their help and their shield.
The LORD has been mindful of us; he will bless us;
he will bless the house of Israel;
he will bless the house of Aaron;
he will bless those who fear the LORD,
both small and great alike.
May the LORD give you increase,
both you and your children.
May you be blessed by the LORD,
who made heaven and earth.
The heavens are the LORD's heavens,
but the earth he has given to human beings.
The dead do not praise the LORD,
nor do any that go down into silence.
But we will bless the LORD from this time on and forevermore. Praise the LORD!"
"I love the LORD, because he has heard my voice and my supplications.
Because he inclined his ear to me,
    therefore I will call on him as long as I live.
The snares of death encompassed me;

the pangs of Sheol laid hold on me;
I suffered distress and anguish.
Then I called on the name of the LORD:
   "O LORD, I pray, save my life!"
Gracious is the LORD, and righteous; our God is merciful.
The LORD protects the simple; when I was brought low, he saved me.
Return, O my soul, to your rest, for the LORD has dealt bountifully with you.
For you have delivered my soul from death,
my eyes from tears, my feet from stumbling.
I walk before the LORD in the land of the living.
I kept my faith, even when I said, "I am greatly afflicted";
I said in my consternation, "Everyone is a liar."
What shall I return to the LORD for all his bounty to me?
I will lift up the cup of salvation and call on the name of the LORD,
I will pay my vows to the LORD in the presence of all his people.
Precious in the sight of the LORD is the death of his faithful ones.
O LORD, I am your servant; I am your servant, the child of your serving girl.
You have loosed my bonds.
I will offer to you a thanksgiving sacrifice and call on the name of the LORD.
I will pay my vows to the LORD in the presence of all his people, in the courts of the house of the LORD, in your midst, O Jerusalem.
Praise the LORD!"
"Praise the LORD, all you nations!
Extol him, all you peoples!
For great is his steadfast love toward us,
   and the faithfulness of the LORD endures forever.

Praise the LORD!"
"O give thanks to the LORD, for he is good;
his steadfast love endures forever!
Let Israel say, "His steadfast love endures forever."
Let the house of Aaron say, "His steadfast love
endures forever."
Let those who fear the LORD say, "His steadfast love
endures forever."
Out of my distress I called on the LORD;
the LORD answered me and set me in a broad place.
With the LORD on my side I do not fear.
What can mortals do to me?
The LORD is on my side to help me;
I shall look in triumph on those who hate me.
It is better to take refuge in the LORD
than to put confidence in mortals.
It is better to take refuge in the LORD
than to put confidence in princes.
All nations surrounded me;
in the name of the LORD I cut them off!
They surrounded me, surrounded me on every side;
in the name of the LORD I cut them off!
They surrounded me like bees; they blazed like a fire
of thorns; in the name of the LORD I cut them off!
I was pushed hard, so that I was falling,
but the LORD helped me.
The LORD is my strength and my might;
he has become my salvation.
There are glad songs of victory in the tents of the
righteous:
"The right hand of the LORD does valiantly;
the right hand of the LORD is exalted;
the right hand of the LORD does valiantly."
I shall not die, but I shall live,
and recount the deeds of the LORD.
The LORD has punished me severely,
but he did not give me over to death.

Open to me the gates of righteousness,
>that I may enter through them
>and give thanks to the LORD.
This is the gate of the LORD;
>the righteous shall enter through it.
I thank you that you have answered me
>and have become my salvation.
The stone that the builders rejected
>has become the chief cornerstone.
This is the LORD's doing; it is marvelous in our eyes.
This is the day that the LORD has made;
>let us rejoice and be glad in it.
Save us, we beseech you, O LORD!
O LORD, we beseech you, give us success!
Blessed is the one who comes in the name of the LORD.
We bless you from the house of the LORD.
The LORD is God, and he has given us light.
Bind the festal procession with branches,
>up to the horns of the altar.
You are my God, and I will give thanks to you;
>you are my God, I will extol you.
O give thanks to the LORD, for he is good,
>for his steadfast love endures forever."

>[Psalms 115-118 NRSV]

The singing goes on until after midnight, and by that time most of the children among them had fallen asleep on the pillows. Even after the Hammat pilgrims had finished singing the Hallel, and some of them are clearing away the platters and the cups that had been used in the meal, they could still hear the joyous sounds of other groups in the city as they also are singing their praises to the Lord in this most special night of the holy festival. It so happens that one of those other groups that was singing included Yeshuah and some of his followers.

The morning of the fifteenth day of Nisan is a time of relaxation in which most people sleep late, spend some time reflecting upon the mighty acts by which the Lord had redeemed His people, and think about their obligations concerning holiness and righteousness. Eliezer,

Reuel and their families return to the home of their Yerushalayim cousin Yehuda and his wife Shira, where they exchange stories about their Pesach dinners. Yehuda comments that it seemed to him that there were more Roman soldiiers in Yerushalayim during this year's festival, because of the crowds of pilgrims, and all of the militant talk about freedom from oppression. When Yehuda said that, Eliezer thinks, *I wonder if Marius also is here in Yerushalayim.*

The Festival of Unleavened Bread continues through the twenty-first day of Nisan, and throughout the seven days no leavened bread is eaten. Yehuda invites Eliezer and his family to stay at his house again in seven weeks for the Shavuot Festival. Some Jews travel to Yerushalayim every year for all three of the pilgrimage festivals (Passover, Shavuot, and Sukkot), but most Jews don't attend all three celebrations. However, Eliezer has been thinking about bringing his first fruits offering to the Temple at Shavuot, but only if he can arrange for Reuel to look after his children again while he would be gone . . . especially since Assurbani has been causing trouble.

On the sixteenth day of Nisan, the barley that is used in the omer offering is ceremonially harvested from a designated field outside of Yerushalayim. Afterwards, the priests take the barley to the inner court of the Temple where the newly ripened grain is thrashed, parched, ground, and sifted until it is very clean flour. Olive oil and frankincense is poured over an omer of the flour, the priest waves the omer before the altar and burns a handful of the ground meal on the altar. After the ceremony of the waving of the omer, the people are allowed to purchase barley in the markets, and seven weeks later the covenant renewal festival of Shavuot (Weeks, or Pentekoste) occurs. But not long after the ceremonial barley for the omer offering is harvested, many bags of barley grain are brought into the Yerushalayim storeroom where some of the Hammat pilgrims have been staying, and the visitors must accommodate themselves to a somewhat smaller space.

Eliezer, Reuel and their families enjoy the hospitality of Yehuda and Shira for five more days, and then on the morning of the twenty-second day of Nisan they rejoin their neighbors from Hammat to begin their long walk together back to their own homes.

Chapter 18

By the time that the pilgrims from Hammat return to their homes, they had been away for most of the month of Nisan, and the condition of their homes reflect their neglect. Some birds and other small animals have made themselves comfortable in Eliezer's home, and everything needs to be swept clean or to be washed thoroughly. Furthermore, Eliezer knows that the five-month-long dry season will begin soon, and that he needs to remove the abundance of weeds that had invaded his terraced garden and fields during his absence. Still, it is good to be home! While they were away, Eliezer had arranged for one of his neighbors to feed his donkeys and his chickens, but that person hadn't done anything beyond animal-feeding. So Eliezer, Miriam, and Yaaqov all go to work, busily reclaiming their home and terraced garden.

The next day, Eliezer goes to the main market for fruits and vegetables in Tiberias, to purchase some food for his family. Zibrah happens to be there and, of course, she immediately comes over to him. "Shalom, Eliezer! I have missed not seeing you for many weeks. How was Yerushalayim?"

Eliezer replies, "Thank you, Zibrah. Yerushalayim was crowded, but magnificent, as always! My family enjoyed a very meaningful time at the festival."

Zibrah says, "It is good that you and your children were able to participate in the festivities, but while you were gone, a few people have been spreading a scandalous story about your daughter, Miriam. I know that you have been having a difficult time finding a husband for her, but this damage to her reputation may make that even more difficult in the future."

Eliezer responds to her, "Zibrah, I assure you that the gossip that you heard about Miriam is not true. She has never done anything that would bring dishonor to her or to my family. People who know her well should disregard the lies that are being spoken about her. Please do what you can to stop the circulation of false stories about Miriam, won't you?"

Zibrah answers, "Eliezer, I will try to stifle the gossip about your daughter, but you must know that many people always seem ready to believe even the most outlandish things that are said about others. I remember another young woman who never married, and about whom some terrible things were spoken -- she finally ended up having to to support herself as a prostitute."

Eliezer had heard stories like that before, but he bristled that Zibrah would even mention such a situation while they were sharing a conversation about his own daughter. He starts to leave Zibrah, but then he turns back to her and says, "I will appreciate it if you never mention such disgraceful circumstances to me again. Surely, the Lord has a wonderful plan for both of my children, and I am patiently waiting for it to be revealed. Good day, Zibrah." Then Eliezer turns homeward, carrying the produce that he had bought, while Zibrah worries that what she said to Eliezer had offended him.

As Eliezer is leaving the crowded Tiberias marketplace, he happens to see Assurbani. Eliezer quickly walks over to where Assurbani is, and he says, "Assurbani, you have been telling lies about Miriam, and you must stop doing such evil things."

Assurbani is surprised by Eliezer's directness, especially in such a public place, but he decides to pretend that he is innocent of any wrongdoing, so he replies, "Your daughter is the one who has disgraced you, not me. Instead of traveling so often, you should have watched her more carefully, or at least found her a husband."

For just a moment, Eliezer thinks, *I would like so much to slap Assurbani's face with the back of my hand while shouting my disgust into his face!* . . . But instead, Eliezer angrily removes his sandals, wipes the dust from his feet with his hands, shakes the dust from his sandals before putting them back on again, and then he turns away from Assurbani and continues on his way towards Hammat. Eliezer did those things without speaking even a single word.

Assurbani understood the public insult that Eliezer had done to him, a demonstration of Eliezer's complete rejection of Assurbani, his symbolic unwillingness to even touch the same dirt that Assurbani may have contacted, and his disdain for even wasting words with such an undeserving person. At this realization, Assurbani's face becomes as red as if it had been slapped, because he had experienced Eliezer's contempt for him as a man. Very quickly, his humiliation turns into anger and, once again, he resolves to find some way to punish Eliezer for having offended him.

CHAPTER 19

Two days later, Zibrah is still concerned about the last time she and Eliezer had spoken, so she decides to attempt to put things right between them by bringing him a gift. She spends several hours cooking a savory stew containing lamb, beans, onions, peppers, garlic, barley, and spices; and she also bakes a loaf of bread with some cut-up olives mixed into the dough. Around midafternoon, she brings the food and another item to Eliezer's house in Hammat.

Yaaqov is playing outside his house, and when he notices Zibrah coming up the path to their home, he goes inside to report this visitation to his father.

Eliezer steps out of the doorway to his home just as Zibrah arrives there. He says to her, "Shalom, Zibrah. Welcome to my family's home. Please come in."

Zibrah replies, "Shalom, Eliezer. Thank you for inviting me into your house. I realize that you weren't expecting to see me this afternoon, but I want to try to repair any damage that my remarks the other day may have caused to our friendship. I need you to know that I have the highest regard for you and your family, including your beautiful daughter, Miriam."

Eliezer says, "Thank you, Zibrah. But you didn't need to walk all of the way from Tiberias to Hammat just to tell me that."

"Well, I felt that I should, just to clear up any hurt feelings or misunderstanding that my remarks may have caused. I brought you some dinner that I prepared for your family, plus a gift for Miriam." She takes off the shoulder bag that she has been carrying, and she places it on the courtyard table.

Just then, Miriam and Yaaqov come out of the interior of the building and into the courtyard, and they greet Zibrah. Zibrah and Miriam hug each other and kiss each other on the cheek. And then

Zibrah reaches into her shoulder bag, brings out a necklace made of colored gemstones and beads and she gives it to Miriam. As Zibrah hands the necklace to Miriam, she says, "Many years ago, my husband gave me this necklace. I have enjoyed wearing it, but now I want you to have it. I hope that you will like it too."

Gasping with surprise, Miriam responds, "It is lovely, Zibrah. Thank you very much!"

And Eliezer adds, "How generous it is for you to give Miriam such a beautiful gift!"

Then Zibrah reaches into her shoulder bag and brings out the loaf of olive bread and a warm, covered ceramic pot containing the savory lamb stew, and she carefully places them on the table, saying, "Eliezer, Miriam, and Yaaqov, I hope that you also will enjoy this meal that I prepared for you to eat." She uncovers the pot and the fragrant smell of warm, cooked lamb and spices waft out of the container. Then Zibrah says, "Please accept this meal as a sign of my affection for all of you. I will leave you now to enjoy it in peace, without any further intrusion by me today."

As she picks up her shoulder bag and starts to move toward the doorway, Eliezer speaks up and says, "Please, Zibrah, don't leave without joining us in eating the delicious feast that you prepared. There is more than enough food for the four of us to share. Miriam will fetch some wine for us to drink with the food."

Eliezer gestures for his guest and family to be seated at the table. Miriam brings a pitcher of wine, and some cups, plates, and utensils to the table. And then she also brings a bowl of water and a towel, for everyone to wash their hands with before eating. Starting with Eliezer, each person, in turn, washes their hands in the bowl of water, saying the handwashing blessing.

Then Eliezer picks up the loaf of bread with one hand, and he touches the pitcher of wine and the pot of stew with the other, and he says the blessing for the meal. Then Eliezer invites Zibrah, Miriam, and Yaaqov to eat.

When Eliezer tastes his first mouthful of stew, he stops chewing briefly and he savors the complex flavors that Zibrah had brought together so skillfully. Then he turns to Zibrah and says, "Zibrah, this lamb stew is beyond delicious! Thank you so much for sharing it with us." And Miriam and Yaaqov enthusiasitically nod their heads in agreement.

Zibrah responds, "I am so pleased that you all are enjoying what I cooked. I was worried that the food wouldn't turn out so well."

The diners cheerfully gobble the stew, the delicious bread, and the pitcher of wine. Miriam asks Zibrah to explain all of the details that went into the preparation of the food, and Zibrah is honored to share her cooking secrets.

The diners each share stories about other memorable meals that they had enjoyed. Eliezer refills the wine pitcher, Miriam lights some oil lamps when the daylight begins to dim, and everyone continues to have a great time until well after dusk. At one point during the evening, Eliezer thinks, *This reminds me of family dinners that we had when my Ahuva was alive. Zibrah is easy to talk with, and Miri and Yaaqov seem to like her.*

When the after-dinner visiting seems to have run its course, Miriam and Zibrah clear the table and wash all of the crockery together, Yaaqov goes to his bed for the night, while Eliezer sits at the table, reading a portion from his Torah scroll by the light of an oil lamp.

After the cleanup is done, Zibrah puts her covered pot back into her shoulder bag, and gets herself ready for a moon-lit walk back to her own home in Tiberias. She thanks Eliezer and Miriam for hospitably allowing her to spend the evening with them, and Eliezer and Miriam thank her for thoughtfully providing such a wonderful meal.

Then Eliezer says, "Zibrah, it isn't right for you to walk to your home all alone in the dark. If you will permit it, I will accompany you back to your home's doorway in Tiberias."

Zibrah replies with a smile, "Thank you, Eliezer. I will enjoy having your company as I walk back to my home."

So Eliezer and Zibrah say "Goodnight" to Miriam, and then they begin walking together towards Tiberias.

As they are walking, Zibrah says, "Eliezer, you have done a wonderful job of raising Miriam and Yaaqov by yourself for the ten years that have passed since your wife died. Miriam and Yaaqov are smart, polite, and very charming. I don't think that many men could have done as well as you have as a parent."

Eliezer replies, "Thank you for your kind words, Zibrah. But I am painfully aware of my failure in finding a suitable husband for Miriam.

I should have been more diligent in handling that responsibility years ago, and now I am worried that it may be too late for her."

Zibrah responds, "Don't be so hard on yourself, Eliezer. Time and chance have a way of bringing new opportunities to all of us. I have been thinking a lot about Miriam lately, and now I really believe that things will work out well for her, though perhaps not in a way that either you or she may have envisioned before."

"What kind of crazy, wishful talk is that? A responsible parent would have made better choices on behalf of his daughter, that would have prevented Miriam's current situation."

"What I am saying to you is this, Eliezer, always be open to new possibilities! The fact that you made some choices that contributed to Miriam's current circumstances may actually have made possible the very *best* outcome for her in the end. You profess to be a man of faith, Eliezer, but you seem to think that, somehow, *everything* depends on you. Instead, you should put more trust in the Lord, who has been guiding both you and your daughter all along."

"I would really like to believe that you are right, Zibrah. But the practical part of me can't help but wish that I knew more about what the end of a life's story might be like, especially concerning my children."

"But, Eliezer, you aren't in a position to determine everything about your children's future. Their future belongs to them, and to the Lord. A wise parent can influence outcomes regarding their children, but he cannot control every outcome."

As Eliezer and Zibrah continue walking in the moonlight, Eliezer thinks quietly about what Zibrah had said, and Zibrah respects his silence. After a few minutes, Eliezer says, "I am really glad that we have had this talk, Zibrah. I have been experiencing a lot of stress recently, and now I realize that I brought most of it upon myself unnecessarily."

Then Zibrah says, "Yeshuah of Natzerat teaches that we should not worry about our external circumstances. Instead, he says that we should live more carefree lives, trusting in the Lord to provide for our needs."

Eliezer stops walking, and he replies, "Oh, no! Not you, too! Who is this Yeshuah, anyway, that so many people pay attention to every word he says? . . . It bothers me that he has so little regard for some of our religious practices, and also that he associates with sinners."

Zibrah replies, "Yeshuah is a wonder-worker who welcomes everybody, and he encourages people to live more righteously, without distracting them with complicated requirements and detailed law codes. I like that such a holy man is so open with tax collectors, prostitutes, and other sinners, and he even eats with them. He values all people."

They resume their walking, and Eliezer counters, "But every one of our Pharisee requirements is derived from a provision in the Torah. Regardless of what Yeshuah says, a person cannot be faithful to the covenant without paying attention to particular details."

Then Zibrah says, "But a person can become so immersed in those details, that he can easily forget what the Torah laws were intended to accomplish in the first place."

Eliezer replies, "I understand what you are saying. But it does seem to me that a righteous person would do *both* things: pay attention to the details and, at the same time, not lose sight of the underlying principles."

Zibrah laughs and says, "Well, to me that seems easier to say than to actually do! Demanding strict adherence to a complicated collection of derived requirements that aren't actually included in the Torah is not a substitute for following the actual commandments to love God and also to love other people."

Eliezer recognizes the truth of what Zibrah had just said. Then he thinks, *I never would have expected to be having a conversation about covenant faithfulness with Zibrah! It is nice having someone else to talk with about such important matters.*

Just then, Zibrah and Eliezer arrive at the entrance to Zibrah's house. Zibrah says, "Thank you, Eliezer, for walking me home. Wouldn't you like to come inside for some refreshment, before you have to walk back to Hammat by yourself?"

Eliezer responds, "Zibrah, the meal that you prepared was wonderful. I don't want to inconvenience you any more tonight. I should just go home now."

With a smile, Zibrah says, "If you liked the meal I fixed for you, then why don't you come inside, and then you can show your appreciation in a way that will be enjoyable for both of us?" Then she reaches out with both of her arms and hugs Eliezer earnestly, and she whispers to him, "Welcome."

Standing in Zibrah's arms, and with her face close to his own, Eliezer mumbles, "I don't think that I should do that. I am feeling very tempted, but I don't believe that I should do that.
. . . . Please don't try to push me in that direction."

Zibrah hears Eliezer's words, but she also could sense his receptiveness to her, if not to her invitation. So she stops hugging Eliezer and, taking his hand in hers, she looks into his eyes and says, "Eliezer, I like you very much, and my desire is to open myself to you in every way. Please don't get scared and start avoiding me, just because I have been so bold with you. I will restrain myself, but I would like for us to continue to be interested in each other and to allow our relationship to develop. Will you allow that to happen?"

And Eliezer replies, "Yes, Zibrah, I will. But, in the future, maybe we should avoid being alone together in private places."

Zibrah says, "If you insist that we observe that rule, then I will comply with it. However, I promise that I won't pressure you into doing anything that might make you uncomfortable, unless you tell me that you are ready."

Eliezer responds, "Very well. Thank you for a very delightful and interesting evening. Good night, Zibrah."

Then Zibrah kisses Eliezer on the cheek and says, "Good night, Eliezer. I am eagerly looking forward to our next encounter." And then Eliezer departs, and Zibrah enters her house.

As Eliezer is walking home, he thinks, *I do not have the same feelings for Zibrah that I had for Ahuva, but I do enjoy being with her. I really wanted to go inside her house with her, but I am glad that I was able to resist her advances.*

And, at that same time, Zibrah is thinking, *Eliezer is such a good man! He definitely is worth waiting for. I will have to find a way to keep him interested, without scaring him away.*

Chapter 20

About two weeks afterwards, it is the late-spring beginning of the dry season, and Marius notices that some of the wheat fields around Capernaum are almost ready for harvest. He remembers that he had offered to help Eliezer with harvesting his crops. Since he hadn't seen Eliezer for more than a month, he decides to take another hike to Hammat on his next day-off, to find out how his friend is getting along.

A couple of days later, Marius puts on his civilian clothes, and he walks the eleven mile distance that separates Capernaum and Hammat. This time, he doesn't stop at the bathhouse. Eliezer, Miriam, and Yaaqov are all outside, working in the garden. When they see Marius walking up the path toward their home, the family stops working and greets Marius warmly. It is midmorning when Marius arrives at Eliezer's house.

Eliezer asks Marius, "What brings you to my home, Marius?"

Marius replies, "If you will permit me, I would like to help with your gardening today. I can see that your wheat is ready to be harvested, and that some of your early vegetables are also ready. Helping you would be a nice change from my everyday military routine. Would that be alright?"

Eliezer smiles and responds, "Yes Marius, I welcome your help. Thank you. As you can see, there is much work that needs to be done and I need to finish it before next week, when I am planning to leave for Yerushalayim. I want to bring my offering of first fruits to the Temple for the festival of Shavuot."

Marius says, "Very well. What would you like me to do?"

Eliezer replies, "Why don't you and I harvest the wheat, while Miriam and Yaaqov continue working in the vegetable garden? Last week, I marked the wheat plants that were the first to ripen by tying a reed around them. We will harvest those plants first, and then we will harvest the others." So Eliezer goes to his shed, gets two sickles for himself and Marius to use, and then the two men work side-by-side, cutting the wheat, gathering and binding the sheaves, and stacking them into piles. There is a separate pile for the early-ripened wheat that Eliezer had previously marked for his first fruits offering. As they work, the men visit about recent events, and they speculate about some future possibilities. Eliezer is pleased by Marius' respect for Jewish ideas, especially concerning society and family life. When they finish harvesting the wheat, Eliezer and Marius will carry the bundles of cut grain into the storeroom of the house, carefully setting aside the portion that will be brought to Yerushalayim for Shavuot.

While Eliezer and Marius are harvesting wheat, Miriam and Yaaqov pull out weeds in the vegetable garden, they harvest some ripe vegetables, and then they water the plants. They finish their fieldwork about an hour past midday, and then Miriam prepares a simple meal of bread, dried fruits, and a pitcher of cold water for all of them to share.

After the harvested wheat is brought into the house, Eliezer, Miriam, Yaaqov, and Marius wash their hands, and then they gather together at the courtyard table. Eliezer says the customary blessing for the bread. Then he picks up the platter containing the dried fruits, and he blesses them: "Blessed art Thou, Lord, our God, King of the universe, who creates the fruit of the tree. Amen." Then Eliezer picks up the pitcher of water and says the general blessing: "Blessed art Thou, Lord, our God, King of the universe, by whose word all things came to be. Amen." After the blessings, Miriam hands the bread to Marius, their guest. After thanking Miriam, Marius breaks off a piece for himself from the loaf before passing the remainder of the loaf to Yaaqov, who is seated next to him. As soon as the bread is passed to Yaaqov, Miriam hands the platter of dried fruit to Marius. As before, Marius thanks Miriam for her kindness, and then he takes some of the fruit before passing the platter on to Yaaqov. In turn, each person receives the foods and then begins eating them. Then Miriam takes the pitcher of water and goes around the table, filling each person's cup from the pitcher. Marius and Eliezer's children look at each other's faces while exchanging the customary meal formalities, but Miriam and Yaaqov don't actually converse with Marius.

During the meal, Marius asks, "Eliezer, when will you be traveling to Jerusalem to make your first-fruits offering?"

Eliezer replies, "The festival of Shavuot is one week from today, so I will have to leave here the day after tomorrow in order to arrive in Yerushalayim for the ceremonies."

Then Marius asks, "Will your family be accompanying you to the festival?"

Eliezer answers, "In some previous years, all of my family would make the pilgrimage to the Temple for Shavuot. But this year, I have been planning to make this journey without them, but along with a few other landowners, while my children will remain here under the protection of my brother Reuel and his wife."

"How long will you be away, Eliezer?"

"I expect to be gone about twelve or fourteen days."

Marius thinks briefly about this interval of time, and then he says, "During the time that you are gone, if you will permit it, I can arrange to spend part of one day here, taking care of your garden and fields."

Eliezer thinks for a moment about what Marius had said and then he responds, "Thank you for your offer, Marius. But Miri and Yaaqov will be able to take care of the plants themselves during my absence. However, you are welcome to visit here again after I return."

Marius says, "Very well. I will try to arrange my schedule so that I will be able to return for another half-day of farm work about three weeks from today. It is very satisfying for me to work in the soil with plants again."

After the meal, Yaaqov invites Marius to join him outside the courtyard for a game of throwing or kicking the leather ball to each other, and either trapping it with their feet or catching it with their hands. Marius and Yaaqov play with the ball and with each other enthusiastically for a little less than an hour, and then Marius realizes that he needs to begin walking back to Capernaum. So Marius and Yaaqov go back to the courtyard, where Eliezer and Miriam are talking with each other, while Miriam is making a basket from some peeled willow-shoots.

She shows her project to Marius and Yaaqov, and she explains that this basket will be used to hold the family's first-fruits offering for Shavuot. Marius compliments Miriam on the quality of her basketry.

While Marius is speaking to Miriam, she looks steadily into his eyes, and she thinks, *He seems sincere, and he is much nicer that I thought he would be. I am surprised.*

Marius sees the look that Miriam gave him, but he doesn't understand what it could mean. Marius thanks the family for allowing him to spend so much of his day with them.

As Marius is taking his leave of Eliezer, Miriam, and Yaaqov, Eliezer asks Marius if he could walk with him as far as Tiberias, and Marius agrees. After saying goodbye to Miriam and Yaaqov, the two men start walking together.

Marius says, "Eliezer, thank you for allowing me to visit your family today. I like being a soldier, but I do miss socializing with people that aren't soldiers. Being with your family is especially enjoyable to me. Moreover, it has been more than five years since the last time that I did any farmwork, and I enjoyed working with plants again."

Eliezer replies, "Marius, thank you for coming to my home today. You were a big help! My children and I have learned to like you. Is your farmland in northern Syria similar to Israel's?"

Marius answers, "In many ways, the farms in your country do remind me of where I grew up. Where I come from, we raise wheat, cotton, grapes, olives, and sheep, just like here. But my homeland also is famous for raising pistachios, and I haven't seen many of those small nut-bearing trees here."

Eliezer says, "We like eating pistachios and cooking with them too, but they are very expensive. Sometimes clusters of pistachio nuts can be found growing wild along roadsides, but the only place where I have noticed them being cultivated in Israel is in the Huleh Valley, about ten miles north of Lake Kinneret. I have seen how much you enjoy farming. Tell me again, why did you leave your family's farm in Syria to become a Roman soldier?"

Marius responds, "I am the youngest of three brothers, and my family's farm is not large enough to be divided between my brothers and me, so I decided to pursue the career of an auxiliary soldier with the Roman army. After I complete my twenty-five years of service, I am planning to buy my own farm."

Eliezer says, "I hope that your two older brothers appreciate the sacrifice that you made on their behalf, in giving up your rightful share of the family farm."

Marius says, "They do. But, at the same time, I believe that my experiences as a soldier in lands far from my homeland also have been beneficial for me. I have been enriched by firsthand experiences among people that are different from my own countrymen. I have learned that just because someone may seem different than me doesn't necessarily make him less important than I am. In fact, I have found that differences can be good."

Eliezer lifts his eyes from the road and, looking directly at Marius, he says, "I am only just beginning to learn that lesson. However, most of my countrymen are very narrow-minded, and feel threatened by ideas that are new to them."

Marius smiles and says, "The people in my homeland are like that too, and they are just as adamant about holding onto their traditional ways as people here are stubborn about yours."

"Maybe that is because both of our peoples are descended from the same Aramaean group," Eliezer speculates.

Marius says, "You may be right about our sharing a common ancestry, but I believe that exclusivism is even deeper than heredity, because I also have witnessed it among the Greeks, the Romans, and the Aegyptians."

"Really? Well, maybe that explains why those people are always trying to get everybody else to do things their way! You and I must share some more talk about cultural differences at a later time. But I have almost arrived at my destination for this afternoon. I am looking forward to seeing you again, Marius, about three weeks from now!"

After saying that, Eliezer leaves the main road and turns toward the Tiberius waterfront, for his afternoon visit at Zibrah's house. Marius waves farewell to Eliezer, and then he continues on his own way back toward Capernaum.

Even before Eliezer arrives at her house, Zibrah goes outside to meet him, and she hugs him vigorously. It is obvious that she has eagerly been watching for him. Excitedly, they go inside her house together, for another chaste visit of sharing conversation, hopes, thoughts, and fruit juice together.

CHAPTER 21

Just as he had planned, two days later, Eliezer packs up a few of his essential belongings, as well as the basket Miriam made to hold his Shavuot first-fruits wheat offering, and he leaves Hammat with a few other men from his town, who also are traveling to Yerushalayim for the festival without their wives and children. They leave Hammat early on the first day of the month of Sivan. They follow the same southerly Yarden River Valley route through Yeriko, before turning west and taking the uphill road to Yerushalayim, as they had traveled previously for Pesach. However, this time they made the eighty-two mile journey in just four days, instead of the five-day trip that they had taken with their families only seven weeks earlier. They traveled faster in order to avoid being out on the road during Shabbat, which always occurs on the day before Shavuot. Many of the pilgrims who live only a short distance from Yerushalayim could wait until the first day of the week for their trip, but not the travelers from Galilee.

During the afternoon of the fourth of Sivan, Eliezer and his fellow-pilgrims from Hammat enter Yerushalayim. As they are entering the city, they sing,

> "I was glad when they said to me, 'Let us go to the
> house of the LORD!'
> Our feet are standing within your gates, O Jerusalem."
> [Psalm 122:1-2 NRSV]

Once inside Yerushalayim, they split-up and go to their temporary accommodations. Eliezer goes to the home of his cousin Yehuda and his wife Shira, with whom he had stayed during Pesach.

When Eliezer arrives at the entrance to Yehuda's two-story house, he knocks on the door and calls to his cousin, "Yehuda and Shira! I am Eliezer, from Hammat."

In response, Yehuda opens the door and says, "Shalom, cousin! As always, you are welcome to come into our house."

Eliezer gives due reverence to the mezuzah box that is attached to the doorpost before entering the house. Then Yehuda and Eliezer hug each other warmly, and also kiss each other on the cheek. Shira is working at the cooking area in a corner of the room, busily preparing food for their Shabbat meals, but she stops working long enough to join her husband in greeting Eliezer.

Next, Yehuda invites Eliezer to go upstairs to the guest room that he had used before, where he could freshen-up and change his clothes before dinner.

Eliezer enjoys his cousin's hospitality, and he experiences the familiar observance of Shabbat with Yehuda and Shira. They share a relaxing, full day together, including lighting the Shabbat lamps, joyful meals, study, worship, and rest.

At one point, Eliezer asks Yehuda and Shira if they can recommend a suitable young man as a possible husband for Miriam, and Yehuda mentions that he knows a forty year-old priest named Nathan, whose wife had died recently and who told him that he was interested in marrying again.

Eliezer thanks his cousin for the suggestion, but he says that Miriam wouldn't want to marry someone who is about the same age as her father. Neither Yeduda nor Shira are able to provide another suggestion, but they tell Eliezer that they will make some inquiries on his behalf in their community.

Shavuot is an annual observance that has many aspects. It commemorates the anniversary of when the Israelites received the revelation of the Torah at Mount Sinai. As such, many rabbis emphasize that Shavuot is a ceremony of covenant renewal. But in practice, Shavuot is mainly a celebration of thanksgiving to God for the produce of the Promised Land, particularly for wheat, barley, grapes, figs, pomegranates, olives, honey, and dates. Detailed instructions pertaining to the first-fruits offering are given in scriptural texts in Vaiyikra [at Leviticus 23:15-22], Bemidbar [at Numbers 10:10, 28:26-31], and Devarim [at Deuteronomy 16:16-17, 26:1-11]. Actually, a first-fruits offering from those designated plant species may be given anytime between Shavuot and Sukkot, but the first-fruits offering of wheat has special significance at Shavuot.

During the evening before the morning of Shavuot, Eliezer takes his offering of bundled stalks of early-ripened wheat and arranges it carefully in the basket that Miriam had made, and that she also had decorated with a narrow strip of dyed linen cloth.

On the first day of the week, the sixth of Sivan, the procession of first-fruits begins in the morning and continues throughout the day, until the last basket of produce is brought to the Temple from outside of the immediate vicinity of Yerushalayim. On that morning, Eliezer awakes while it is still dark outside, and he takes his basket containing the bundled stalks of his first-fruits wheat offering, and he carries it to the arched staircase that leads to the Temple Mount, and he joins some other pilgrims that are gathered there. Eliezer sees that some pilgrims also brought other types of offerings besides wheat. And at the same time, another group of pilgrims is gathering by the stairway outside the Huldah Gates.

As the first rays of sunlight begin to illuminate the sky, the priests at the Temple offer their daily sacrifice of a lamb, their recitation of morning prayers and the appointed scriptures (which on this day includes the Ten Commandments and the Sh'mah Yisrael) and the blessings, and they also burn some incense.

When these daily duties are completed, an ensemble of Levite musicians announces the beginning of the Shavuot ceremony by blowing shofars and flutes at the Temple, and the Temple guards open the doors of the outer gates of the Temple. Then the procession of pilgrims goes across the outer court, passes through the soreg balustrade (partition), up the steps to the platform, through the Beautiful Gate and across the Court of the Women, through Nicanor's Gate to the Court of Israelites, and into the Court of the Priests. When it is his turn, Eliezer, carries his first-fruits offering basket to the place between the altar and the entrance to the Sanctuary, and there he announces to the officiating priest,

> "Today I declare to the LORD your God that I have
> come into the land that the LORD swore to our
> ancestors to give us."
>
> [Deuteronomy 26:3b NRSV]

Then Eliezer lowers the basket from his shoulder and he holds the basket from underneath. The priest recites each verse of the Devarim portion for Shavuot, and Eliezer responds by repeating each verse after the priest:

> "A wandering Aramean was my ancestor;
> he went down into Egypt and lived there as an alien,
>   few in number,
> and there he became a great nation, mighty and populous.
> When the Egyptians treated us harshly and afflicted us,
> by imposing hard labor on us,
>   we cried to the LORD, the God of our ancestors;
> the LORD heard our voice and saw our affliction,
>   our toil, and our oppression.
> The LORD brought us out of Egypt with a mighty hand
>   and an outstretched arm,
> with a terrifying display of power,
>   and with signs and wonders;
> and he brought us into this place and gave us this land,
>   a land flowing with milk and honey.
> So now I bring the first of the fruit of the ground
>   that you, O LORD, have given me."
> [Deuteronomy 26:5-10 NRSV]

Then the priest places his hands under Eliezer's hands that already were beneath the basket, and together Eliezer and the officiating priest wave the first-fruits offering before God -- moving the basket in four directions, and also raising and lowering it. Afterwards, the priest takes the basket from Eliezer, and places it momentarily on the corner of the altar, while Eliezer prostrates himself before the Lord. And then Eliezer gets up and leaves the Temple. He has fulfilled his Shavuot obligation.

Eliezer knows that some of the newly-harvested wheat that was offered by the Shavuot pilgrims will be made into flour, and baked into two loaves of bread by the priests. Then the two loaves will be offered, along with a sacrifice of two sheep, at the Temple altar while the Levite musicians play special music with trumpets, flutes, and singing. And afterwards, the two loaves and the sacrificial meat will be eaten by the priests in the Temple, as an important part of the festival observance.

Eliezer returns to Yehuda's house, to partake of a light midday meal with his cousins, during which Eliezer describes for Yehuda and Shira his experience of how this year's ceremony had gone. After the meal, Yehuda and Eliezer read together the Torah portion from Shemot that is designated for this festival day:

> "On the third new moon after the Israelites had gone out of the land of Egypt, on that very day, they came into the wilderness of Sinai. They had journeyed from Rephidim, entered the wilderness of Sinai, and camped in the wilderness; Israel camped there in front of the mountain.
>
> Then Moses went up to God; the LORD called to him from the mountain, saying,
>
> 'Thus you shall say to the house of Jacob, and tell the Israelites: You have seen what I did to the Egyptians, and how I bore you on eagles' wings and brought you to myself. Now therefore, if you obey my voice and keep my covenant, you shall be my treasured possession out of all the peoples. Indeed, the whole earth is mine, but you shall be for me a priestly kingdom and a holy nation. These are the words that you shall speak to the Israelites.'
>
> So Moses came, summoned the elders of the people, and set before them all these words that the LORD had commanded him. The people all answered as one: 'Everything that the LORD has spoken we will do.' Moses reported the words of the people to the LORD. Then the LORD said to Moses, 'I am going to come to you in a dense cloud, in order that the people may hear when I speak with you and so trust you ever after.'

When Moses had told the words of the people to the LORD, the LORD said to Moses: "Go to the people and consecrate them today and tomorrow. Have them wash their clothes and prepare for the third day, because on the third day the LORD will come down upon Mount Sinai in the sight of all the people. You shall set limits for the people all around, saying, 'Be careful not to go up the mountain or to touch the edge of it. Any who touch the mountain shall be put to death. No hand shall touch them, but they shall be stoned or shot with arrows; whether animal or human being, they shall not live.' When the trumpet sounds a long blast, they may go up on the mountain." So Moses went down from the mountain to the people. He consecrated the people, and they washed their clothes. And he said to the people, 'Prepare for the third day; do not go near a woman.'

On the morning of the third day there was thunder and lightning, as well as a thick cloud on the mountain, and a blast of a trumpet so loud that all the people who were in the camp trembled. Moses brought the people out of the camp to meet God. They took their stand at the foot of the mountain. Now Mount Sinai was wrapped in smoke, because the LORD had descended upon it in fire; the smoke went up like the smoke of a kiln, while the whole mountain shook violently. As the blast of the trumpet grew louder and louder, Moses would speak and God would answer him in thunder. When the LORD descended upon Mount Sinai, to the top of the mountain, the LORD summoned Moses to the top of the mountain, and Moses went up. Then the LORD said to Moses, 'Go down and warn the people not to break through to the LORD to look; otherwise many of them will perish. Even the priests who approach the LORD must consecrate themselves or the LORD will break out against them.' Moses said to the LORD, "The people are not permitted to come up to Mount Sinai; for you yourself warned us, saying, 'Set limits around the mountain and keep it holy.'" The LORD said to him, "Go down, and come up bringing Aaron with you; but do not let either the priests or the people break through to come up to the LORD; otherwise he will break out against them." So Moses went down to the people and told them.

Then God spoke all these words:

'I am the LORD your God, who brought you out of the land of Egypt, out of the house of slavery; you shall have no other gods before me.

You shall not make for yourself an idol, whether in the form of anything that is in heaven above, or that is on the earth beneath, or that is in the water under the earth.

You shall not bow down to them or worship them; for I the LORD your God am a jealous God, punishing children for the iniquity of parents, to the third and the fourth generation of those who reject me, but showing steadfast love to the thousandth generation of those who love me and keep my commandments.

You shall not make wrongful use of the name of the LORD your God, for the LORD will not acquit anyone who misuses his name.

Remember the sabbath day, and keep it holy. Six days you shall labor and do all your work. But the seventh day is a sabbath to the LORD your God; you shall not do any work -- you, your son or your daughter, your male or female slave, your livestock, or the alien resident in your towns. For in six days the LORD made heaven and earth, the sea, and all that is in them, but rested the seventh day; therefore the LORD blessed the sabbath day and consecrated it.

Honor your father and your mother, so that your days may be long in the land that the LORD your God is giving you.
You shall not murder.
You shall not commit adultery.
You shall not steal.
You shall not bear false witness against your neighbor.
You shall not covet your neighbor's house; you shall not covet your neighbor's wife, or male or female slave, or ox, or donkey, or anything that belongs to your neighbor.'

When all the people witnessed the thunder and lightning, the sound of the trumpet, and the mountain smoking, they were afraid and trembled and stood at a distance, and said to Moses, 'You speak to us, and we will listen; but do not let God speak to us, or we will die.' Moses said to the people, 'Do not be afraid; for God has come only to test you and to put the fear of him upon you so that you do not sin.' Then the people stood at a distance, while Moses drew near to the thick darkness where God was."
[Exodus 19:1-25 & 20:1-21 NRSV]

While Eliezer and Yehuda are discussing this Torah portion, they hear music from the Temple signalling that the two loaves and the sheep are being offered by the priests. Then, after Eliezer and Yehuda finish their discussion, they recite the Sh'mah Yisrael, from Devarim:

"Hear, O Israel: The LORD is our God, the LORD alone. You shall love the LORD your God with all your heart, and with all your soul, and with all your might."
[Deuteronomy 6:4-5 NRSV]

As arranged previously, the next morning, Eliezer thanks Yehuda and Shira for their hospitality, and then he goes to the Gate of Ephraim,

101

that also is called the Fish Gate, to meet with the other pilgrims from Hammat, in order to begin their homeward journey together.

They arrive in Hammat early in the afternoon of the eleventh day of Sivan. When he arrives at his house, Eliezer is greeted enthusiastically by Miriam and Yaaqov.

Miriam had already begun her preparations for the family's observance of Shabbat, that will begin at sundown. While Miriam is working, Eliezer tells her and Yaaqov all about his Shavuot trip, and his brief visit with Yehuda and Shira. Eliezer tells Miriam that Yehuda knows a forty year-old priest who is a widower and also interested in marrying again, but Miriam reminds him that she would prefer someone closer to her own age.

The following day, Eliezer's brother, Reuel, comes by to tell Eliezer that he had been keeping an eye on Eliezer's family and home while he was gone. He also reports that he had heard a rumor that Assurbani had raped a thirteen year-old girl in Tiberias. However, because he is a profoi, Assurbani will not be accused of any wrongdoing. Eliezer reminds himself about the unreliability of rumors, and he resolves to leave Assurbani's fate to the Lord.

CHAPTER 22

On the first day of the week, the thirteenth of Sivan, Eliezer awakes early to work in his terraced garden. There is much to do, the dry season has been underway for about a month, and the produce that Eliezer had planted is growing vigorously. After a light breakfast and prayers, Eliezer and Yaaqov spend most of that morning weeding and watering in the garden.

That afternoon, Eliezer goes to Hammat's synagogue, where he finds his brother Reuel, his friend Reuben, and Rabbi Yitzhak sitting outside, discussing that day's Torah portion from Bemidbar, about the offerings of the leaders for the dedication of the altar [Numbers 7] for the Tabernacle. At the end of the reading, Moses is described as conversing with the Lord in the tabernacle, and the voice speaking to him was heard as from above and between the two cherubim on the Ark of the Covenant.

Reuel says, "Having a device for talking to God would be wonderful! Rabbi Yitzhak, what happened to the Ark of the Covenant?"

Yitzhak explains, "The Ark of the Covenant is never mentioned in our authoritative writings after the destruction of the Temple by the Babylonians. Some rabbis have speculated that the Ark was captured by the Babylonians, and was taken back to Babylon. Other rabbis have the opinion that the Ark, together with certain other sacred vessels, were hidden by King Josiah or by a priest, in order to prevent their capture by the Babylonians, and that the location of the hiding-place could either be beneath the Temple plaza, or at another undisclosed location. But we do not know what happened to the Ark of the Covenant."

Reuben says, "I heard some speculation that the prophet Yirmiyahu (Jeremiah) had been involved with hiding the Ark from the Babylonians, and that the Lord himself also had spoken to His people through Yirmiyahu throughout that terrible period."

Then Eliezer reminds his friends, "The Lord has often spoken to people through prophets in the history of our people. I wonder if there are any prophets in our present time."

Reuel asks, "What about Yohanan the Baptizer, or even Yeshuah? Could they be prophets of the Lord?"

Yitzhak replies, "Some rabbis have the opinion that no authentic prophets have arisen since Malachi, who was a messenger of God more than 450 years ago; however, I believe that it certainly is possible that the Lord could be speaking through prophets in our own time, including Yohanan and Yeshuah. We should ask the Lord for discernment, and then listen very carefully to those voices that seem to be speaking to us authoritatively."

Eliezer responds, "Rabbi, I understand what you are saying about the need for discernment, and I agree with you. But my discernment regarding Yeshuah is influenced by the fact that he openly associates with sinners. Surely someone like that could not be a prophet, could he?"

Yitzhak thinks for just a moment, and then he says, "A follower of Yeshuah told me that, one day when someone was complaining about his master eating with tax collectors and sinners, Yeshuah had heard what the man said and he interjected, 'Those who are well have no need of a physician, but those who are sick. Go and learn what this means, "I desire mercy, not sacrifice." For I have come not to call the righteous but sinners.'"

Eliezer carefully considers this saying briefly, and then he replies, "But the prophet that Yeshuah was quoting was saying that acceptable worship should be performed only by people who are loyal, sincere, and faithful. That is not the same thing as disregarding our purity regulations."

Then Yitzhak says, "If Yeshuah is an authentic spokesman of the Lord, then perhaps he is advocating a higher form of righteousness and loyalty than exclusive ritual purity."

Eliezer thinks deeply about what Yitzhak said, but he has trouble disassociating righteousness from ritual purity. It always seems to him that those concepts were two parts of the same thing, and therefore they always should be found together. But he thinks, *Maybe Yitzhak is right. I must try to find out about righteousness that is higher than ritual deeds.*

Eliezer thanks Yitzhak, Reuel, and Reuben for the discussion that they had shared, and then he goes home to be with his family. But he continues to think about the idea of a righteousness which transcends ceremonial acts. Later that evening, Eliezer realizes that Yitzhak was talking about heart-obedience, which is different from the habitual performance of rituals and practices.

As Miriam is preparing the family's evening meal of stewed vegetables and bread, she also is thinking about her life. Her father hasn't found a husband for her yet, even after conferring with Uncle Aharon and Aunt Bilhah, and their cousins Yehuda and Shira. She doesn't personally know any unmarried men her own age. Then she remembers her father's friend, Marius. He isn't a Jew, so her father would never approve of him as a suitor for her, but he does seem to be a good person, and handsome too. Despite their differences in upbringing and religion, she likes him. Then Yaaqov interrupts her thinking, by asking her what they would be eating for dinner. So she shows him the bread dough that she is kneading, and the vegetable stew that is cooking. And Yaaqov says, "Oh no, not again!"

At that same time, Marius is marching with his sentries from post to post, supervising the changing of the guard in Capernaum. As he carries out this duty, he also is thinking about Eliezer and his family. He is pretty sure that Eliezer would have returned to his home by now, after participating in the Shavuot ceremony in Jerusalem. Marius decides to visit his friends in Hammat on his next day off, to do some more agricultural work with Eliezer.

And, while Zibrah is preparing her evening meal, she is thinking about Eliezer. She hasn't seen him since before he went to Yerushalayim, and she has missed his visits. She reminds herself how fortunate she is to have such a good man as Eliezer in her life, even if only for brief, occasional visits.

After dinner that evening, Eliezer finds himself thinking about Zibrah. So he takes leave from his children and begins walking towards Tiberias, to spend some more time with Zibrah. But as he walks along, Eliezer asks himself questions about his relationship with Zibrah, and about where it is going. However, he doesn't turn back. When he arrives at her house, Zibrah is very happy to welcome him inside again. Eliezer temporarily suppresses his concerns as he enters her home.

Later that evening, Zibrah senses Eliezer's pensiveness, so she says, "Eliezer, I can see that you are uncomfortable about something. As you requested, I haven't pressured you about physical intimacy. So, what is bothering you?"

Eliezer responds, "I enjoy our occasional visits together, and I understand that you want more from me. I would enjoy that too, but not without our being married."

Zibrah says, "If you and I decided to have a sexual relationship, it wouldn't be adultery because you and I are both unmarried persons. It wouldn't hurt anybody, so I don't think that it would be wrong."

Eliezer replies, "Strictly speaking, it may not be adultery, but fornication is immoral, and is itself regarded as an offense against marriage. Also, some of our neighbors would begin talking about us, which would create a scandal."

She laughs and responds, "Actually, our neighbors might already be talking about us! But it wouldn't bother me if someone became upset about our relationship. What we do privately, or don't do for that matter, shouldn't be of concern to anyone but you and me!"

"But, at the very least, immorality would cause problems for my children, and some people would avoid doing business with both of us."

Zibrah says, "Why are we spending our time talking about the consequences of a sexual relationship that we do not have, since we are carefully observing lives of abstinence?"

Eliezer takes a deep breath and then he replies, "Well, it turns out that you aren't the only one in this relationship who is interested in greater intimacy. I think that we *should* marry each other. I enjoy our friendship, and my children like you too. So, will you marry me?"

She says, "Well, as far as I am concerned, that shouldn't be necessary. I still think that we should be able to live our lives any way that we want, without getting married. But if you think that is what you want us to do, then I will do that."

Eliezer reaches out, hugs and kisses Zibrah, and he says, "Thank you, Zibrah! I believe that we will be very happy together. . . . Wait. I remember when you told me that your father had died. Do you have an older brother, or somebody else, that I should contact, in order to obtain permission to marry you?"

"No, Eliezer, mine is the only permission that you need, and I have already given you my consent."

"Well, I want to do everything in the right way. I realize that our situation is a lot different than when young people get married. But we still need to prepare our marriage agreement, and make arrangements for our betrothal, and also for our wedding feast."

"Yes. And we also will have to figure out our living arrangements for after the wedding: here at my home in Tiberias, or at your family home in Hammat, or switching back and forth between both places, whenever it seems most convenient. But, before we address all of those details, I think that you should hug and kiss me again. This is kind of an important moment, don't you think?" And Eliezer responds cheerfully to her suggestion.

Later that evening, as he is walking home, Eliezer thinks about how he will tell Miriam and Yaaqov about the wedding that he was planning.

CHAPTER 23

The following morning, as Eliezer and his children are eating their breakfast of bread and fruit, Eliezer tells them that he is planning to marry Zibrah.

Miri exclaims, "Good for you! I am very happy about your decision. I like Zibrah myself, and I think that you and Zibrah will be very good together. And I will especially appreciate having another woman in our household to talk with. When will the betrothal occur, and how soon after that will the wedding be?"

Before Eliezer could answer Miriam's questions, Yaaqov says, "Yes. I also like Zibrah. I especially like the good food that she makes! Is she going to be living here with us?"

Eliezer chuckles and says, "I don't know how long it will take for all of us to make preparations for the betrothal and wedding. But I don't think that it will require a very long period of time for us to be ready. After the wedding, either Zibrah will be living here with us, or we all will be living with her in Tiberias. We will figure that out later."

Miri thinks for a moment, and then says, "Well, I hope that Zibrah will come here, to our home, because I would prefer not having to live in the same city as Assurbani."

And Yaaqov says, "I don't care about Assurbani, but I would like for all of us to live in this house, because this is the place where I have lived all of my life."

Eliezer says, "Thank you, children, for your support, and for your thoughts about our possible living arrangements after the wedding. Zibrah and I will consider what you have said when we make our decision about where we all should live together."

After breakfast, Eliezer leaves his home, and goes to meet with Rabbi Yitzhak, to seek his help in writing the ketubah, or marriage agreement, for Eliezer and Zibrah to sign in the presence of witnesses.

He finds Yitzhak in the synagogue; where he happens to be reading from the scroll of Yirmiyahu [Jeremiah].

Eliezer tells his friend Yitzhak, "Rabbi, I have decided to marry the widow Zibrah, from Tiberias. And I would appreciate your wisdom in helping me to make necessary arrangements for the betrothal and wedding."

Yitzhak replies, "Eliezer, your decision pleases me. But I am not very surprised. One of our congregants told me that, several times, she has seen you traveling between here and Tiberias at night. And I also have observed that you have been a lot more relaxed during the past six weeks than I remember last winter, when you were so upset."

"Rabbi, Zibrah and I have not had intercourse together, although several times we werr tempted to do so. Isn't it interesting that, in small towns like ours, it isn't easy for anyone to keep his private actions secret, and people are inclined to assume the worst about others."

"Well, I think that it is a good thing that you are planning to marry again. So, how may I help you?"

"I remember that many years ago, when I married Ahuva, first a marriage contract called a ketubah had to be drawn-up and signed, after which there was a public acknowledgment of our new status as betrothed husband and wife to each other, although we weren't even living together yet, and several months later came the actual wedding celebration, including the consummation. So getting married is a process, in which various social rules and traditions are expected to be followed. But this won't be the first wedding for Zibrah either. So, what would the process be in our situation?"

"Eliezer, I think that it is a good idea to have a ketubah, and the official signing of that document could be combined with a simple betrothal ceremony involving you, Zibrah, and family members and friends of both of you. As soon as you and Zibrah consent to marry each other in the presence of at least two witnesses, then you and Zibrah could privately consummate the marriage immediately. But most rabbis recommend a betrothal period involving a widow of between several days to a month, to allow enough time for making preparations and for acquiring gifts. What timeframe did you and Zibrah have in mind?"

"I was planning to make one of my seasonal marketing trips around the middle of next month, so how about having our betrothal around the end of Tammuz, about thirty days from now, and having our wedding feast two or three weeks after that?"

"Eliezer, you shouldn't have either the betrothal or wedding feast during the three weeks between the seventeenth of Tammuz and the ninth day of Ab (Tisha B'Ab), which commemorate the destruction of our first Temple by the Babylonians. It probably would be too soon to try to get everything done before the middle of next month, so wouldn't it be better to have the betrothal after Tisha B'Ab? That would give me plenty of time to help you with the wording of the ketubah, and it also gives you and Zibrah time to contact your relatives and friends about the celebration."

"That's right! I hadn't thought about avoiding those three sorrowful weeks. However, another possibility might be for us to have the betrothal around the fifteenth of Tammuz, and the wedding feast around the twelfth of Ab? The betrothal would not have to involve the whole community or our out-of-town relatives."

"Yes, Eliezer, that schedule seems feasible. That wouldn't give us a lot of time to write your ketubah. But I am confident that we could get it done."

"And I also would have to do my marketing trip earlier in the month than I had been planning, but I could make that work, too. I must talk about all of this with Zibrah and my family!"

That evening, the beginning of the fifteenth of Sivan, Eliezer returns to Zibrah's house in Tiberias, to discuss the scheduling of their marriage events. He says to her, "I was planning to take my early-summer marketing trip around the middle of the month of Tammuz, and Rabbi Yitzhak reminded me that we shouldn't have any of our wedding events between the three sorrowful weeks between the seventeenth of Tammuz and the ninth of Ab, so we should schedule our festivities around those dates. Yitzhak suggested that we postpone our betrothal and wedding feast until after Tisha B'Ab. But I have been thinking about other possibilities. What do you think?"

Zibrah replies, "If we are going to do this, then I would prefer not having to delay too long. Couldn't we sign the ketubah and have our betrothal early next month, before your marketing trip, and then we could have our wedding feast about four weeks after the betrothal, just before the middle of the month of Ab?"

"Yes, I was thinking about something like that, too. That would give me a little more than three weeks to prepare our marriage agreement, so that we could have our signing and betrothal ceremony on the tenth day of next month. Then I could do my marketing trip between the twelfth and the sixteenth, and we could hold our wedding feast on the eleventh or twelfth day of the following month, after Tisha B'Ab!"

"Eliezer, that sounds great! You are going to be very busy during the next few weeks, writing our marriage agreement, and getting your crops ready for sale. And I am going to have to begin putting together some special clothes and furnishings for our wedding. Now, have you thought any more about our future living arrangements?"

"Yes, I talked about that with Miriam and Yaaqov this morning. They are excited about our getting married soon, and also about getting a new mother. But both of them said that they would prefer having you come to live with us in Hammat, instead of having them move to Tiberias. Do you think that we could do that?"

Zibrah replies, "Maybe we should plan to live in both houses, as determined by our seasonal business activities, mine with managing my fishing operation, and yours with agriculture, but we could try to spend most of our days living in your house in Hammat. Our two homes are really not very far apart, but switching back and forth between them will give all of us an interesting change from time-to-time."

Eliezer says, "Yes, I think that we will be able to make those living arrangements work out for us all."

A couple of days later, while Eliezer and his family are working in their garden, Marius walks up the path to their property. He says, "Hello, Eliezer, Miriam, and Yaaqov! May I work with you today?"

Eliezer, Miri, and Yaaqov smile and wave their greetings to Marius, and Eliezer says, "Shalom, Marius! Of course you may join us in our gardening."

Marius says, "I can see that you are busy weeding and watering your vegetables and melons. What would you like me to do?"

Eliezer replies, "Some of our early figs are ripe, and ready to be picked. Would you harvest them for me?"

Marius asks, "Fine, but how do I know which ones are ready, and how do I pick them?"

Eliezer replies, "First of all, here are some shears for you to use; and over there next to that tree are some shallow baskets for collecting the figs after you harvest them. Ripe figs droop as their necks begin to wilt, and their fruit is a little soft to the touch. Be careful to handle the fruit gently, and to cut them from the tree, leaving a small part of the stem attached to each fig if possible. If the fruit breaks free from the stem by itself in your hand, that is alright. Miri will help you with the baskets. She knows how to handle the figs, and how to put them in the baskets."

Looking first at Miriam, and then at Eliezer, Marius says, "Very well. We will harvest your figs together."

Then Marius and Miri cheerfully go to work collecting the ripe figs. And as they are working, they talk with each other. Miri tells Marius about her father's plan to marry Zibrah. Marius is a little bit surprised. He tells Miriam that he met Zibrah, and found her to be a very matter-of-fact person. All the while, Eliezer and Yaaqov continue their weeding and watering.

Miri notices that Marius is following her father's instructions perfectly. So she says, "Are you sure that you haven't done this before? You are harvesting figs like an expert!"

Marius replies, "Thanks for the compliment. But your praise really should be for your father's good directions. I enjoy doing farmwork. I like being a soldier, but I do miss not being able to regularly work in soil, like when I was younger. I am happy that your father allows me to help in your family's garden."

Miriam thinks for a moment, and then she says, "I was surprised when my father opened himself to you. Ordinarily, Pharasaic Jews don't even speak with gentiles, and especially with Roman soldiers, unless it is absolutely necessary. It pleases me that my father is becoming more open-minded."

Marius says, "Believe me, I understand. My own country also was conquered by Rome, and my people hate the occupying soldiers too, just like here in Judaea."

"Then why did you become a soldier? Wait, I remember when you told my father about your family's farm not being large enough to divide between you and your brothers."

"That's right. And I also enjoy being able to experience other countries. And, after I complete my twenty-five years as a soldier, I will become a Roman citizen and I also will receive a bonus payment that will allow me to purchase my own small farm."

"So, after you retire from the army, will you be moving to Rome?"

"No, the Roman Senate wouldn't be comfortable having a large number of former soldiers living in the vicinity of their capitol -- which is fine with me. I look forward to being able to buy my farmland someplace else. There are Roman colonies in Macedonia, Achaia, Asia, and Aegyptus, where retired soldiers are able to live comfortably. And the Roman Empire likes to create these enclaves, as a way of peaceably extending their presence throughout the empire. Maybe they will establish a colony for former soldiers here in your country."

"Please don't take this personally, but my countrymen certainly hope that won't happen."

Marius laughs, and says, "I understand! Believe me, I experience the hatred of your countrymen every day. But your family is an exception, and also your prophet, Jesus, who lives in Capernaum. He and some of his followers are kind and welcoming towards everyone, including us soldiers."

Miri asks him, "Do you know Yeshuah?"

"Not personally, but he has been friendly toward me and my men. He always greets us warmly as he passes by us. And several of his disciples also try to follow his example."

"That is interesting. I haven't met Yeshuah myself, or heard him preach, but I would like to someday. I know many people who have seen him in public, and most of them say that they like him."

Marius says, "During the past few weeks, I acquired another new friend, a follower of Jesus named Othniel ben Obed. He originally came from Jericho, but now he lives in Capernaum. Othniel told me that he believes that Jesus could become the anointed leader of your country. He would be even more important that Herod Antipas."

Miriam responds, "Well, my father told me that Antipas may be a son of his father, who was our king, but that your Roman authorities will never allow us to have another king. So how could Yeshuah ever become more important than Antipas? Yeshuah is not a prince or a general, so I doubt that he will be able to overthrow Antipas and Rome."

"Maybe Jesus' authority isn't political or military."

"You may be right, but I don't understand how moral excellence and a few miraculous deeds could make Yeshuah more powerful than other leaders."

"Neither do I. But, for some reason, Othniel really believes that Jesus is capable of changing things for the better."

"Marius, let's change the subject. Have you considered leaving the army, and trying another occupation? Soldiering for another nineteen years seems like a very long time to me, and even if you survive to retirement, you might be too old to start a new career then."

"Miriam, there isn't an honorable way for me to leave the army before the completion of my twenty-five year enlistment, unless the condition of my health renders me incapable of continuing to serve. I have no other options."

"What about your private life? Do you have to wait until you retire before starting a family?"

"As a soldier, I'm not supposed to have a private life. I am not allowed to get married, but I know soldiers who have sired children with women who aren't their wives, but they are planning to marry them after they retire."

Miri exclaims, "That is outrageous! You can't take a wife, but it is permissible for you to have a concubine and produce illegitimate children?"

"Yes, I am ashamed to admit that you are correct. What are your future plans?"

"Marius, someday I hope to marry a good man who is about my same age, and to have children of my own. But at this time, I don't seem to have any prospects for my husband. Perhaps my father and I are both a bit too particular about qualifications."

"Miriam, you are a wonderful woman, and you deserve someone equally special to spend the rest of your life with."

"Thank you, Marius. You wouldn't happen to know anyone who might be suitable, would you?"

"Well, I am not a Jew, and we have already talked about how I cannot marry anyone until about nineteen years from now. And you were quite clear concerning your thoughts about that situation, so I suppose that I couldn't be regarded as a suitor, myself. However, my new friend, Othniel, is about the same age as you. He is an unmarried Jew who is friendly to everyone, and quite idealistic. I like him. Except for being one of Jesus' followers, I don't know what other future plans he might have."

"He sounds interesting, and because you have a good opinion about him, then perhaps I would like him too. Would you please introduce me to him sometime?"

"Yes, I would, definitely."

Marius and Miriam finish harvesting the figs, and Eliezer and Yaaqov finish their weeding and watering of the entire garden. After that, Eliezer insists that Marius join them for dinner, and Marius agrees. After dinner, Marius hikes back to his garrison at Capernaum. Eliezer walks along with him as far as Tiberias.

During the next two weeks, Eliezer keeps himself busy harvesting vegetables and melons from his garden, and meeting with Rabbi Yitzhak about the wording of his marriage agreement. Zibrah visits Hammat several times, to get better acquainted with Miriam and Yaaqov. Yeshuah's reputation continues to grow as he is attracting large crowds teaching and healing wherever he goes in Galilee. And Marius tells Othniel about his friends from Hammat.

CHAPTER 24

On the morning of the first day of Tammuz, Marius brings Othniel along with him for a visit to Hammat. Besides telling Othniel about Eliezer and his family, Marius also mentioned the bathhouse. So when they arrive in Hammat, instead of going directly up the path to Eliezer's property, they stop at the bathhouse first. Marius pays the bathing fee to the attendant for himself and also for Othniel, and the two men enjoy their refreshing baths. Afterwards, Marius and Othniel walk up the hill to Eliezer's home and terraced gardens. When they arrive at the door to Eliezer's home, Marius calls, "Hello, Eliezer. I am Marius, and I have brought a friend with me."

Eliezer opens the door and, seeing his friend Marius, invites the two men to come into the courtyard, saying, "Welcome, Marius. And welcome, friend of Marius."

Eliezer notices that, before entering, Marius' friend reverences the mezuzah box on the doorpost and he says, "Shalom be upon this house, and upon all who dwell here."

Then Marius says to Eliezer, "I want to introduce you to my friend, Othniel. He is from Jericho, but we met in Capernaum."

Eliezer greets Othniel and says to him, "Othniel, I see that you are a Jew. How did you meet our friend, Marius?"

Othniel replies, "I am a disciple of Yeshuah from Natzerat, and we have been staying in Kfar Nahum while Yeshuah is teaching in Galilee. Yeshuah tells us that we should be kind to everyone, and so I introduced myself to Marius while he was on guard duty. And, as we talked with each other, I realized that he and I could be friends, and not enemies."

Just then, Miriam comes into the courtyard from one of the interior rooms of the house, and Marius greets her, as if she is his sister, and then he says, "Miri, I would like you to meet my friend, Othniel." And turning to Othniel, he says, "Othniel, this is the charming woman that I told you about. She is Eliezer's daughter, and her name is Miriam."

Othniel and Miriam greet each other politely. And then Miriam invites everyone to be seated at the family table, while she goes to fetch some refreshing cups of fruit-flavored water to serve them.

As Miriam is preparing the refreshments, she is thinking about how good-looking, polite, and friendly Othniel seems to be. And how nice it was that Marius followed-through on her request to introduce her to Othniel.

Eliezer asks, "Othniel, what is Yeshuah really like?"

Othniel replies, "Yeshuah is the most extraordinary person I ever met. He is sensitive, wise, brilliant, and compassionate. He deeply cares about everyone he encounters, and he reaches out to them according to their individual needs. When he speaks to you, it is as if nothing else matters. He is the only truly holy man I have ever known."

Eliezer says, "Well, if he is so holy, then why does he associate with sinful people. And why is he so critical of Pharisees and other religious leaders?"

"I think that you should ask him that question yourself. But, from what I have understood about Yeshuah's teaching, I think that he would say that the kingdom of heaven is more than an exclusive collective of religious people who believe that they are good at keeping rules. Repentant sinners realize their need for grace and mercy, but many religious people are overly proud of their own accomplishments. A person can never justify himself through his own righteousness, but instead will be justified only through humility, compassion, forgiveness and mercy."

Eliezer replies, "I think that I am beginning to understand something important! A few weeks ago, my rabbi was trying to teach me about a form of righteousness that is higher than ritual purity and habitual ceremonies. It sounds like your Yeshuah and my rabbi are expressing similar ideas. Perhaps Pharisees like me should stop being so defensive about our traditions, and instead should become more open to alternative ideas."

Then Eliezer turns toward where Marius is sitting at the table, and he says, "Marius, I like your friend, Othniel! Thank you for bringing him along with you today."

Marius replies, "You are very welcome, Eliezer. I don't think that I understand what is so controversial between different branches of your religion, but that probably is because I am an outsider."

"Neverthess, both of you are welcome in my house. I have learned something important from each of you."

Just then Miriam returns with cups of cold, fruit-flavored water, and she is pleased to see the cheerful friendliness which prevails at the table.

Miriam asks Othniel, "Marius told us that you are from Yeriko. Our family usually stays overnight in Yeriko when we are traveling to Yerushalayim for the pilgrim festivals. Yeriko is a unique city, and a very interesting place to visit. What was it like growing up there?"

Othniel says, "Yeriko is a very old city, and it is the most important trading center in the southern portion of the Yarden River valley. Yeriko has many palm trees, and several beautiful palaces. Because Yeriko is close to our neighboring countries to the east, we frequently receive visitors from the Decapolis, Peraea, Nabataea, Arabia, and other countries, and it is interesting to observe the differences and similarities between those people and ourselves. Yeriko also has a bathhouse, that is more elaborate than your bathhouse here in Hammat. My father's name is Obed, and he is a well-known producer of aromatic oils and spices. I have one older brother, another brother that is younger than me, and I also have two sisters that are younger than me. Our whole family works in the family's business. We are a religious family, but we aren't members of a particular Jewish sect. When I was growing up, I remember traveling with my family almost every year to Yerushalayim for Pesach, Shavuot, and Sukkot. When Yohanan the Baptizer was preaching by the Yarden River south of our city, I went out to hear him, and I was there when he said that Yeshuah is the Lamb of God. And a few weeks after that, I left my home to become one of Yeshuah's disciples."

She asks, "How old are you, and why aren't you married?"

Othniel replies, "I am twenty-four years old. A few years ago, my parents were planning for me to become betrothed to a girl from our city but, for financial reasons, those arrangements didn't work out, and I haven't thought too much about marriage since then. I realize that many men my age are married, but Yeshuah is older than me and he isn't married either, and neither are some of the other disciples. But while we are discussing personal questions, what about you?"

Miriam says, "I am twenty-one years old, and am still unmarried, because my father and I have probably been too picky. I have been the woman of our family home ever since my mother died eleven years ago. But that situation will be changing soon, because my father is planning to marry again about five or six weeks from now."

Othniel says, "Well, that will be a big change for all of you!"

While Miriam and Othniel are getting acquainted, Eliezer and Marius are intently listening to their conversation, and both of them remain silent. But then, Yaaqov bursts into the courtyard from outside, where he had been playing ball games with some other children his age. Yaaqov is happy to see his friend Marius again, and Marius introduces him to Othniel.

Othniel says, "Yaaqov, I remember you! You are the boy whose bread loaves and fish were used by Yeshuah to feed a very large crowd of people at Ein Sheva!"

Yaaqov replies, "Yes, that's right. So, you were there, too?"

"Yes, I was. What an astounding event! Everyone who was there that day learned that the Lord can accomplish great things from even small offerings, when we are willing to share what we have. You made that lesson possible!"

"But it wasn't me, it was Yeshuah who did it!"

"You are correct. But Yeshuah was able to use what you gave him. Most people would have said, 'This little amount that I have couldn't possibly make a difference, so I might as well keep all that I have for my own use.' But you gave what you had, without holding back. It was like a miracle of a small seed becoming a whole orchard, full of fruit. The seed of your small meal really did make a difference!"

At that point, Eliezer exclaims, "I have heard the story about the feeding of many people from Yaaqov's little meal, but since I am not able to understand how that could have happened, I cannot accept that there wasn't some kind of trickery involved. I am a practical man, and I have learned that things aren't always as they seem to be."

Othniel answers, "I can see that you are skeptical. But I also perceive that you are a godly man. Is anything too difficult for God to do?"

"No. Of course not! But why would the Lord choose to act through a man who so openly associates with sinners, and who is critical of people who are passionate about faithfulness to the covenant?"

"Eliezer, that simply brings us back to what we were talking about before . . . the importance of humility, compassion, forgiveness, and mercy. This is the higher form of righteousness that your Rabbi was trying to teach you about. I believe that Yeshuah is revealing the heart of God to us, and that we need to simply trust God to receive it . . . like a young boy offering his small meal for thousands of people to eat. Sometimes God's ways just don't make sense to us, but we should trust Him anyway, and stop trying to figure everything out, in order to justify ourselves."

Eliezer becomes quiet, thinking about what Othniel had said. And no one interrupted his personal deliberation. After a few moments, Eliezer says, "I have been a sincere Pharisee for all of my adult life, and I have learned to consider faith and religious practices according to the standards and values that I was taught. But now, I realize that my pride led me to be overly judgmental of the faith of other persons. I apologize for my closed mind and lack of spiritual discernment. All of this is very unsettling for me. I feel like an important part of my life has been uprooted. I will need some time to sort everything out, but now I realize that your teacher, Yeshuah of Natzerat, could very well be a worthy teacher of Israel."

During the afternoon, Eliezer, Miriam, Yaaqov, Marius, and Othniel spend a couple of hours working together in the garden, with friendliness and laughter accompanying their watering and weeding. That evening, after dinner, Marius and Othniel hike back to Capernaum. And Eliezer walks along with them as far as Tiberias. He is eager to share his new understandings about humility, mercy, and righteousness with Zibrah.

CHAPTER 25

On the morning of the tenth day of Tammuz, Eliezer, his children, his brother Reuel, and Rabbi Yitzhak walk together to Zibrah's house in Tiberias for the betrothal. Zibrah is waiting for them at her table, on which she has placed a cup of wine. After the group gathers around the table, Eliezer lays a cloth bag containing silver coins on the table, and then he presents the marriage agreement that he had prepared, with some help provided by Rabbi Yitzhak.

Eliezer opens the ketubah scroll, and he reads aloud from it, "On the sixth day of the week, the tenth day of the month of Tammuz in the year 3788 since the creation of the world according to the reckoning that is used here in the city of Tiberias, Eliezer, son of Eliab, said to Zibrah, daughter of Zebulun, be my wife according to the laws of Moses and Israel, and I will cherish, honor, support, and maintain you in accordance with the custom of Jewish husbands who cherish, honor, support, and maintain their wives faithfully. And I here present you with a marriage gift of one hundred Tyrian silver shekels, which belongs to you according to the laws of Moses and Israel; and I will also give you food, clothing, and other necessities, and live with you as husband and wife. And Zibrah consented and became the wife of Eliezer."

Zibrah responds by picking up the bag of coins and saying to Eliezer, "I accept your marriage gift, and I give my willing consent to your proposal of marriage."

Then Eliezer picks up the cup of wine from the table, and says the blessing for wine.

Eliezer sips some wine from the cup, and then he lifts the cup to Zibrah's lips, for her to also drink from it. The sipping of the wine from the shared cup symbolizes that their lives are now entwined.

Then Eliezer says the blessing, "We bless you, O God, Sovereign of the Universe, who has commanded us regarding sexual propriety, but permitting to us those who are sanctified for us through marriage. Amen."

Turning toward Zibrah, Eliezer says, "Behold, you are betrothed unto me according to the laws of Moses and Israel." After he finishes that declaration, Eliezer and Zibrah embrace, each telling the other of their love.

Then, one at a time, Reuel and Yitzhak affix their signatures to the marriage agreement as witnesses to the betrothal of Eliezer and Zibrah. Following that, Zibrah brings out some sweet cakes and cups of fruit juice for all of them to partake of. And Zibrah and Eliezer hug and kiss each person who is there, thanking them for their attendance at the betrothal.

And Eliezer and Zibrah announce that their wedding feast will be celebrated the following month, on the twelfth day of Ab.

As Eliezer and the other persons from Hammat are about to leave Zibrah's house, Eliezer sees Assurbani standing in the street that leads from Tiberias' main market to the waterfront. He seems to be waiting for them. Eliezer walks purposefully toward Assurbani, and as he is doing so Assurbani says to him, "I heard that you and Zibrah were becoming betrothed today. So, how soon will you and your family be moving to Tiberias?"

Eliezer responds, "Where I live with my family should not be of any concern to you. Stay away from my family. And, as of now, my family also includes Zibrah."

"Are you threatening me?"

"No, I am giving you a warning. And I advise you to take it very seriously. You would not like what will happen if you don't."

"As a profoi of this city, I should be attentive to everything that happens here."

Looking intensely at Assurbani, Eliezer says, "I am telling you to consider my family as outside of your jurisdiction. Do you understand me? Now, go!"

Assurbani hurriedly retreats back up the street, toward the marketplace. And Eliezer returns to Zibrah, his children, Reuel, and Yitzhak, who are standing together by the door. Eliezer gives Zibrah

122

another hug, and then he takes the hands of Miriam and Yaaqov into his own hands, and then he leads them toward Hammat. As they are walking homeward, they talk about the upcoming wedding, and they try to dismiss Assurbani from their thoughts. Eliezer asks Reuel to check on his children during his upcoming absence for his marketing journey, and Reuel agrees to do so.

CHAPTER 26

Two days later, on the twelfth day of Tammuz, Eliezer leaves Hammat on his early-summer marketing trip with his donkeys, Amit and Marit, carrying bags and baskets loaded with lentils, peas, beans, cucumbers, onions, leeks, garlic, figs, and melons. His first stop is the main market agora in Tiberias, that is about two miles from his home.

When Eliezer arrrives at the marketplace, he quickly surveys the area, selects an open stall to setup in, and observes that Assurbani is nowhere in sight. After spreading his cloak, and displaying samples of his produce on it, his first customer is Zibrah.

Zibrah says, "Shalom, Eliezer! It is so good for me to see you today! I want to buy some cucumbers from you."

"Shalom, Zibrah! You will always be my best customer! How many cucumbers would you like? For you, they are free."

"What a bargain! I would like three of them . . . and a nice ripe fig too, please."

Eliezer gives her the cucumbers and the fig that she said she wanted, and then several other customers arrive at his stall. He gives Zibrah his warmest smile, and then he turns his attention to the other customers. Zibrah steps back and watches with appreciation as her betrothed husband handles his business dealings with several of her neighbors.

By midday, Eliezer had sold about one-tenth of his vegetables and fruit. And, at that time, Zibrah brought Eliezer a loaf of freshly-baked bread and a pomegranate for them to share. They sat down on the paved surface of the agora and ate the meal that she had brought, and they talked about who they wanted to invite to their wedding feast. After they finished eating, Zibrah went to her home, and Eliezer became more attentive to the circulating customers. During the afternoon, the number of customers in the marketplace diminishes and, about half-way through the afternoon, Eliezer decides to close down his sales operation. He reloads his goods onto his donkeys, and he starts walking with them to Kfar Nahum, on the road that is on the northwest side of Lake Kinneret.

~ /// ~

Almost three hours later, Eliezer arrives at Aharon's home in Kfar Nahum. Aharon welcomes his brother-in-law to his house, and then he helps him to unload the containers of vegetables and fruit that Eliezer brought with him to sell. They put Amit and Marit in a pen next to Aharon's house, and they give the donkeys some water and food. Then Aharon invites his brother-in-law to join him in washing hands and faces before eating the dinner that Bilhah had prepared for them. Eliezer thanks Aharon and Bilhah for their hospitality.

At dinner, Eliezer says to Aharon and Bilhah, "Two days ago, I became betrothed to the widow Zibrah, from Tiberias."

With a look of surprise on his face, Aharon responds, "What good news, Eliezer! I hope that you will be very happy with your new wife, and I believe that my sister Ahuva would be pleased with your decision. While she was alive, her greatest desire always was your happiness."

Eliezer says, "Thank you, Aharon. I always will treasure the special relationship that I had with your sister, but I have come to understand that my relationship with Zibrah does not dishonor Ahuva, or my memory of her. Instead, my relationship with Zibrah helps me to deal with the changing circumstances of my present life without having Ahuva beside me."

Bilhah asks, "How do Miriam and Yaaqov feel about you getting married again?"

"I have been surprised by my children's willingness to welcome another person into our family life. They both have expressed appreciation for Zibrah, and they also have been enthusiastic about my decision. Miriam told me that she is looking forward to having another woman in our home, and Yaaqov says that he likes Zibrah's cooking."

"Well, that is wonderful, Eliezer! When will the wedding feast be held?"

"Exactly one month from today, on the twelfth day of Ab. And I hope that you both will be able to attend the festivities."

Aharon says, "Thank you for inviting us! We will try to be there."

Then Bilhah asks, "Eliezer, have you found a husband for Miriam yet?"

"No, I haven't. However, last week we met a very nice young man from Yeriko, named Othniel, who is unmarried and twenty-four years old. He is one of Yeshuah's disciples."

Aharon exclaims, "I know Othniel! He lives here in Kfar Nahum with some other followers of Yeshuah. And I also am acquinted with his father, Obed. I agree that Othniel seems to be a very nice man. Is he interested in marrying Miriam?"

"I don't know. We only just met him last week. You didn't mention Othniel last winter, when we talked with you about helping us to find a husband for Miriam."

Aharon replies, "I don't think that Othniel was living here in Kfar Nahum then, so I didn't think of him at that time. However, I have been buying spices from Obed for several years. Would you like for me to contact Othniel's parents on your behalf about Miriam?"

"Yes, I would appreciate it if you would do that for me. Thank you."

Aharon says, "Eliezer, I recall that the last time that we talked, you had some serious reservations about Yeshuah. Are you sure that you want to consider one of Yeshuah's disciples as a possible suitor for Miriam?"

"I have had long conversations with my rabbi and also with Othniel about Yeshuah and, as a result, I am now much more open-minded than I was before. I haven't personally witnessed Yeshuah's ministry but, based on everything that I have heard about him, I am now willing to regard him as a worthy teacher of Israel."

"But what about Yeshuah's criticism of Pharisaic practices?"

Eliezer says, "My rabbi has reminded me of the greater importance of humility, mercy, and forgiveness over the habitual performance of rituals and practices. In light of this realization, I accept that Yeshuah's criticism of Pharisaic intolerance and hypocrisy may be justified."

"It sounds like you have experienced an epiphany which is similar to my own. Now we both will think about our faith practices with more discernment."

Eliezer nods his head in agreement with what Aharon said.

Then Bilhah asks, "What does Miriam think about these matters?"

"Miri always has been more open-minded and less judgmental about others than me. I think that she is curious about Yeshuah, but she also is faithful to our traditions. In the end, she will make her own decisions about what she believes are the right things to do. I admire her greatly."

Eliezer, Aharon, and Bilhah smile together, and then Aharon says, "Congratulations, Eliezer. You have raised her very well."

Eliezer spends the following morning selling some of his produce in the Kfar Nahum market agora, and at midday he fastens his cloth bags and baskets to Amit and Marit, and starts walking away from the Kfar Nahum market, and toward the western entrance to the city. On his way out of Kfar Nahum, he sees Marius by the city gate and he speaks with him briefly, as one friend to another. Eliezer asks Marius about Othniel, and Marius tells him that Yeshuah and his followers, including Othniel, had left Capernaum to visit Bethsaida, Caesarea Philippi, and other places in Gaulanitis. Then Eliezer resumes walking towards the next stop on his marketing trip, Tzipori, that is almost twenty-three miles from Kfar Nahum.

~ /// ~

After about six and one-half hours of steady walking, Eliezer arrives at the place where he and his donkeys will spend the night. It is a meadow with a nearby spring that is only a short distance from Tzipori, and not too far from the road. Eliezer is tired, hot, and hungry. He unloads his produce, waters and feeds Amit and Marit, washes his hands and feet and face, and then he eats his supper of bread, fruit, dried meat, and wine. After dinner, Eliezer says his prayers, and then he lays down on his cloak and goes to sleep.

The next morning, after his morning prayers and a quick breakfast, Eliezer loads his donkeys with the containers of vegetables and fruit, and they walk through the city entrance, past the synagogue, several luxurious homes and commercial shops, and along paved, colonnaded streets to the city's open-air market and public forum, which is a paved courtyard that is surrounded by columns and beautifully decorated buildings.

Tzipori (also known as Sepphoris) was a small settlement during the Hasmonean period, but after the Land of Israel was conquered by the Roman army under Pompey, a Roman governor declared Tzipori to be the capital of the Galilee district. After the death of Herod the Great, Jewish rioters seized Tzipori from the Romans, but this revolt led to the destruction of Tzipori by the Romans, and the enslavement of its Jewish inhabitants. But about thirty years ago, Herod Antipas began rebuilding the city of Tzipori, and he restored its former status as the capital of Galilee. Of course, Herod Antipas also established the newer city of Tiberias only ten years ago, and he moved his capital from Tzipori to Tiberias. Nevertehless, Tzipori still has the lustre of an important city that is new and beautiful. The total population of Tzipori currently is about 8,000 persons, but the city is continuing to grow.

Eliezer sets up his stall in the open-air market, and soon persons from many prosperous households in the city are queueing-up to purchase lentils, peas, beans, cucumbers, onions, leeks, garlic, figs, and melons from him. One of Eliezer's repeat customers is a man named Ephron, who is reputed to be an exceptionally talented artist and musician. Ephron buys all of the figs that Eliezer brought with him. Another Tzipori customer that Eliezer remembers from previous marketing trips is a socialite woman named Ruth -- she purchases several of Eliezer's onions, leeks, garlics, and melons. Eliezer's business is steady throughout the morning, and intermittent after midday. The Tzipori customers are willing to pay good prices for high quality produce. By midafternoon, Eliezer had sold about half of the vegetables that he had brought with him from Hammat. Eliezer purchases several delicious pomegranates for himself from a Tzipori merchant named Talmai. Then he packs-up his remaining produce, and walks with Amit and Marit to Natzerat, that is only about three and one-half miles away. He finds a good resting place just outside of the village, where he spends the night.

~ /// ~

Natzerat is an agricultural village with a total population of about 400 residents that is built on a rocky hillside and extends into a valley that opens to the south. Natzerat only has one spring, and this water source is augmented by several local cisterns. Nearby are gardens, vineyards, orchards, fields, and pastures. There is a small open-air market in the southwestern part of the village.

The following morning, as Eliezer walks through the village of Natzerat, he wonders about the location of Yeshuah's family home. And, as he passes by the synagogue, he remembers that the Natzerat synagogue has a reputation of being very conservative, and this realization makes it difficult to understand how Yeshuah came to his own liberal interpretation of Torah. When Eliezer arrives at the open-air market, there is only one stall in operation, and that belongs to a local olive oil producer whose name is Amos. Eliezer introduces himself to Amos, and then he begins displaying the vegetables he wants to sell. After a while, a few customers arrive and make their purchases. Whenever there is a lull in sales activity, Eliezer and Amos talk to each other. Eliezer asks Amos for his opinion concerning Yeshuah.

Amos tells him, "The last time Yeshuah visited here, he was invited to address our congregation, and our local congregants were appalled and offended when Yeshuah actually referred to himself as the fulfillment of some messianic prophecies. Our people became furious towards him, and he only narrowly escaped from being killed. Around here, people have a difficult time regarding Yeshuah as anyone more special than the young boy that we knew when he was growing up here. I think that is why he hasn't returned to his hometown since then."

Eliezer says, "Well, Yeshuah has become a very important teacher in Israel, and many people claim that he has performed miraculous deeds."

Amos asks, "You seem to be very interested in Yeshuah. Are you one of his followers?"

"No, I have never heard him preach, and I have never witnessed any of his alleged miracles."

"None of our local residents have ever seen him perform miracles either."

Eliezer comments, "I heard that Yeshuah's father is a builder here in Natzerat, but it doesn't look to me like there is enough development in this village to support a construction craftsman and his family."

Amos responds, "Yes, when Yeshuah's father, Yosef, was alive, he was a respected builder in our village. However, most of the carpentry and stonework that he and Yeshuah created was over in Tzipori, because that city has been growing steadily ever since it was reestablished by Herod Antipas thirty years ago. Tzipori has provided economic opportunity for craftsmen from throughout Galilee."

"Thanks for telling me about Natzerat and its people, Amos. I enjoyed it."

At midday, Eliezer determined that he had sold enough vegetables in Natzerat to have made that part of his marketing trip worthwhile. Most customers prefer shopping during the cooler morning hours, instead of in the warm summer afternoons, so Eliezer decides to close down his sales business in Natzerat, and to move on to the next stop of his marketing trip.

Eliezer buys a jug of olive oil from Amos, and then he fastens his bags and baskets to Amit and Marit, and begins walking southward, toward the Plain of Esdraelon, and the road that leads through the Harod Valley to Beit Shean. Beit Shean is twenty-two miles from Natzerat, and Eliezer knows that it will take more than six hours for him and his donkeys to travel that distance.

~ /// ~

After walking for almost five and one-half hours, Eliezer decides to rest for the night by the spring of Harod, at the foot of Mount Gilboa, and only three miles from Beit Shean (Scythopolis). He waters and feeds his donkeys, he washes his hands, feet, and face, and then he eats his supper of bread, wine, olives, and salt. He knows that he still has a good selection of vegetables and a few melons to sell. At dusk, after saying his prayers, he wraps himself in his cloak and lies down between Amit and Marit to sleep.

Early the next morning, Eliezer awakens and prays thankfully for this new day, for his health, his children, and also for Zibrah. After washing himself, he eats his breakfast, and then he packs-up his goods for the short walk to Beit Shean.

A little less than one hour later, Eliezer and his donkeys pass through the entrance to the Scythopolis, with its white marble buildings, and paved streets. Eliezer follows Palladius Street to the entrance of the commercial agora. Eliezer finds his friend Peleg, and he goes over to where Peleg's stall is, hoping to join him in a combined sales operation, as they had done before. Peleg and Eliezer greet each other warmly, and Peleg helps Eliezer to set up his display of beans, cucumbers, onions, garlics, and melons. Peleg is selling wheat and figs, as usual for this time of year.

Customers keep Eliezer and Peleg busy all morning. Several customers recognize Eliezer from previous marketing trips, and most of those customers purchase more vegetables this time than they bought before. Business is very good. In fact, after only three and one-half hours, Eliezer and Peleg sell all of the produce that they had brought with them to sell.

Since it was midday, Eliezer and Peleg decide to eat a meal together in Beit Shean before returning to their homes, and Peleg recommends a merchant that he knows who sells very tasty stewed vegetables with pancakes. They wash their hands, say a food blessing, and sit down to eat together.

As they are eating, Eliezer says, "Peleg, I must share my good news with you! I am going to marry again, on the twelfth of Ab. I hope that you will be able to attend my wedding feast in Hammat. It would honor me if you do."

"Thank you for the invitation, Eliezer. I will try to be there. But why get married at your age?"

"Because, despite my age, I am in love with a woman named Zibrah who loves me and I want to share what is left of my life with her at my side."

"Good for you, Eliezer! Is Zibrah a young woman?"

"Peleg, she is not a youthful maiden, but she is young enough for me. She is a widow who is about three years younger than me. But she does make me feel like I am young again!"

"Well, I am impressed that you and your betrothed wife share such a youthful perspective!"

"Thank you, Peleg. I am blessed to have her in my life."

"Your announcement does seem to be quite sudden. Why haven't you mentioned Zibrah to me before this?"

"Actually, Peleg, until two months ago, Zibrah was just one of my regular customers. But then, something happened, and our relationship has been becoming more serious ever since."

Then Peleg says, "Well, Eliezer, that sounds very interesting. And perhaps you will tell me the rest of that story someday. But now, I want to talk with you about another matter. I have heard mixed reports about Yeshuah of Natzeret. Some people say that Yeshuah could be the Maschiah because of his miraculous deeds, but many also have reported that Yeshuah has referred to us Pharisees as hypocrites. I want to know what you think about him."

Eliezer replies, "Peleg, I haven't personally witnessed Yeshuah's preaching or his miracles, so I cannot say much about either of those things. However, according to information that I received from several persons having firsthand experiences of Yeshuah's ministry, it seems that Yeshuah is a remarkable teacher whose interpretation of Torah is less conservative than our Pharisaic principles, but still is consistent with the teachings of some other well-regarded rabbis. I do not believe that Yeshuah and his followers are capable of overthrowing the Roman government; therefore, he cannot be the Maschiah that we have been expecting."

"Yeshuah may not be a military leader, but he does appear to be growing in popularity with ordinary people, although not with the Pharisees. So, what do you think about Yeshuah being critical about us Pharisees?"

"You know, that used to bother me, but I have decided that most of the criticisms that Yeshuah makes about Pharisees are actually well-deserved. Besides making guidelines and rules, we Pharisees also like to judge everyone according to our requirements. We are very adept at finding faults in others, but not in ourselves. Instead of always trying to justify ourselves, we should bave been emphasizing humility and mercy."

After thoughtful consideration of what Eliezer said, Peleg responds, "So, does this mean that you have stopped being a Pharisee?"

"No, but I am trying to be more open-minded about many things, especially people."

Peleg says, "Eliezer, that may sound like a good thing, but real righteousness requires standards. Who decides what is right?"

"Each person is responsible for his own covenant faithfulness, based upon a proper understanding of Torah."

"But Eliezer, wouldn't it be easier if everyone just followed the same rules?"

"My rabbi taught me, 'A righteous person has a duty to make righteous choices.'"

"Thank you for sharing your thoughts with me, Eliezer. I am looking forward to selling with you again the next time you come to Beit Shean. When will you be coming back?"

"I anticipate being here again about two months from now, in late-summer. But I do hope that the next time that I will see you will be next month, at my wedding banquet in Hammat."

Then Eliezer and Peleg say "Farewell" to each other, and they begin walking toward their respective homes -- Eliezer and his donkeys are walking along Valley Street toward the Yarden River road that turns to the north, and Peleg is traveling westward toward the Yizreel Valley road. Eliezer knows that he is about nineteen miles from his home but, since it is early in the afternoon, he figures that he and his donkeys should be able to make it to his home in about five and one-half hours, just before the setting of the sun at the ending of the sixteenth of Tammuz. This would be a half-day earlier than he had planned. As he is walking, Eliezer remembers that homecomings are always the best part of every trip, but he also reminds himself that tomorrow, the seventeenth day of Tammuz, will be a day of fasting in preparation for Tisha B'Ab.

CHAPTER 27

Just after sunset on the twelfth day of Ab, Eliezer dresses himself in his most splendid clothes and, accompanied by Yaaqov, Reuel, Yitzhak, Reuben, Kenan, Aharon, Yehuda, Peleg, Marius, and Othniel, they walk together from Hammat to Zibrah's house in Tiberias.

Zibrah is dressed in bridal clothing and wearing jewelry, and she has been waiting for Eliezer and his friends to arrive. Waiting with Zibrah are Miriam, Serah, Bilhah, Shira, and Zibrah's friends, Salome, Mayim, Milkah, and Joanna.

As Eliezer and his companions are approaching Zibrah's house, they hear the women inside laughing and singing. Their song is from Shir Eshirim, and it is sung in praise of Zibrah's beauty:

"How beautiful you are, my love, how very beautiful!
Your eyes are doves behind your veil.
Your hair is like a flock of goats,
moving down the slopes of Gilead.
Your teeth are like a flock of shorn ewes that have
come up from the washing, all of which bear twins,
and not one among them is bereaved.
Your lips are like a crimson thread, and your mouth
is lovely.
Your cheeks are like halves of a pomegranate behind
your veil.
Your neck is like the tower of David, built in courses;
on it hang a thousand bucklers, all of them shields
of warriors.
Your two breasts are like two fawns, twins of a gazelle,
that feed among the lilies.

Until the day breathes and the shadows flee, I will hasten to the mountain of myrrh and the hill of frankincense.
You are altogether beautiful, my love;
there is no flaw in you."

[Song of Solomon 4:1-7 NRSV]

Then, when the women see Eliezer and the other men enter the house, with even more merriment they sing:

"What is that coming up from the wilderness,
like a column of smoke,
perfumed with myrrh and frankincense,
with all the fragrant powders of the merchant?
Look, it is the litter of Solomon!
Around it are sixty mighty men of the mighty men of Israel,"

[Song of Solomon 3:6-7 NRSV]

"My beloved is all radiant and ruddy,
distinguished among ten thousand.
His head is the finest gold; his locks are wavy,
black as a raven.
His eyes are like doves beside springs of water,
bathed in milk, fitly set.
His cheeks are like beds of spices, yielding fragrance.
His lips are lilies, distilling liquid myrrh.
His arms are rounded gold, set with jewels.
His body is ivory work, encrusted with sapphires.
His legs are alabaster columns, set upon bases of gold.
His appearance is like Lebanon, choice as the cedars.
His speech is most sweet, and he is altogether desirable.
This is my beloved and this is my friend,
O daughters of Jerusalem."

[Song of Solomon 5:10-16 NRSV]

After the song ends, all of the men and women are laughing and hugging each other merrily. Finally, when everyone is ready, Eliezer takes Zibrah's hands into his, and then he leads her out of her house. When everyone in the wedding party is outside, Eliezer's companions and Zibrah's attendants light their torches and lamps, and then the procession goes from Tiberias to Eliezer's house in Hammat, singing joyfully from Tehillim as they went:

> "My heart overflows with a goodly theme;
> I address my verses to the king;
> my tongue is like the pen of a ready scribe.
> You are the most handsome of men;
> grace is poured upon your lips;
> therefore God has blessed you forever.
> Gird your sword on your thigh, O mighty one,
> in your glory and majesty.
> In your majesty ride on victoriously for the cause of
> truth and to defend the right;
> let your right hand teach you dread deeds.
> Your arrows are sharp in the heart of the king's enemies;
> the peoples fall under you.
> Your throne, O God, endures forever and ever.
> Your royal scepter is a scepter of equity;
> you love righteousness and hate wickedness.
> Therefore God, your God, has anointed you with the
> oil of gladness beyond your companions;
> your robes are all fragrant with myrrh and aloes and
> cassia.
> From ivory palaces stringed instruments make you glad;
> daughters of kings are among your ladies of honor;
> at your right hand stands the queen in gold of Ophir.
> Hear, O daughter, consider and incline your ear;
> forget your people and your father's house,
> and the king will desire your beauty.
> Since he is your lord, bow to him;
> the people of Tyre will seek your favor with gifts,
> the richest of the people with all kinds of wealth.

The princess is decked in her chamber with gold-
woven robes;
in many-colored robes she is led to the king;
behind her the virgins, her companions, follow.
With joy and gladness they are led along as they enter
the palace of the king.
In the place of ancestors you, O king, shall have sons;
you will make them princes in all the earth.
I will cause your name to be celebrated in all
generations;
therefore the peoples will praise you forever and ever."
[Psalm 45:1-17 NRSV]

As the noisy procession passes by houses along the street, people come outside to see the commotion, and they enthusiastically shout their congratulations to the bridegroom and his bride. Many of them recognize Eliezer and or Zibrah as their neighbors and friends.

When the procession arrives at Eliezer's house, they go inside and enjoy the wedding feast, and much drinking of wine. A few prayers, blessings, and toasts are offered, and some of the guests give gifts to the newly married couple. While eating dinner, Marius and Yaaqov sit together and visit about Marius' soldiering experiences.

After the dinner, Othniel asks Miriam if she will step outside with him for a private conversation. When they are alone, Othniel says, "Miriam, my father told me that he was contacted by your uncle Aharon about discussing the possibility of marriage arrangements involving me and you. Were you aware of that?"

Miriam replies, "No. But I am not too surprised. Recently, my father has become very anxious about finding a prospective husband for me. For many years, he rejected every young man who ever expressed any interest in me, but about a year ago he realized that with a shortage of good prospects, there is a very good chance that his daughter might never marry. And then you walked into our lives, fulfilling most of my father's qualifications."

"I thought that might be the situation. I will tell you a secret. My father also is worried that I may have missed my best opportunities for finding a wife. He isn't completely desperate yet, but I don't think that he is too far from there."

"I remember when you told us that, a few years ago, you were very close to becoming betrothed but that those financial arrangements didn't work out. I thought that perhaps your father's financial situation was the reason."

"Oh, no! My father has an abundance of financial resources, so that wasn't the problem. The actual situation was that the girl decided that she wanted someone else for a husband, and so her father kept raising the bride price, until my father finally refused to continue negotiating with him. So now my father worries that I have become so deeply involved with following Yeshuah, that I won't ever settle down and give him grandchildren."

Miriam exclaims, "So our fathers' failure to develop alternative plans might actually bring them together to seek a mutual solution to their matchmaking problems!"

Othniel says, "Yes, I think that you may be correct about that. But we don't know very much about each other, and I don't believe that my parents ever met either of your parents. However, I do find myself to be very impressed by you."

Miriam shyly responds, "Thank you . . . I like you, too. And you also have made a very good impression with my Abba. So what did you tell your father?"

Othniel replies, "I told him that I had met you, and that you and your family seemed very nice."

"Well, what happens next?"

"I think that we should get better acquainted with each other, and that we should encourage our parents to discuss this matter with each other."

"Then we are in agreement with each other. Were you in love with the girl with whom you almost became betrothed?"

"No, I wasn't. But it did hurt my feelings when she told me that she wanted to marry someone else instead of me. . . . Were you disappointed when you learned that your father had rejected marriage proposals from those men that were seeking to marry you?"

Miriam smiles and then says, "No, I wasn't disappointed. I knew that my father didn't think that any of them were good enough for me, and I actually agreed with him."

"Oh, no! What if your father decides that I am not good enough to marry his daughter?"

Miriam chuckles and touches Othniel's hand, and then she says, "Well, I don't think that will happen, but if it does, then you and I will just have to convince him otherwise." As she said that, Miriam and Othniel smile at each other.

Then Othniel says, "Well, then let us get better acquainted, as we agreed. Tell me about the most important things in your life."

Miriam answers, "I would say that the most important things in my life are: life itself, loving God, and serving my family. I love my life, and I am very happy with it. My father taught me and my brother to read, and he always shares his Torah studies with me. I enjoy learning about God and what He wants from His children. Until today, as the woman of this house I have been responsible for most of the cooking, baking, housecleaning, laundering, and other housekeeping duties. I also help my father with the work in our garden. And I actually enjoy doing all of those things. What about you?"

And Othniel says, "As I told you before, I come from a religious family and I am a dedicated disciple of Yeshuah. Now, even more than when we met last month, I am convinced that Yeshuah is an extraordinary person, perhaps the most extraordinary person who ever lived."

Miriam asks, "What happened since last month, to make you more convinced than before about Yeshuah?"

Othniel replies, "Last month, I went with Yeshuah and the other disciples to Caesarea Philippi and, while we were there, Yeshuah shared some very important secrets with us. I cannot tell you everything that he said but, more than ever before, now I am convinced about Yeshuah's importance in the kingdom of God. However, some of the things that he told us also are very disturbing. He said that he was going to be killed horribly, but that afterwards he would be raised from the dead. And he said that all of us who are his disciples will have to deny ourselves, take up our own crosses, and follow him. None of us really understood what he meant by that."

"Othniel, I cannot imagine what any of that means. So I believe that we will have to wait and see what happens before we will be able to understand. But until then, it is clear that Yeshuah is calling for a much deeper commitment from his followers. Are you prepared for that?"

"I certainly hope that I am. What about you? If you and I become married, then my commitment to Yeshuah would have serious consequences for you. And you have never even met Yeshuah."

"If I become your wife, then your commitments will also become my commitments. And I will accept that, wherever they might lead us."

The party goes on until very late, and everyone has a very good time. And after all of the guests either left the party or laid down to sleep, Eliezer and Zibrah go to his sleeping room and they consummate their marriage.

And the folllowing morning, Aharon tells Eliezer about the matchmaking conversation that he had with Othniel's father, Obed. After checking with Miriam about her desires, Eliezer tells Aharon that he and Zibrah are looking forward to meeting with Othniel's parents regarding Miriam, and he asks Aharon to arrange that meeting.

~ /// ~

That same morning, Assurbani hears about Eliezer's and Zibrah's wedding procession that had taken place the night before. He remembers when Eliezer insulted him four months ago, and he also remembers a conversation that he had with Eliezer last month, in which Eliezer warned him to stay away from his family. He hates Eliezer, but he also is afraid of him. Assurbani sensed that Eliezer was quite close to becoming violent last month, and Assurbani knows that Eliezer is much stronger than himself, so he likely would be hurt more than Eliezer!

He thinks, *I would like to find a way to hurt Eliezer somehow, but I know that I must be careful, so that Eliezer will never know who is responsible for his misfortune, and especially so that Antipas will not find out. I would like to indulge my lust with Miriam, but that could have some very negative consequences for me. . . . I could have someone else ravage her -- that would punish both Eliezer and Miriam! . . . No, that might be too obvious. . . . I know what I will do! I will pay someone to kidnap Yaaqov, and sell him as a slave in Ptolemais. Eliezer won't be able to find him, or to get him back. That will cause great pain to Eliezer and his family! . . . Now, who can I get to do that job for me?*

Then he remembers a Phoenician ruffian named Baraket, who works in the fish processing facility at Magdala, also called Taricheae.

Later that day, Assurbani goes to Taricheae to find Baraket.

CHAPTER 28

About one month later, on the morning of the first day of the week, Eliezer departs from Hammat with Amit and Marit on his customary late-summer marketing tour of five Galileean cities over six days. Zibrah travels with him to Tiberias. While Eliezer sells produce in Tiberias' main marketplace, Zibrah meets with her fishing crews about her fishing business, and she also visits some of her friends, and the house that she owns there. Meanwhile, at the agora, a couple of times Eliezer notices that the policeman that he had previously seen with Assurbani seemed to be watching him.

That afternoon, Eliezer travels on to Kfar Nahum, and to Aharon's house in that city.

Aharon asks him, "So Eliezer, how is your marriage to Zibrah working out?"

"Very well, on several levels. Zibrah and I are really happy together, and Zibrah and my children also seem to enjoy our new circumstances in our house."

"That is great! I have heard that, sometimes, second marriages have a more difficult time blending their lives, because older folks are often more set in their ways than younger people."

Eliezer replies, "I can see how that might be true of many older people but, with each other, Zibrah and I seem to be young again. And each of us always tries very hard to accommodate the other."

"That is excellent! I remember that my sister, Ahuva, used to say how considerate you were with her. And it pleases me to think that you are still considerate with the other people that are in your life."

"Thank you. Were you able to contact Othniel's father, Obed, about setting up a meeting to discuss possible marriage arrangements between Othniel and Miriam?"

"Yes, I did. And Obed suggested that he, his wife Adah, and you, and Zibrah meet together in Yerushalayim on the fourth day of Sukkot. He said that the meeting could occur in his sukkah, and that he would arrange for dinner to be served."

Eliezer responds, "What a great idea! Having our meeting during the joyous celebration of Sukkot will provide a happy setting for us to discuss our childrens' future."

And Aharon says, "Then I will communicate your acceptance of Obed's invitation to him. And I also will plan to be there at the beginning of your meeting, to introduce you and Zibrah to Obed and Adah."

"Thank you, Aharon. I appreciate all that you are doing on our behalf."

Then Aharon, Bilhah, and Eliezer enjoy eating the dinner that Bilhah had prepared.

The next morning, Eliezer sells some of his produce in the commercial agora at Kfar Nahum. While he is at the market, Marius visits Eliezer's display of vegetables, and they enjoy chatting together briefly. During the afternoon, Eliezer and his donkeys walk to Tzipori, and they spend the night at his customary resting place.

On day three, Eliezer sells a large quantity of his vegetables in the paved, open-air market, and he enjoys talking with some of his familiar Tzipori customers. At the end of that day, he walks to Natzerat.

Eliezer spends the morning of day four selling produce in Natzerat. And that afternoon, he travels to his resting place by the spring of Harod, at the foot of Mount Gilboa, and only a short distance from Beit Shean.

~ /// ~

While Eliezer was traveling between Natzerat and Mount Gilboa, Yaaqov went missing back in Hammat. Around midafternoon, Zibrah and Miriam told Yaaqov he could go outside to play with some of his friends. But when Yaaqov didn't return to their home at his usual time just before dinner, Zibrah and Miriam went looking for him. But they did not find Yaaqov. They found Yaaqov's friends; however, those boys said that they hadn't seen Yaaqov at all that afternoon. Zibrah and Miriam became frantic.

Zibrah says, "Miriam, what do you think happened to Yaaqov? Does Yaaqov have any other friends besides those boys that he might have been visiting this afternoon?"

"Zibrah, those boys that we were talking with are the only playmates of Yaaqov that I know about. Furthermore, I can't think of a single occasion when Yaaqov was late in coming home for dinner when he wasn't playing with his friends. So, there must be some other explanation."

"Do you think that he could have gone off somewhere by himself, and become injured somehow?"

Miriam thinks for a moment, and then she says, "Sometimes, Yaaqov does keep to himself, but I don't think that he would have gone too far from our home. Let's look down by the lake."

"That's a good idea."

So, Miriam and Zibrah walk to the water's edge, and they walk alongside the lake in both directions, looking carefully. After a few minutes, Miriam finds Yaaqov's leather ball lying on the ground next to the water. And right next to it, she notices some marks in the mud that appear to have been made by the keel of a small boat. So they go to the house that is closest to where they found the ball, and they ask the man who lives there if he can remember seeing a twelve year old boy by the water this afternoon, or perhaps a small boat nearby.

The man thinks for a while, and then he says, "I didn't see any boy there this afternoon, but I did notice a small sailboat with a man in it who was wearing a conical-shaped hat. I remember thinking that kind of hat is quite unusual around here."

Then Zibrah says, "Phoenician men typically wear conical hats. I remember seeing a man from Phoenicia who works at the fish pickling operation in Magdala, and I have observed him wearing a hat like the one that you described. We will find him, to see if he knows anything about our boy. Sir, would you please tell us your name, in case we need to talk with you again about this matter."

The man tells Zibrah, "My name is Yehoezer. I hope that you will find your boy. Please contact me again if you think that I might be helpful."

Miriam and Zibrah each say, "Thank you, Yehoezer", and then they return to their home, because the sky had become dark while they were visiting with Yehoezer. They tell each other that there is a chance that Yaaqov might come home by himself. Perhaps he might even be there already, waiting for them.

But when they arrive at their home, no one is waiting there. Miriam and Zibrah pray earnestly for the Lord's protection of Yaaqov, and for his safe return to their home. That night, when Miriam laid herself down for sleep, she cried.

~ /// ~

At that same time, Eliezer is at his campsite by the spring of Harod, laying down between his donkeys, and saying his bedtime prayers. He doesn't know that his son was kidnapped earlier that day.

The next morning, Eliezer wakes up early, says his prayers, washes himself, eats a light breakfast, loads his goods on Amit and Marit, and walks to the commercial agora in Scythopolis. He finds Peleg, and asks him if they could sell their goods together again, and Peleg agrees. Eliezer spreads his cloak on the paved market floor, and he displays his remaining vegetables on the cloak. During lulls between dealing with customers, Eliezer and Peleg visit with each other about their lives, and about their hopes for the future. As in their previous conversations, Peleg again expresses hope that the Maschiah will be revealed soon. And Eliezer tells Peleg that he expects marriage negotiations on behalf of his daughter will begin soon. Peleg agrees that would be a good thing.

Meanwhile, Zibrah and Miriam ask Rabbi Yitzhak to help them find Yaaqov. And then they walk to Tiberias to find out if anyone there may have seen Yaaqov. When they arrive in Tiberias, Zibrah suggests to Miriam that they visit the main marketplace first, before going to any of her friends' homes.

At the market, Zibrah sees her friend Salome, so Zibrah and Miriam go over to where Salome is and they greet her, "Shalom, Salome! We are looking for Eliezer's son, Yaaqov. Yaaqov has been missing since yesterday afternoon. Have you seen him?"

Salome replies, "No, I haven't. Was he here in Tiberias when he became missing?"

"No, the last time we saw him was at our house in Hammat. But we think that it is possible that he could have been in this city after he went missing. So we are asking our friends to help us to find him."

Salome responds, "I am very sorry to hear that Yaaqov has become missing. I will be watchful for Yaaqov."

"Thank you, Salome. Would you also please notify Mayim, Milkah, and Joanna about Yaaqov's disappearance for us?"

"Yes, I will ask all of our friends to watch for Yaaqov."

"Thanks. And now, Miriam and I will walk over to Magdala, to contact someone there who may know something about Yaaqov's disappearance."

Just then, Assurbani notices Miriam and Zibrah in the marketplace, and he walks over to where they are. Then he says, "Hello, ladies! It is nice for me to see you again. What brings you to my city? May I help you?"

Miriam declines to acknowledge Assurbani, but Zibrah says to him, "Assurbani, yesterday afternoon, Eliezer's son Yaaqov went missing, and we are asking all of our friends to help us to find him."

Assurbani says, "Oh my, that is terrible! I imagine that Eliezer, and all of your family, must be very upset about Yaaqov's disappearance. Do you think that Yaaqov ran away from home? Or perhaps that some harm has befallen him?"

Zibrah replies, "Eliezer doesn't know about Yaaqov's disappearance yet, because he still is away from our home on a business trip. We do not believe that Yaaqov ran away from home. We suspect that Yaaqov may have been kidnapped."

"But who would do such a thing? Do you have proof that Yaaqov was kidnapped? Has anybody contacted you, demanding money for Yaaqov's return?"

"We do not know who did this, but we will try to find out. No one has contacted us demanding money."

Assurbani turns to Miriam and says, "I know that you and Yaaqov are very close. His disappearance must be especially painful for you. I think you realize that you probably will never see Yaaqov again. He could even be dead already. So, how will you ever get through this?"

Miriam says, "Assurbani, you seem to be enjoying this situation way too much. Take your false sympathy and get away from us! We believe that God will help us, and until this situation is resolved, we will do everything that we can to bring Yaaqov home. That is how we will get through it!"

Assurbani turns back to Zibrah, and he says, "When you see Eliezer, please tell him that I am very sorrowful about Yaaqov's disappearance, and the suffering that it has caused."

Zibrah replies, "Assurbani, I will tell Eliezer what you said, but he might not believe that you meant it." Then Zibrah and Miriam leave the Tiberias commercial agora, and continue on their way to Magdala. Miriam's eyes are reddened and moist.

~ /// ~

After spending less than three hours in the Beit Shean marketplace with Peleg, Eliezer sells all of the produce that he brought with him. Because of his eagerness to be with his wife and children, he decides to say "farewell" to Peleg, and to proceed directly to his home. So he leads Amit and Marit out of Beit Shean and onto the road that leads to the Yarden River and then northward towards Hammat. He is confident that he will cover the distance in about five and one-half hours.

~ /// ~

Magdala also is known by the Greek name Taricheae, which means "fish factory", after the important facility in that town for drying, salting, and pickling fish. When Miriam and Zibrah arrive in Magdala, they go to the fish processing center there. Because of her fishing business, Zibrah is familiar with the fish factory, as well as some of the people who work there.

Zibrah finds the facility manager, and greets him, "Shalom, Beor."

Beor replies, "Shalom, Zibrah. I heard that you got married again. Is that right?"

"Yes, it is true. Last month, I married Eliezer, who is a widower and a farmer from Hammat. We are very happy together. This woman with me is Eliezer's daughter, Miriam."

"Greetings, Miriam. It is a pleasure for me to meet you."

Miriam replies, "Thank you. I also am pleased to make your acquaintance."

Then Beor says, "Zibrah and Miriam, what brings you to my fish factory today? Would you like to buy a container of pickled fish?"

Zibrah answers, "No, thank you. We are looking for one of your workers. I don't know his name, but I remember seeing him here before. I recall that his beard is arranged in rows of small tight curls, and he usually wears a conical-shaped hat. We were hoping to be able to talk with him."

Beor replies, "That would be Baraket, our worker from Phoenicia. I'm sorry to have to tell you that he isn't at work with us today. In fact, he hasn't been here for the past few days, and I don't expect him to return to work for several more days. He told me that he was planning to visit his relatives in Acco during this week."

Zibrah says, "Do you know anything about Baraket's family in Acco?"

"I believe that they are fishermen. And Baraket said that his father's name is Resheph."

Then Zibrah says, "Acco is at least thirty miles from here. Do you think that Baraket was going to walk that distance?"

"No, I don't think so. Baraket doesn't like walking. He usually travels from place to place on Lake Kinneret in his small sailboat. And Baraket also has a mule-drawn cart that he sometimes uses for transportation on land."

Zibrah and Miriam look at each other and nod, without speaking any words. Then Zibrah says to Beor, "Beor, where does Baraket live?"

"He lives in a small house in the southern portion of Magdala, right next to the shore. . . . Why are you asking all of these questions about Baraket? What is this about?"

Zibrah answers, "My husband's son went missing yesterday afternoon, and we think that he may have been kidnapped."

"So what does that have to do with Baraket?"

"Someone told us that he saw a man with Baraket's description around the time and place that our boy disappeared. We want to talk to Baraket, because he may know something about what happened."

"Well, that certainly is a very serious matter. I am a father and grandfather myself, and I would be quite upset if any of my offspring were taken. So, if there is anything that I can do that might help you to get your boy back, then you can count on me to do it. Just tell me what you want to do."

"Thank you, Beor. We would appreciate it very much if you would ask your suppliers, customers, and neighbors if they have seen anything suspicious in the past couple of days involving a twelve-year-old boy. And when Baraket does return to Magdala please don't tell him that we were asking about him. We will contact him ourselves."

"I will do as you have requested. And I also will pray for the safe return of your husband's son to your family."

Zibrah and Miriam both say, "Thank you for helping us, Beor. We appreciate your cooperation with us in this time of our crisis. But now, we must return to our home in Hammat."

As Zibrah and Miriam are preparing to leave the fish processing facility, Beor says, "Shalom, Zibrah and Miriam. May peace be with you, and with your family." And then he went back to supervising his workers.

Zibrah and Miriam reply, "And may peace also be with you, Beor." They leave the fish factory, and depart for Hammat. On their way, they stop for a brief period at the house that Beor described as belonging to Baraket. They notice a small sailboat that had been pulled up on the shore, and a small, empty pen attached to the house that could be used for keeping a mule. But they don't see any sign that Yaaqov may have been there.

~ /// ~

Later that afternoon, Eliezer and his donkeys, Amit and Marit, walk up the path to his home in Hammat. Miriam hears them approaching, and she runs outside to greet her father. She says, "Abba, Yaaqov disappeared yesterday afternoon, and we have not been able to find him!"

Shocked by what Miri said, Eliezer stops in his tracks and he responds, "What happened?"

At that moment, Zibrah comes out of the house and greets her husband with sympathetic hugs and kissses.

With anxiety and a little impatience, Eliezer asks, "Tell me, what happened to Yaaqov?"

While the ladies are unloading baskets and bags from the donkeys, and are putting Amit and Marit back into the pen alongside the house, Miriam begins explaining what had happened: "Yesterday, at midafternoon, we told Yaaqov that he could go outside to play with his friends. But he didn't return home at dinnertime, so Zibrah and I went out looking for him. We found Yaaqov's friends, but they said that they hadn't seen Yaaqov. We thought that perhaps he had wandered off somewhere to be by himself, and the next place that we went was down by the shoreline, close to Yehoezer's house. There, next to the water, we found Yaaqov's leather ball and, right next to it, we saw some marks in the mud that appeared to have been made by a small boat."

Eliezer is listening very carefully.

Continuing the story, Zibrah says, "Then we visited with Yehoezer, and asked him if he had seen Yaaqov yesterday afternoon, or perhaps a small boat, in the vicinity of his house. He said that he hadn't noticed a twelve year-old boy, but he did remember seeing a small sailboat being operated by a man wearing a conical-shaped hat. Then I remembered seeing a Phoenician man working at the fish processing facility in Magdala, and that he usually wears a conical hat."

Eliezer responds, "That kind of hat is very unusual in this part of Galilee, but I have seen Phoenician men wearing hats like that elsewhere."

Then Miriam says, "After talking with Yehoezer, it was dusk, and so we returned home, in case Yaaqov might have come home himself. But he wasn't there. We suspect that Yaaqov may have been kidnapped. This morning, we asked Rabbi Yitzhak to spread the word about Yaaqov's disappearance, and then we went to Tiberias, to ask some other people to watch for Yaaqov. Assurbani was there, and he asked us to tell you that he is very sorry to learn about Yaaqov being missing."

Eliezer interrupts, "Do you think that Assurbani had anything to do with Yaaqov's disappearance?"

Miriam says, "Abba, I don't know anything about that. But, we do know that he is a despicable man, and it seemed to me that his sympathy wasn't genuine."

Then Zibrah tells Eliezer, "This morning we also went to Magdala, and we talked with the manager of the fish factory about his Phoenician employee. The manager's name is Beor, and he was very cooperative. It turns out that his Pheonician worker is named Baraket, and Baraket has been away from his work the past couple of days, and is reported to be visiting his relatives in Acco this week. We saw the house in Magdala where he lives, and we also saw his sailboat, that was next to his house. We were told that Baraket drives a mule-driven cart, but he must have it with him, because it wasn't at his house."

Eliezer sits down on the ground outside of his home, and he thinks about all that Zibrah and Miriam had said. Zibrah and Miriam sit down with him. Then Eliezer says, "We must find Baraket, to see what he may know about this situation, and we also need to continue spreading the word about Yaaqov's disappearance throughout our region. Shabbat begins tomorrow evening at sundown. Tomorrow, let's spend most of the daylight hours talking with our Hammat neighbors, to see if anyone else has any information relating to Yaaqov's disappearance. On the first day of the week, I will begin searching for Baraket."

Zibrah says, "I will go with you. I can identify him."

Eliezer replies, "All right, but I don't want to leave Miriam alone, so she should stay with Reuel and Serah while we are gone. But, right now, please join me in praying for Yaaqov: 'Blessed are you, O Lord, for listening to the prayers of your people with mercy and compassion. We are deeply troubled because Yaaqov has been taken from us, but nothing is hidden from you, O Lord. Please help, protect, and save Yaaqov, and guide us as we strive to find him. We put all of our trust in you. Blessed are you, O Lord, who answers our prayers. Amen.'"

Zibrah and Miriam say, "Amen."

Then Eliezer, Zibrah, and Miriam get back on their feet, and they go into their home and eat the dinner that Zibrah had prepared before Eliezer's arrival.

CHAPTER 29

On the first day of the week, after saying their morning prayers, Eliezer and Zibrah escort Miriam to Reuel's and Serah's house, and then they walk to Tiberias and, from there, on to Magdala.

Zibrah shows Eliezer the house in which Baraket lives, on the outskirts of Magdala. Eliezer verifies that no one is in the house now, and he inspects Baraket's sailboat, the pen where he keeps his mule, and the place where he customarily keeps his cart.

Then they walk to the house that is closest to Baraket's house, and Eliezer knocks on the door, and calls out, "Hello! I am Eliezer, from Hammat, and I would like to have a visit with you."

A moment later, the door opens, and the woman who opened it says, "Did you say your name is Eliezer? Aren't you the farmer who sometimes sells his produce at the markets in Tiberias and Magdala?"

Eliezer says, "Yes, I am that Eliezer, and this lovely woman is my wife, Zibrah."

Then the woman at the house says, "Eliezer, I remember buying some melons and vegetables from you! And Zibrah, I am pleased to meet you. My name is Anah. But why did you come to my house today?"

Zibrah says, "Anah, four days ago, our twelve year-old son, Yaaqov, went missing, and we think that he may have been kidnapped. Have you recently noticed a twelve year-old boy that you didn't recognize? It is possible that he may have been near here."

Then Anah says, "Yes, about three days ago, in the morning, I noticed my neighbor, Baraket, leaving his home in his cart, with a boy beside him that I hadn't seen before. The boy looked distressed to me."

Eliezer says, "Anah, do you know which direction they were going?"

"They were going to the west on the main highway, toward the coastal plains of Acco."

Then, in unison, Eliezer and Zibrah say, "Thank you, Anah! You have been very helpful. And now, we must be on our way."

Eliezer and Zibrah left Magdala immediately and they begin walking towards Acco.

After about five hours of walking, Eliezer and Zibrah arrive at the familiar meadow with a spring that is near Tzipori, the same resting place that Eliezer customarily uses on his marketing tours. They wash their feet, hands, and faces, and they eat a small meal of bread and fruit that they had brought with them. Then they walk over to Tzipori, enter the city, and go directly to the open-air market and public forum. Eliezer introduces Zibrah to the people who are there that he knows, including Ephron, Talmai and some others. And he asks them if they had seen an unfamiliar twelve year-old boy that was traveling with a man with a curly beard, and wearing a conical-shaped hat. He explains that his son had been kidnapped, and that he and the man are believed to be traveling to Acco in a mule-drawn cart. But none of those people could remember having seen a boy and man traveling together that looked like what Eliezer had described. They express their sympathy to Eliezer and Zibrah, and they say that they hope that Eliezer and Zibrah will succeed in finding their son, and getting him back unharmed. Eliezer and Zibrah thank the people for their kind thoughts, and then they go back to their campsite outside the city, say their bedtime prayers, and lay down, intending to sleep.

As they lay there on their cloaks on the grassy ground, Eliezer and Zibrah are both deep into their own thoughts, and there is no conversation between them. Eliezer and Zibrah are both thinking that no one that they had spoken with, either on the road or in Tzipori, had actually seen Yaaqov or the elusive character wearing a strange hat. Perhaps the persons they are seeking aren't actually on their way to Acco, as was thought. Maybe Baraket had turned off of the road somewhere, and had taken Yaaqov in a different direction. Then Eliezer sighs despairingly, and quietly speaks to himself, "What if we *never* find Yaaqov? What if he isn't at Acco?"

Even though Eliezer's quiet exclamation was barely audible, Zibrah heard it and understood. She rolls her body closer to Eliezer's, she touches his face with her own hands, she brings her face very close to his face, and then she says, "Eliezer, we must follow this trail of information wherever it leads us. If we don't find Yaaqov at Acco, *then* we will turn our consideration to other possibilities. But until then, let us hold on to the hope that we are on the right path."

Eliezer says, "I understand that what you said is right."

Then they hug each other in silence and, after a while, they both fall asleep.

Eliezer and Zibrah wake up early the next morning, say their prayers, eat a light breakfast, and then continue on their way towards Acco. Five hours later, at midday, they arrive at Acco. It is the twenty-third day of Elul, and the second day of the week.

Acco is a fortified city that is located on the north side of a large bay in the eastern side of the Mediterranean Sea. It is a Phoenician city, with a mixed population that includes Phoenicians, Syrians, Canaanites, Egyptians, Greeks, Romans, and some Jews. The city has been in continuous existence for more than 1,900 years, and its natural harbor is an important port for regional and international shipping. However, the importance of Acco is overshadowed by Tyre and Sidon, located farther north. About 250 years ago the name of the city was changed from Acco to Ptolemais, and that is the name that is used by Egyptians, Greeks and Romans, but most Phoenicians, Syrians, Canaanites, and Jews still prefer to call it Acco. The large, high-walled, wedge-shaped city projects out into the sea and faces the water on three sides. Acco's seaport is the bay south of the promontory. There is no dock. Ships anchor in the cove. There is a sandy beach on the bay south of the city, and a small town is near the shore of the bay that serves the seaport. There are inns, taverns, and other diversions in the shoreline town that cater to the needs of sailors and transients whose work brings them to the seaport.

Eliezer and Zibrah had already decided that they probably will need several days, at least, to search for Baraket and Yaaqov in the vicinity of Acco, so they rent sleeping accommodations at an inn in the shoreline town. Then they found an establishment selling kosher ready-to-eat food, where they are able to purchase a meal for themselves, and to sit on benches at a table in order to eat it. There also are a few other customers eating, so Eliezer talks with them about how he might be able to contact some of the local fishermen at Acco. They tell him the location of a tavern where many local fishermen like to gather when they aren't working.

When Eliezer and Zibrah enter the tavern, they sit down at one end of a long table at which some men also are sitting, and Eliezer orders two cups of the wine that is being served. When the wine is served to Eliezer and Zibrah, they start drinking it. The other men at the table appear to be fishermen, or at least they smell like fish, so Eliezer asks, "Excuse me for interrupting, but do any of you know a local fisherman named Resheph?"

The oldest-looking man in the group answers, "I used to know a fisherman named Resheph, but he died. One of Resheph's sons, a man named Mitten, took over Resheph's business after his father died."

Eliezer says, "How could I get in touch with Mitten? I am trying to contact his brother, Baraket."

The old fisherman replies, "I don't believe that Baraket lives in Acco any more. And I don't know where he lives now."

"You are right. Baraket lives in Magdala now, but I heard that he currently is visiting his relatives here in Acco. Perhaps Mitten will know where I can find Baraket."

"After entering the city, turn left onto the second street that goes in that direction, and then follow that street as it curves back to the right and toward the far end of the city. Mitten's house has a sign in the shape of a fish over the door, and the name "Mitten ben Resheph" is painted on the fish sign."

Eliezer says, "Thank you very much. You seem to be very familiar with Acco and its residents. Do you also happen to know where the Jewish synagogue is in Acco?"

"Yes, I do. After you enter the city, instead of turning at the second street that goes to the left, go straight until you come to a park, then turn to your right and look for a building with pillars on the left and right sides of the doorway, with a sign in the shape of a menorah over the door, and a design of a six-pointed star on the door. That will be the synagogue."

"Thanks again, for providing us with directions." Then Eliezer and Zibrah finish their wine, depart from the tavern, and then walk over to the city gate. As they enter the city, they see a few policemen by the gate. Eliezer thinks about asking the police to help him, but he worries that, as a foreigner, they might not treat him with impartiality. So they enter the city and follow the directions to the synagogue that the old fisherman had given to them. They notice that inside the walls, Acco is comprised of many very old buildings that are built right next to each other, and that the city has narrow, paved streets.

It is midafternoon. Eliezer and Zibrah give proper reverence to the mezuzah box that is attached to the doorpost of the synagogue. Then they open the door and enter the synagogue. Inside they find a group of men engaged in a lively discussion about the Torah. Zibrah goes over to a bench at the side of the hall, sits down, and quietly listens to the discussion. And Eliezer goes over to the table where the men are seated, sits down in a vacant chair, introduces himself to the group, and joins the discussion. They are talking about a scriptural portion from Shemot [Exodus 21-23] pertaining to laws about slaves, personal injury, property, and justice.

In the course of the discussion, a man named Tomar says, "A righteous person has an obligation to do everything in his power to protect those who are vulnerable."

Another discussant, a man named Kemuel, responds, "Yes, and during this season of repentance leading up to Rosh Hashanah and Yom Kippur, we all need to be especially mindful of those requirements, as well as the more prominent commandments."

Then Eliezer says, "It is a pleasure for me to be in the company of spiritual brothers whose minds and hearts are attuned to the needs of others. As it happens, I may be a person in need of your wise advice, and perhaps even more substantive help. Will you allow me to share my situation with you?"

Tomar says, "Eliezer, our Torah discussions must not be limited to esoteric ideals. We also must consider practical applications of our principles. So please tell us about your situation."

Eliezer replies, "I am Eliezer, from Hammat. My wife, Zibrah, is sitting over there *(pointing to her)*. I have a twelve year-old son named Yaaqov but, five days ago, he was taken from us. We believe that the man who did this is Baraket ben Resheph, who originated in this city. We think that Baraket may have brought Yaaqov here to Acco. We have come to Acco to find Yaaqov, to get him back, and to bring him home with us. Of course, we also would like the person who kidnapped him

156

to be held accountable for what he did but, for us, the most important thing is to have our son returned to us unharmed."

Tomar asks, "Why do you believe that the man named Baraket kidnapped your son, and brought him here?"

"Because one witness saw him at the time and place where Yaaqov was kidnapped, and another witness saw him leave his home with Yaaqov in his mule-driven cart. And Baraket told his employer that he was going to visit his family here in Acco."

"Why would Baraket have done such a terrible thing?"

"I don't know. But I certainly would like to ask him why. Do you think that the Acco police would arrest Baraket and interrogate him, if I reported this situation to them?"

"I am truly sorry that I have to tell you this. They might ask him some questions, but because you are a foreigner they probably would not charge a fellow Phoenician with a crime solely on the basis of your report."

Eliezer asks Tomar, "What do you advise me to do?"

Tomar replies, "I advise you to try to find your son yourself, without first contacting the local or Phoenician authorities. If you are successful in getting your son back, then bring him home with you and seek justice in Israel, where the kidnapping occurred. However, if you aren't able to have your son returned to you through your own efforts, then you could contact the Acco authorities, but only as a last resort. If it comes to that, I will recommend a local magistrate that may be less corrupt than the others."

Then Kemuel interjects, "Eliezer, in the portion from Shemot that we were studying this afternoon, it says, 'Whoever kidnaps a person, whether that person has been sold or is still held in possession, shall be put to death.'"   [Exodus 21:16 NRSV]

Eliezer says, "Yes, Kemuel, I knew that. But that provision is not enforceable in this gentile country of Phoenicia. . . . Thank you, Tomar, for your very good advice about dealing with the local authorities. I am planning to contact a member of Baraket's family tomorrow. Depending on how well, or how badly, that visit turns out, I may want to consult with you again."

Then Eliezer and Zibrah leave the synagogue, and they take a stroll through some of the streets of Acco, thinking all the while about the possibility that their son could be there. Then they return to the kosher food vendor in the shoreline town to eat their dinner. After their evening meal, they take a walk on the beach, and then they go back to their rented room at the inn.

CHAPTER 30

The next morning, Eliezer and Zibrah eat a light breakfast in their rented room, and then they walk from the shoreline town to the fortified city of Acco, pass through the gate, and turn off of the main street at the second left turn and follow that winding street until they come to the fishermens' district. They look carefully at each of the fish-shaped signs over the doors, until they find the one that had the words, "Mitten ben Resheph". Eliezer knocks on the door, and then he waits a couple of minutes. Then he knocks again. Eliezer and Zibrah hear someone moving around inside the house, and after a couple additional minutes the door is opened by a woman.

Eliezer says, "Good morning, lady. We are Eliezer and Zibrah. We are looking for Baraket ben Resheph. Will you help us?"

"Baraket is my brother-in-law, but he doesn't live here. He lives in Taricheae, over by the large Galilean lake."

"We were informed that Baraket is visiting his relatives in Acco this week. So we assumed that he would be staying with his brother, Mitten. If he isn't here, can you tell us where he is?"

"Well, I might be able to help you, but why do you want to talk with him?"

"We heard that he brought a boy with him to Acco, and we are interested in acquiring that boy from him."

"Oh, you mean his slave! Baraket doesn't own that boy anymore. Yesterday, he sold the boy to Bodo."

Eliezer and Zibrah look at each other with surprise. Then Zibrah says, "We are still pretty new to Acco, so we aren't familiar with anyone named Bodo. Can you tell us where we might find him?"

Then the lady says, "Bodo runs the largest cargo-handling operation in Acco. He employs many people who load and unload shipments to and from commercial ships that drop anchor in the cove, using several smaller transport vessels. He also transfers cargo between sea and land carriers through his warehouse in the shoreline town."

Eliezer says, "Thank you very much. You are so nice! We really appreciate your helping us. I'm certain that we will be able to find Bodo now. But what about Baraket? Where is he today?"

"Oh, I may as well tell you, Baraket is out on the Great Sea today, on Mitten's fishing boat. They went to sea before dawn this morning, and I don't expect them to return to the port until midafternoon."

Zibrah responds, "Thanks, again, for all of the information! Have a good day!"

Mitten's wife cheerfully says, in return, "And the same to you, Zibrah! Goodbye."

Then Eliezer says to Zibrah, "Yaaqov is here, someplace! Let's go find Bodo's warehouse, to see if he could be there." And Zibrah is just as excited as her husband. They go through the streets of Acco to the city gate, past the guards at the entrance, and over to the shoreline town. Then they see a fairly large building with a sign on it that says, "Bodo's Cargo Handling."

Eliezer and Zibrah walk through the double doors to the warehouse with their eyes wide-open, looking for Yaaqov inside. One side of the warehouse is for imports, and the other side for exports. They see stacks of crates, and clusters of bales, bundles, and large, sealed clay jars, all containing goods received for shipment to, or from, Acco. They see a few men searching through the various containers, looking for particular items of freight. And a small party of muscular men is struggling to bring a wheeled cart laden with crates through the doors of the warehouse from the outside. Eliezer looks carefully, trying to identify someone who appears to be directing the activities in this establishment. However, finding no evident director, Eliezer opens his mouth, and says in a loud voice, "Can someone please tell me how I may talk with Bodo?"

Just then, a man walks through the doors, and says, "Who is it that wants a visit with Bodo?"

Eliezer says, "My name is Eliezer, and I would like to meet Bodo."

The man responds, "Bodo is not here this morning. I am Azmalqart, the warehouse foreman. How may I help you?"

"We were informed that, yesterday, Bodo bought a young Galilean boy as a slave from a man named Baraket. That boy never should have been sold for a slave. He is my son, and a free person. I want my son returned to me."

Azmalqart responds, "I was there when Bodo purchased the boy from Baraket. We decided that the boy was too young, and too slight to be of much use as a freight hauler. So he currently is serving as a house slave in Bodo's personal residence."

Eliezer replies, "Where is Bodo's home?"

Azmalqart says, "If you create a disturbance at Bodo's home, you will be arrested as a troublemaker."

"Then would you please make arrangements for a peaceable meeting between Bodo and me and my wife?"

"I will ask Bodo if he is willing to meet with you. How may I get in touch with you after I obtain Bodo's response?"

"My wife and I are staying at the inn, here in this shoreline town."

Azmalqart says, "I will let you know, soon after I talk with Bodo about your request."

Eliezer responds, "Thank you, Azmalqart." Then Eliezer and Zibrah go back to their room at the inn to wait for Bodo's response.

Eliezer and Zibrah waited all afternoon that day, and half of the following day, for word of a meeting with Bodo about Yaaqov. However, no one contacted them about their requested meeting with Bodo. So, early in the afternoon of the twenty-fifth of Elul, Eliezer and Zibrah go back to Bodo's warehouse, looking for Azmalqart, or Bodo himself.

Upon entering Bodo's warehouse, Eliezer does not see Azmalqart, so he opens his mouth and says in a loud voice, "Can someone please tell me how I might be able to talk with Bodo?"

From the rear of the building, a voice answers, "I am Bodo. Who is it that wants to speak with me?"

"My name is Eliezer. I am the father of a twelve year-old boy named Yaaqov who was kidnapped from our home in Hammat by a man named Baraket, who brought him to Acco against his will and sold him to you as a slave. I want him returned to me unharmed."

Bodo walks over to where Eliezer is standing, and he looks directly into Eliezer's eyes and says to him, "The boy that I bought was represented to me as a slave, and I purchased him as such in good faith. I paid good money for my slave, and I am not going to just give him back to you. If you create a disturbance in Acco then you will be arrested and jailed as a troublemaker. If you seek any kind of legal action against me in Acco, you will lose. Therefore, I don't think that we have anything further to discuss about this matter."

Then Zibrah speaks up, asking Bodo, "How much money did you pay for our son?"

Bodo replies, "I paid Baraket seventy-five silver shekels for the boy."

Zibrah says, "Then I would like to purchase him from you for one hundred silver shekels. If you accept my offer, then you actually will make a profit from this transaction."

Eliezer gasps and says to her, "Zibrah, are you spending the marriage gift that I gave to you for your personal security?"

Zibrah replies, "Our marriage agreement says that I can spend that money for anything that I want, and I cannot think of a better way for me to spend it than for our son."

Bodo thinks about what Zibrah had said, and then he says to her, "I accept your offer of one hundred silver shekels for the boy that you say is your son."

Then Eliezer interjects, "Of course, we first must verify that the boy that you have in your possession is our son. How soon can we do that?"

Bodo replies, "Whenever you are ready to pay me the money that you offered."

Zibrah says, "I have it with me right now. Let us complete this business as soon as possible."

Less than one hour later, Eliezer and Zibrah exchange the one hundred silver shekels for Yaaqov, who is found to be in good health, despite his ordeal. And Zibrah also insists that Bodo endorse over to them the original Bill of Sale that Bodo had received from Baraket. Shortly afterward, Eliezer, Zibrah, and Yaaqov are walking on the highway that leads from Acco to Tzipori.

Eliezer offers a prayer of thanksgiving for Yaaqov's return: "Blessed are you, O Lord, for answering our prayers and supplications, and for not turning us away from your presence empty-handed. We thank you for helping all of us throughout Yaaqov's ordeal. We bless and thank you for your mercy and your loving kindness which never cease. Amen."

Then Eliezer says, "Zibrah, that was a very generous thing that you did, giving your marriage money to redeem Yaaqov."

Zibrah replies, "Not at all! Yaaqov is your son by birth, and my son by marriage. But now, since I bought him, Yaaqov is more truly a son to both of us."

While they are on the way, Zibrah asks, "Yaaqov, what happened on the day that you were kidnapped?"

Yaaqov replies, "I remember that you and Miriam suggested that I go outside to play with my friends. But I didn't see any of them playing nearby, and so I went down to the shore of Lake Kinneret, because sometimes I like watching the fishermen throwing their nets from their boats and then hauling in the fish that they catch. But that afternoon, I didn't see any fishing boats. However, there was a sailboat nearby, and it was interesting for me to watch how the man sailing it was able to make the sailboat go exactly where he wanted it to go. Then I realized that the man driving the sailboat also was watching me. He brought his boat directly to the spot where I was standing. He said something to me that I didn't hear clearly, and when I leaned closer to him so that I could hear better, he grabbed me, and he pulled me into the boat with him."

Eliezer asks, "Why didn't you cry out when he grabbed you?"

"I tried to shout, but he covered my mouth with his hand, and then he stuffed some cloth into my mouth, and he tied another piece of cloth around my head and over my mouth. He also tied my wrists together behind my back."

Zibrah asks, "What did the man look like?"

"He is a big man with a beard that was carefully trimmed and wavy, and he was wearing a conical-shaped hat made out of cloth that had red and white stripes."

Zibrah says, "What happened next?

"The man showed me his knife, and he told me that if I resisted him in any way, or if I tried to escape from him, that he would kill me immediately. I was very scared, becuase I believed that he would do what he said. Then he sailed his boat to the north, past Tiberias, and he brought the boat to his house, that is next to the lake, on the southernmost part of the town of Magdala. He brought me inside his house, and he told me again to be very quiet, or he would kill me. Then he removed the gag from my mouth, and gave me some bread to eat, and some water to drink. Then he put the gag back over my mouth, and he tied my feet together, and joined my feet with my hands using the rope that was behind my back. Once, he let me urinate into his chamber pot. I prayed for someone to help me, but mostly I slept. The next morning, he gave me some more water to drink, and then he carried me outside and put me into his cart. Then he drove the cart for many hours, until we arrived at the city of Acco. When we entered Acco, some soldiers asked about me, and he told them that I was his slave. Then he brought me to another man's house, where he removed the gag and the ropes that held my hands and legs. Again he reminded me that if I tried to escape, he would kill me. Two or three days later, he brought me to another man's house, and he sold me to that man. The man that bought me didn't hurt me, but he was very strict. I kept praying that somehow you would find me."

Eliezer says, "Yaaqov, when we started searching for you, we decided that we would never stop until we found you, no matter how long it might take!"

Yaaqov responds, "Thank you, Abba!

Zibrah asks, "Did you cry when you were taken":

"Yes, I cried through part of the first night, when I was in the kidnapper's house. And I also cried a little while we were riding in the cart, because I knew that I was being taken far from our home. I was afraid that I might never see my family again, and that idea made me very sad."

Then Eliezer asks, "Do you know the names of the man that kidnapped you, and the man that bought you in Acco?"

"Yes, the people who knew the man that kidnapped me called him Baraket, and the man that bought me is called Bodo. Will they be punished for what they did to me?"

Eliezer answers, "We don't know if Baraket will be punished or not. But he certainly deserves to be punished. Bodo won't be punished, because when he bought you he didn't know that you weren't a slave.

Did Baraket ever say anything to you about *why* he kidnapped you, and brought you so far away from us?"

"Once he mentioned that another person had paid him to kidnap me and to take me far away from my family in Hammat."

"Did he say who had paid him to do such a mean thing?"

"No, he didn't."

Eliezer and Zibrah wondered who would do something so awful, and why. Evidently, it was someone who wanted to hurt them very much. And it almost did. Eliezer thought to himself, "If ever we find that Baraket has returned to Magdala, we could have him arrested and interrogated thoroughly about this incident."

Eliezer, Zibrah, and Yaaqov spent that night at an inn in Zipori, and Eliezer told many of his friends in that city that he and Zibrah had retrieved Yaaqov from Acco. The following day, the twenty-sixth day of Elul, Eliezer's family is reunited at their home in Hammat. And during the next couple of days, they share the good news about Yaaqov's return with their friends and neighbors.

When Assurbani hears that Eliezer had succeeded in retrieving Yaaqov from slavery in Acco, he becomes worried that Eliezer may have found out from Baraket about his own role in Yaaqov's kidnapping, or that he would find out if Baraket is interrogated by people who sympathize with Eliezer. So Assurbani tells his policeman colleague, Mibzar, to be alert for Baraket's return to Magdala, and to discreetly capture and hold Baraket for questioning, just as soon as that is possible. And after he is questioned, to kill him.

CHAPTER 31

A few days later, on the first day of Tishri, Eliezer and his family celebrate Rosh Hashanah at their home, as a day of holy rest and of sounding the shofar. This particular observance of Rosh Hashanah is especially meaningful because of Yaaqov's redemption from slavery in Phoenicia during the previous week. And nine days later, they share a solemn participation in observance of Yom Kippur, the Day of Atonement. And on the day after Yom Kippur, the family begins their five-day journey to Yerushalayim for the seven-day pilgrim festival of Sukkot (also known as Booths, and Tabernacles). It is raining when they depart from Hammat. However, the rain does not dampen the joyful enthusiasm of the pilgrims on their way to celebrating Sukkot.

They arrive in Yerushalayim on the fifteenth day of Tishri, just as the festival is getting underway. Eliezer leads his family through the winding streets of the holy city to the familiar two-story home of his cousin Yehuda, and Yehuda's wife Shira. After visiting briefly with Yehuda and Shira, Eliezer and Yaaqov get to work assembling the sukkah (booth) in which they will eat, sleep, and spend much of their time during the next seven days. The reusable materials that are used to construct the frame and sides of the shelter are owned by Eliezer, but they are stored for him at Yehuda's house. For the roof, they use freshly cut palm branches, leaving spaces between them, so that the sky may be seen from inside the sukkah. After the sukkah is set up, Zibrah and Miriam decorate the inside with etrogs, palm fronds, and branches of willow and myrtle -- the "four species" of Sukkot. Eliezer's sukkah is set up behind Yehuda's home, and right next to Yehuda's own sukkah.

When Eliezer sees that his sukkah is ready, he takes two willow branches, three myrtle branches, a ripe, green, closed palm frond that is longer than the willow and myrtle branches, and several single strips of palm leaves. He makes a woven cylindrical holder using the palm strips, folding the ends inside after the cylindrical shape is formed. Then he creates a bundle from the tree branches, putting the closed palm frond in the middle, the two willow branches on the left side, and the three myrtle branches on the right side. He ties the bundle together with some palm strips, and then he passes the stems of the bundle through the woven holder, so that the top of the holder is just below the leafy portions of the willow and myrtle branches. The resulting bouquet is referred to as a lulav. At Sukkot, each man holds the lulav in one of his hands and an etrog in his other hand for the "four species" procession at the Temple. At certain times during the recitation of the Hallel psalms, the lulav is shaken lightly, or waved in several directions. Some rabbis have given various interpretations of what the "four species" symbolize, but for Eliezer the most important thing is keeping the commandment.

When Eliezer finishes the preparations, he brings his family into the sukkah, and he reads the following portion from Vaiyikra to them:

> "Now, the fifteenth day of the seventh month, when you have gathered in the produce of the land, you shall keep the festival of the LORD, lasting seven days; a complete rest on the first day, and a complete rest on the eighth day.
>
> On the first day you shall take the fruit of majestic trees, branches of palm trees, boughs of leafy trees, and willows of the brook; and you shall rejoice before the LORD your God for seven days.
>
> You shall keep it as a festival to the LORD seven days in the year; you shall keep it in the seventh month as a statute forever throughout your generations.
>
> You shall live in booths for seven days; all Israelites shall live in booths, so that your generations may know that I made the people of Israel live in booths when I brought them out of the land of Egypt: I am the LORD your God."
>
> [Leviticus 23:39-43 NRSV]

Then Eliezer says the blessing for Sukkot, "Blessed art Thou, Lord, our God, King of the universe, who has sanctified us with His commandments, and commanded us to dwell in the sukkah. Amen." He tells his family that Sukkot is a festival for rejoicing, and a reminder of our dependence on God. Sukkot is the great fall harvest festival, but the central theme of Sukkot is the pure joy that comes from having a relationship with God. For Eliezer and his family, this particular Sukkot is special because of Yaaqov's redemption from slavery, Eliezer's having found love again with Zibrah, and the new prospect of a life partner for Miriam. God is good, and His resources, love, and concern are without limits!

Eliezer takes his lulav and etrog, and goes to the Temple with Yaaqov to participate in the festivities at the Temple, while Zibrah and Miriam have an enjoyable time with Shira and Shira's daughters, visiting with each other and preparing food for their men.

Each day of Sukkot, the participants at the Temple pray, sing hymns and psalms, and watch and participate in religious processions. One of the hymns that is sung as the priests march around the altar, that is covered with freshly cut willow branches, has a refrain that begins with "Hosha nah", which means "Please save us."

Every morning during Sukkot, the High Priest and two priests playing trumpets lead the procession of pilgrims to the Pool of Siloam, where the High Priest fills a golden picher with water, and then the procession returns to the courtyard of the Temple, where the water is poured on the altar, while each person in the procession waves his lulav and sings,

"Save us, we beseech you, O LORD! O LORD, we beseech you, give us success! Blessed is the one who comes in the name of the LORD. We bless you from the house of the LORD."

[Psalm 118:25-26 NRSV]

Evening festivities during Sukkot are illuminated by large oil lamps that tower over the Women's Court of the Temple, and these produce a bright light that can be seen from a great distance.

Daily during the festival, and also on the eighth day, large numbers of animals are sacrificed, with accompanying grain offerings, and drink offerings. Not all of the Sukkot sacrifices are offered on behalf of the people of Israel. Many of them are offered as atonement on behalf of people from all of the nations of the world.

During the first few days of Sukkot, Eliezer overhears some people talking about Yeshuah. They seemed to be expecting that Yeshuah will attend the festival, but no one has seen him there yet. From the way they are talking about Yeshuah, it sounds like the people have very strong opinions about him, some are positive and some negative.

On the afternoon of the fourth day, Aharon accompanies Eliezer and Zibrah to their meeting with Obed and his wife Adah at Obed's sukkah, to discuss the possibility of marriage between Othniel and Miriam. After introducing the two sets of parents to each other, Aharon leaves them.

Zibrah says, "Obed, your sukkah is very beautiful! The white interior walls look like what I imagine the clouds of glory might look like! I like your decorations of fruit and flowers. And I have never seen a sukkah with comfortable reclining couches, or a fine table like this one!"

Obed replies, "Thank you for your generous compliments, Zibrah! I hope that you and Eliezer don't think that it is too extravagant."

Eliezer says, "No, your sukkah isn't too extravagant! It is comfortable in some ways, but I think those ways probably enhance your experience of Sukkot, and don't detract from it. Your sukkah still seems enough like a temporary lodging."

Obed responds, "Thank you, Eliezer. Well, let us turn our attention to the matter at hand. Your brother-in-law, Aharon, contacted me to see if my wife and I would consider making arrangements for a marriage between our son, Othniel, and your daughter, Miriam. Is that what what you are interested in discussing today?"

Eliezer says, "Yes, it is. I have not been diligent in seeking to find a suitable person to marry our daughter, Miriam. We have met your son, Othniel, and he seems to be a very fine young man who fulfills the qualifications that are most important to us. However, we are aware that we still aren't very well-acquainted with Othniel, and also that you have never even met Miriam. Therefore, I think that it may be premature for us to prepare a contract for marriage now. But I would like to suggest that we consider the possibility of entering into such an agreement after our children have become better acquainted with each other, and also after each of us becomes better acquainted with the other's child."

Then Obed's wife, Adah, says, "I asked Othniel what he thought about the possibility of marrying your daughter, Miriam. He told me that, even though he has been around Miriam only a few times, nevertheless, he believes that they share a very deep connection with each other, and he hopes that we *will* make a contract. . . . I was surprised by his hastiness in this matter, because he usually is very careful about making decisions."

And Obed adds, "Othniel surprised me, too. He told me how much he likes Miriam and her family, and he said that all of us should get used to the idea of having our families joined together by marriage."

Zibrah looks at Eliezer and says to him, "Well, I am not at all surprised by any of this. In fact, I have been expecting something like this for Miriam for many months."

Adah says, "I just want what will be best for my son."

Zibrah responds, "We all want that. Every parent wants to know that they did everything they could to help their child become a person with good values who is able to take care of himself or herself, and also to see that they have a suitable companion who will help them to face life's challenges, and to give them the love that they need."

Adah says, "Yes, Zibrah. What you said expresses my desire perfectly!"

Eliezer says, "When I asked Aharon to contact Obed about the possibility of arranging a marriage between Miriam and Othniel, I was feeling pretty desperate. And afterwards, I worried that I had been reckless."

Obed responds, "Eliezer, I sympathize with you about desperation. A few years ago, a pending marriage agreement between Othniel and another young woman fell apart, and I was frustrated about that failure. Then, when Othniel became so passionate about becoming a disciple of Yeshuah, I became worried that Othniel might never want to become married. So, I was desperate too. But when Aharon contacted me about Miriam, and especially after Othniel told me that he welcomed the idea, I became more hopeful. So I certainly don't regard you as having behaved recklessly."

Eliezer says, "So what do you and Adah think that we should do next?"

Obed smiles at Adah, and says, "Eliezer, Zibrah, and Adah, I think that we already are doing the right thing, by spending this time getting aquainted with each other. But I would like for us to expand this conversation by including Othniel and Miriam in our familiarization process. So, after the seven-day festival of Sukkot, and the Solemn Assembly on the eighth day, Adah and I would like to have you and your family, spend a few days with us at our home in Yeriko. Othniel also will be there. This will give all of us an opportunity to become better acquainted, and our time together will guide all of us as to what steps should follow."

Eliezer replies, "Thank you for your generous offer of hospitality to us. We are looking forward to visiting your home. And we are completely open to whatever decisions our children may make."

Obed says, "Wonderful! Now, let us finish preparations for our dinner."

That afternoon, While Eliezer, Zibrah, Obed, and Adah were discussing the possibility of a marriage between Othniel and Miriam, Yeshuah came to the Temple and spoke to a crowd of pilgrims about himself and about the One who had sent him, mentioning prophecies about the end of days. Some of the people were talking about that anyway, because they had been reading scriptural portions from Zecharyahu [Zechariah] and Yechezkel [Ezekiel], and there was speculation concerning whether this Yeshuah could be the Maschiah. The chief priests and Pharisees sent temple guards to arrest Yeshuah, but they returned empty-handed because they were astonished by what Yeshuah had said. After Yeshuah's teaching, his hearers were even more divided than before. Othniel was with Yeshuah at the Temple.

Four days later, on the twenty-second day of Tishri, is Shemini Atzeret (which means "Eighth Day of Assembly"), a separate holy day in which the Jewish people spend an additional day with God after Sukkot, to underscore the spiritual themes and messages of Sukkot, and also to celebrate the special relationship that exists between God and the people of Israel. But on this day, the participants no longer dwell in booths, they no longer wave the lulav, and the daily water libation is not offered at the Temple. For that day, Eliezer and Yaaqov join Zibrah and Miriam in Yehuda's and Shira's house in Yerushalayim.

On the morning of the following day, Eliezer thanks Yehuda and Shira for their hospitality during the previous eight days. Yehuda tells Eliezer that he is looking forward to hosting Eliezer and his family again at Pesach, which is less than six months away. Eliezer, Zibrah, Miriam, and Yaaqov each embrace Yehuda, Shira, and their children, before departing from Yerushalayim for Yeriko. Yeriko is about fifteen miles away, but the curving desert road is mostly downhill, so they arrive in Yeriko in less than four hours.

They carefully follow the directions that Obed gave Eliezer, and they walk through the city of palm trees to an expensive neighborhood that is located south of the spring of Elisha. They find Obed's villa, and walk to a beautifully-carved, wooden door with a mezuzah box attached to the doorpost. Shortly after Eliezer knocks on the door, Obed opens the door and invites Eliezer and his family to enter his home. Eliezer, Zibrah, Miriam, and Yaaqov each give proper attention to the mezuzah box before stepping inside to receive a warm greeting from Obed. Upon entering, each one says, "Peace be to this house!."

As Miriam steps accross the threshold, Obed hugs her, kisses her cheek, and then he holds both of her hands in his own hands and he looks at her carefully, while smiling. Then he says, "Miriam, I am especially happy to meet you. You are just as lovely as Othniel said. Welcome!"

Miriam blushes shyly and responds, "Thank you, Obed. I am very pleased to meet the parents of my special friend, Othniel."

At that moment, Adah comes out of an interior room of the house, and into the great room that is adjacent to the entryway. She sees Eliezer and his family, and she rushes over to greet each of them.

When Yaaqov walks through the doorway, Obed hugs him vigorously and exclaims, "You must be Yaaqov, that brave young man who was kidnapped, enslaved, and redeemed, just like our ancestors! The Lord surely was with you, helping you to get through it! It is an honor to have you visit my home!"

Yaaqov replies, "Thank you, Sir. I am happy to be here."

Then Eliezer says, "Thank you, Obed and Adah, for welcoming all of us to your home. Is Othniel here already?"

Adah replies, "No, he hasn't arrived yet, but we expect him to be here later this afternoon. Until then, let us help you to be comfortable in our home, and to become better acquainted." Then she calls out, "Micah! Deborah! Mereth! Come, and meet Othniel's friends!"

They hear sounds from elsewhere in the house, and a teeenage boy and two teenage girls hurry into the great room. Then Adah says, "This handsome young man is Othniel's younger brother, Micah. And these beautiful girls are Othniel's sisters, Deborah and Mereth. Children, I am pleased to introduce you to Eliezer, Zibrah, Miriam, and Yaaqov. They are friends of Othniel from Hammat." The new acquaintances all greet each other cheerfully.

Obed says, "Othniel's older brother, Onan, is visiting Nabataea this week, buying spices for our business."

After the newly acquainted persons visit together for a few minutes, Adah turns to Eliezer, Zibrah, Miriam, and Yaaqov, and says, "Come, I will show you the rooms that have been prepared for you to use." Then she leads them down a hallway, and she shows them which room was intended for Eliezer and Zibrah, and which room would be shared by Miriam and Yaaqov.

Micah, Deborah and Mereth ask Miriam and Yaaqov if they may join them for some fun in their guest room, and Miri and Yaaqov welcome them. Othniel's siblings are curious about their brother's relationship with Miriam and Yaaqov, and Miriam and Yaaqov want more information about what Othniel is really like. After a while, Micah, Deborah, and Mereth leave Miriam's and Yaaqov's guest room, so that their guests may catch up on some needed rest.

After washing their hands, faces, and feet, Eliezer and Zibrah return to the great room, where they join Obed and Adah for some more conversation, and some light refreshments. They talk about family, faith, business, and politics. They share their own personal stories, as well as their future hopes. It is a good time together, and they discover that they all believe in the same important ideas. Then Eliezer and Zibrah return to their room, to take an afternoon nap.

Around the middle of the afternoon, Othniel arrives at his parents' home. He is delighted to learn that Eliezer and his family are there, and that his parents are getting along so well with Eliezer and Zibrah.

Obed asks Othniel about Yeshuah, and Othniel responds, "Yeshuah is amazing! During the festival, Yeshuah explained to his disciples that Sukkot is a celebration of all that God has done for us, and he explained how many of the symbols and themes of Sukkot relate to the Maschiah: tabernacle, glory, water, light, and redemption."

Obed asks, "But what about your living expenses? Does your discipleship provide you with income to cover those costs?"

Othniel answers, "Yeshuah's disciples do not receive income from the ministry, but most of our meals and lodging are provided for us, either as charitable gifts, or the costs are covered by payments made out of our common treasury."

Obed says, "Niel, haven't you spent enough time with this Yeshuah? When are you planning to return to our house, and to handle your share of family responsibilities?"

Othniel responds, "Abba, I don't know. It is exciting for me to be learning from Yeshuah, and to participate in his ministry. I am not ready to give that up. And I'm not sure that I ever will be."

"What about Miriam? You told me that you might be interested in marrying her. That is why her parents are visiting with us for a few days. What kind of life would that be for her, following after you, as you travel from town to town with Yeshuah?"

"Abba, I don't expect that Yeshuah's ministry will continue to involve much traveling after it becomes more established. But none of us disciples really knows what to expect."

"That is exactly my point! You don't know *anything* about where your discipleship with Yeshuah is going! If you are thinking about settling down with Miriam as your wife, and building a life together with her, then you need to start living more responsibly. Your mother and I both think that it is time for you to settle down."

"Abba, Miriam told me that if we do marry each other, then my commitments would also become her commitments, wherever those might lead us."

"When a woman gives her consent to marry according to the laws of Moses and Israel, she has a right to be well cared for. I cannot imagine that would include living arrangements like those you have been experiencing."

"Abba, our ancestors were nomadic herders, and they didn't need permanent dwellings."

"That is true, but Miriam isn't a nomadic herder, and neither are you. So when will you be ready to settle down?"

"I would hope to be ready before the end of the betrothal period."

Obed replies, "I was hoping that you would be returning to the family business before then, but perhaps that timeframe would work. Where will you be living when you marry? You know that you and your wife would always be welcome to live with us, in this home. But you should talk with Miriam about her desires."

Othniel says, "If I decide to return here to help you with the family's business, then I probably will want to live in this house until Miriam and I marry. I suspect that Miriam and I might prefer living in our own house after our betrothal period. But that is one of many details that she and I need to talk about."

Then Eliezer and Zibrah return to the great room, and greet Othniel and his parents. Eliezer says, "Othniel, your father, mother, Zibrah, and I have been talking about the possibility of marriage between you and our daughter, Miriam. Do you give your consent to us having these discussions?"

Othniel, responds, "Yes, sir, I do."

"Have you discussed this matter with Miriam?

"Miriam and I did talk briefly about the idea of marrying each other, and we agreed to encourage our parents to discuss this matter further."

"If your parents, and Zibrah and I reach an agreement about marriage, where would you live after your wedding celebration, and how would you provide for our daughter?"

"Miriam and I have not talked about any possible living arrangements, but I would hope to be able to live with her in our own house here in Yeriko. I am planning to resume my work in our family business, and I expect that employment will provide a comfortable life for us."

Obed says, "Niel, your mother and I are very happy to hear about your future intentions! We will do everything that we can to help you to make preparations for your married life."

Zibrah asks, "Othniel, you and Miriam have only known each other a very short time. Why do you feel that you and Miriam would be a good match for each other?"

Othniel responds, "Zibrah, Eliezer, father, and mother, it is true that Miriam and I first met each other only about fifteen weeks ago, and that we haven't had many conversations together. But I do feel that each time that we have been together, Miriam and I have been able to connect with each other in ways that were surprising to both of us. Never before have I experienced anything like the attraction that I feel towards her. I do not know what feelings she may have, but to me it seems like we were made for each other!"

Obed responds, "Niel, you couldn't possibly know that about Miriam! It takes many years to develop that kind of closeness with another person!"

But Zibrah believes what Othniel said.

Just then, Miriam comes down the hallway and into the great room. Seeing Othniel, she rushes to hug him. Then, she says to all, "I realize that I did not hear all of the conversation that you have been having, but I did hear some of it, and I want to say a few things that I believe are pertinent to the conversation that you have been having. First, I consent to marry Othniel. Next, it is true that Othniel and I have not known each other for a very long time, but I also have been very surprised by the closeness of our relationship. As illogical as it may sound, I agree with Othniel that it feels like we were made for each other!"

Then Othniel hugs Miriam. And Eliezer hugs Othniel.

And Obed says to Miriam, "Daughter, welcome to our family!" Then everyone takes turns hugging everyone else in the room.

Both sets of parents, Othniel, and Miriam spent the rest of the day clarifying their hopes, desires, and commitments, and at dinner that evening, Obed and Eliezer announced to their combined families that a ketubah (marriage agreement) is being prepared.

Later that evening, Eliezer asks Othniel to join him for a walk in the city, and he does. As they are walking, Eliezer asks Othniel, "Please tell me about your rabbi, Yeshuah."

Othniel responds, "For me, being one of Yeshuah's followers is both exciting and challenging! He is an amazing teacher, and the wondrous things that he does for people in need are always astonishing! At about the same time that you were trying to figure out where Yaaqov had been taken, Yeshuah separated all of us disciples into pairs, and he sent us out to towns throughout Galilee and Samaria to preach and to heal in the same manner that we have seen him do many times. At that time, none of us thought that we were capable of doing anything like what Yeshuah does, but he gave us authority and we were obedient. My companion was a disciple named Mattaniah, and we were sent to minister in Sepph, Biri, and Jamnith. Not everyone in those towns wanted to hear what we had to say about the Kingdom of God, but many did, and we saw some miraculous healings! And when we returned to Yeshuah at Kfar Nahum, most of the other pairs of disciples reported similar results."

Eliezer comments, "What a remarkable experience that must have been!"

"Yes, it certainly was."

"Do you know anything about Yeshuah's future plans?"

Othniel responds, "We do not have any information about Yeshuah's future plans. Some of us believed that Yeshuah would become an important leader in Israel. And I had been thinking that Yeshuah's ministry would take a different form after it became more established, perhaps as a distinct Jewish sect. However, recently Yeshuah has been saying repeatedly that he expects to be killed by his enemies. We hope that he is mistaken about that!"

Eliezer says, "Yes, I hope so, too. I finally got to see Yeshuah speak on the last day of Sukkot, when he came to the Temple. In the water ceremony, the High Priest poured out water from the golden pitcher, and everyone in the great crowd of people waved their lulav, and sang, 'Save us, we beseech you, O Lord! O Lord, we beseech you, give us success!' And then Yeshuah shouted, 'Let anyone who is thirsty come to me, and let the one who believes in me drink. As the scripture has said, "Out of the believer's heart shall flow rivers of living water." ' I understand that Yeshuah was talking about providing refreshment for people who are spiritually thirsty, but what did he mean when he said 'Out of the believer's heart shall flow rivers of living water'?"

Othniel replies, "Yeshuah later explained to us that certain end-times prophecies will be fulfilled when the living water of the Holy

Spirit is manifested among his followers, as a result of their trusting in him. Some of us were confused about that too, but he told us that the fulfillment hasn't happened yet."

Eliezer says, "Sometimes Yeshuah's teaching is easy to understand, but at other times his sayings are quite mysterious."

"Yes. He has said that we will understand many of his sayings at a later time."

"Where did he learn these things? I have visited Natzerat. I don't see how he could have acquired his wisdom there."

"Yeshuah speaks on his own authority, from the depths of his special relationship with God."

Eliezer says, "You might be right, but Yeshuah's outburst on that final day of Sukkot certainly produced a mixed response from the crowd."

Othniel says, "That is what usually happens when Yeshuah speaks to large numbers of people."

At that same time, Marius is making an evening tour of sentry posts at Capernaum, and the soldier who is patroling the southeastern sector of that city reports that he discovered a dead body that had washed up on the shore of the Sea of Tiberius. The dead man's hands and feet had been bound with ropes, and his throat had been cut. Marius organizes a group of soldiers, and they wrap the dead body in a large piece of cloth, and move it to a storeroom located near their barracks. Then Marius reports the incident to Centurion Gaius, who tells him that they will begin an investigation tomorrow.

Two days later, on the twenty-fifth day of Tishri, Othniel and Miriam were betrothed to each other at Obed's and Adah's villa in Yeriko. Miriam was wearing a new dress, along with the gemstone necklace that Zibrah had given to her. She looked very beautiful, and Othniel was exceptionally joyful. Each of them sipped wine from a shared cup. Othniel said to Miriam, "You are hereby betrothed unto me according to the laws of Moses and Israel." And Miriam gave him her consent. And it was so.

CHAPTER 32

The morning after the betrothal party, Eliezer, his family, and Othniel leave Obed's and Adah's house in Yeriko, and they begin walking northward toward Galilee. Four days later, they arrive in Hammat. Othniel stays overnight in the covered portion of Eliezer's courtyard, before taking his leave from Miriam and her family on the following day, and traveling on to Kfar Nahum.

When he arrives in Kfar Nahum, Othniel finds Marius by the city gate, and he says to him, "Marius, I am so excited to tell you that Miriam and I are now betrothed!"

Marius enthusiastically grabs Othniel's arms, and replies, "I wish that I was betrothed to her instead. But I am happy for both of you. You are so fortunate to be betrothed to Miriam! She is the most excellent woman I know!"

"Yes, I realize how blessed I am that she gave her consent to marry me. And did you hear that Yaaqov was kidnapped and sold into slavery, and that Eliezer and Zibrah were able to redeem him in Acco around the end of Elul?"

"No, I hadn't heard that about Yaaqov. But I did hear something that might be connected to Yaaqov's disappearance. About a week ago, one of my sentries discovered the body of a dead man by the lakeshore. It was estimated that the man had been murdered around the twenty-first or twenty-second day of Tishri, and the dead man was identified as a Phoenician fish processing worker named Baraket from Acco. When the investigator talked to Baraket's neighbor in Magdala, she told him that she had seen Baraket taking a sad young boy in his cart towards Phoenicia around the nineteenth day of Elul. Maybe the sad young boy was Yaaqov, and Baraket was his kidnapper!"

"Hmmm. You may be right about that! That date when the neighbor saw the boy in the cart with the man from Phoenicia does seem to fit the period when Yaaqov was kidnapped."

Then Marius says, "What about when Baraket was murdered? Do you think that Eliezer could have killed him, as punishment for kidnapping his son, Yaaqov?"

Othniel hesitates for only a moment, and then he says, "No, I don't believe that Eliezer is capable of murder. Furthermore, Eliezer wasn't even in Galilee when that man was killed, because he was in Yerushalayim for Sukkot and Shemini Atzeret, and after that, he spent several days at my parents' home in Yeriko. Someone else must have wanted to be rid of Baraket."

Marius says, "I will tell the investigator about Yaaqov's kidnapping, and also about where you and Eliezer's family were when the man was murdered. It is good to see you again. I am glad that you have returned to Capernaum."

"Shalom, Marius. I am on my way to the room that I share with three other disciples of Yeshuah."

After Marius completed his morning tour of Capernaum's sentry stations, Marius reported to Optio Titus, who also was serving as lead investigator regarding Baraket's murder, and he gave a report of the information that Othniel had told him.

A week later, Othniel comes to Hammat for another visit with his betrothed. Miriam and Othniel enjoy talking with each other about their interests and hopes. They are discovering that some of their interests are similar, while others are different or complementary. In these exploratory conversations, they have uncovered a few tensions, but no serious conflicts. The more they find out about each other, they discover there is so much more to be learned. Sometimes, they enjoy being together without even talking, not because they can't think of anything to say, but because words aren't always necessary. During their visits, Eliezer usually stays near enough to observe them, but not close enough to hear everything that they say to each other. On the other hand, Zibrah usually tries to give Miriam and Othniel more privacy with each other. Zibrah has talked with Miriam about intimate matters, but Miriam has not initiated physical actions with Othniel except holding hands with him; and Othniel is content to wait for further intimacies, because of his deep respect for her virtue, and his sincere desire not to spoil their relationship.

It is the second week of the midautumn month of Marchesvan, and while Eliezer is harvesting his winter figs and late olives, he observes that the etrog trees in his garden are blossoming, and this reminds him that it also is time for him to begin plowing and planting. He knows that these tasks need to be completed before the onset of winter. Fortunately, Marius and Othniel also notice the changes, and on the fifth day of that week, they walk together to Hammat, so that they can help Eliezer with his seasonal agricultural work.

Eliezer is busy plowing the upper terrace of his garden with Marit, so he doesn't notice Marius and Othniel as they walk up the path to his house. However, Yaaqov sees them, and he shouts, "Shalom, Marius and Othniel!" Then he runs to greet them while they are still approaching.

Miriam and Zibrah hear Yaaqov's shout, and they happily come out of the house to meet the young men as they walk toward the door to the courtyard. Affectionate hugs are exchanged, and then the group goes inside to share some refreshments that Zibrah had prepared..

Marius says to Miriam, "Congratulations for your betrothal to our friend, Othniel."

Miriam responded, "Thank you, Marius. I am very happy to be betrothed to such a good man. Thank you for introducing us to each other."

Then Marius asks Yaaqov about his kidnapping ordeal, and everyone listens while Yaaqov tells the story of his abduction by Baraket and his enslavement.

After Yaaqov told his story, Marius says to him, "Last month, one of my soldiers found Baraket's body by the shore of Lake Kinneret. Someone killed him, so you don't need to worry that he might try to kidnap you again."

Yaaqov says, "Baraket told me that someone else paid him to kidnap me and to take me far away from my family and home. So I am worried that person might decide to cause more problems for us."

Marius replies, "Did Baraket mention the name of the person who paid him to kidnap you?"

"No, he didn't. Maybe that person killed Baraket, so that Baraket would not be able to tell the authorities about what happened and why."

"You may be right about that. Right now, my deputy commander is trying to figure out who killed Baraket."

"Do you think that he will be successful?"

"I certainly hope so. Optio Titus is a very smart man, and he says that searching for truth always is about paying careful attention to the details, and asking the right questions to people who are able to provide useful information."

Then Othniel says, "Well, let us hope that Titus is thinking about those questions now. But, as for us, why don't we help Eliezer with his harvesting, plowing, and planting? We can spend some more time visiting together afterwards."

Marius says, "Yes! I am very eager to get my hands back into some dirt." And Marius, Othniel, and Yaaqov go outside to help Eliezer in the garden.

While they are working in the garden, Marius says to Eliezer, "My deputy commander, Titus, is investigating Baraket's murder. I told him that Baraket kidnapped Yaaqov, and he said that he would like to talk with you and Yaaqov about what happened. Maybe he will be able to figure out who paid Baraket to kidnap Yaaqov. Would you and Yaaqov come to Capernaum, to be interviewed by Titus?"

Eliezer replies, "Ordinarily, I would avoid talking to a Roman soldier, but I will pray about it."

About an hour later, Eliezer says to Marius, "While we have been working, I have been praying about whether or not Yaaqov and I should meet with your investigator. I have decided that we will meet with him, because of the possibility that he might be able to identify the person who was behind Yaaqov's disappearance."

"Excellent! When can I tell Optio Titus to expect that you and Yaaqov will come to the military garrison in Capernaum for a meeting with him?"

"Please tell him that we expect to be there at midmorning tomorrow."

"Thank you. I will tell him that when I give him my updated report this evening."

After several hours of working together in the garden, the men returned to Eliezer's home. Eliezer removed the plowing harness from Marit, and put some hay in the trough in her stall. Marius played a game of catch with Yaaqov. Othniel told Miriam that he was planning to go to Yerushalayim with Yeshuah and many of the other disciples next month, for the winter Festival of Chanukah (also known as Dedication). And Zibrah prepared a late afternoon supper for the family and their friends to share. At dinner, Eliezer mentioned that he and Yaaqov would be visiting Kfar Nahum tomorrow, to be interviewed regarding the kidnapping. Then Zibrah and Miriam declared that they also would go with Eliezer and Yaaqov for the interview, because they were the ones who uncovered the clues that pointed to Baraket.

After dinner, Marius and Othniel leave Hammat to return to Kfar Nahum.

Upon his arrival at the Capernaum military garrison, Marius immediately reports to Optio Titus, about Eliezer's and Yaaqov's plans to be interviewed by him.

CHAPTER 33

The following day, Eliezer and his family walk together from Hammat on their way to Kfar Nahum. As they pass through Tiberias, Zibrah encounters her friends Salome and Joanna by the market agora.

Salome says, "Zibrah, it is so good to see you again! We heard that you and your husband were able to retrieve your son from Acco. What good news!" And then, turning toward Yaaqov, Salome says, "Yaaqov, I am so happy that you were rescued by your parents. You must realize how fortunate you are, that they were able to find you, and bring you home!"

Yaaqov nods to Salome, and then Joanna adds, "We were praying for your safe return from the time when we found out that you had been taken, until we heard that you were brought home safely! Thanks to the Lord for bringing this situation to a good conclusion!"

Zibrah says to her friends, "Thank you Joanna and Salome, for your prayers and your friendship! It is such a blessing for us to have the support of friends like you! And I am happy to tell you that our daughter, Miriam, now is betrothed to a man named Othniel, from Yeriko."

Joanna responds, "Congratulations, Miriam! I know Othniel! He and I are both disciples of Yeshuah. Othniel is a very good man."

Miriam says, "Thank you, Joanna. I am very happy to be betrothed to Othniel."

Zibrah says, "Joanna and Salome, I would like to spend more time visiting with you now, but my family and I have an appointment in Kfar Nahum. Let's get together again soon."

And then Zibrah and her family continue on their way.

At the next intersection of streets, they came to the Tiberias administrative building, and they see Assurbani standing in front of the building, talking with Mibzar, his policeman-colleague.

Seeing Eliezer and his family, Assurbani smiles and says to them, "Eliezer, Zibrah, Miriam, and Yaaqov, it is good to see all of you together again! We heard that something bad happened to you recently. We are pleased that everything turned out well, but it must have been extremely upsetting for you all while it was happening."

Eliezer replies, "Yes, it was very disturbing. Thank you for caring. We do realize that Yaaqov's disappearance could have turned out quite differently than it did."

Assurbani says, "Yes, sometimes the world is a very wicked place, especially for powerless people."

"What are you saying, Assurbani? If you think that you are exempt from trouble yourself, then you are mistaken!"

"Well, good luck to you then, Eliezer. Until we meet again, that is."

"Good bye, Assurbani." And then Eliezer and his family resume their walking towards Kfar Nahum. Assurbani and Mibzar are smiling confidently at each other.

As Eliezer and his family enter Magdala, they see Baraket's house. They notice that the door is open, and the sailboat, mule, and cart are gone. They keep walking.

When they arrive at Kfar Nahum, they walk through the city until they reach the entrance to the military garrison that is located in the city's northeast quadrant. Marius is there waiting for them; he is standing next to one of his sentries. Marius welcomes them to the fort, and he escorts them to the headquarters building. In front of the headquarters door is a pole with a carved golden eagle at the top, and a square cloth banner called a vexillum suspended from a crossbar beneath the eagle. The banner contains Roman words and military symbols. Marius knocks at the door, and a voice from inside commands him to enter, along with the guests that he is accompanying.

Inside, a very impressive, tall, strong-looking man with a short haircut, and wearing a toga, introduces himself as Titus Aelius Magnus, a Roman citizen, and the deputy commander of this garrison. He extends his right arm to Eliezer, and when Eliezer extends his own right arm in return, each man grasps the other's arm as a friendly sign of greeting. Then, Eliezer introduces himself and each member of his family to Titus. Titus orders Marius to bring enough chairs so that everyone may sit comfortably, and when this is done, Titus dismisses

Marius from the proceeding. Then Titus looks at Yaaqov and says to him, "I was told that you were kidnapped by a man from Phoenicia named Baraket. Please tell me what happened."

Yaaqov tells the story of his abduction, his transfer to Acco, and his enslavement to Bodo. Titus listens to his story very carefully, and interrupts him a few times, asking for additional clarifying details.

When Yaaqov completes his explanation, Titus asks him, "Did Baraket say why he was kidnapping you?"

"Baraket told me that someone else had paid him money to kidnap me and to take me far away from my family and my home."

"Did he say that the person who paid him wanted him to kidnap you, specifically, or to find and kidnap any boy that he could find?"

"He said that he was told to kidnap me. He knew my name, my description, and where I live in Hammat."

"Did he mention who it was that paid him to do those things?"

"No, Sir. He did not."

"Why do you think that someone paid him to do those things?"

"I don't think that the person who was behind my kidnapping wanted to hurt me, I think that he wanted to hurt my family."

"Has anyone ever told you that they wanted to hurt you, or your family?"

"No, no one ever told me that."

"Thank you, Yaaqov. You are a very brave young man."

Turning his face toward Eliezer, Titus asks, "Did you ever meet, encounter, or talk with Baraket yourself?"

"No, I have no knowledge of ever having encountered Baraket personally."

"Did you, or anyone that you know, kill Baraket?"

"Marius told me that a man had been murdered, and that the dead man was identified as Baraket. But I did not kill him, and I do not have any information about who may have killed him."

Titus says, "We estimate that Baraket was killed around the twenty-first or twenty-second day of Tishri. Where were you on those dates?"

Eliezer replies, "On those specific dates, I was in Yerushalayim, participating in religious observances for Sukkot and Solemn Assembly. My famiy and I left our home in Hammat on the eleventh day of Tishri, and we did not return to it until the thirtieth of that month. We were in Yerushalayim from the fifteenth until the morning of the twenty-third, and afterwards we spent three days in Yeriko, visiting with the family of our daughter's betrothed husband."

"Marius told me that you were away from Galilee when Baraket was killed, and I do not have any doubts about that information. But my responsibility as investigator requires that I must ask you myself. What is your occupation?"

"I am a farmer in Hammat, and I sell my produce on a seasonal basis at public markets in Tiberias, Kfar Nahum, Tzipori, Natzerat, Beit Shean, and occasionally Magdala."

"So your work does bring you to Magdala sometimes. You said that you never encountered Baraket. Are you certain about that?"

"I do not recall ever having met a man having Baraket's name or description."

"Are you aware of any conflicts or tensions that may exist between you and your neighbors, or with competing farmers or agricultural merchants?"

"No, I am not."

"Are you aware of any conflicts or tensions that you may have with other persons because of your religious or political beliefs?"

"I am a Pharisee, and there are many people whose religious beliefs and practices are different from my own, but I am not aware of any hatred or animosity towards me because of my religious beliefs and practices."

"What about your political beliefs?"

"I am not involved with any political organization, and I am not a promoter of any political philosophy or belief system."

"Have you exchanged angry words with any acquaintance of yours?"

"Yes, I have been confronted aggressively by a man from a neighboring community who expressed an interest in my daughter that I regarded as unwelcome and inappropriate. This person also attacked my daughter's reputation. I have refrained from responding aggressively toward him, but I have assertively tried to maintain a certain distance between him and my family."

"Who is this person?"

"His name is Assurbani. He is one of the profoi of Tiberias, and he is a member of the Herodians."

"Are you aware of any relationship or connection between Baraket and Assurbani?"

"No, I am not."

"Are you aware of Assurbani having used any other individual or agent in his quarrel with you?"

"Yes, my family has become aware of the presence and involvement of a man named Mibzar, who is a colleague of Assurbani's. He is a protective bodyguard of Herod Antipas who also functions like a policeman in Tiberias."

"Thank you, Eliezer. I understand that you would have preferred not having this talk with me today, but the fact that you did may help us to promote justice in this province."

Then, turning his attention to Zibrah and Miriam, Titus asks, "Ladies, are you aware of any conflicts or tensions toward you or your family from individuals or groups in this region?"

After a moment of hesitation, Miriam replies, "The only person who has ever behaved badly toward any of us is Assurbani. A few years ago, he told my father that he was interested in marrying me, and my father rejected his proposal of marriage. Assurbani did not receive this rejection graciously. Assurbani consistently makes inappropriate sexual remarks to me, and he also has threatened me. Last year, one time he put his hands on me, and afterwards he spread nasty, untrue rumors about my character. When my father confronted Assurbani about his lies, he denied having lied about me, and then, in a nonviolent way, my father insulted him publicly. And this humiliating offense to Assurbani's pride seemed to increase his anger toward us."

"Do you think that Assurbani is capable of violence?"

"I don't know about that. I think that Assurbani is afraid of my father, but he is even more afraid of having his true character exposed, and losing whatever status and power he has acquired. And I think that he would do whatever he thought was necessary in order to cover up his misdeeds."

"What do you think about Mibzar?"

"I have noticed that policeman often is with Assurbani, and occasionally I also have observed him alone, sneaking around and spying on my family. I believe that Assurbani uses Mibzar to do things on his behalf. He looks mean."

Then Titus asks, "How about you, Zibrah? Do you have anything to add, regarding anyone who might want to harm your family?"

Zibrah responds, "I have only been married to Eliezer for about three months, and my hometown is Tiberias, so I have had more encounters with Assurbani and Mibzar than Eliezer or his children. Assurbani is ambitious and decisive, he has a scandalous reputation with young girls, and he has a strong dislike for my husband. Mibzar is a ruthless thug who does Assurbani's dirty work. Eliezer has an excellent reputation, and the only person that I know of who speaks badly about him is Assurbani."

Titus says, "It is extraordinary that you were able to find Yaaqov, and to recover him. How were you able to do that so quickly?"

Zibrah replies, "When Yaaqov disappeared, Eliezer was away from our home, on business. Miriam and I noticed that Yaaqov was missing, and we went looking for him, and we talked with many of our neighbors. We knew that Yaaqov is fond of watching the fishing boats from the lakeshore and, when we searched there, we found his favorite toy, a leather ball, right next to some marks in the mud that appeared to have been made by a boat. A neighbor named Yehoezer, who lives near to where we found the ball, said that although he hadn't noticed our son, he did see a small sailboat near that spot that was being piloted by a man wearing a conical-shaped hat. I realized that kind of hat is unusual around here, but I remembered having seen a Phoenician man working at the fish processing facility in Magdala who wore a conical-shaped hat. So, the day after Yaaqov went missing, Miriam and I went to Magdala, and we talked with the fish factory manager about that employee. The manager's name is Beor, and he told us about Baraket, where he lived in Magdala, and that he was visiting his family in Acco for a few days. We went to Baraket's house, and we saw his sailboat, and the empty pen in which he kept his mule. Eliezer arrived home that same afternoon, just before Shabbat. On the first day of the following week, Eliezer and I started walking towards Acco. On our way, we talked to several people about the disappearance of our son. Eliezer and I stopped in Magdala, and we visited with Baraket's neighbor, Anah. She told us that Baraket had departed from Magdala in the morning three days earlier in his mule-driven cart, that a sad-looking boy was in the cart with him when he left, and that he was heading west, towards Phoenicia. Two days later, we arrived in Acco, and we began searching for Baraket's family. We visited the synagogue in Acco, and we were advised not to contact Acco's local officials about the disappearance of our son, except as a last resort, because we are foreigners. Eventually, we met with Baraket's sister-in-law, and she told us that Baraket had sold Yaaqov as a slave to a man named Bodo, who runs a large cargo-handling operation in Acco. We contacted Bodo, and we explained to him that Yaaqov is our son, and that Yaaqov should not have been sold as a slave. He said that he had paid good money for Yaaqov, and that he was not going to just give him back to us. At that point, I offered him one hundred silver shekels to purchase Yaaqov from him, and he accepted my offer. I paid him the money, and we made the exchange. I insisted that he endorse the original bill of sale that he had received from Baraket over to me, and he did so. Then we immediately left Acco, and we began our two-day journey home."

Titus says, "That is quite a story. May I see the bill-of-sale that Bodo gave you?"

Zibrah replies, "Yes, you may. I have it with me today. Here it is. . . . You can see where Baraket signed the original bill-of-sale, and also where Bodo signed Yaaqov over to me, for the price of one hundred shekels."

Titus says, "Thank you, Zibrah. Here, you may have your bill-of-sale back. Well, it is clear to me that Baraket did indeed kidnap your son Yaaqov from your town of Hammat, that he transported him to Acco in Phoenicia for the purpose of selling him as a slave, that he sold Yaaqov as a slave to a man named Bodo, and that you redeemed Yaaqov from enslavement by purchasing him back from Bodo."

Eliezer says, "Thank you, Optio Titus, for listening to our testimony, and for believing what we told you. I would like to know what will happen next."

Titus replies, "This is a very delicate situation, since Herod Antipas has jurisdiction in this portion of the Province of Judaea. Assurbani is a member of Herod's political faction, and Mibzar is one of Herod's protective bodyguards. I will continue investigating the kidnapping of Yaaqov and the murder of Baraket and, when it is completed, I will give a report of my findings and recommendations to Centurion Gaius

Cornelius Crescens. He will decide what will happen next. If there is a trial, some of you may be required to testify."

Eliezer says, "When you question Assurbani and Mibzar, they will deny any wrongdoing."

Titus smiles and replies, "When we interrogate suspects, we almost always are able to persuade them to tell us the truth."

Eliezer says, "Thank you, Titus. We are looking forward to learning about your centurion's decision. . . . One more thing, this morning when we walked through Magdala, we noticed that Baraket's sailboat, mule, and cart were missing. Did you seize those items as evidence?"

Titus responds, "No. I do not know what happened to those items of Baraket's property. Perhaps we will locate them as our investigation continues." Titus calls for his aide to summon Tesserarius Marius to escort his guests back to the entrance of the military garrison. And then Titus says, "Thank you all for visiting with me today. You are a very nice family. Good bye."

Eliezer and his family decide to visit the house of Aharon and Bilhah, to thank them for their help in arranging the betrothal of Miriam and Othniel, and to tell them about their interview with Optio Titus. Eliezer found himself thinking about the curious circumstance of his family having consulted with a pagan military officer from an occupying army in order to seek justice in their own Holy Land. He never imagined *that* would happen!

CHAPTER 34

Two months later, it is the middle of the month of Tebeth, and the winter rainy season is well underway. Eliezer is happy that he was able to complete his planting during the preceding month, before the heavy rains began. He enjoys his winter routine of weeding and careful study of Torah, the Prophets, and the Psalms. In this season, he is able to meet with his study partners at the synagogue two or three times every week, but he also spends some time every day studying at his home, either on his own or with his family.

It is late-morning of the first day in the third week of Tebeth, and Marius and Othniel are walking to Hammat for another visit. It is raining. Eliezer and his family are seated at their table discussing a portion of the great poem of Yishayahu [Isaiah] when Marius and Othniel knock on their door. Eliezer and his family haven't seen these men for more than a month, and they happily postpone their discussion regarding the meaning of the servant in the song, who is called to be a light to the nations [Isaiah 42] until later. Miriam is especially delighted to be able to spend a few hours with her betrothed husband, and she also is happy to see her friend Marius again. After welcoming them, Zibrah invites Othniel and Marius to eat their midday meal with the family.

Eliezer says, "We haven't seen you since Marius helped me to complete my grain planting, and Othniel was leaving for Yerushalayim with Yeshuah for Chanukah, the Festival of Dedication. So, what have you men been doing since the last time we were together?"

Marius is eager to speak first, so he says, "Well, I have some news for you! One day last month Centurion Gaius ordered me to organize two groups of soldiers to simultaneously arrest Assurbani and Mibzar in Tiberias, and to bring them to our Capernaum military garrison for interrogation by Optio Titus. And two weeks ago, based on information that was extracted from Mibzar, we recovered Baraket's mule and sailboat. Evidently, after killing Baraket and dumping his body, weighed down with rocks, into the lake, Mibzar also sunk Baraket's sailboat, and then he confiscated Baraket's mule for his own personal use. The ropes that were used to bind Baraket's hands and feet are identical to some rope that we found in the shed where Mibzar was keeping Baraket's mule. Mibzar is definitely not very smart. While being interrogated with torture, Assurbani confessed that he paid Baraket one hundred shekels to kidnap Yaaqov and to remove him to Phoenicia. Baraket's neighbor, Anah, identified Assurbani as having visited Baraket at Baraket's house in Magdala before the kidnapping. It looks like the next step is for Centurion Gaius and Optio Titus to meet with Herod Antipas about the evidence that they have uncovered concerning the kidnapping and murder. They will insist that Antipas make a right judgment himself regarding both criminals, or else these cases will be referred to Roman authorities for disposition, which would be an even greater disgrace for Antipas."

Eliezer slaps his own thigh with excitement and says, "I am very pleased to hear that justice is being served in our Holy Land! It is unfortunate that it has to come through foreigners, but I am pleased nevertheless."

Zibrah says, "I can hardly wait to talk with my friend Joanna about this news, to find out how Antipas will respond. Her husband, Chuza, is the steward to Herod Antipas."

Marius asks Eiliezer, "What is the penalty for their crimes under your laws?"

Eliezer responds, "According to the laws of Moses and Israel, murder and kidnapping are both punishable by death."

> *[murder: Exodus 21:12. Leviticus 24:17, & Numbers 35:31; kidnapping & kidnapping for enslavement: Exodus 21:16 & Deuteronomy 24:7]*

Miriam hugs her brother and says, "Yaaqov, how wonderful it is for us to have the prospect, at least, of having the persons who caused us so much torment to be judged!"

Yaaqov responds, "To me, vindication does feel good, but I also am a little bit sad for Assurbani, and even for Baraket and his family. These things never should have happened in the first place."

Then Othniel says, "Yaaqov, you are absolutely right, but all of us make choices in our lives, and those choices have consequences. We should always pray for God's help in the choices that we make, and then trust that they will work out for the best."

Yaaqov responds, "But not everything that happens to us is because of choices that we make ourselves."

"Of course, but whatever does happen, each of us is able to decide how we will respond. No matter what, know that God is with you, and that He will help you to deal with it. But you must trust God, and obey Him when He tells you what to do."

"Yes, I do believe that. But sometimes it is difficult to know what God wants us to do."

"It becomes easier when you spend more time praying, earnestly studying the Scriptures, and listening for God to speak."

Then Eliezer asks, "Othniel, how was your visit to Yerushalayim for Chanukah?"

Othniel says, "Well, we went to Yerushalayim intending to be there for the entire eight-day festival, observing the progressive lighting of lamps during each of the days, and the retelling of the story of the Maccabees. However, Yeshuah was walking in the portico of Solomon at the Temple, and some religious opponents challenged him there. They tried to interrogate Yeshuah about his identity as the Maschiah and as God's Son, and Yeshuah responded by saying that he and the Father are united in the work that they are doing. When they heard Yeshuah say that, they picked up stones in order to stone him, because they thought that Yeshuah was making himself to be the same as God. Then Yeshuah explained that as God's Son, he was only doing the works that the Father gave him to do. As the religious authorities were preparing to arrest Yeshuah, we were able to get away from them, and it was a good thing that we escaped. So, instead of remaining in Yerushalayim, we left there and went across the Yarden River to Bethabara, the place where Yohanan the Baptizer had baptized people during his ministry. I stayed there with Yeshuah for several days, ministering to the people who came to see him. But then

I left Bethabara and I visited my parents at Yeriko, before returning to Galilee to be with all of you."

Eliezer says, "Do you know what prompted those religious oppenents of Yeshuah to confront him?"

Othniel replies, "Someone said that he thought they were agitated because Yeshuah had previously healed a man who had been born blind."

"Why would that have agitated them?"

"Because he healed that man during Shabbat, and when they asked the man about his healer, he told them that his healer's name is Yeshuah, and that Yeshuah must have come from God."

"But can't you see why those religious people were upset?"

"All I can tell you is that in Yeshuah, I have experienced God's presence. And I haven't experienced that to the same extent in anything or anyone else. Somehow, God is uniquely at work in and through Yeshuah. Do you believe in the Son of Man?"

"Yes, I believe that the coming of the Son of Man will mark the beginning of the Final Judgment, as foretold in the Book of Daniyel [Daniel 7]"

"So do I. And I believe that, somehow, the Future Judgment is already present and at work in Yeshuah, even though it has not yet come in all of its fullness."

"What are you saying? I do not understand."

"I am not yet able to understand it fully myself, but I believe that Yeshuah is himself the climax of God's plan for the redemption of all creation! And even though I lack understanding about this, nevertheless, I do believe that it is true!"

"That sounds like heresy to me. It doesn't even make sense!"

"Think about it. It didn't make any sense when God told Noah to build an ark. It didn't make sense when God told Abraham to leave his home to go a place that God would show him. It didn't make sense when Moses led the Israelites out of Egypt and into the wilderness. A whole generation of Jews had to die off because they didn't believe that they could be successful in their campaign against the Canaanites. And it didn't make any sense that exiled Jews in Babylon would ever be able to return to our Holy Land to renew the covenant promises. But here we are, the descendants of all of those people who experienced those unanticipated events! Let us wait and see what God is doing before rejecting it beforehand."

"Alright. Once again, you are telling me to keep an open mind about Yeshuah. I will try to do so, but how will we recognize the climax of God's plan, when it occurs?"

"At this time, we can't even know what to look for. But it certainly will be an unprecedented event. Let us wait and see, trusting God to work out the details. Yeshuah says that the Kingdom of God is in our midst!"

Eliezer is bewildered by the direction of this conversation with Othniel, and Zibrah had stopped listening when Othniel mentioned the beginning of the Final Judgment. But Miriam accepted the possibility of experiencing the presence of God in Yeshuah, and of Yeshuah as somehow being the climax of God's plan. Although she doesn't understand it yet either, she says, "I believe it." And Othniel is overjoyed by her response, because once again, it feels like they were made for each other.

Then Zibrah announces that it must be time for lunch.

A week after Marius' and Othniel's visit, Zibrah puts on a rain-repelling cloak, and she walks through the rain to Tiberias, for a visit with her friend Joanna. When she arrives at Joanna's and Chuza's house, she knocks on the door, and waits for Joanna to invite her in.

The door opens and Joanna says, "Zibrah, how good it is for me to see you again! And, what a nice surprise, since today is such a miserable, rainy day! Please, come in."

Zibrah gives proper respect to the mezuzah box on the doorpost, then she steps inside, and hugs her friend, saying, "Shalom, Joanna! Thank you for opening your home to me."

Joanna says, "I think that this is the first time that I have seen you since two months ago, when you were on your way to Kfar Nahum for an appointment. I remember thinking that it was so good to know that you and Eliezer were able to rescue your son after he was kidnapped, and also to hear that Miriam is betrothed."

"Thank you. Yes, my family is very happy about those outcomes."

"And my husband told me that he has learned some more information about the circumstances of your son's kidnapping."

"What did he tell you?"

"Well, he said that Herod Antipas told him that Assurbani paid someone to kidnap your son, and then, in order to cover-up what he had done, he had Herod's own bodyguard kill the kidnapper."

"Do you know how Herod found out those things?"

"My husband told me that two Roman officers had a meeting with Herod last week, and they told him their findings from an investigation of the kidnapping and murder. Apparently, their investigation led them to arrest Assurbani and Mibzar, and when those suspects were interrogated, they confessed to what they had done."

Zibrah asks, "Did Chuza tell you what he thinks will happen next?"

"Well, Herod Antipas is very upset. He is angry that people he trusted committed crimes, and that this will reflect badly upon his administration. He is worried that the Roman emperor may remove him from his position as Tetrarch, like they did with his brother, Archelaus. The Roman soldiers told him that they will return Assurbani and Mibzar to his custody, provided that he will make an appropriate judicial determination concerning the criminals. Otherwise, the Romans will take action themselves, and that this would not be good for Herod Antipas."

"So, will there be a trial?"

"Chuza said that he believes there will be some kind of legal proceeding, over which Herod Antipas will preside, and in which the confessions of conspiring to kidnap and enslave, and of murder will be presented. Since those are capital crimes under our laws, it is expected that Herod will sentence Assurbani and Mibzar to death, and that those sentences will be carried out immediately."

Zibrah says, "Thank you Joanna, for letting me know. My family will be pleased to learn that justice may finally be done."

Joanna asks, "Zibrah, did you know that Assurbani and Mibzar did those things?"

"Joanna, about two months ago we became aware of some clues that pointed in their direction, but we didn't find out that they had confessed their crimes until last week."

"It must be a great relief to finally have this matter settled."

"We knew that someone paid the kidnapper to take our son from us, but we didn't know who would have done such a thing. We had hoped that the kidnapper would be captured and interrogated concerning the identity of the person who had paid him. And then we heard that the kidnapper had been murdered. Because of the possibility that those two crimes were connected, we were fearful that our family would still be vulnerable to additional violence from an unknown person. So it is a great relief for us to know what actually happened, but now we still must wait to see if those two criminals will be fairly judged."

"Don't you believe that Herod Antipas will handle these cases correctly?"

"I certainly hope that he will, but there remains the possibility that he might not condemn two persons who have been closely associated with him and his administration."

Joanna says, "I don't think that you need to worry. My husband told me that Antipas is experiencing a lot of pressure from the Romans to declare Assurbani and Mibzar as being guilty. If he doesn't, he might lose his status as Tetrarch and, if that happens, my husband might also lose his position."

Zibrah responds, "Both of us seem to be hoping for the same outcome."

CHAPTER 35

During the last two days of Tebeth, an announcement was proclaimed throughout Galilee that a judicial hearing would be held in the theater in Tiberias at midafternoon on the first day of the first complete week in Shebat, and that everyone was invited to attend. As one might expect, there were lots of rumors concerning the subject of the proceeding, and some, though not all, of the people actually had heard the correct information that a Herodian and one of Herod's own bodyguards had been accused of serious crimes for which the death penalty could be ordered by Herod Antipas himself. As it sometimes happens, on the fateful day, the rain stopped. There was considerable interest in what might happen, so the theater was full of people before the appointed time. Eliezer and his family had been sitting in their places since midday. An elaborate gilded chair was placed at the center of the theater's platform, and the left and right front ends of the platform each contain a large pile of stones.

At the ninth hour of the day, Herod Antipas, Tetrarch of Galilee and Peraea, walks onto the platform of the theater with several of his minor officials, and everyone stands until he is seated on the throne. Then the people in the audience sit down again. Antipas waves his hand and, in response to that gesture, several members of his protective security force lead Assurbani and Mibzar in chains onto the platform. Assurbani and Mibzar both appear very different to people who knew them before this day. Now they look gaunt, dirty, and visibly frightened. Some of the members of the audience comment softly to persons nearby, and the sound of their combined muffled voices resonate in the theater.

Then, looking at the notes held in his hand, Herod Antipas says in a loud voice, "The taller of the two chained men that you see before you is named Assurbani. I am ashamed to admit that he used to be a member of the party of the Herodians, and he also was a profoi of this city. The other man in chains is named Mibzar. He used to be one of my protective guards. Officers from the Roman military garrison at Capernaum conducted a careful investigation of the facts surrounding two crimes that were committed in our jurisdiction, and these are their findings: On the twelfth day of Ab, Assurbani contacted a Phoenician man named Baraket in Taricheae and paid him one hundred shekels to kdnap a twelve year old freeborn boy named Yaaqov from Hammat and to sell him as a slave in Ptolemais. On the eighteenth day of Elul, Baraket captured Yaaqov in Hammat, bound him with ropes and forcibly brought him to Taricheae. On the morning of the nineteenth of Elul, Baraket took Yaaqov to Prolemais. On the twenty-third of Elul, Baraket sold Yaaqov as a slave for seventy-five shekels to a man named Bodo, who operates a cargo-handling business in Ptolemais. Yaaqov's parents, Eliezer and Zibrah, were able to find Yaaqov in Ptolemais, and on the twenty-fifth of Elul, they paid Bodo one hundred shekels to redeem their son from his illegal enslavement. The family returned to Hammat on the following day. Shortly after Baraket returned to Taricheae, Mibzar murdered Baraket by cutting his throat during the night of the twenty-second day of Tishri, and dumped his body into the Sea of Tiberias. On the tenth day of Chislev, Assurbani and Mibzar were arrested by soldiers from the Roman military garrison at Capernaum, and their interrogation began. On the sixteenth day of Chislev, Assurbani confessed that he had paid Baraket to kidnap Yaaqov, and Mibzar confessed that he had murdered Baraket, in order to conceal Assurbani's role in the kidnapping and enslavement. These crimes were done with intent and with full knowledge of the consequences, and they have brought disgrace to me, our country, and our people. Is there anyone here who will attest to the truth of the allegations that I have spoken about these two men? If so, please stand and say, 'I do.'"

Eliezer, his family, Centurion Gaius, Optio Titus, and Marius all stand and said, "I do."

Then Herod Antipas says, "The crimes of kidnapping to enslavement, and of murder are both capital offenses under the laws of Israel and also of Rome. Is there any reason why these men should not be condemned to death for their crimes?"

Rabbi Yitzhak and two other rabbis in the audience stand. Herod Antipas points toward Yitzhak and says, "What reason can you give?"

Yitzhak replies, "First of all, if it is true that these men did those things, then their actions are terrible and cannot be condoned. However, these are human beings, and taking away their lives would be an offense to our God, because they were created in His likeness. Therefore, I ask for mercy, so that they may turn their lives away from wickedness and learn to do good. And secondly, I have been informed that the accused mens' own confessions are the only non-circumstantial evidence against them. Following oral traditions that have been passed down to us for many generations, our own religious court proceedings do not permit accused persons to testify against themselves. So I object to condemning these men on the basis of their confessions."

Herod Antipas points to the other two rabbis and asks, "Are your reasons the same as what Rabbi Yitzhak said?"

The other two men nod their heads and say, "Yes, they are."

Herod Antipas says, "With respect, I thank you for giving your reasons. But I am persuaded that they are, in fact, guilty of the charges made against them and, under Roman law, they should be condemned."

Rabbi Yitzhak stands and says, "But we are not Romans. We are Jewish citizens of Judaea, and I believe that our traditions do not justify judicial executions in these particular cases. Therefore, we ask for leniency." And a large number of persons in the audience vocalize their agreement with what Yitzhak said.

Herod Antipas spends several moments considering his options. Then he says, "Thank you, Rabbi Yitzhak, for your wise counsel. In deference to our religious traditions, I will not impose death sentences upon Assurbani and Mibzar. But I do hereby sentence them to enslavement for the duration of their lives on Roman galley ships. They are to be taken immediately to the port of Caesarea Maritima by soldiers from my protective security force, and arrangements will be made for their assignment as galley slaves for the duration of their lives. Until those assignments are made, they will be held as criminals in the prison at Caesarea Maritima. Let it be done as I have said!" Then he waves his hand, and the same soldiers who escorted Assurbani and Mibzhar into the theater lead them away from it.

Assurbani and Mibzar are relieved to learn that they will not die today, but they also are worried about the grim fates that await them as slaves on a galley ship.

A few people in the audience are disappointed that they will not get to witness the judicial executions that they were expecting. But practically everyone is pleased about having their own traditions upheld over the application of Roman laws.

Optio Titus finds Eliezer, Zibrah, Miriam, and Yaaqov together in the crowd, and he asks them, "Are you satisfied with the sentences that Herod Antipas gave today?"

Speaking on behalf of the family, Eliezer responds, "Yes, Titus. We believe that those sentences are just. Thank you for your role in producing the judgments. I don't think that any of my family members were eager to throw stones at either of those men. Shalom!"

Titus says, "I am pleased that those men will never again be able to cause trouble for your family. And I also offer you my best wishes for your peace, happiness, and prosperity! Good day."

As Eliezer and his family walk back to their home, Eliezer says a familiar prayer, "Blessed are you, O Lord, for uprooting and humbling the arrogant enemies of your Divine Will, and for causing salvation to flourish. Amen."

Later that month, Eliezer noticed that the almond trees were again starting to show their familiar white blossoms. He remembered telling Yaaqov last year that the almond blossoms are a reminder of the Lord's eagerness to fulfill His promises to His people, and he offered a prayer that it would happen soon. He had no idea how truly that hope would be fulfilled.

CHAPTER 36

Five weeks later, it is the thirteenth day of the late-winter month of Adar, and Eliezer and Yaaqov are harvesting citrus fruit from the etrog trees in their garden. The following day, which starts at sundown, is the Festival of Purim, and Othniel arrives at their home in the early-afternoon, so that he will be able to enjoy the whole day of Purim with his new family. In addition to being Purim, the fourteenth of Adar also is a Shabbat, so this seems to be a particularly holy occasion, even though Purim is only regarded as a minor festival by the religious leaders in Yerushalayim. Zibrah and Miriam have been making preparations for this special day of celebration in which both creation and salvation are themes, with an abundance of special foods and drinks to enjoy. During the afternoon, Eliezer takes out his Megillah Esther (Esther scroll), and prepares himself for chanting from it at the evening service at the synagogue, because Rabbi Yitzhak had requested that Eliezer serve as the cantor.

Zibrah sets the table with the two oil lamps, a cup of wine, two bread loaves that she had baked with extra braiding representing Haman's rope, a bowl of water, a towel, and the family's best stone plates and wooden eating implements. She covers the loaves of bread with a linen covering. Then, just as the sun is setting, Eliezer, Miriam, Yaaqov, and Othniel join her at the table. They all cover their heads, and then Zibrah lights the two oil lamps. She waves her hands in welcome over the lit lamps. Then she covers her eyes, and recites the Shabbat blessing, after which she removes her hands from her eyes and looks at the flames of the oil lamps. This familiar ritual always feels special to the participants. This is Shabbat, a precious time of rest and rejoicing with people that we love, and a glimpse of the world to come!

After partaking of the delicious dinner of vegetable soup, roasted fish, several tasty side dishes, and bread and wine, the family sang together:

"You who live in the shelter of the Most High,
　who abide in the shadow of the Almighty,
will say to the LORD,
　'My refuge and my fortress; my God, in whom I trust.'
For he will deliver you from the snare of the fowler
　and from the deadly pestilence;
he will cover you with his pinions,
　and under his wings you will find refuge;
his faithfulness is a shield and buckler.
You will not fear the terror of the night,
　or the arrow that flies by day,
or the pestilence that stalks in darkness,
　or the destruction that wastes at noonday.
A thousand may fall at your side,
　ten thousand at your right hand,
but it will not come near you.
You will only look with your eyes
　and see the punishment of the wicked.
Because you have made the LORD your refuge,
　the Most High your dwelling place,
no evil shall befall you, no scourge come near your tent.
For he will command his angels concerning you
　to guard you in all your ways.
On their hands they will bear you up,
　so that you will not dash your foot against a stone.
You will tread on the lion and the adder,
　the young lion and the serpent
　you will trample under foot.
Those who love me, I will deliver;
　I will protect those who know my name.
When they call to me, I will answer them;
　I will be with them in trouble,
I will rescue them and honor them.

> With long life I will satisfy them,
> and show them my salvation."
>
> [Psalm 91:1-16 NRSV]

Othniel and Miriam go outside for a brief walk in the evening air. They have been hoping to share some precious time and a little conversation together away from the others. They return to the house about one-third of an hour later.

When Eliezer estimates that it is shortly after the second hour of the night, Eliezer, his family, and Othniel walk down the path to the synagogue, where the congregation was beginning to assemble for its first observance of this Purim.

Inside the synagogue, the room is lit by lamps that are attached to many of the pillars that support the roof. The back wall of the room is where shelves and cabinets are located, where the sacred scrolls and other religious writings are kept when they are not in use. The prominent and ornately decorated ark that is used for Torah scrolls is called the Aron Kodesh. The Prophetic and Ketuvim scrolls are kept in special cabinets next to the Aron Kodesh. Commentaries and other religious scrolls are stored on the shelves. A tall table that is used as a reading desk is located in front of the Aron Kodesh. There is a shorter table in the center of the room that is used for study and discussion purposes at other times during the week. The men sit in rows along both sides of the room, facing the reading desk, and fairly close to it.. And the women and children sit in rows by the front wall, on either side of the entrance door, and facing the reading desk and the area where the men are sitting.

When it seems that everyone is in their places, Eliezer stands with his head covered, and he steps over to the cabinet where the five shortest Ketuvim scrolls are kept together. He removes the Megillah Esther and takes it to the reading desk. Eliezer bows his head momentarily and then he looks upward and says, "Blessed are You, Lord our God, King of the universe, who has sanctified us with His commandments, and commanded us concerning the reading of the Megillah."

And the congregation responds, "Amen."

Eliezer says, "Blesssed are you, Lord our God, King of the universe, who performed miracles for our forefathers in those days at this season."

And the congregation responds, "Amen."

Eliezer lifts up his hands and says, "Blessed are you, Lord our God, King of the universe, who has granted us life, sustained us, and brought us to this season."

And the congregation responds, "Amen."

Then Eliezer unrolls the scroll, and he begins chanting the words,

> "This happened in the days of Ahasuerus, the same Ahasuerus who ruled over one hundred twenty-seven provinces from India to Ethiopia. In those days when King Ahasuerus sat on his royal throne in the citadel of Susa, in the third year of his reign, he gave a banquet for all his officials and ministers. . . ."
>
> [Esther 1:1-3a NRSV]

Eliezer continues chanting the story of the great banquet in the king's palace, Queen Vashti's refusal to display her beauty for the entertainment of the king's friends, the king becoming furious about her disobedience, and the search for a new queen. Then Eliezer pauses, and the congregation recites,

> "Now there was a Jew in the citadel of Susa whose name was *Mordecai* son of Jair son of Shimei son of Kish, a Benjaminite."
>
> [Esther 2:5 NRSV]

After the congregation recites this verse, Eliezer chants it and then goes on to chant about how Mordecai had adopted his beautiful cousin, Esther, when her parents had died. Because of her great beauty, Esther is chosen to become the new queen, but Mordecai had told her not to reveal her heritage. Mordecai becomes a hero by uncovering a plot to kill the king. Then Eliezer chants,

> "After these things King Ahasuerus promoted *Haman* son of Hammedatha the Agagite, and advanced him and set his seat above all the officials who were with him. And all the king's servants who were at the king's gate bowed down and did obeisance to *Haman*; for the king had so commanded concerning him. But *Mordecai* did not bow down or do obeisance. Then the king's servants who were at the king's gate said to *Mordecai*, "Why do you disobey the king's command?" When they spoke to him day after day and he would not listen to them, they told *Haman*, in order to see whether *Mordecai's* words would avail; for he had told them that he was a Jew. When *Haman* saw that *Mordecai* did not bow down or do obeisance to him, *Haman* was infuriated. But he thought it beneath him to lay hands on *Mordecai* alone. So, having been told who *Mordecai's* people were, *Haman* plotted to destroy all the Jews, the people of *Mordecai*, throughout the whole kingdom of Ahasuerus."
>
> [Esther 3:1-6 NRSV]

At every mention of Haman's name, members of the congregation wave their wooden noisemakers, shout "Boo!" or hiss, and stomp their feet, to express their displeasure with this evil enemy of Jews. And every time Mordecai's name is heard they cheer.

Then Eliezer chants about how Haman falsely told the king that, since the Jews do not obey the kings's laws they should be destroyed, and that lots had been used to determine the date for their destruction, and the king tells Haman to proceed with his plans. So Mordecai appeals to Esther to save her people. Esther explains that according to the laws, not even the queen may go to the king unless she is summoned by him, under penalty of death. So Esther called for a fast that her appeal to the king would be successful. Esther does go to the king. She invites him and Haman to a banquet, at which she pleads for her people and accuses Haman. Then the king condemns Haman to die on the same gallows that Haman had constructed to execute Mordecai, and the king gives permission for Jews to defend themselves against any oppressors who attempt to destroy them. So, on the day that the Jews were to have been destroyed, the Jews in Persia killed five hundred of their enemies, including all of Haman's ten sons. And that day, the fourteenth of Adar was established as the holiday of Purim.

And Eliezer's chanting pauses for the congregation to recite the final declaration of the scroll, about Mordecai's vindication:

> "For *Mordecai* the Jew was next in rank to King
> Ahasuerus, and he was powerful among the Jews
> and popular with his many kindred, for he sought the
> good of his people and interceded for the welfare of
> all his descendants." [Esther 10:3 NRSV]

And then Eliezer chants his repetition of this verse.

After the reading, Eliezer says this final blessing, "Blessed are you, Lord our God, King of the universe, who takes up our grievance, judges our claim, avenges our wrong; who brings just retribution upon all our mortal enemies. Blessed are you Lord, who exacts vengeance for his people Israel from all their oppressors; the God who delivers."

And the congregation responds, "Amen."

Then the people sing joyous songs, share humorous skits based on the story of Purim, partake of special refreshments, and laugh together. The party lasts until well after most people's customary bedtime.

The Megilla is read again in the same manner on the following morning, and the celebration afterward is even more elaborate, with many people wearing costumes.

CHAPTER 37

During the morning of the fifteenth of Adar, the day after Purim, Othniel departs for Yeriko. He is planning to meet up with Yeshuah and the other disciples at Bethabara, the place where they have been staying, near the Yarden River.

On the sixteenth of Adar, two days after Purim and the second day of the week, Eliezer loads Amit and Marit with etrogs, winter figs, and onions. Then he hugs and kisses his family before leaving Hammat for his late-winter marketing trip. As he walks toward Tiberias, he remembers that it has been six months since his late-summer marketing trip, during which Yaaqov was kidnapped. Eliezer is relieved to know that the person who had initiated that awful episode won't be able to cause any more problems for his family.

At that same time, Centurion Gaius informs his assembled soldiers, "Because of heightened concerns about potential unrest in Jerusalem during Passover, the Prefect of Judaea, Pontius Pilate, has ordered all available soldiers to be placed under his direct control in Jerusalem for three consecutive weeks, starting on the 5th day of Nisan. During that period, Optio Titus will supervise a small crew of ten soldiers at our Capernaum garrison, to provide minimal security here. The list of soldiers who will remain here with him is posted at our headquarters. All other soldiers will be prepared for the march to Jerusalem that will commence on the first day of Nisan."

At the main market agora in Tiberias, Eliezer sells some of his vegetables and fruits, but many of the people in the marketplace are more eager to talk with him about Yaaqov's kidnapping, and the the sentencing of Assurbani and Mibzar, than to purchase produce. Eliezer is informed that Assurbani's replacement as profoi is another

Herodian. He enjoys visiting with Zibrah's friends, Joanna and Salome. They tell him that they are looking forward to this year's Pesach Festival, because of Yeshuah's anticipated presence there.

Later that afternoon, Eliezer reloads his produce onto Amit and Marit, and he departs from Tiberias for Kfar Nahum. When he walks by the entrance to the military garrison, he looks at the sentry who is guarding the gate, but he doesn't recognize him.

So he continues walking until he arrives at Aharon's and Bilhah's house, where he is welcomed, and he and his animals are cared-for. After Eliezer, Aharon and Bilhah are finally able to relax together, Aharon asks, "What are the plans for Miriam's and Othniel's wedding."

Eliezer replies, "The wedding celebration won't be held until about seven months from now, in the month of Tishri, but we still haven't made any specific arrangements."

Then Bilhah says, "There is plenty of time to work out all of the details. Aharon and I are just so happy that the Lord has brought Miriam and Othniel together!"

Eliezer responds "Yes, they do seem to be very well-matched. And you and Aharon helped, by putting us in contact with Obed and Adah. Zibrah likes to say that important things always happen at just the right time, and that is because the Lord is guiding us."

Aharon says, "I certainly agree with Zibrah about that!"

The following day, Eliezer sells more of his produce at the market in Kfar Nahum in the morning. During a lull in sales activity, Marius visits with Eliezer about the judicial proceeding, and also about his upcoming trip to Jerusalem. At midday, Eliezer packs up his goods, and leads Amit and Marit for several hours to his customary resting place near Tzipori.

On the morning of the third day of his late-winter marketing trip, Eliezer sells a large amount of his etrogs and onions, and some of his winter figs to customers at the Tzipori market. He particularly enjoys visiting with his repeat customers, several of whom want to hear about how Yaaqov is getting along now, six months after his ordeal during Elul. Most of them hadn't heard about the judicial conclusion of that story, so Eliezer tells them about it. And he also proudly tells his friends about his daughter's betrothal. In the afternoon, Eliezer walks with his donkeys to an inviting meadow just outside of Natzerat.

The next morning, Eliezer walks with his donkeys to Natzerat's open-air market, and he sets up a display of the remaining etrogs, winter figs, and onions that he brought with him. His acquaintance, Amos, comes to Eliezer's stall for a visit and, this time, Eliezer knows better than to mention Yeshuah to him. Eliezer trades some of his winter figs for another jug of Amos' olive oil, and they talk together about their experiences with the Romans. Eliezer sells some of his produce to a few other customers, and at midday he decides to close his sales operation at Natzerat, and to travel for several hours to the spring of Harod, that is at the foot of Mount Gilboa, and only about an hour away from Beit Shean.

Day five of Eliezer's marketing journey is the sixth day of the week, and Eliezer knows that he must complete the final stage of his sales tour in Beit Shean before middday, and return to his home by late-afternoon. He expects to sell all of his remaining onions and fruits this morning, and he is looking forward to seeing his friend, Peleg, at the commercial agora. After entering Beit Shean, Eliezer goes directly to the commercial agora, and he finds Peleg at his customary stall.

Peleg notices Eliezer approaching, and he says, "Shalom, Eliezer! I am happy to see you. Would you like to sell your produce in my stall again?"

Peleg's warm invitation makes Eliezer smile, and he says in reply, "Yes, of course. As you will see, I don't have too many etrogs, winter figs, or onions left, so I don't think that I will burden you for very long today."

"I will enjoy being with you for as long as it takes for you to sell the produce that you brought. How is your family?"

Eliezer replies, "Peleg, my family is well now, but so much has happened since you and I were together six months ago! Yaaqov was kidnapped, removed to Acco, and sold as a slave. Zibrah and I found him and redeemed him. After Sukkot, Miriam became betrothed in Yeriko. Yaaqov's kidnapper was murdered, to conceal the identity of the person who initiated Yaaqov's disappearance. The Roman officers who investigated the murder and kidnapping found out who was responsible, and Herod Antipas sentenced the guilty persons to enslavement on a Roman galley ship. So, it has been a very eventful six months for my family!"

Peleg says, "What an amazing story! You are truly blessed, since everything turned out so well! It could have been so much worse. I am overjoyed that Yaaqov is restored to you, and also to hear about Miriam's betrothal!"

Eliezer spreads his cloak on the pavement inside Peleg's stall, and arranges what is left of his produce on his cloak. Then some customers arrive and purchase produce from Peleg and Eliezer.

About an hour later, there is a lull in sales activity, and Peleg says, "Eliezer, have you heard that Yeshuah recently has been preaching and healing at Bethabara?"

Eliezer replies, "Yes, I did hear about that. Miriam's betrothed husband is one of Yeshuah's disciples. He told us that there was an incident at the Temple during Chanukah, after which Yeshuah departed from Yerushalayim for Bethabara."

"Well, I am looking forward to Pesach. Yeshuah's ministry has attracted a very large number of followers, and I don't see how the Temple officials can continue disregarding him. I am hoping to see Yeshuah myself at Yerushalayim. This Pesach could be even more exciting than others I have attended! Maybe this is what we have been hoping for!"

Two hours later, Eliezer sells the last of the produce that he had brought with him to Beit Shean. He buys an ephah of wheat from Peleg, and thanks him for his hospitality. They each express the hope that they will see one another in Yerushalayim during Pesach, now only a few weeks away. Then Eliezer attaches his goods to Amit, and he leads both of his donkeys towards the Yarden River road that goes to Hammat. A little more than five hours later, he arrives at his home, in plenty of time before Shabbat. He has missed not being with Zibrah and his children for many days, and he is looking forward to spending Shabbat with them.

CHAPTER 38

On the morning of the first day of Nisan, Centurion Gaius leads a contingent of seventy Roman soldiers as they depart in two side-by-side columns from their garrison at Capernaum, and begin marching toward Jerusalem. Each soldier is dressed in his complete uniform and is carrying his equipment, with his spear in one hand, and any essential additional items in a pack on his back, along with his shield. Since Optio Titus is staying behind with the security detail at the military garrison, Marius is serving as Gaius' second-in-command for the Jerusalem deployment. Marius is calling out a cadence, to help the soldiers to keep in step with one another while they are marching through the town. Their route will take them through the territory of Samaria to Antipatris, and from there to Gophna, before turning southward to Jerusalem. They are planning to arrive in Jerusalem on the fifth day of Nisan. While they are marching toward Jerusalem, a crew of military engineers is setting up their camp on Mount Scopus, just north of the holy city.

On the third day of Nisan, which is the second day of this week, Eliezer, his family, and the other members of their light-hearted fellowship group of twenty pilgrims from Hammat, are beginning their travel along the Yarden River Valley road towards Yeriko. As they are walking along, some of them talk with each other, or sing songs. All of them notice the brilliant spring flowers in the fields and hillsides, especially in Galilee. They haven't seen many field flowers for several months. Everyone loves springtime -- nature just seems to be filled with promise, hope, and beauty! And as they move further south, they continue to see beautiful flowers, although their quantity, variety, and color are more subdued as their distance from Galilee increases. As before, the pilgrims spend the first three nights sleeping in improvised shelters alongside the road, or next to the river, with the men taking turns guarding their campsites.

On the fourth day of their trip, they arrive in Yeriko, and the group goes directly to the inn where they had stayed previously.

Eliezer asks the innkeeper, "Do you have available lodging space for twenty pilgrims?"

The innkeeper responds, "I am sorry, but there only is enough space remaining to accommodate fifteen or sixteen persons for this night."

Eliezer says, "That will take care of most of our group. Thank you, we will take it! The rest of us will find other accommodations."

Then, while most of the group of Hammat pilgrims make themselves comfortable at the inn, Eliezer, Zibrah, Miriam, and Yaaqov walk over to Obed's and Adah's house, to see if they could stay there again. Eliezer knocks at the door, and when Adah opens it, she cheerfully welcomes them in, and invites them to stay. One by one, each member of the family gives proper reverence to the mezuzah box attached to the doorpost of the house, and then they step inside and hug Adah, saying "Thank you."

Adah calls toward the inside the house, "Obed! Our daughter-in-law, Miriam, and her family are here!"

And Obed rushes into the large room, smiling broadly at his unexpected guests, the members of his other family. Starting with Miriam, he hugs each one and says, "Shalom! We are so happy to have you visit our home again."

After Obed greets all of them, Miriam asks, "Is Othniel here?"

Obed responds, "No, during part of last month, he was staying nearby, at Bethabara with Yeshuah and the other disciples. Then, quite suddenly, all of them left to go to Bethany. But, we expect to see Othniel in Yerushalayim during Pesach."

Adah says, "You all must be hungry from your trip! Will you have dinner with us?"

Zibrah responded, "Thank you very much. That would be very nice, but we don't want to be a problem for you."

"Zibrah, I assure you, sharing our family meal with your family would be a joy for us, and not a problem! You are always welcome in this house!"

Hearing the conversation taking place in the great room, Obed's and Adah's youngest children, Micah, Deborah, and Mereth, come to see who is visiting. When they see Yaaqov and Miriam, they squeal with delight and run to embrace their relatives.

Adah says to everyone, "Would you like to wash your hands, and eat some fruit and drink a little juice before we all partake of our meal?"

Obed says, "What an excellent idea! Deborah and Mereth, please get the wash basin, a jug of water, and a few clean towels for all of us to use."

Deborah and Mereth respond in unison, "Yes, Abba!" And then they go to fetch the specified items.

A few minutes later, Deborah carries a wash basin and several towels, Mereth brings a jug of water, and Adah brings a large plate containing apricots. They put them on the family table, and then everyone gathers around the table. Mereth pours water into the basin. Then, one at a time, each person washes their hands while saying the handwashing blessing, and then dries them with the towel.

After all of them had washed their hands, they sit down, and Adah brings a plate with two loaves of bread and puts it into the center of the table. Obed blesses the bread and the fruit, and then they pass the plate of apricots and a loaf of bread around the table, and each person takes some of each of them. Then Adah brings a tray containing cups filled with pomegranate juice.

Adah says, "This is not our meal. It is just some light refreshments. After this, we would like for Eliezer, Zibrah, Miriam, and Yaaqov to take some time to get some rest and to make themselves comfortable. We will eat our evening meal just as the sun is setting."

Early the next morning, the seventh day of Nisan, which is the sixth day of this week, Eliezer and his family thank Obed and Adah for their hospitality, and they agree to get together in Yerushalayim during the Feast of Unleavened Bread. Then Eliezer, Zibrah, Miriam, and Yaaqov walk to the inn, to gather with their fellow pilgrims from Hammat. And as soon as everyone is ready for the long, mostly uphill climb to Yerushalayim, they depart from Yeriko. Their journey through the dry Judean desert mountains takes about seven hours, and by late-afternoon, they are quite weary, but excited. As they are approaching Yerushalayim, they sing,

> "I was glad when they said to me, 'Let us go to the house of the LORD!' Our feet are standing within your gates, O Jerusalem."
>
> [Psalm 122:1-2 NRSV]

But when they arrive at the entrance to the city, they are surprised by the unexpected presence of Roman soldiers who are searching for, and confiscating, any swords and long knives that they find. And anyone that the soldiers' supervisor thinks looks like he might be a troublemaker is carefully questioned before being allowed into the city. So there is a line of pilgrims waiting to be inspected, and this delays their entry into Yerushalayim. But most of the waiting pilgrims are happy anyway -- their journey to the holiest of cities for the most sacred of festivals is almost completed, and they are trying hard not to let minor annoyances spoil their pilgrimage experience.

At this same time, Marius and several of his Capernaum-based soldiers are conducting the same kind of inspection, weapons confiscation, and questioning at gates at the northern and western entrances to the city.

Once inside the city, the Hammat pilgrims split-up and go to their temporary accommodations.. Eliezer and Reuel and their families go to the home of their cousin Yehuda and his wife Shira, with whom they had stayed during previous pilgrim festivals. A few of the other Hammat pilgrims also have relatives in Yerushalayim that they will stay with, but most of the members of their group return to the same grain merchant's storeroom that they had rented for last year's Pesach.

When Eliezer and Reuel and their families arrive at the entrance to Yehuda's two-story house, Eliezer knocks on the door and calls to his cousin, "Yehuda and Shira! We are your cousins from Hammat."

In response, Yehuda opens the door and says, "Shalom, cousins! We have been looking forward to your arrival!"

The visiting pilgrims each take turns giving due reverence to the mezuzah box attached to the doorpost of the house, before stepping across the threshold to greet Yehuda with a hug and a kiss on the cheek. After everyone is inside, Yehuda closes the door.

Then Shira calls from the kitchen corner of the great room, "Welcome to our home! I apologize for not greeting you properly at the door but, as you can see, I am busy preparing our food for Shabbat, only about an hour and one-half from now. Please come over here and let me greet each of you, and then make yourselves comfortable in the same rooms upstairs that you used before. And, if you want, you also may take turns using our family miqveh before dinner."

While the women and children go upstairs to the guest sleeping rooms, Eliezer and Reuel go to the miqveh located in a separate room at the rear of the first floor of the house. Eliezer removes his clothes, steps into the water, and then says, "Blessed are You, O Lord, our God, King of the universe, who has sanctified us with your commandments and commanded us concerning the immersion. Amen." Then he submerges himself completely in the water for a moment. He steps out of the miqveh, dries himself with a towel, and dresses himself in a clean change of clothes that he brought with him, and then he says some other prayers before going upstairs to be with his wife and children. Then Reuel disrobes, performs the same ritual immersion, and dresses himself in his clean clothes.

After Eliezer rejoins Zibrah, Miriam, and Yaaqov, Miriam leaves to visit the miqveh herself. She brings her shoulder bag containing her extra clothes and other essentials with her to the miqveh, and she performs the same procedure that her father and uncle did before her.

Just before sunset, the three families gather around the large table in the great room for Shabbat, and they all cover their heads. The table is ready with two oil lamps, bread loaves, cups of wine, other prepared foods, and a basin of water with towels beside it. How precious it is to celebrate Shabbat together in Yerushalayim, seven days before the sacred Festival of Pesach!

During the following afternoon, while most of the people staying at Yehuda's home are taking naps or short walks, Othniel finds the house and knocks at its door. Shira opens the door, and recognizes

Othniel from meeting him at the celebration of Eliezer's and Zibrah's wedding. She says, "Shabbat Shalom, Othniel! Please come in."

Othniel first gives proper veneration to the mezuzah scroll, then he steps inside, greets Shira with a hug, and says, "Shabbat Shalom, Shira! Is Miriam here?"

"Yes, she is. I will tell her that you are here." Then Shira closes the door, goes into a side room off of the great room and finds Miriam reading the Torah with her father. She tells both of them, "Othniel is here. I'm certain that both of you would like to visit with him."

Miriam hurries out of the room, with Eliezer following her and, when she sees her betrothed husband, she shouts, "Niel, how wonderful it is for me to be with you again!" Miri and Othniel hug each other enthusiastically and kiss each other on the cheeks.

When the other members of the combined families in the house at this time hear Miriam's exclamation, they all come to greet Othniel.

Eliezer and Othniel hug each other, and kiss one another on the cheek. Both of them say, "Shabbat Shalom!" to each other.

Then Eliezer says, "Zibrah and Yaaqov are enjoying a stroll together in this crowded city. They will want to visit with you too, when they return, if you can remain here a little longer."

Othniel replies, "And I also am looking forward to seeing them. I am very excited to tell all of you about what happened two weeks ago!"

Shira says, "Please let us all sit down, and listen comfortably to what Othniel wants to tell us. I will get some refreshments."

When everyone is sitting down quietly in the great room, and enjoying a cup of fruit juice, Othniel says, "After spending Purim with Miriam and her family in Hammat, I had a very brief visit at my parents' home in Yeriko, and then I went to Bethabara, to be with Yeshuah and my fellow disciples. Yohanan ben Zebedee told me that Yeshuah had received word that a good friend of his in Bethany, a man named Elazar, was very sick, and that Elazar's family had requested that Yeshuah come to him right away. But Yeshuah did not leave Bethabara until two days later. While we were walking toward Bethany, Yeshuah told us that Elazar had died. And when we arrived at Bethany, we learned that Elazar's body had already been in his tomb for four days. Yeshuah was very sad, but he asked to be shown where the body was, and so we were brought to the tomb. Yeshuah asked that the stone that was used to seal the tomb be removed and, when it was moved, we could smell the stench of death. Yeshuah prayed earnestly, and then with a loud voice he commanded Elazar to come out of his tomb, and shortly afterwards, Elazar did come out, though with difficulty because his hands and feet were wrapped with strips of cloth and his face was covered. Elazar was truly dead, but Yeshuah had restored his life to him and given him back to his family! What an astonishing thing this was! Some of the witnesses were shocked and speechless, while others became excited and ran to tell everyone about the miraculous act that they had seen. After that, Yeshuah and us disciples withdrew to the town of Ephraim. We have been in seclusion there until today. Right now, Yeshuah is in Bethany having dinner with Elazar and his family, and making preparations for his entry into Yerushalayim tomorrow. I came here to be with you all, and to tell you what happened."

Eliezer says, "I don't know what to think about this story. What can it mean for a man to have power over death? Only God has the ability to give life!"

Othniel replies, "Yeshuah's prayer was for God to raise the man, so that shows that Yeshuah acknowledges that God is the real miracle worker. But, the fact that God raised him in response to Yeshuah's prayer must mean that Yeshuah is no ordinary man."

Just then, Zibrah and Yaaqov return from their walk, and Zibrah excitedly says to the gathered group, "In the city we have heard people saying that Yeshuah raised someone who was dead back to life! And we have heard that Yeshuah is coming to Yerushalayim for Pesach, and that some people want to proclaim him as our Maschiah and king!"

Miriam says to Zibrah, "Othniel is here, and he just told us that he was there when Yeshuah raised that dead man back to life. So it is true!"

Yaaqov says, "And I also believe it."

Eliezer shakes his head and says, "I'm sorry Othniel, but I just don't know if I can believe your story. Maybe there is another explanation for what happened."

Miriam responds, "Abba, what other explanation can there be?"

Eliezer says, "I don't know . . . Maybe the man just seemed to be dead, and that somehow he revived in the tomb, all by himself."

Othniel says, "Believe me, he was dead and stinking because the decomposition of his body was underway. But now, he is whole again."

Reuel and Yehuda just shake their heads, without giving any other response to what had been said.

Shira says, "I would like to believe that it happened. Wouldn't it be wonderful if it did?"

With exasperation, Othniel says, "It happened just the way I said. I was there. The man was truly dead, and Yeshuah raised him back to life."

Other people in the city also are talking about the story of Yeshuah raising Elazar from the dead and back to life. And people also recall other wonderful things that Yeshuah is said to have done. People are excited about the prophet from Galilee, and they are eager to see him for themselves! But the people's leaders are worried about the people becoming too excited, and the potential commotion that might generate. Their fear is that Rome will deal harshly with any violation of their peace and order.

CHAPTER 39

The following day is the ninth of Nisan, and the first day of the week that leads to Pesach. Shabbat is past, and businesses are back in operation. And everyone in Yerushalayim is thinking about Pesach being only six days from today: Pesach -- the celebration of Israel's freedom from Egypt, and of hope for her release from domination by the pagans!

It is Reuel's turn to preside at this year's Pesach dinner for their chaburah of Hammat pilgrims. So Reuel, Eliezer, Serah, and Zibrah are in the markets of Yerushalayim, purchasing vegetables, fruits, nuts, and wine for the special meal. It probably is a little early in the week for them to be buying vegetables for the dinner, but they are eager with anticipation. They overhear some people talking about Yeshuah, wondering when he will come into the city.

Miriam is at Yehuda's and Shira's house, washing the clothes that the family was wearing while they were traveling, so that they all will have clean clothes to wear for Pesach. Yaaqov also is at Yehuda's and Shira's house. He is organizing his cousins to do a skit based on the story of the Exodus. Othniel went back to Bethany last night, to be with Yeshuah. And Marius is on duty at the Ephraim Gate, on the north side of the city.

Reuel, Eliezer, Serah, and Zibrah are bringing the food and wine that they purchased to the storeroon that they had rented from the grain merchant for the festival. Their friend and neighbor, Reuben, is there.

Eliezer says, "Shalom, Reuben! Here are some vegetables, fruits, and wine for our Pesach dinner. We will leave them here with you, until it is time for us to start preparing that meal."

Reuben replies, "Very well. Did you hear that Yeshuah raised a man from death to life in Bethany a couple of weeks ago?"

Eliezer says, "Yes, we heard about that last night. But, I am having a difficult time believing that it really happened."

Reuben replies, "Not me. I believe it."

And Serah and Zibrah nod their heads in agreement with Reuben.

Then Reuel says, "I'm not as skeptical as my brother. Yeshuah has already performed so many remarkable deeds! Anyone who could do all of those things probably also could bring someone back from death to life!"

Eliezer responds, "You may be right, Reuben. But this Yeshuah really stretches the limits of credibility for me. I just can't figure out why the Lord would choose to work through someone who isn't as meticulous as we are in keeping His commandments. And Yeshuah never has anything good to say about us Pharisees."

Reuben adds, "Eliezer, you always have the same objection! Maybe God isn't a Pharisee, after all!"

Eliezer smiles and says, "Well, if He isn't, He should be!"

While Eliezer and the others are talking, suddenly Kenan bursts into the storeroom, and announces, "Yeshuah just rode into the city on the foal of a donkey, and there were crowds of people welcoming him enthusiastically. They were shouting, 'Hosanna to the Son of David! Blessed is the king who comes in the name of the Lord! Hosanna in the highest heaven!' Some people in the crowds were waving palm branches, and putting those branches, and their cloaks, on the path in front of him."

Reuben says, "I understand the crowd's enthusiasm. People are excited about seeing the man who has done so many wondrous deeds, and who has captivated his hearers with his preaching. But why did Yeshuah choose to arrive in Yerusahalayim in this manner?"

Eliezer replies, "That is a very good question. We have been told that Yeshuah always walks or boats from place to place in his public ministry, and that it is not his custom to travel by other types of conveyances. Therefore, I believe that his decision to ride into the city on a donkey actually was a very provocative act. The prophet Zecharyahu wrote,

'Rejoice greatly, O daughter Zion! Shout aloud, O daughter Jerusalem!

Lo, your king comes to you; triumphant and victorious
is he, humble and riding on a donkey, on a colt, the
foal of a donkey.' [Zechariah 9:9 NRSV]

I believe that Yeshuah was intentionally presenting himself
as Israel's king, when he arrived riding on the foal of a donkey, in
fulfillment of the prophecy. Yeshuah has been traveling around
preaching about the kingdom of God, and we have heard of people
clamoring for him to be proclaimed as king. But this may be the first
time that he actually openly claims to be a king. Therefore, I think that
the real question is: was Yeshuah's presentation of himself sincerely
politically motivated, or was he deliberately seeking to incur the wrath
of the chief priests and the Roman authorities? I wonder which of these
alternatives was his real intention, or was his purpose something else,
that I haven't even considered?"

Reuben responds, "I would not have thought about all of that on
my own. But what you said does sound correct."

Zibrah says, "Perhaps Yeshuah's real intention was simply to do
what God told him to do. That would be consistent with everything
we ever heard Yeshuah say about the things that he does."

Then Eliezer turns to Kenan and he asks, "What did Yeshuah do
after his dramatic royal entrance into Yerushalayim?"

Kenan replies, "After he entered the city, he spent some time
looking around, he spoke to a few people about his death, and then he
returned to Bethany."

Reuben exclaims, "He talked to some people about his *death*? That
doesn't sound like what an aspiring king would do."

Eliezer says, "Othniel told me that Yeshuah has been speaking to
his disciples about his death for several months. As you can imagine,
it has been very unsettling for them."

On the afternoon of the tenth day of Nisan, Reuel and Eliezer
go to the marketplace in the Court of the Gentiles at the Temple to
purchase a one-year old unblemished male lamb as the designated
sacrificial animal for their chaburah. After selecting a large lamb and
determining its price, they exchange their normal currency for Temple
money and they buy the lamb, and then they bring it back to Yehuda's
and Shira's house. Then Reuel places the lamb into the arms of his son,

Yonah, and tells him to take special care of it for the next four days, being particularly careful that it not becomes injured in any way. Yonah agrees to accept that responsibility, just as Yaaqov had done in the preceding year. Yaaqov tells his cousin, Yonah, that he will help him.

On the eleventh day of Nisan, Reuel, Eliezer, and their wives visit the market and purchase fresh vegetables for the Pesach dinner that members of their Hammat chaburah will share. When they bring the food they bought to the storeroom, Reuben tells them that he had visited the Temple earlier that day, and that Yeshuah also was there. Yeshuah was being confronted by the chief priests and the elders of the people who challenged his authority in various ways. Yeshuah answered all of their questions through an extended discourse in which he denounced the Scribes and Pharisees as being hypocrites, and then he returned to Bethany.

When Eliezer heard what Yeshuah said about the Scribes and Pharisees, his only comment was, "Well, Yeshuah is consistent, that is certainly true! And you know, I am beginning to think that he also is right in many cases."

After dinner on the evening of the thirteenth day of Nisan, all of the pilgrims in the Hammat chaburah meet together in the storeroom where they were planning to share the Pesach dinner on the following night. Then, by the light of an oil lamp, Reuel led the members of the chaburah in a cheerful search of every corner of the premises for any hametz (leaven). They didn't find any leaven, of course, because the owner of the storeroom had already removed all of the yeast and leavened grain, but this is part of their Pesach observance. After their search, the pilgrims share some refreshments before returning to the Yerushalayim houses where they have been staying,

CHAPTER 40

Very early in the morning of the fourteenth of Nisan, more than two hours before sunrise, there is a frantic sound of pounding at the door to Yehuda's and Shira's house. Yehuda gets out of his bed and comes to the door with a lit oil lamp. When he opens the door, he sees Othniel, and he can tell that Othniel is very distraught. Yehuda says, "Othniel, why are you here in the darkest time of night, while everyone else is sleeping?"

Othniel replies, "Yeshuah's enemies came and took him away during the night. We believe that they are seeking to kill him. May I please come in? I would like to talk to Miriam and her family. I am very upset."

"Yes, I can see that you are in great distress. Can you come back later, during the daylight?"

"That may be too late! Please, won't you let me speak with my betrothed wife and her parents?"

"Oh. All right, you may come in. I will awaken Eliezer, and tell him that you are here." Yehuda opens the door wide to let him come in.

Othniel shows due respect to the mezuzah box before he steps inside the house. And then he says, "Peace be to this house!"

Yehuda points to a chair in his great room, and says, "Please, sit here while I wake Eliezer for you."

Othniel says, "Thank you. I will." Then Yehuda lights an oil lamp for Othniel, and he goes upstairs.

A couple of minutes later, Eliezer comes down the stairs, rubbing his eyelids and temples to help him wake up. When he comes into the great room, he sits down next to Othniel, and he says, "Othniel, what has happened, that you are here in the middle of the night?"

"Eliezer, Yeshuah's enemies came and took him away during the night. We believe that they intend to get rid of him."

"Where and when did this happen, who came to get him, and where did they take him?"

Othniel replies, "Last night, about an hour or two after dinner, Yeshuah asked some of his closest followers to go with him to a garden in the place of the oil press, on the side of the Mount of Olives. He went there to pray, and he asked them to accompany him. After they had been there a few hours, a group of men with torches came, accompanied by some Temple police. They were being directed to that place by Yehuda Iscariot, who also is one of Yeshuah's closest followers. He knew where Yeshuah would be. The Temple guards bound Yeshuah's arms with rope, and they led him away to be interrogated by the high priest."

"How do you know about this?"

"One of Yeshuah's closest followers, a man named Yohanan ben Zebedee, came to the rented room that I share with three other disciples of Yeshuah and he woke us up and told us what happened. He was there when it happened."

"According to what you said, Yeshuah was taken into custody by people who are associated with the Temple. So he is being attacked for religious reasons by religious people. I would like to think that religious people always behave justly, but I know that they don't. Unfortunately, people who believe in the rightness of their cause too often have no difficulty justifying anything that they do. The good thing is that the Sanhedrin includes some people who do believe in fairness. You should make sure that they are present at any hearing or proceeding in which Yeshuah is to be judged."

Othniel says, "Yes, I know that some of the Sanhedrin members actually are sympathetic with Yeshuah and his teaching."

Then Eliezer says, "Then I hope that having them there will make a difference. His accusers will turn his own words against him. And some of the things that Yeshuah has said are considered offensive by many people."

Othniel responds, "What do you mean?"

"From what people have told me, Yeshuah frequently mentions the special relationship he has with God, even to the point of saying, 'The Father and I are one,' and 'I am God's Son.' Doesn't that sound like blasphemy to you?"

"It isn't blasphemy if it is true! And I do believe it to be so."

"You should be careful who you say that to!"

Othniel asks, "Do you think that the Sanhedrin would sentence Yeshuah to death?"

Eliezer replies, "No, I don't think so. Even though the Torah prescribes the death penalty for many types of offences, including religious offenses, the death penalty is almost never imposed by any properly constituted religious court. And I heard that the Roman authorities actually took away the power of Jewish courts to sentence anyone to death."

"But what about the Roman authorities? They don't seem to hesitate from crucifying people. Do you think that the Roman prefect would sentence Yeshuah to death?"

"No, I don't. The Romans crucify criminals that are non-Roman citizens who are convicted of heinous crimes or treason, but they would not execute someone just for breaking a Jewish religious law."

Othniel says, "Well, I certainly hope that you are right!"

Just then, Miriam walks into the great room and says, "And I also hope that you are right, Abba. I was awakened by the sound of talking down here, and I came down to see who was here. But I only heard the last part of your conversation. What is going on, that I find my betrothed busband talking with my father about possible executions in the middle of the night?" She sits in a chair next to where Othniel is sitting, and opposite to her father's chair.

Othniel and Eliezer look at each other, and Eliezer says to Othniel, "You tell her what has happened."

Othniel looks into Miriam's eyes and says, "Late last night, some of Yeshuah's enemies came and took him away by force. Yeshuah's closest followers are concerned that his enemies are seeking to eliminate him, and that they might succeed."

Greatly concerned, Miriam says, "Who would want to do such a thing, and why?"

"Yeshuah was arrested by a detachment of Temple guards, and he was taken away to be interrogated by the high priest. Therefore, we believe that he is being attacked for religious reasons."

Miriam asks, "So, what happens next?"

Othniel replies, "We don't know for certain. But, we think that the next step may be some kind of hearing before the Great Sanhedrin, the highest court in Israel. The Sanhedrin is made up of seventy eminent men, plus the high priest. Today is the Day of Preparation for Pesach, so they may decide to judge this matter today. As soon as the sun rises, I will contact Yeshuah's closest followers, to find out what they may know about this situation."

Miriam says, "Then you should try to get some rest, between now and daybreak. Why don't you just curl up over there, in the corner of the room? I will wake you when it is time for all of us to eat some breakfast."

"Alright, I will do that. Thank you."

Eliezer and Miriam blow out the light and go upstairs.

As the first light of dawn becomes visible over the Mount of Olives, Yehuda and Shira arise from their bed, and come downstairs. They find Othniel sleeping in a corner of their great room, and Yehuda quietly tells Shira about what had happened during the night. They begin preparing the morning meal.

A few minutes later, Eliezer, Zibrah, Reuel, and Serah also awake and come down. Without waking Othniel, the six parents talk softly about Yeshuah's arrest. Yehuda mentions that one of his neighbors is a member of the Sanhedrin, and that he will try to get some more information about what is going on from that neighbor after breakfast. Then Eliezer leads them in prayer, saying, "Blessed are you, O Lord our God and God of our fathers. May your will be done in heaven above and also here on earth. Grant peace of mind to those who fear you, and do what seems best to you. We are your humble people, and we trust you. Blessed are you, O Lord, who hears and answers prayer. Amen."

Miriam wakens Othniel and invites him to join the combined families at the table for their shared morning meal. There is a side table, with a basin of water and a towel. All of the others had already washed their hands, and are now sitting at the table, waiting. Miriam and Othniel wash their hands while saying the handwashing blessing, and then they dry their hands with the towel, and sit down.

Yehuda says a blessing for the meal, and then platters of bread and sliced fruit, and pitchers of cold water, are passed around the people seated at the table, and the family members begin eating and talking with each other.

Yehuda says to Othniel, "Othniel, I know that you are very upset about your rabbi being arrested last night, and that you are anxious to find out what has happened. One of my neighbors is a member of the Sanhedrin. His name is Yehonatan. After our meal, I will visit him at his house, to find out if there is anything that he can tell us about Yeshuah's arrest, and what may happen next."

Othniel responds, "Thank you, Yehuda. I would appreciate receiving any information about that situation. I was planning to leave right away, to find out what my fellow disciples may know, but I will wait here until your return from visiting with your neighbor."

Meanwhile, most of the other members of the combined families were discussing the preparations that would be made today for this evening's Pesach dinner. Eliezer and Reuel and their families will partake of the special dinner at the rented storeroom, with the other members of their chaburah of pilgrims from Hammat. Most of the food preparations for that dinner will be completed during this morning. Reuel and Eliezer will bring the large lamb that Yonah has been caring for to the Temple this afternoon as their sacrifice and to be slaughtered. And afterwards, they will roast the lamb in one of the public clay ovens. Yehuda and Shira will have their own separate observance of the Pesach dinner at their home, with their children. Othniel had planned to partake of the Pesach dinner with his parents and his siblings at the house where they are staying, but now he is less certain about those plans.

When Yehuda returns from visiting with his neighbor, he requests that Othniel, Miriam, Eliezer, Zibrah, Reuel, Serah, and Shira sit down with him in the great room, so that he could give them his report of what Yehonatan had told him. When they are all seated, Yehuda says, "Yehonatan told me that the Sanhedrin has been greatly concerned about the growing public excitement that has been generated by Yeshuah's traveling ministry, including enthusiastic reports of messianic expectations, and they have been monitoring certain blasphemous statements that reportedly were made by Yeshuah. There is considerable fear that, given our current, tense relationship with the Romans, any substantial public disturbance would be interpreted by the Romans as evidence of a political insurrection, and would be met with a violent response that could be disastrous for the people of Israel.

After receiving the report that Yeshuah had raised a dead man back to life in Bethany, and all of the speculation that caused, the Sanhedrin decided to seek to have Yeshuah put to death, but without stirring up a large public outcry."

Eliezer responded, "What? The Sanhedrin voted to plot the death of a rabbi in Israel because he is too popular? And they did that without conducting a trial?"

Yehuda says, "You must understand, the Sanhedrin has to do what will be best for all of the people of Israel. Their concern was that Yeshuah's miraculous deeds might attract even more followers, and that could provoke some kind of trouble. Their fear was further magnified by Yeshuah's triumphal entry into Yerushalayim. Even the Romans noticed that Yeshuah was welcomed as Israel's King. Last night, with the aid of one of Yeshuah's own followers, Temple guards were able to arrest him and brought him to the High Priest for questioning. During his interrogation last night, Yeshuah said that he is the Messiah and the Son of God, and that utimately he would be recognized as the Son of Man coming with the clouds of heaven. That is blasphemy!"

Othniel asks, "So, what happens next? I heard that the Romans took away the ability of Jewish judges to impose the death penalty."

Yehuda replies, "This morning, probably while we were eating breakfast, Yeshuah was taken to Pontius Pilate for judgement."

Eliezer says, "But the Romans would not prosecute someone for a religious offense like blasphemy."

Yehuda, "Maybe not, but they might if that person claimed to be a king. Treason against Rome is an offense punishable by crucifixion. I think that our prefect, Pontius Pilate, may be considering that accusation right now!"

Othniel responds, "Oh, no! I have to leave here right now, to go to Pilate's headquarters!"

Miriam immediately stands up and says, "I will go with you!"

Eliezer says, "Miriam and Othniel, please be very careful! Do not put yourself in jeopardy! I will be praying for you, and also for Yeshuah."

Miriam replies, "Don't worry about us. I will make sure that neither of us does anything drastic. We will return." And then Miriam and Othniel leave, rushing across Yerushalayim towards the Roman headquarters.

CHAPTER 41

When they arrive at the plaza of the Praetorium, Miriam and Othniel encounter a large, very agitated crowd of onlookers, and many stern-faced Roman soldiers who are trying to keep order. Othniel looks through the crowd and finds his fellow-disciple, Yohanan ben Zebedee.

Othniel and Miriam go over to where his friend is standing, and Othniel asks him, "Yohanan, what is happening?"

Yohanan is distressed, but he replies, "The High Priest, Caiaphas, and the Sanhedrin declared Yeshuah to be guiilty of blasphemy. This morning, Caiaphas and the Temple guards brought Yeshuah to Pilate, the Roman governor of Judea, to request that the death sentence be imposed. Caiaphas told Pilate that as a self-declared king of the Jews, Yeshuah was setting himself against Rome, and therefore he deserves to be crucified. Pilate questioned Yeshuah himself, and then Pilate told the crowd that he found no case against Yeshuah. So Pilate offered the crowd a choice: he was prepared to release either Yeshuah or a notorious bandit named Barabbas, and the crowd demanded that Barabbas be released instead of Yeshuah. Then Pilate ordered that Yeshuah be scourged, and that is about to happen."

They watch as Yeshuah's hands are fastened to a stone pillar, he is stripped of his clothing, and beaten with a whip, called a flagellum, from his shoulders to his loins. Instead of a single leather thong, the flagellum has many leather strands, and each of them is weighted with lead balls or tipped with sharp pieces of bone. The effect of being struck with the flagellum is devastatingly violent; the skin is torn and bruised, and the pain is unbearable. The first strike with the flagellum lacerates Yeshuah's shoulders and back, and the pain causes him to slump against the pillar, with his legs sprawling. With difficulty, he gets his feet back underneath him and he stands back up to receive the next three strikes on his back, sides, and hips. The repeated strikes of the flagellum are shredding his skin and the underlying muscle. Several of his ribs are exposed, and his involuntary cries are unlike any other sound Miriam or Othniel had ever heard. Yeshuah loses consciousness and collapses against the pillar. He is revived with cold water being poured upon him, and he is helped back to his feet. Then the merciless whip strikes again, and again, and again, pounding and tearing at the trunk of his body, his buttocks, and his groin. The soldier swinging the flagellum is perspiring heavily, and is becoming exhausted himself. The many lacerations and bruises, the blood flowing down, and the agonizing howls are too much for many people in the crowd to bear, but the flagellation does not stop, except when it again becomes necessary to revive Yeshuah from unconsciousness, and then the torturous beating resumes. The torment finally ends when the soldiers are unable to revive Yeshuah, and they decide that he is near death. Then some soldiers come and unfasten Yeshuah's body from the post, and they carry it back inside the building.

Miriam and Othniel are horrified! They have never seen brutality like this, and it has been done to someone who is dear to them! Throughout the ordeal, they were praying for Yeshuah, and for mercy.

> About a half hour later, Pilate comes out again and says, "Look, I am bringing him out to you to let you know that I find no case against him." [John 19:4b NRSV] Then Yeshuah is led out to him, wearing a purple robe and a crown of thorns. This time, Yeshuah's face also is bloody, bruised, and swollen. He looks ghastly, repulsive, and pitifully inhuman. Pilate says, "Here is the man!"
>
> [John 19:5b NRSV]

Pilate wants to release Yeshuah, and he appears to have hoped that the crowd would consider that Yeshuah already had been punished enough.

Some people in the crowd are shouting, "Mercy! Release him!"

But many more people in the crowd are shouting, "Crucify him! Crucify him!"

[John 19:6b NRSV]

Then someone shouts, "If you release this man, you are no friend of the emperor. Everyone who claims to be a king sets himself against the emperor!"

[John 19:12b NRSV]

Pilate is yielding to pressure, but he also wants to taunt the religious leaders who have been stirring up the crowd. So, turning to the crowd, he says, "Here is your king!"

[John 19:14b NRSV]

The crowd answers, "Away with him! Away with him! Crucify him!"

[John 19:15a NRSV]

Pilate asks, "Shall I crucify your king?"

[John 19:15b NRSV]

And the chief priests respond, "We have no king but the emperor."

[John 19:15b NRSV]

So Pilate gives the order for Yeshuah to be crucified. It is about the sixth hour of the day, noon.

And Othniel and Miriam are shocked. This is not how either of them imagined that this saga would turn out.

Four Roman soldiers are assigned the task of carrying out Pilate's crucifixion order. Pilate has a titulus inscribed in three languages to be placed on Yeshuah's cross. It says "Jesus of Nazareth, the King of the Jews." [John 19:19b NRSV]

Yeshuah carries his own cross through the northwestern portion of Yerushalayim, and through the Gannath Gath to the place of execution,

Golgotha. All along the route, there are groups of onlookers, some of them are jeering and mocking Yeshuah, while others are providing tear-filled encouragement to their Master. And when Yeshuah and his executioners pass through the Gannath Gate, Marius is on duty there, with his head bowed and his fist at his chest, offering a respectful salute to his friend that is passing by and dragging a cross. Miriam and Othniel follow the solemn procession along the route to Golgotha.

As they are passing through the gate, Marius embraces Othniel and Miriam, and he says to Othniel, "I am so ashamed that this is happening, and I am especially sorry for you, because I know that you love him."

By the time that Miriam and Othniel arrive at the hill of Golgotha, they see that Yeshuah has been stripped of his clothing, his hands and feet have been nailed to the cross, and the cross has been raised, with its base inserted into a hole in the rock and firmly held in its place with wedges. Yeshuah is crucified between two other condemned men. Miriam and Othniel see the inscription that Pilate ordered to be put on Yeshuah's cross, and they hear the protests of the chief priests regarding its message. A soldier tells them to take their complaint to Pilate, since he is the one who specified how the inscription should be written.

Seeing Yeshuah's suffering, both Miriam and Othniel are unable to keep from crying. But, after a while, Miriam and Othniel look around at the other people close to Yeshuah's cross. Besides the soldiers and the chief priests, they also see Yohanan ben Zebedee, Yeshuah's mother, and a few other grieving women. While Yeshuah is hanging on the cross, the sky becomes ominously darkened. The onlookers listen as Yeshuah is forgiving the men who are crucifying him, and they also hear him entrust the future care of his mother to Yohanan. Yeshuah says that he is thirsty, and he groans about having been forsaken by God. Finally, at about the ninth hour of the day, Yeshuah says, "It is finished," [John 19:30b NRSV] and then he bows his head and dies.

They hear the sound of the shofar from the Temple, and Othniel realizes that, at that very moment, the Passover sacrificial lambs are being slain at the Temple, and he remembers that Yohanan the Baptizer referred to Yeshuah as the "Lamb of God". And Othniel and Miriam join several others in crying for their loss. Miriam notices beautiful wildflowers growing on some nearby hillsides, and the contrast between that beauty and the hideous things she has seen today seems incongruous to her.

Late in the afternoon, the soldiers break the legs of the men on either side of Yeshuah, to hasten their death. But when they come to Yeshuah, they see that he is already dead, but to make sure they thrust a spear into his chest, and immediately a mixture of blood and water flows out of the wound, as proof of Yeshuah's death. Afterwards, they take Yeshuah's body down from the cross, and some of Yeshuah's friends anoint his body with a mixture of myrrh and aloes, they wrap it in linen cloths, and they lay it in a new tomb in a nearby garden. It is just before sunset, which marks the beginning of the fifteenth day of Nisan, which is Pesach, and also Shabbat.

Later, Miriam and Othniel are walking back to Yehuda's and Shira's house, so Miriam can wash herself and put on her clean clothes to participate in the Pesach meal with the other Hammat pilgrims. And, after escorting Miriam to Yehuda's house, Othniel will go to the house where his family will be celebrating Pesach. But as they are walking, they share their feelings about what has happened. Both of them are profoundly shaken by the horrific things that they had witnessed being done to a very great, very good, and very gentle man.

Miriam says, "I just can't believe the meanness of so many people: of the chief priests who kept the crowd clamoring for Yeshuah to be crucified, of the Roman governor who condemned Yeshuah despite the fact that he found nothing in him deserving of death, of the soldiers who inflicted such terrible punishments, and of the crowd that kept jeering at Yeshuah and mocking him throughout his ordeal!"

Othniel responds, "Yes, it is very disturbing to discover such evil in the hearts of so many people. I loved Yeshuah, and I loved being his disciple. But I think the worst thing for me about what happened today is that when Yeshuah died, all of the dreams that I had for the future of his ministry died with him!"

Miriam says, "Didn't you say that Yeshuah had repeatedly been predicting his death?"

"Yes, he did. But all of us were hoping that he was mistaken!"

"And I also recall you telling me that he said he would rise again on the third day. What about that?"

"I believe that all of the righteous dead will rise again, at the end of the age, for new life in the world that is to come!"

Miriam says, "I believe that too! But Yeshuah said that he would arise on the third day. Do you believe that he meant that would happen two days from now?"

"Perhaps that is what he meant. But, right now, with all that has happened, it is difficult for me to hope for anything."

"Well, Yeshuah said that he would be put to death by his enemies, and that happened. And he also said that he would rise again. We know that he was able to raise Elazar of Bethany from being four-days-dead back to life. Maybe that same power will raise him in two days. If it is difficult for you to have hope, then let us at least agree to wait and see what will happen."

"Miriam, your faith is amazing!"

"No, at this point, I wouldn't call what I have faith, because I am not confident that what we would like to hope for will actually happen. But at least I am open to the possibility that it could be true."

"I would like to believe that it is possible that Yeshuah will rise from the dead in two more days, but I don't understand why he would have thought that would happen."

"Well, we know that Yeshuah sometimes understands and applies the Torah, Prophets, and Writings differently than many other rabbis. Maybe if we could understand why he was so convinced that the scriptures pointed to his death, then we would better comprehend his ideas about resurrection."

When they arrive at Yehuda's and Shira's house, Othniel and Miriam hug each other for a long time, each saying to the other how sorry they are that the other also had to witness Yeshuah's awful suffering. And they agree that Othniel would return here at midmorning tomorrow to escort Miriam to the home where his parents are staying. Then she goes inside, to get her clean clothes, and to visit the miqveh for another immersion. After the day's events, she feels soiled, and she believes that she needs the spiritual benefit of ritual immersion. Then she wishes Yehuda, Shira, and their family a blessed Pesach, and she leaves to go to the rented storeroom where her fellow pilgrims from Hammat are observing Pesach.

When Miriam arrives at the storeroom-dining hall, she sees the familiar configuration of a large table whose top surface is only one cubit above the floor, and that extends around most of the room, with an opening at one end. The two oil lamps for Shabbat had already been lit, and a linen-covered platter of unleavened bread is on the table next to them, Reuel and Eliezer haven't finished roasting the lamb yet, so the other members of the chaburah are visiting with each other in small groups.

Zibrah had heard that Yeshuah had been crucified, and she knew that Miriam had gone with Othniel to observe the judicial proceeding. She asks Miriam what had happened, and Miriam begins telling her. A few other people overhear Miriam sharing her story, and they come over to where she and Zibrah are talking, so that they also may know the details. Several of them had seen Yeshuah teach. All of them agreed that crucifying Yeshuah was a terrible thing.

After about two hours, Reuel and Eliezer arrive with the roasted lamb. The chaburah of twenty Hammat pilgrims take their places around the outside of the table, reclining on pillows, starting with Reuel as the designated head of the chaburah at one end of the table, and continuing around the table from the oldest to the youngest at the other end. Serah and Zibrah are serving as attendants for the Pesach dinner. Miriam finds her place at the table.

After everyone else has reclined, Serah and Zibrah pour the first cup of wine for each pilgrim. Then, Serah brings out a bowl of water, and Zibrah a towel. Starting at the head of the table, and then going around the table, one at a time, each pilgrim put their hands into the bowl of water that Serah is holding, and then they dry them with the towel in Zibrah's hands. As each person washes their own hands, they say the handwashing blessing.

After all of them have washed their hands, Reuel picks up his cup of wine and says the blessing. "Blessed are you, O Lord our God, king of the universe, who has created the fruit of the vine, and brought us out from under the yoke of the Egyptians. And you, O Lord our God have given us festival days for joy, this feast of unleavened bread, the time of our deliverance in remembrance of the departure from Egypt. Blessed are you, O Lord our God, who has kept us alive, sustained us, and enabled us to enjoy this season." Then everyone said, "Amen," and drank their first cup of wine. Their Pesach dinner is underway. But none of these pilgrims will ever forget this Pesach.

CHAPTER 42

As with previous Passover celebrations, this year's morning of the fifteenth day of Nisan is a relaxing time of reflecting about the mighty acts of God in delivering His people from bondage in Egypt. But this year, many people are also thinking about yesterday's crucifixions, which spoiled the solemnity and joy of their Passover commemoration. The seven-day Feast of Unleavened Bread, which began with last night's Pesach dinner, is continuing. However, this morning, Eliezer, Reuel and their families are returning to the home of their Yerushalayim cousin Yehuda and his wife Shira. Miriam anticipates a visit by Othniel, and going with him for a visit with his parents, Obed and Adah.

As they are walking from the storeroom to Yehuda's house, Eliezer says, "Miriam, yesterday included some very terrible experiences for you! Did you sleep well last night, or did you have to relive those memories in your dreams?"

Miriam replies, "Last night, I was exhausted in every way, so I was able to sleep relatively soundly, and without nightmares. However, I will be thinking about what happened for a very long time."

"Do you think that you will be able to put that experience behind you, so that it will not continue troubling you emotionally?"

"I hope to be able to distance myself enough from that horrific experience, so that I will be able to function normally; but I don't ever want to forget what happened."

"Why don't you try to just put it out of your mind?"

"Because I need to understand why it happened, and what benefit it provides."

"We were told that members of the Sanhedrin believed that Yeshuah needed to be eliminated for the greater good of our Land and its people."

"Yes, I heard that too, and it still doesn't make sense to me. But Othniel says that Yeshuah predicted that it would happen, and it is possible that Yeshuah may have deliberately acted in some ways to ensure that it *would* happen. At the very least, he allowed it to happen. I would like to understand why he would have done that."

"What? You think that Yeshuah actually made himself the victim of such an awful death?"

"I believe that Yeshuah could have avoided it, but he didn't. And I would like to know why."

Then Zibrah says, "If what you are saying is true, then I believe that the reason why Yeshuah went through with it is because that is what God told him to do."

Miriam says, "But why would God's plan require the death of Yeshuah?"

Eliezer responds, "Miriam, I would like to remind you that God's ways are higher than our ways. We cannot know the will of God unless He reveals it to us."

Miriam says, "I'm having a difficult time understanding how the will of God could include the awful things that I witnessed yesterday."

Zibrah says, "Perhaps all of the reasons will be revealed someday. Until then, I advise you to let this matter go, because if you don't, it will only make you more upset."

Miriam responds, "Thank you, Zibrah and Abba, for talking with me about this. Our conversation has been very helpful for me."

At midmorning, Othniel arrives at Yehuda's and Shira's house, and Miriam leaves with him for a visit with Obed and Adah. As they are walking to the house where Othniel's parents are staying, Miriam says, "I had a good talk with my parents about Yeshuah's suffering."

Othniel replies, "What was it about that conversation that made it so good?"

"Because I needed to talk about what has been bothering me, and they really listened to me."

"What did you say was bothering you?"

Miriam replies, "I told them that Yeshuah predicted his own violent death and that, instead of avoiding provocative encounters that led to his death, he appears to have purposely pursued them. Why did he allow his death to happen?"

"So, what did they say?"

"Zibrah said that she thinks that God told him to do it."

Othniel says, "You know, I think that once again Zibrah is right!"

"Well, if she is right, then why would God's plan require the death of Yeshuah?"

"I don't know, but let's study our scriptures carefully, and pray for insight."

Miriam says, "Yes. And let us also remember to wait and see what happens, about Yeshuah's other prediction."

"Yes, but it is difficult for me to expect Yeshuah to be raised from the dead."

"Which brings us to how *you* are dealing with the violence that we witnessed yesterday?"

Othniel says, "Well, it feels like my heart has been ripped into pieces. My spiritual leader suffered a brutal, humiliating, and excruciatingly painful death. His message of grace, compassion, forgiveness, mercy, and peace was swept aside by intolerance, fear, hatred, and evil. The dream of being part of a great spiritual awakening died, along with Yeshuah. I am disappointed with God, and my faith has been replaced by hopelessness. So, to answer your question about how I am doing, I must say that I am deeply hurting. At this point, the only two things that I am desperately clinging to are my family, and you -- my beautiful, sensitive, courageous, and intelligent future wife. Miriam, I love you, and I am so thankful that I don't have to endure this pain without you."

Miriam says, "Thank you, Othniel. I have known for quite a while that I love you too, and I believed that you also love me, even though neither of us said it until now. . . . I also am hurting. We are both dealing with disillusionment. But I do believe that we will get through this. My abba is fond of saying that, as a farmer he has learned the importance of continuing to trust God, even when doing that may not seem to make any sense. He says that going through a process of having our lives uprooted is never easy, but it always produces good results if we keep focusing on God. I believe that, somehow, God will bring good out of what has happened, and He will replace the dream that we had with a new vision. But, in the meantime, we need to hold on to Him, and to each other, as we are waiting for the benefit to be revealed."

After a few moments of walking in silence, Othniel says, "Miriam, as Yeshuah was dying on the cross, he said, 'My God, my God, why have you forsaken me?' Now, I know that he was suffering terribly, but his complaint about abandonment was really uncharacteristic of him."

Miriam responds, "I wondered about that too, but then I realized that he was praying from the Psalms. The twenty-second Psalm starts with

> 'My God, my God, why have you forsaken me?
> Why are you so far from helping me, from the words
> of my groaning?'
>
> [Psalms 22:1 NRSV]

but it ends

> 'All the ends of the earth shall remember and turn
> to the LORD;
> and all the families of the nations shall worship
> before him.
> For dominion belongs to the LORD, and he rules
> over the nations.
> To him, indeed, shall all who sleep in the earth bow
> down;
> before him shall bow all who go down to the dust,
> and I shall live for him.
> Posterity will serve him; future generations will be
> told about the Lord,
> and proclaim his deliverance to a people yet unborn,
> saying that he has done it.'
>
> [Psalms 22:27-31 NRSV]

We only heard Yeshuah say the first part of that Psalm, but I would like to think that he was on his way to also reciting the thanksgiving at the end."

Othniel says, "Thank you, my beloved! That is a remarkable observation, but it makes sense to me, because it is consistent with Yeshuah's customary prayers."

When Othniel and Miriam arrive at the house where his parents are staying, but before going to the door, Othniel says to her, "Besides our family home in Yeriko, my father also owns this house, it is very convenient for my family during the pilgrim festivals."

"Then why did you come to Yehuda's house two nights ago?"

"It is because I wanted to be close to you during that night of awful uncertainty."

"Thank you for saying that, Othniel. It is quite a compliment!"

They go to the door, give reverence to the mezuzah box on the doorpost, and then Othniel opens the door for Miriam to enter the house first. And he announces, "Father and Mother, Miriam and I are here!"

Othniel's younger siblings, Micah, Deborah, and Mereth, are the first to respond to their brother's announcement. They come running, eager for another visit with their future sister-in-law. There is a joyful round of hugs and kisses. Then Othniel's older brother, Onan, and his wife Hannah, also come to greet Othniel and Miriam. Othniel introduces Miriam to his brother and sister-in-law, and they warmly greet one another. And finally, Obed and Adah come into the living room, and they also affectionately greet Othniel and Miriam. It is about midday on the fifteenth of Nisan, and it is still Shabbat and Pesach.

Obed invites the family to take turns washing their hands at the nearby side table, and then to seat themselves at a large table, to partake of a meal that Adah had carefully prepared during the preceding afternoon. The younger children all want to sit by Miriam, but Othniel insists that instead Miriam should sit between himself and Onan, so that Onan and Miriam will be able to get better acquainted.

Obed gives the blessing of the meal, and also of the wine, and then a platter of unleavened bread, and bowls of cooked vegetables are passed around the table, and everyone starts eating and enjoying being together.

Adah asks Miriam, "Did you have an enjoyable Pesach meal last night with your family and the other pilgrims from Hammat?"

Miriam replies, "Yes, we had a very nice commemoration of the Passover last night, but it was overshadowed by yesterday's crucifixions."

Obed says, "That was a terrible thing to do, especially just before Pesach!"

Then Adah says, "Let us all try to put that terrible event out of our minds, so that we won't be distracted from our observance of today's religious themes."

Miriam and Othniel look at each other for a moment then, without saying anything, they nod their heads in agreement and they continue eating, and talking about anything besides the death of the prophet Yeshuah.

Miriam asks Onan to tell her about the work that he does in his father's business, and he happily describes how spices and aromatics are produced, including the extraction of balsam essence from the trimmings of balsam trees, extracting the oil and resin from lignum aloes, harvesting the bark of cassia, wood of cinnamon, syrup from rose leaves, and seeds of cummin, and also extracting sticky gum resins from balm trees, galbanum and myrrh plants. And he also told her about his travels to import exotic spices from Nabataea and Arabia.

Obed proudly listens as his oldest son explains the scope of his family's enterprise, and then he shares his expectation that Othniel will soon find his own place in the business.

Othniel and Miriam hear everything that is said about the thriving business that Obed has built, but their comments avoid the expression of any future commitments to the business. Until they are able to sort out their own priorities, they are politely interested, but non-committal regarding the family's business.

Later that afternoon, Obed takes Othniel aside and says to him, "Othniel, six months ago you told me that you expected to be ready to settle down before the end of the betrothal period, that now is only six months away. I am very sorry about what happened to your rabbi, and I know that you must be very sad about that. I would think that Yeshuah's death might have changed your timetable. Take the time that you need to grieve the loss of your teacher, and to separate yourself from your friends in the ministry that Yeshuah founded. You are my son. When you are ready, there is work for you to do here. If you and

Miriam want to have your own separate home her in Yeriko, I will help you to make that possible. Do you understand me?"

Othniel replies,"Yes, Abba. I understand what you are saying, and I am grateful for your patience with me."

Obed says, "Good. Then go and kiss that pretty future wife of yours. And talk with her about your future together."

Othniel smiles and responds, "Yes, Abba. I will do that!"

CHAPTER 43

It is the sixteenth day of Nisan, and the first day of the week. This is the day that the barley is ceremonially harvested from a particular field outside of Yerushalayim, and then it is converted into flour by the priests, and it is mixed with oil and frankincense. An omer of the special flour is waved before the altar, and a handful of it is burned on the altar. The Omer Offering marks the official beginning of the barley harvest, and seven weeks later the festival of Shavuot (also called Weeks, or Pentekoste) will occur.

Besides the ceremonial Omer Offering, there is even a greater excitement, and much confusion, in the city as rumors are spreading about some women having found Yeshuah's tomb to be empty this morning. One of those women was Zibrah's friend, Joanna. At midmorning, Joanna excitedly comes to Yehuda's and Shira's house to share what has happened with Zibrah and Eliezer, and anyone else there who will listen to her.

There is a noise of pounding upon Yehuda's door, and Shira opens it. She recognizes Joanna as someone she had met previously. Shira says, "Hello! I remember you from Eliezer's and Zibrah's wedding celebration."

Joanna says, "Thank you very much. I am Joanna of Tiberias, and a friend of Zibrah. I would like to speak with Zibrah. Is she here?"

Shira responds, "Yes, she is here. I will get her for you. Please come in."

Joanna gives due respect to the mezuzah box on the doorpost, and she steps inside the house, while Shira goes upstairs to tell Zibrah that her friend, Joanna, is here to visit with her.

A few minutes later, Zibrah, Eliezer, Miriam, and Yaaqov come down the stairs and greet Joanna warmly. And Yehuda also comes down to join them. Shira asks all of them to be seated in the great room, while she gets them some refreshments.

When all of them are seated, and with a cup of fruit juice in their hands, Joanna says, "Early this morning, I accompanied Miriam of Magdala, and Mariah the wife of Clopas to Yeshuah's tomb, so that we could complete the anointing of his body, that they had only been able to begin two days previously. We were very sad with grieving. As we were walking towards the tomb, we wondered who we could ask to roll away the heavy stone that covers the entrance to the tomb, but when we arrived there we saw that the stone had already been rolled away, and that the tomb was open. When we entered the tomb, we were shocked to discover that Yeshuah's body wasn't there. But then, suddenly two men appeared before us, wearing dazzling clothes, and they said, 'Why are you looking for someone who is living in this place for the dead? He is not here, because he has risen. Remember that he told you that he would be handed over to sinners, and be crucified, and that on the third day he would rise again.' And we did remember how he had said this to us while we all were with him in Galilee. Then the men said, 'Go quickly, and tell his disciples that he has been raised.' So we left immediately and went to all of the disciples that we could find, and we told them that Yeshuah had risen from the dead. At first, they did not believe us, but after Simeon Petros and Yohanan went to the tomb themselves and saw that it was empty, then they also believed. Later, Miriam of Magdala said that she saw Yeshuah alive, and that she had talked with him. This is very exciting! Yeshuah is alive! He has arisen, just as he said!"

Miriam speaks first, and she says, "Thank you, Joanna, for telling this news to us. I was there when Yeshuah was crucified, and I have been desperately hoping to hear this news. I do believe that Yeshuah is alive! Does Othniel know?"

Joanna replies, "No, I don't think that Othniel was with any of the other disciples this morning, so he may not have heard this news."

Miriam stands up and says, "I must go to the house where Othniel is staying with his parents, so that he will know that Yeshuah is alive again!" And she leaves.

Then Zibrah says, "Thank you, Joanna, for sharing this with us. I believe you, but I would like to see him again, myself."

While everyone was speaking, Eliezer was very quiet. Now he says, "Joanna, I would like to believe that what you said is true, but maybe there is another explanation for the tomb being empty. Who were those men that talked to you? And couldn't the being that Miriam of Magdala saw, and talked with, have been Yeshuah's ghost, and not a live Yeshuah?"

Yaaqov says, "I believe that Yeshuah is alive!"

Shira says, "Joanna, I would like to believe that he is alive again, but you didn't actually see him alive yourself."

Yehuda just shakes his head, without saying anything.

Miriam runs all the way to Obed's and Adah's house in Yerushalayim, and she goes straight to the door and knocks on it. In just a few moments, Obed opens the door, and says, "Miriam! How wonderful to see you again! Please, come in!"

She gives respect to the mezuzah box, and then she steps inside, hugs Obed, and says, "Shalom, Obed. Is Othniel here?"

"Yes, he is. Please sit down, and I will tell him that you are here."

With great anticipation, Miriam sits while Obed goes down the hallway.

Othniel quickly comes into the living room, eager to be with his betrothed wife. As soon as she sees him, she doesn't wait for him to come to her, but she jumps up and runs into his arms and, when his face is next to her own, she says, "He is risen!"

Othniel replies, "What did you say?"

"I said, he is risen! Yeshuah is alive again! This morning, Miriam of Magdala saw him, and talked with him."

"We were there when they put his dead body into the tomb."

"I know. But that tomb is empty now."

"Who told this to you?"

"Our friend, Joanna of Tiberias came to Yehuda's house, and she told us that she went to the tomb this morning with Miriam of Magdala, and Mariah the wife of Clopas, to complete the anointing of Yeshuah's body. But the tomb was empty, and two messengers appeared and gave them the news that Yeshuah had arisen, just as he said that he would. They were told to go quickly and tell the disciples. Simeon Petros and Yohanan did not believe them until they went to the tomb themselves. And Miriam of Magdala is said to have seen and talked with Yeshuah herself. He is risen! It is true!"

Othniel says, "You know, this changes everything! But I have no idea what happens next. Right now, I think that I should be with the other disciples. Do you want to come with me?"

"Yes, I will go with you. But first, let me tell my parents where we will be."

"Yes, of course." Then they hastily left that house together.

Obed heard what Miriam told his son, but he was bewildered by what she had said. He thought to himself, "Yeshuah died, and now he is alive again? How can that be?"

Miriam and Othniel stopped at Yehuda's and Shira's house long enough to tell Eliezer, Zibrah, and Yaaqov that they were going to the residence where many of the other disciples of Yeshuah were staying. Reuel and Serah, Yehuda and Shira, and all of their children also were there, with Eliezer, Zibrah, and Yaaqov. All of them were talking about Joanna's announcement. Most of them were perplexed. But Joanna was not there. Miriam thought that she must have gone to tell some of her other friends about the news.

That evening, Miriam returns to Yehuda's and Shira's house. Everyone else staying in that house had already eaten their dinner. It has been a long, exciting day for Miriam, but she still is energized. Shira offers Miriam some food, so Miriam washes her hands, and then they all sit down with her at the table while she eats her late dinner.

Eliezer asks, "Where did you go?"

Miriam says, "I went with Othniel to a house in the city on Mount Zion, which has a large enclosed room that appears to have been constructed on top of what once was the flat roof of the dwelling. Some of the disciples of Yeshuah rented that upper room for the Festival of Unleavened Bread, and many of them are staying there. They are afraid of the Romans, and also of the chief priests and other enemies of Yeshuah. They heard about the empty tomb from Miriam of Magdala and the other women who went with her to the tomb. Simeon Petros and Yohanan had gone to the tomb themselves, and they also were in the upper room when Othniel and Miriam arrived. Othniel asked what happens next, and no one was able to give him an answer. Then two more disciples arrived. They said that they had been walking towards a village about seven miles west of Yerushalayim, and that they had encountered a man on the road who talked with them about all that has happened. When they sat down at a table with him in the village and he broke bread with them, they suddenly realized that the man was Yeshuah, and then he disappeared. They said that then they ran all the way back to Yerushalayim, so that they could tell the other disciples that they had seen Yeshuah. And while everyone in the upper room was talking about that report, suddenly Yeshuah was standing there among us! Everyone became really frightened, because we thought we were seeing a ghost. But Yeshuah showed us that it was really him. He reminded the disciples that his death and resurrection had been foretold in the scriptures, and he also told them that they would be sent to proclaim repentance and forgiveness in his name throughout the world. Then, just as suddenly as he had appeared to us, he vanished from our presence! His resurrected body has some different properties than before, but it still shows the marks of his crucifixion. Yeshuah is alive!"

Eliezer says, "What an incredible story! But, since you are the one who personally experienced it, then I believe it! I am going to have to reconsider everything I ever thought about Yeshuah!"

Zibrah asks Eliezer, "Does that mean that you will be more willing to tolerate people who don't follow the same religious practices as you, or to associate with known sinners, like Yeshuah does?"

"Probably not as well as Yeshuah does, but I certainly will be less critical of others."

Yehuda says, "Eliezer, what does this mean? Only God has power to bring the dead back to life."

Eliezer replies, "I do not know, Yehuda. But, at the very least, Yeshuah is no ordinary man."

Zibrah nods her head in agreement with what her husband said.

Yaaqov says, "I think that Yeshuah is the Son of God."

Eliezer says, "Yaaqov, I don't know what that means. In our tradition, sometimes that term is used to describe angels, kings, or especially righteous persons, but not in a unique sense, because our God is one and there is no other besides Him. The Romans call their emperor a son of god and that is wrong, and it also would be wrong for us to regard Yeshuah as being of the same nature as God."

And Yehuda and Reuel nod their heads in agreement with what Eliezer said.

Zibrah looks at Eliezer and says, "Eliezer, you always like to make definitive statements about what you think our traditions say, even when those traditions fall short of explaining our present reality. It is good to hold on to tradition, but not when God is trying to introduce us to new ideas. You shouldn't be so quick to deny what people are saying, especially when the old answers don't seem to fit."

Shira says, "Well, I think that Yeshuah must be a prophet."

Reuel responds, "No prophet ever rose from the dead."

Miriam says, "Only someone sent from God could do the things that Yeshuah does."

Eliezer responds, "Yes, he is someone who has received exceptional favor from God."

Zibrah, Miriam, and Yaaqov all nod their heads in agreement with Eliezer.

Serah says, "It will be interesting to see what happens with the movement that Yeshuah started. Maybe it will become a separate sect, like the Essenes."

Miriam responds, "Yes, I agree that it will be interesting. But I also hope that Yeshuah's enemies will not try to eliminate him again."

Zibrah says, "I don't think that they would be able to kill him again."

The next morning, on the seventeenth of Nisan, Othniel is with his fellow disciples. So Miriam joins the other members of her family walking through parts of Yerushalayim. They visit the Temple, and while there they hear some people saying that Yeshuah's disciples had removed Yeshuah's body from the tomb and hidden it somewhere else, so that they could say that he had risen from the dead.

Miriam tells her family, "Yeshuah's enemies are spreading false rumors to cover up the truth that Yeshuah has risen." They leave the Temple and walk to the Ephraim Gate, on the north side of the city, and to their surprise, they see that their friend Marius is on duty there.

When Marius sees his friends from Hammat, he tells another soldier that he wishes to speak with his friends for a few minutes, and he asks him to be especially vigilant until he returns, and the soldier agrees. Then Marius steps away from the gate a few paces, and he greets Eliezer, Zibrah, Miriam, and Yaaqov warmly.

Then Mariius turns to Miriam and says, "When I saw you and Othniel the other day by the Gannath Gate, I was ashamed to be a soldier. There may be people in this world who deserve to suffer like that, probably including a few soldiers that I have known -- but not Jesus. He was truly good, kind, and gentle, and I do not understand how that terrible sentence could have been imposed on him. I have been deeply troubled by what happened, and so I talked with my commanding officer about it. Centurion Gaius also admired Jesus, but he told me that, as soldiers, we must follow orders that are given to us, or suffer the same fate ourselves. He told me that individual soldiers will not be blamed for carrying out difficult orders, but I don't feel right about that, and I am beginning to think that I shouldn't be a soldier."

Eliezer says, "So, what are your options?"

Marius responds, "Well, I cannot resign from the Roman army. I signed a contract to serve for twenty-five years, and the only way for me to not complete that contract is if I should die before the twenty-five year enlistment period ends, or if I should become disabled. If I became a deserter, the Romans would hunt me down and kill me. I wish that I could just resign from the military and come help you to farm your land, but I can't do that."

Eliezer says, "So, according to what you said, either you stay in the army, or else you die or become disabled. You can't choose to be disabled, so your real choices are: to stay in the army, or to die. Of those two bad choices, which is least favorable to you, and which is more favorable?"

Marius replies, "When you put it that way, the better of my two bad choices is for me to stay in the army, and for me to try to complete my contract. That also is what Centurion Gaius advised."

Miriam responds, "Well, there you are! It appears that you have made your decision."

"But I still feel very bad about the death of your prophet, Jesus."

Miriam says, "Yes, that was awful. But the good news is that he is alive again!"

"No, I am sorry, but that can't be true. I was told that some of Jesus' followers removed his body from the tomb so that they could say that he had risen."

"Marius, the real truth is that Yeshuah is alive! I saw him myself, yesterday!"

"What? How can that be?"

"Because God raised him from death to new life!"

"Well, I don't understand it, but that certainly is good news!"

Zibrah says, "None of us understands it, either! But, now that you know, maybe it will be easier for you to go back to your soldiering. Because Yeshuah still lives, maybe there is hope for all of us!"

Marius smiles and says, "I don't understand that either, but thank you for telling me about Jesus. I need to get back on duty. Farewell!"

Eliezer says, "Shalom, Marius! When you return to Galilee, come to Hammat for another visit with us!" Then Marius is hugged by each member of the family, before he goes back to guarding the gate.

On the fourth day of that week, the nineteenth of Nisan, Eliezer and his family walk to Obed's and Adah's house in Yerushalayim to meet with Othniel and his parents about planning the upcoming wedding celebration. Eliezer knocks at the door, and Obed opens it, saying, "Eliezer, Zibrah, Miriam, and Yaaqov, we have been expecting you! Shalom! Please, come inside."

Speaking for his family, Eliezer responds, "Shalom, Obed. Thank you very much for inviting us!" Then, Eliezer and each member of his family reverence the mezuzah, and step through the doorway.

Once inside, there are exchanges of hugs, kisses on the cheek, and personal greetings involving Obed, Adah, and Othniel, with Eliezer, Zibrah, Miriam, and Yaaqov. Then Adah says, "Please come into the great room and have a seat. Our daughters, Deborah and Mereth will bring some refreshments for all of us."

When everyone is seated, Obed says, "The purpose of this meeting is to plan Othniel's and Miriam's marriage celebration. Are we all still agreed to go forward with that celebration on the twenty-fifth day of Tishri?"

Othniel and Miriam are sitting next to each other. Smiling widely, they look at each other and they say, "Yes."

Eliezer, Zibrah, Yaaqov, and Adah also say, "Yes!"

Then Obed says, "We all are familiar with the custom of having the wedding procession begin at the groom's house, proceed to the bride's parents' house, and then having everybody process back to the groom's house for the party. And we all are aware that there are sixty-seven miles separating Hammat and Yeriko. So the traditional arrangement just isn't practical for this wedding celebration. Are we all in agreement about that?"

Everyone responds, "Yes, of course."

Obed continues, "Well, I would like to suggest an alternative arrangement. I anticipate that by the twenty-fifth of Tishri, Othniel will have his own separate home in Yeriko. I suggest that Miriam and her family regard our family villa in Yeriko as their temporary home. I suggest that you plan to arrive there after Shemini Atzerat, the Eighth Day Assembly. If you leave Yerushalayim early on the morning of the twenty-third of Tishri, you could be at our house around midday. Othniel, his brother Onan, and Onan's wife, Hannah, will be at Othniel's new house getting everything ready for the celebration. Adah and I, and our other children also will be at your temporary home in Yeriko. Then, in the evening of the twenty-fifth, Othniel, his friends, and other attendants will process from his house to your temporary home, where the rest of us all will be waiting. Any of your friends and other guests may also wait at your temporary home, beginning at about sundown. When Othniel and his party arrive, they will be greeted appropriately, everybody will partake of some refreshments. and then the full procession will depart for Othniel's and Miriam's new home, where the wedding feast will continue at least until Shabbat, on the twenty-seventh of Tishri, or, if you want, perhaps for as long as a week. How does that sound to you?"

Eliezer replies, "That sounds very nice. It is generous of you to offer us the hospitality of your home for such an occasion."

Zibrah says, "If we don't arrive at your villa in Yeriko until midday on the twenty-third, that does not give us enough time for preparing food for the party. Maybe we should delay the wedding until several days after the twenty-fifth."

Adah responds, "Please don't be concerned about food preparation. We will see to it that all of the food is prepared beforehand by caterers that we have used before in Yeriko."

Eliezer asks, "What will my share of the cost of this celebration be?"

Obed replies, "I would appreciate it if you would consider that to be part of Othniel's mohar, or bridal payment, to you."

Eliezer asks, "What about the cost of necessary furnishings, housewares, and supplies for Othniel's and Miriam's new house? I could help with that."

Obed says, "Thank you for offering, but I also want to take care of that for my son and new daughter-in-law. I am just delighted that our two families will be joined by our childrens' marriage."

Eliezer says, "Thank you very much, Obed. I am overwhelmed by your generosity!"

Obed says, "You are very welcome. The Lord has been very generous with me!"

The next two days, through the twenty-first of Nisan, the pilgrims in Yerushalayim continue their observance of the Feast of Unleavened Bread by eating matzah, and by reflecting about God's mighty acts which brought the Israelites out of their bondage and into freedom, even though today's Israelites aren't completely free presently. And for the followers of Yeshuah, this festival now has an additional meaning, although Yeshuah's appearances are very scarce, and the disciples are continuing to be afraid of the authorities. Eliezer and Zibrah invited Yehuda and Shira to Miriam's and Othniel's wedding celebration in Yeriko, to be held on the twenty-fifth day of Tishri.

CHAPTER 44

As the sun is setting, marking the beginning of the twenty-second of Nisan and Shabbat, the combined families of Yehuda, Eliezer, and Reuel gather around the table and Shira lights the two oil lamps, welcomes the Sabbath, and says the blessing.

And then Yehuda picks up the cup of wine and says,

> "And there was evening and there was morning, the sixth day. The heavens and the earth were finished, and all their multitude. And on the seventh day God finished the work that He had done, and He rested on the seventh day from all the work that He had done. So God blessed the seventh day and sanctified it because in it God rested from all the work that He had done in creation. Blessed art Thou, Lord, our God, King of the universe, Who creates the fruit of the vine. Amen."

Yehuda puts the cup back on the table. Then he raises his hands and says,

> "Blessed art Thou, Lord, our God, King of the universe, who sanctifies us with His commandments, and has been pleased with us. You have lovingly and willingly given us Your holy Shabbat as an inheritance in memory of creation, because it is the first day of our holy assemblies in memory of our exodus from Egypt, because You have chosen us and made us holy from all peoples and have willingly and lovingly given

255

us Your holy Shabbat for an inheritance. Blessed art
Thou, who sanctifies Shabbat. Amen."

Then, one at a time, each person puts their their hands into a bowl
of water, and then dries them with a towel. As each one washes their
hands, they say the blessing, "Blessed art Thou, Lord, our God, King
of the universe, who has sanctified us with His commandments and
commanded us concerning washing of hands."

After all of them had washed their hands, Yehuda removes the
linen covering from two loaves of braided challah bread, because the
Feast of Unleavened Bread had ended at sundown. He lifts up the
loaves in his two hands and says, "Blessed art Thou, Lord, our God,
King of the universe, who brings forth bread from the earth. Amen."
Then he breaks a piece off of one of the loaves for himself, and the loaf
is passed around the table, so that each person may break off their own
piece. With this, the Shabbat dinner begins. And more food is brought
to the table for the families to share.

After dinner, Yehuda says the grace-after-meals prayer:

> "Blessed art Thou, Lord, our God, King of the
> universe, Who nourishes the whole world in goodness
> with grace, kindness, and compassion. He gives bread
> to all flesh, for His mercy endures forever. And
> through His great goodness we have never lacked, nor
> will we, lack food forever, for the sake of His great
> Name. For He is God, who nourishes and sustains all,
> and does good to all, and prepares food for all His
> creatures which He created. Blessed art Thou, Lord,
> who nourishes all. Amen."

Then the families sing together:

> 'O give thanks to the LORD, for he is good;
> his steadfast love endures forever!
> Let Israel say, "His steadfast love endures forever."
> Let the house of Aaron say, "His steadfast love
> endures forever."

Let those who fear the LORD say, "His steadfast love
endures forever."
Out of my distress I called on the LORD;
the LORD answered me and set me in a broad place.
With the LORD on my side I do not fear.
What can mortals do to me?
The LORD is on my side to help me;
I shall look in triumph on those who hate me.
It is better to take refuge in the LORD than to put
confidence in mortals.
It is better to take refuge in the LORD than to put
confidence in princes.
All nations surrounded me;
in the name of the LORD I cut them off!
They surrounded me, surrounded me on every side;
in the name of the LORD I cut them off!
They surrounded me like bees;
they blazed like a fire of thorns;
in the name of the LORD I cut them off!
I was pushed hard, so that I was falling,
but the LORD helped me.
The LORD is my strength and my might;
he has become my salvation.
There are glad songs of victory in the tents of the
righteous:
"The right hand of the LORD does valiantly;
the right hand of the LORD is exalted;
the right hand of the LORD does valiantly."
I shall not die, but I shall live,
and recount the deeds of the LORD.
The LORD has punished me severely,
but he did not give me over to death.
Open to me the gates of righteousness,
that I may enter through them and give thanks to
the LORD.
This is the gate of the LORD;
the righteous shall enter through it.

I thank you that you have answered me and have
become my salvation.
The stone that the builders rejected has become the
chief cornerstone.
This is the LORD's doing; it is marvelous in our eyes.
This is the day that the LORD has made;
let us rejoice and be glad in it.
Save us, we beseech you, O LORD!
O LORD, we beseech you, give us success!
Blessed is the one who comes in the name of the
LORD.
We bless you from the house of the LORD.
The LORD is God, and he has given us light.
Bind the festal procession with branches,
up to the horns of the altar.
You are my God, and I will give thanks to you;
you are my God, I will extol you.
O give thanks to the LORD, for he is good,
for his steadfast love endures forever.'

[Psalm 118:1-29 NRSV]

After the singing, the combined families spend another hour
talking and listening to each other, before blowing out all but the two
Shabbat oil lamps and going to their own beds for sleep.

The following morning, the families share a light breakfast of fresh
fruit and bread, and then they spend some time discussing portions of
the Torah together, remembering the Creation of the heavens and the
earth, God's loving provision of a covenant for His chosen people, and
the exodus from slavery in Egypt to freedom. And they also talk about
God's deliverance of His people from exile in Babylonia.

At midmorning, Othniel arrives for a visit to Yehuda's and Shira's
house, and he brings with him a copy of the Scroll of Yishayahu
[Isaiah]. Miriam is delighted to see her betrothed husband again. It
has been six days since the last time she was with him, on the day that
Yeshuah rose from the dead. And the other members of the combined

families also are pleased to see Othniel again. They are all gathered together in the great room.

Othniel says to Miriam, "Do you remember when we were wondering why Yeshuah was so adamant that the scriptures pointed to his death, and about what his suffering accomplished?"

Miriam replies, "Yes, I do. We talked about that during the evening following Yeshuah's death. Have you figured out the answers to those questions?"

"I think that I may have realized something that directly relates to our puzzlement. It starts with some portions of the Scroll of Yishayahu, which seem to have been written to provide encouragement to the people of Israel during the final years of their Exile in Babylonia. The prophets had proclaimed that Israel was exiled for idolatry, unfaithfulness, and disobedience. Israel in exile was like when Adam and Eve were expelled from the Garden of Eden. But God did not forget the covenant that He made with Abraham and his descendents. God called Israel to be the people through whom He would undo the sin of Adam, and thereby redeem all of creation. But how would God accomplish those things? The clues to the solution may be in the four 'Servant Songs' of Yishayahu."

Eliezer says, "Our family discussed some of those passages three months ago. In the poem, the servant is identified as Israel, who was chosen by God to bring justice and light to the nations." [Isaiah:42:1-4, and 49:1-6]

Othniel responds, "Yes, that is exactly what the first two servant songs say. But there is more. The third song describes the servant's humiliating suffering and his vindication, and the fourth song explains that the servant's suffering unto death was borne on behalf of others" [Isaiah 52:13-15, and 53:1-12]

Eliezer says, "Rabbi Yitzhak has taught us that, through many centuries, Israel has suffered greatly under the oppression of pagans, and that it is our fate to continue suffering until the Maschiah appears."

Othniel replies, "But Israel's suffering doesn't fit Yishayahu's description: it was not unto death, nor was it experienced on behalf of others. It probably was written almost 600 years ago, but it describes exactly what Miriam and I observed on the day that Yeshuah died. Let me read Yishayahu's third and fourth servant songs to you."

Othniel opens the Scroll and reads,

> "The Lord God has given me the tongue of a teacher,
> that I may know how to sustain the weary with a word.
> Morning by morning he wakens-- wakens my ear to
> listen as those who are taught.
> The Lord God has opened my ear, and I was not
> rebellious, I did not turn backward.
> I gave my back to those who struck me, and my
> cheeks to those who pulled out the beard;
> I did not hide my face from insult and spitting.
> The Lord God helps me; therefore I have not been
> disgraced;
> therefore I have set my face like flint, and I know that
> I shall not be put to shame;
> he who vindicates me is near. Who will contend with
> me? Let us stand up together.
> Who are my adversaries? Let them confront me.
> It is the Lord God who helps me; who will declare
> me guilty?
> All of them will wear out like a garment; the moth
> will eat them up"
>
> [Isaiah 50:4-9 NRSV]

Then, Othniel turns to another portion, and he continues reading:

> "See, my servant shall prosper;
> he shall be exalted and lifted up, and shall be very high.
> Just as there were many who were astonished at him
> --so marred was his appearance, beyond human
> semblance, and his form beyond that of mortals-- so
> he shall startle many nations;
> kings shall shut their mouths because of him;
> for that which had not been told them they shall see,
> and that which they had not heard they shall
> contemplate."
>
> [Isaiah 52:13-15 NRSV]

"Who has believed what we have heard?

And to whom has the arm of the LORD been revealed?

For he grew up before him like a young plant, and like a root out of dry ground;

he had no form or majesty that we should look at him, nothing in his appearance that we should desire him.

He was despised and rejected by others; a man of suffering and acquainted with infirmity;

and as one from whom others hide their faces he was despised, and we held him of no account.

Surely he has borne our infirmities and carried our diseases;

yet we accounted him stricken, struck down by God, and afflicted.

But he was wounded for our transgressions, crushed for our iniquities;

upon him was the punishment that made us whole, and by his bruises we are healed.

All we like sheep have gone astray; we have all turned to our own way,

and the LORD has laid on him the iniquity of us all.

He was oppressed, and he was afflicted, yet he did not open his mouth;

like a lamb that is led to the slaughter, and like a sheep that before its shearers is silent,

so he did not open his mouth.

By a perversion of justice he was taken away. Who could have imagined his future?

For he was cut off from the land of the living, stricken for the transgression of my people.

They made his grave with the wicked and his tomb with the rich,

although he had done no violence, and there was no deceit in his mouth.

Yet it was the will of the LORD to crush him with pain.

When you make his life an offering for sin,

he shall see his offspring, and shall prolong his days;
through him the will of the LORD shall prosper.
Out of his anguish he shall see light; he shall find
satisfaction through his knowledge.
The righteous one, my servant, shall make many
righteous, and he shall bear their iniquities.
Therefore I will allot him a portion with the great,
and he shall divide the spoil with the strong;
because he poured out himself to death, and was
numbered with the transgressors;
yet he bore the sin of many, and made intercession for
the transgressors."

[Isaiah 53:1-12 NRSV]

Eliezer says, "But we believe that Yishayahu's prophecy concerns Israel as a whole, and not just a single individual. Why would you think that it pertains to Yeshuah?"

Othniel responds, "Eliezer, if you read the entire Scroll of Yishayahu, it is evident that the people of Israel as a whole are not capable of undoing the sin of Adam. Indeed, Yishayahu repeatedly points out that Israel has failed in its vocation of covenant faithfulness, and of being the nation through whom God's light would shine to the ends of the earth, and God's justice would spread. Therefore, the servant is an individual who must stand in Israel's place, doing the redemptive work of rescuing humanity on behalf of the Israel that had failed, through his own humiliating, sacrificial death. Through the suffering servant, God himself would do what needed to be done. Yeshuah is the servant, and he died for all of humanity's sins."

Miriam says, "Oh! Now I understand the prophecy of the Suffering Servant, and I can see why Yeshuah could have believed that he had to die. But how did he know that he would rise on the third day?"

Othniel replies, "There are numerous scriptures regarding resurrection, including several passages in Yishayahu [Isaiah 25:6-9, 26:19, 65:17-25, and 66:22-23], Yechezkel's prophecy of the valley of dry bones [Ezekiel 37], and also in Daniyel [Daniel 12:1-3], but all of those appear to pertain to Olam Ha-Ba, the 'World to Come'. However, I think that Yeshuah may have been especially mindful of:

'For you do not give me up to Sheol,
or let your faithful one see the Pit.'

[Psalm 16:10 NRSV]

'Come, let us return to the LORD;
for it is he who has torn, and he will heal us;
he has struck down, and he will bind us up.
After two days he will revive us;
on the third day he will raise us up,
that we may live before him.'"

[Hosea 6:1-2 NRSV]

Miriam asks, "Besides that verse in Hosea, what is the significance of the third day in scripture?"

Othniel replies, "Miriam, in scripture, the third day is often associated with special acts of divine intervention. The dry land was separated from the waters and the earth brought forth vegetation on the third day of creation, the Pharaoh's cupbearer was restored to his position on the third day after Joseph prophesied it, God revealed himself at Mount Sinai on the third day after the people arrived there, Joshua led the people across the Jordan River on the third day after they had arrived by its banks, Esther boldly went before the king on behalf of her people on the third day of a fast, and Jonah prayed to the Lord from the belly of the fish on the third day. And Yeshuah believed that God would raise him from the dead on the third day. It all fits together!"

Then Eliezer says, "The followers of Yeshuah like to proclaim that Yeshuah is the Maschiah, but our messianic prophecies do not mention the death of Maschiah, instead they speak of his victory over God's enemies. Yeshuah has no military or political power, and he was executed by the Romans. So, how could he have been the Maschiah?"

Othniel replied, "I think that we all have been looking for the wrong kind of Maschiah. Yeshuah defeated the powers of sin and death through his death on the cross, and his resurrection. He is alive today!

And someday, he will be acknowledged as ruler over all nations. But his final victory will not be won by military or political power, it will be won by God's love. I don't think that any of us can fully understand it yet, but Yeshuah's death and resurrection are essential elements of God's plan to redeem *all* of His creation."

"That all sounds very nice, but it is not how real victories are won!"

"I suspect that people in the times of Noah, Avraham, Moshe, Eliyahu, Yirmiyahu, and Yisayahu also thought that they were unrealistic about what they were trying to accomplish."

And Eliezer, Reuel, Yehuda, Zibrah, Serah, Shira, and Miriam all nod their heads in agreement with the last thing that Othniel had said, but with confusion about some or all of the other things that he had said.

Then Miriam says, "Othniel, my family and I will be starting our journey back to our home in Hammat tomorrow morning, and I don't know when the next time will be for you and me to be together. So, let us take a walk together while we are able to do so."

Othniel says, "Good idea! Let's go now. And then I need to have a visit with my family, before they return to Yeriko tomorrow."

Then Eliezer says, "Won't you also be going back to Yeriko tomorrow?"

Othniel replies, "No, I think that I will remain here in Yerushalayim with the other disciples for a while longer." Then Othniel and Miriam left Yehuda's and Shira's house for a stroll together.

CHAPTER 45

On the twenty-third day of Nisan, that also is the first day of the week, Eliezer and Reuel and their families rejoined their neighbors from Hammat to begin their long walk together back to their own homes. When they returned to Hammat four days later, they were tired, but eager to re-establish their daily routines in their own homes. They had been away twenty-five days and there was much work waiting for them to do. Eliezer and his family immediately went to work cleaning their house, washing clothes, and pulling weeds out of their garden.

The following day, while the other members of her family were still working to reclaim their home from nature, Zibrah went to Tiberias to buy food at the market, and also to check the status of her former home and her fishing boats. When she got there, she wasn't surprised to discover that her house and boats needed maintenance. She thought, *Next week, I will get Eliezer to spend a few days with me in Tiberias, to help me to get my things back in order, and also so we can enjoy some privacy together. It has been a long time since the last time that happened! Now that Assurbani has been taken care of, we shouldn't have to worry about Miriam and Yaaqov spending a few days without us.*

When she returned to Hammat, she shared her idea with the family, and all of them were excited about the idea.

The family enjoyed spending Shabbat together and then, on the last day of Nisan, Eliezer and Zibrah went to Tiberias to perform some essential maintenance on Zibrah's house, her fishing boats, and also on their relationship with each other. When they weren't working, sleeping, or eating, they frolicked with one another in every room of her house, like people half their age.

Meanwhile, Miriam and Yaaqov devoted their attention to preparing the family's vegetable garden and wheat field for the spring and early-summer harvest.

As each of them was working at their separate tasks, they unknowingly shared the same thought: *what a wondrous season this is, in which the plants and all living things seem to revel in fresh hope for exciting and fruitful future possibilities! God is great, and God is good! Thanks be to God for all of His blessings!*

Yaaqov is looking forward to his thirteenth birthday, that now is only about two months away, when he will begin assuming some new responsibilities in his personal and community life.

Miriam is looking forward to her wedding celebration, that now is less than six months away, and she tries to imagine what it will be like to live intimately with Othniel, and to accommodate herself to new circumstances and new experiences.

Zibrah is enjoying the realization of how blessed she is, to be young enough to enjoy the best experiences of life, old enough to appreciate them, a wonderful man to share life with, and a renewed expectation that her best years are still in her future.

Eliezer is proud of the thoughtful, independent young adults that his children are becoming, and he also is happy to have gotten this second opportunity in his life to experience marital joy with his beloved, insightful, and surprising wife, Zibrah. He is looking forward to growing old together with her.

After spending five nights apart from Miriam and Yaaqov, there is a happy homecoming on the fifth day of Iyyar when Eliezer and Zibrah return to their home in Hammat. After rounds of hugs and kisses between both of the parents with their children, Yaaqov says, "Abba, Miriam and I want you to see the good work that we did in the terraced vegetable garden and wheat field while you and Zibrah were away. Will you go with us, so that we may show you?"

Eliezer replies, "Of course I want to see it. Let's go."

So they all went outside, and up the hill to the vegetable garden. Eliezer saw that the plants all looked healthy, and that they were free of weeds and well-watered.

Eliezer says, "Yaaqov and Miriam, I compliment you for the thoroughness of the work that you did. I don't think that our garden has ever looked this well before, at the beginning of the dry season! Thank you for doing such a great job!"

Yaaqov and Miriam give each other congratulatory hugs, and then they respond to Eliezer's compliment by saying, "You are very welcome!"

Then they walk farther up the hill to the wheat field, and Eliezer can see that the stems of new wheat plants have begun to appear, but they haven't yet developed any bearded heads containing kernels. Eliezer says, "Yaaqov, we need to check this field every day. But it probably will be another week or two before we will be able to harvest the first-fruits for our offering. But our field does look good. Thanks for taking care of it while I was gone."

Yaaqov says, "Yes, I will continue to check it every day."

As the family is walking back down the hill toward their home, Miriam asks, "Zibrah, tell us about the work that you and Abba did in Tiberias during this week."

Zibrah replies, "While your father and I were in Tiberias, I gave my house a thorough cleaning, and your father made extensive repairs to the two fishing boats that I own, and he also did some minor repairs to my house. So, we kept ourselves pretty busy."

Eliezer says, "It looks to me like all of us were very busy this week!."

Miriam says, "Well, in just a few hours we will be welcoming Shabbat together, and we still haven't done all of the necessary preparations for our Shabbat meals."

Zibrah responds, "You are correct, Miriam! But I am sure that, if we all work together, we will get everything done in time."

As usual, Miriam and Zibrah were both right. After they completed all of their preparations, the family's Shabbat was memorable, inspiring, and relaxing.

Less than a week later, in the afternoon of the eleventh of Iyyar, Othniel walks up the path to the door of Eliezer's family home, and he knocks on it. Yaaqov opens the door to see who is there, and when he sees that it is his future brother-in-law, he shouts, "Othniel!" And he hugs him affectionately.

Othniel asks, "Yaaqov, it also is good for me to see you again! May I please come into your home? I just arrived here from Yerusahalayim, and I am a tired traveler in need of some hospitality."

Yaaqov replies, "Of course you may enter. You always are welcome here!"

Othniel venerates the mezuzah box on the doorpost, and then he steps across the threshold while carrying Yaaqov with his left arm. And Yaaqov laughs with pleasure.

Miriam and Zibrah heard the sounds of Othniel's arrival, and they come into the courtyard excitedly.

Miriam and Othniel greet each other affectionately. And then Zibrah and Othniel hug each other, each one kissing the other on the cheek.

Miriam invites Othniel to sit with her on two adjacent chairs, and Zibrah gets him a cup of cold water.

Then Miriam says, "I thought that you were in Yerushalayim with Yeshuah and your fellow disciples. Is anything wrong?"

Othniel responds, "No, nothing bad happened after you and your family left Yerushalayim to return to your home. All of the disciples have been waiting together in that upper room for another of Yeshuah's appearances, but it has been more than two weeks since we saw him last. Simeon Petros, both of Zebedee's sons, Tom, Nathanael, and two others all were feeling restless from being cooped-up together in that upper room, and they wanted to return to Galilee for a fishing outing. So I decided to tag along with them, so that I could be with you."

Just then, Eliezer walks into the courtyard and says, "And all of us are glad that you did! I was up in my wheat field, marking the plants that I expect will be the first to ripen. Then, as I was walking back to the house, I heard a commotion. I am delighted to find that your arrival is its cause! How long can you stay with us?"

"I am planning to join Simeon Petros, Yohanan, and the others at midmorning on the first day of the week, to return with them to Yerushalayim. May I stay here until then?"

Without any hesitation, Eliezer and Zibrah both say, "Yes! You are always welcome here!"

Miriam is smiling.

Eliezer asks, "Othniel, have you decided about your future plans yet? Your father says that you are planning to work in his family business, and to live in Yeriko after the wedding celebration. Is that right?"

Othniel replies, "Yes, I did tell him that, and I meant it when I said it. I want you to know that I always will do what Miriam and I decide will be best for the both of us."

"You have personally invested yourself in Yeshuah's ministry, and in being his disciple. Are you prepared to give all of that up when you and Miriam are married?"

"I thought that the ministry that Yeshuah started would develop into a separate religious movement within our Jewish tradition, but then Yeshuah was killed, and it seemed like everything had ended. Then, when Yeshuah rose from the dead, I thought that everything might pick back up where it was before his death. However, since then, Yeshuah has only been with us very briefly, and right now absolutely nothing seems to be happening. I expect to keep in touch with Yeshuah and my fellow disciples for a few additional weeks, and then I will return to working in my father's business. I won't give up the new perspectives that I learned from Yeshuah, because I don't think that any of them are incompatible with the Jewish traditions that I grew up with."

Eliezer turns to Miriam and asks, "How does all of this sound to you, Miriam? Will you be happy living in Yeriko, and being married to a man in the aromatic oils and spices business?"

Miriam replies, "Abba, I believe that I will be happy with Othniel, wherever we may be living, and in whatever occupation he works. I still think that Othniel and I were made for each other, and I am continuing to trust in God's plan for all of us."

Zibrah says, "Well said, Miriam! I believe in you, and I also believe in Othniel. And I trust that, with God's help, both of you will make choices together that will be right for you both."

After dinner, Miriam and Othniel take a stroll down to the lakeshore, and they talk about their individual preferences concerning some of the future choices that they anticipate making. Among other things, they talk about priorities, living arrangements, money decisions, children, and getting along with relatives. As in their previous conversations, they find that their individual ideas concerning each topic are compatible.

When they return from their walk, Zibrah says, "Othniel, I made a bed for you to sleep on in the storeroom. Let me show you." And she showed him the large, interior, shared-use room.

Then Zibrah points at a large piece of pottery on the floor in that room, and she says, "You may use that chamber pot when you need it."

Othniel says, "Thank you, Zibrah. You are very thoughtful."

Zibrah responds, "You are welcome, Othniel. You and Yaaqov are both like sons to me!"

Othniel returns to the courtyard and sits down at the table next to Miriam.

Miriam asks him, "When you return to Yerushalayim with your friends, what will you find there?"

Othniel replies, "I don't know. Maybe Yeshuah will appear again, and tell us what he is expecting us to do next."

"And if he does, what do you think that will be?"

"I am afraid that he will tell us that he is sending us out into the world to proclaim repentance and forgiveness in his name."

"Why does that make you feel afraid?"

"I am afraid because I don't believe that I am ready to be sent out to proclaim anything."

Miriam asks, "Then why are you planning to go back to Yerushalayim?"

Othniel replies, "Because I love Yeshuah, and I desperately want to see him again."

"Then, despite your fear, you must return to Yerushalayim."

"But what will I do, or say, if he sends me out?"

Miriam says, "I don't think that you should worry about that. I remember you telling me about when Yeshuah separated all of his disciples into pairs and sent you all out to preach and heal just like he does. As I recall, after that experience, you were very excited about your success."

Othniel says, "I don't know. That was a very limited mission, and we felt supported, almost as if he had gone along with us."

"I don't see how being sent out now would be much different from the way it was back then."

"It felt much different before, when Yeshuah was with us all of the time. But during the past couple of weeks, being huddled together in the upper room without Yeshuah has really underscored our feelings of helplessness apart from him. I do want to see Yeshuah again, but I don't want him to leave us again."

Miriam says, "So, you really want to see Yeshuah again, but you would prefer having everything go back to the way it was before he was crucified. He has risen from the dead but, since then, he hasn't been with all of you very much, and you are afraid that when he does come back again he will just send you all away on some far-flung mission without him. Is that about it?"

"Yes, I think that you have summarized the situation perfectly. As much as I want to see Yeshuah again, I don't know what I will say or do when he tells me he wants to send me out. I don't want to disappoint him, but I don't think that I can do what he expects."

"Othniel, when that time comes, I believe that you will know how to respond." And she touches his hand, and kisses his face.

Othniel says, "Thank you for listening. Good night." And he kisses her cheek, and then he goes to the bed that Zibrah provided for him in the storeroom.

During the following afternoon, Eliezer, his family, and Othniel are gathered together around the table in the courtyard. They have been talking about recent events concerning Yeshuah.

Eliezer says to Othniel, "Our pharisaic traditions use the term 'resurrection' to refer to a new type of bodily existence for the righteous dead in the World to Come, after the Maschiah has come and God has judged both the living and the dead at the end of the age. I know that there are a few instances in our prophetic scriptures where God used the prophets Eliyahu [Elijah] or Elisha to raise certain people back to life after they had died. But the people whose lives had been restored all died again later. I presume that the man from Bethany that Yeshuah raised from the dead also will die again someday. So, it seems to me that resurrection is not the same thing as resuscitating a dead body to the same sort of life that it had before, but rather a transformation into a new kind of physical existence. Therefore, strictly speaking, the term 'resurrection' should not be used except in reference to the World to Come. I have heard you refer to Yeshuah's having being raised from death to life as resurrection, but the end of the age has not yet come. Shouldn't Yeshuah's followers be using a different term for what happened to him?"

Othniel replies, "Eliezer, you are correct about the need for a distinction between when the souls of the righteous dead are re-embodied with new bodies for the World to Come, and when Eliyahu raised the son of the widow from Zarephath from the dead [1 Kings17:17-22], or Elisha raised the son of the Shunammite woman from the dead [2 Kings 4:32-35], or even when Yeshuah raised Elazar of Bethany from the dead. But we believe that Yeshuah has been resurrected, and that his resurrected body is itself the beginning of God's new creation which will find its fulfillment at the end of the age, when we also will be transformed!"

"What are you saying?"

"I am saying that, after his resurrection, Yeshuah's body appeared to be quite normal in many ways, but we also observed that it was able to come and go through locked doors, and it wasn't always recognized. His body was transformed. We believe that he never will die again. Yeshuah already is alive forevermore!"

Zibrah says, "Yes, I believe that what you said is true." And Miriam and Yaaqov nod in agreement with her.

Eliezer responds, "But that isn't what our sages and scholars expected!"

And Zibrah says, "Exactly!"

Miriam adds, "When we receive our resurrected bodies, we won't return to living in the same ways as we did previously. We will be changed. Yeshuah has already conquered death. I can't wait to find out what will happen next!"

Eliezer thought about Othniel's explanation, plus the responses to it by the other members of his family, but he is not convinced that they could be true. He is still troubled about the claims of resurrection.

Othniel, Miriam, and her family had an enjoyable Shabbat together on the thirteenth of Iyyar. Eliezer kept checking on the status of his growing wheat stems, and on the evening of the fourteenth, he announced that his first-fruits of wheat would finally be ready to be harvested around midday. But at midmorning, Simeon Petros, Yohanan ben Zebedee, and the other five fishing buddies came for Othniel, to have him accompany them back to Yerushalayim.

Eliezer, Zibrah, Miriam, and Othniel lined-up outside the courtyard door to give hugs and kisses to Othniel and to send him on his way. Eliezer says, "Thank you for coming to spend a few days with us. We always enjoy being with you. And we are looking forward to seeing you again in about two and one-half weeks, after our arrival in Yerushalayim for Shavuot."

Othniel replies to Eliezer, "Yes, I will visit with all of you again at Yehuda's and Shira's house!"

Zibrah says, "Don't forget, Othniel, we believe in you!"

Miriam whispers to her betrothed, "Don't worry about anything, my beloved. Our future together will be wonderful!"

And Yaaqov punches Othniel playfully, saying, "Let's you and me have some more fun the next time we are together!"

And, just as they are waving goodbye to Othniel and his companions, Marius comes walking up the path toward Eliezer's house. Othniel and Marius greet each other enthusiastically, and the other disciples and Marius exchange polite, but awkward, greetings as they recognize one another.

Eliezer calls to his friend, "Marius, what an unexpected pleasure to have you visiting with us again! What brings you here?"

Marius replies, "Thank you, Eliezer! I noticed that the fields around Capernaum are ready to be harvested again, and I remembered helping you at this same time last year. Can you use my help again today?"

"Marius, you are just in time! Yaaqov and I were just about to get started when Othniel had to leave with his friends. But, let's all go inside, and have something to eat before we begin working."

"Thank you. That sounds great!" Then, in turn, Marius hugs Eliezer, Zibrah, Miriam, and Yaaqov, saying "Hello" or "Shalom" to each of them.

After enjoying a snack together, Marius says to Eliezer, "How can I help you today?"

Eliezer responds by speaking to all of them, "How about if Marius and I harvest the wheat, while Miriam and Yaaqov harvest the ripe vegetables, and do weeding and watering in the garden. And Zibrah will clean-up the kitchen and dining area." Everyone agrees with those assignments.

Eliezer goes to his shed and gets two sickles, and then he and Marius go to work in the wheat field, carefully separating the wheat plants that Eliezer had marked as first to ripen from those that are unmarked. Working side-by-side, Eliezer and Marius are cutting the wheat, gathering and binding the sheaves, and stacking them. There are separate piles for the early-ripened wheat that will become Eliezer's first-fruits offering, and for the wheat that ripened later, that will be consumed by the family.

As they are working, Marius wants to talk with Eliezer about what had happened in Jerusalem. He still feels badly about Jesus' crucifixion.

Marius says, "I was told that Pontius Pilate tried to release Jesus, but that your Jewish priests stirred up the crowd to demand that he be crucified. Why were they so insistent that Jesus should be killed?"

Eliezer replies, "Marius, the religious authorities in Yerushalayim found Yeshuah guilty of a very serious religious offense, the crime of blasphemy, which means insulting or speaking irreverently about God or sacred things. According to Jewish laws, blasphemy is punishable by death."

Marius says, "Since I arrived in Judaea, I have gotten to know Jesus, and I do not believe that he could possibly be guilty of a religious offense that is so terrible as to require a sentence of death. Was he found guilty at a proper trial, with witnesses and evidence presented?"

Eliezer answers, "I was told that there was some kind of legal proceeding, but that a proper trial was not held."

"Then his execution truly was a huge miscarriage of justice."

"Yes, I think that most people do believe that to be the case. And most people also recognize that politics also was involved: our leaders were afraid of more harsh Roman oppression if Yeshuah's movement became too popular."

Marius says, "Let me tell you something. I know that you and your countrymen regard me as a pagan, and that is what I am. However, I do recognize truth when I see it. I have observed that, in every culture, most of the people that present themselves as religious authorities very often do not really know about the things they say. Each one seems to have his own interpretation of sacred teachings, and each one also feels threatened by anyone whose ideas are different from his own. But your Jesus is an authentic spiritual guide. His wisdom and his power are not new things, they are very old and they are deep. Your priests could not tolerate his existence because his teachings and actions challenged their own authority, so they tried to get rid of him. I don't know how all of this will ultimately turn out, but I believe that the movement founded by Jesus will prevail, unless its leaders themselves become like all of the other exclusive religious authorities."

Eliezer thinks carefully about what Marius said, and after being very quiet for a few moments, he says, "Marius, I believe that your observations and conclusions are correct. Those of us who care deeply about what we believe to be true are often very quick to reject other ideas. We convince ourselves that our core beliefs are absolute truths, and we close our minds to considering other possibilities. And when we encounter someone like Yeshuah, we really don't know what to think about him, and this becomes very disturbing for us. We should be thankful for having our minds opened to new ways of thinking, but that never is our first reaction."

Marius responds, "Yes, that is it! Except for the part where you said 'someone like Yeshuah.' Quite simply, it seems to me that there aren't any others like him. He really is what he seems to be!"

Eliezer says, "You probably are right about that, too. But I haven't figured out what he is yet. Maybe I never will."

"Me neither. But I don't think that I have to figure him out. I just need to open myself to the truths that he wants to reveal. Perhaps that is the good thing about being a pagan!"

Eliezer laughs. And then he and Marius carry the bundles of cut grain into the storeroom of the house, carefully setting aside the portion that would be brought to Yerushalayim as the first-fruits offering.

Zibrah and Miriam are making Miriam's wedding clothes. They also are making a decorative basket to hold Eliezer's first fruits offering.

CHAPTER 46

Nineteen days later, it is the fourth day of the late-spring month of Sivan, and Eliezer, his family, and some other pilgrims from Hammat arrive together in Yerushalayim for Shavuot, that is only two days away. Shavuot (also called Weeks, or Pentekoste) is a many-faceted, one-day festival that commemorates the giving of the Torah to the Israelites, and a renewal of the covenant that God made with Noah, and because of those significant events, some Jews refer to Shavuot as the "Feast of Revelation." But Shavuot also is a celebration of the presentation of first fruits offerings of grapes & wine, figs, pomegranates, olives & oil, honey, barley, and wheat. Except for the ceremonial offering of a special omer of barley on the day after Pesach, individual offerings of agricultural produce can be made only on, or after, Shavuot.

Walking through Yerushalayim, Eliezer notices that there aren't as many pilgrims in the city as he remembered that there were at Pesach, but there still are many pilgrims and, from the sounds of the diverse languages that he is hearing, some of them have come to Yerushalayim from distant lands.

Eliezer, Zibrah, Miriam, and Yaaqov walk to the Yerusahalayim cousin's house, where they are greeted warmly by Yehuda.

Yehuda says, "Shalom, cousin!" as he hugs Eliezer, and Eliezer responds with "Shalom, Yehuda! Thank you very much for allowing us to stay at your home again."

"How else am I going to find out what is going on in Galilee?"

Eliezer says, "Spring is in full bloom, our vegetable garden is ahead of last year at this time, and fishing operations on Lake Kinneret are back in full swing. Zibrah and I spent five days in Tiberias away from our children. And we had a nice visit from Othniel about three weeks ago. What has been happening here in Yerushalayim?"

Yehuda replies, "The chief priests are still trying to get the people to believe that Yeshuah's disciples stole the body from the tomb, and some people do believe that. But there also have been additional reports circulating about people who claim to have seen Yeshush alive."

Yehuda also greets Zibrah, Miriam, and Yaaqov with hugs and kisses on their cheeks.

And then Shira comes out of another room and she also welcomes these members of her extended family. While Yehuda and Eliezer are continuing their conversation about recent events, Shira says, "Zibrah, Miriam, and Yaaqov, perhaps you might want to go upstairs to put your belongings down, and also to freshen up before our Shabbat eve dinner."

Zibrah responds, "Thank you, Shira. Is there anything that we can do to help you with dinner preparations, or anything else that you need to have done?"

Shira laughs and says, "No, everything is ready. We have been looking forward to this visit with you and, for once, Yehuda actually helped me to set the table and to fix the meal!"

Zibrah says, "Good for both of you!"

About two hours later, just as the sun is setting, Yehuda, Shira, Eliezer, Zibrah, and their children all gather around the table. Shira lights the two oil lamps, welcomes the Sabbath, and says the blessing.

And then Yehuda picks up the cup of wine and says the Shabbat blessing for wine. Then he puts the cup back on the table, and he says the prayer of thanksgiving for Shabbat.

Each person, in turn, washes their hands in the bowl of water while saying the blessing for handwashing, and then dries their hands with the towel.

Finally, Yehuda uncovers the two challah loaves, and he lifts them up and says the blessing for food. One of the loaves is passed around the table, and each person breaks off a piece for himself or herself. And pots containing stew and cooked vegetables are uncovered and passed around the table for each person to ladle servings onto their individual plates. Their Shabbat dinner is underway! The family eats, and talks, and laughs, enjoying this lovely, blessed time together.

After dinner, Yehuda says the grace-after-meals prayer.

Then the combined families sing together:

"Praise the LORD, all you nations!
Extol him, all you peoples!
For great is his steadfast love toward us,
and the faithfulness of the LORD endures forever.
Praise the LORD!"

[Psalm 117:1-2 NRSV]

After singing the psalm, the families gather in the great room while Yehuda and Eliezer take turns reading portions from Devarim [Deuteronomy 5 & 6] concerning the Lord's provision of the Ten Living Words, His Commandments.

After listening to the long reading from the Torah, Yehuda's and Eliezer's families go to their beds for sleep.

In the morning, after eating a light breakfast, the families spent some time talking about the Israelites' journey through the wilderness following their exodus from Egypt, covenant faithfulness, covenant renewal, and problems with living under Roman domination.

At midmorning, Othniel arrives for another visit to Yehuda's and Shira's house. It has been almost three weeks since the last time Othniel and Miriam had talked with each other. Of course, the other gathered members of Eliezer's and Yehuda's families also are eager to visit with Othniel. They all are gathered together in the great room.

Yehuda invites Othniel to sit next to Miriam in the gathering, And Shira hands him a cup of pomegranate juice.

Miriam asks, "How are you, Othniel? What have you been doing since the last time I saw you?"

Othniel replies, "The last time that we visited was at your family house in Hammat, when several of the other disciples decided to return to Galilee for a fishing outing. It turns out that while they were fishing at Lake Kinneret, Yeshuah found them, and he told them that he still had work for them to do. After they dropped-by to get me, we returned to Yerushalayim. Later that week, Yeshuah made another appearance with us in the upper room, and he talked with us about the kingdom of God. Then nine days ago, he came to us again. He reminded us us that the scriptures had foretold that the Maschiah would suffer, and that he would rise from the dead on the third day, and that repentance and forgiveness is to be proclaimed in his name to all nations, beginning from Yerushalayim. He called us his witnesses, and he told us to stay in the city until the promised Holy Spirit comes upon us with power. He led all of us outside, up the Mount of Olives and on to Bethany. Then he lifted up his hands and blessed us, and he was lifted up to heaven."

Eliezer is startled by Othniel's report. He says, "Are you certain that really happened?"

Othniel responds, "Yes, I am. And this event also was witnessed by a very large number of people. We all saw it."

Yaaqov asks, "So, has Yeshuah gone away, and is he never going to be with us again?"

Othniel replies, "Yes, he has gone to heaven, but the scriptures say that he will return at the end of the age, when the kingdom of God will come in all of its fullness. But, until then, the Holy Spirit will come and stay with each believer, guiding us and helping us."

Yehuda asks, "What is the Holy Spirit? I don't remember hearing about that in synagogue."

Othniel explained, "The rabbis use the term 'Ruach ha-Kodesh' to refer to what our scriptures call the Spirit of the Lord. God pours out His own Spirit upon all whom He has chosen to carry out His will, or to speak on His behalf. The Holy Spirit rested upon the prophets, but after the death of the last of the prophets the Holy Spirit was not continually present and did not rest upon any individual for a long period of time. The prophet Yehoel [Joel] foretold that, in the days of the Maschiah, the Holy Spirit would be poured out upon all mankind. Yeshuah told us to wait in Yerushalayim until the Holy Spirit comes."

Yaaqov says, "That sounds exciting! When will that happen?"

Othniel replies, "We don't know when, but nine days ago, Yeshuah told us that it wouldn't be too many days from the last time we saw him."

Eliezer says, "I would think that if Yeshuah really is the Maschiah, then he would not have gone away. The Maschiah is supposed to put everything back to the way God intended them to be in the first place."

Othniel responds, "Yes, you are correct. Yeshuah already did take care of the most important part, by redeeming humanity from the sin of Adam through his own suffering. And he will take care of everything else when he returns to bring justice to the world. Until then, he wants his followers to spread the good news of forgiveness to all."

Yehuda says, "What kind of plan is that? That will never work!"

Zibrah says, "I believe that it is God's plan, and that it will succeed!"

And Miriam nods her head in agreement with Zibrah and Othniel, and she says, "Yes!"

Later that day, Miriam and Othniel are able to spend some time together, apart from the others, and she asks him, "Othniel, I recall that you were hoping that everything could go back to the way it was before Yeshuah's death, and you dreaded the idea of being sent out to proclaim his message without his actually being present with you. But now Yeshuah has gone away. So, how are you feeling about that?"

Othniel responds, "When he was taken up into the clouds, we were happy for him. I still am not very confident about my ability to proclaim his message, but let's wait and see what happens when the Holy Spirit comes."

Miriam smiles and says, "Once again, we find ourselves back in wait-and-see mode! For what it is worth, you do a pretty good job of explaining things to my family. To be a witness, it isn't necessary to be a great orator or a scholar, but just to tell the story of what happened. And, I believe that you do that very well!"

The following day, the sixth day of Sivan and the first day of the week, is Shavuot, and pilgrims all over the city of Yerushalayim are getting ready to present their first fruits offerings at the Temple. There is a sound of shofars and flutes from the Temple, announcing the beginning of the Shavuot ceremony.

It is still dark outside as Eliezer takes the basket containing the bundled stallks of his first-fruits wheat offering, and he carries it to the arched staircase that leads to the Temple Mount, and he joins some other pilgrims that are gathered there with their offerings. While he is standing there in line, suddenly he hears a loud sound like that of a dangerous and destructive windstorm, and he sees flashes of light in the sky over the city. Other people in the line see it too, and the crowd makes a noise like a great sigh, or a collective gasp. He looks around, and from where he is standing on the mountain of the Temple, it looks like flashes of light are emanating from a single two-story building on nearby Mount Zion. He wonders what is happening, but then the line starts moving again, and he follows it into the Temple courtyard, up the steps to the platform, and through the gates leading to the Court of the Priests.

When his turn comes, Eliezer carries his first-fruits offering basket to the place between the altar and the entrance to the Sanctuary, and there he declares to the officiating priest his intention to make his offering.

Then Eliezer lowers the basket from his shoulder and he holds it with his hands under the basket. The priest recites each verse of the Devarim portion for Shavuot, and Eliezer responds by repeating each verse after the priest.

Then the priest places his hands under Eliezer's hands, and together Eliezer and the priest wave the first-fruits offering before God -- moving the basket in four directions, and also raising and lowering it. After that, the priest takes the basket from Eliezer, and places it momentarily on the corner of the altar, while Eliezer prostrates himself before the Lord. And then Eliezer stands up again and leaves the Temple. He has fulfilled his Shavuot obligation.

As Eliezer is leaving the Temple, he remembers the sound of the wind and the flashes of light, and he decides to walk over to Mount Zion, to see what the commotion was about. He finds the two-story building, and he sees a very large crowd gathered outside, listening to a man who is speaking to them all. The speaker looks familiar to Eliezer, and then he realizes that this is one of the fishermen who came to his house three weeks ago to get Othniel!

> Eliezer moves closer, and he listens intently as the man says, "Therefore, let the entire house of Israel know with certainly that God has made him both Lord and Maschiah, this Yeshuah whom you crucified."
> [Acts 2:36 NRSV]

> Then someone in the crowd shouts, "Brothers, what should we do?"
> [Acts 2:37b NRSV]

And the speaker answers in a loud voice, "Repent, and be baptized every one of you in the name of Yeshuah the Maschiah, so that your sins may be forgiven, and you will receive the gift of the Holy Spirit. For the promise is for you, for your children, and for all who are far away, everyone whom the Lord our God calls to him."

[Acts 2:38-39 NRSV]

Then Eliezer sees the excitement of the crowd as they are clamoring to receive the promise that the fisherman had offered to them. Eliezer decides to continue on his way to Yehuda's and Shira's house, but he reminds himself to ask Othniel about what happened, the next time that he sees him.

That afternoon, Othniel comes to Yehuda's and Shira's house, and Miriam opens the door to welcome him. She has been expecting his visit. Othniel touches the mezuzah with his right hand, he kisses those fingertips, and then he steps inside to hug his betrothed wife. He seems very eager to tell her about the dramatic events of this day.

Yehuda, Shira, Eliezer, and Zibrah are sitting together in the great room, talking. Yaaqov is somewhere else, playing a game with his cousins.

Othniel and Miriam sit down next to each other on chairs that are facing where Eliezer and Zibrah are seated. And Miriam says, "Please tell us what happened today, Othniel."

And Othniel says, "This morning, I was with a large group of disciples in the upper room on Mount Zion. We were praying, and suddenly there was a sound like a furious windstorm, and it got louder and louder until it sounded like a roar. It seemed like the storm was inside of the building that we were in, and not just outside. And along with the noise of the wind there also were bright lights flashing over all of us like flames. And then, as the power of the Holy Spirit came over all of us, each of us began speaking in languages that we had never spoken before. Pilgrims from many different countries were outside of the building, and they heard us talking. And each one of those foreigners heard about God's deeds of power in their own native language. They were exclaiming about these phenomena, and we came outside to them. And then more people came to see what the commotion was all about. Then Simeon Petros made a speech about how all of this was in fulfillment of what the prophet Yehoel had prophesied. And he told them about how Yeshuah had performed many powerful signs and wonders among the people, and through the treachery of some of them he had been crucified and killed, but that God has raised him from the dead according to the scriptures, and now he is exalted at the right hand of God. Then he said, let all Israel know that God has made him both Lord and Maschiah, this Yeshuah whom you crucified. Then about three thousand persons repented of their sins, they were baptized in the name of Yeshuah the Maschiah, and they were saved. It was very exciting!"

Eliezer says, "I was at the Temple, and I heard the wind, and I saw the light flashes. After I presented my first fruit offering, I walked over to Mount Zion, to see for myself what had happened, and I saw the crowd, and I heard the last part of the fisherman's speech to them."

Yehuda asks, "What does all of this mean? I don't understand."

And Shira says, "I don't understand either."

Zibrah answers, "It means that Yeshuah, the one who was crucified and who rose from the dead, now is exalted as both Lord and Maschiah! This truly has been a day of revelation!"

Othniel and Miriam both nod their heads, and they look into each other's smiling faces, without speaking.

Eliezer had nothing else to say. He was going to have to think about these events for a while, in order to reconcile them with everything else that he thought that he knew about the ways of God.

Othniel and Miriam spent another couple of hours talking about everything. Then Othniel left Yehuda's house to tell his parents what had happened that day.

The next morning, the seventh day of Sivan, Eliezer and his family thank Yehuda, Shira, and their children for their hospitality, and then they mret their fellow pilgrims from Hammat at the Fish Gate, before beginning their homeward journey together. They arrive in Hammat during the afternoon of the eleventh day of Sivan.

A little more than three weeks later, it is the fifth day of the early-summer month of Tammuz, and the second day of the week. This is Yaaqov's thirteenth birthday, the long-awaited day when he finally reaches his legal maturity under Jewish laws. He hasn't actually reached puberty yet, but according to the rabbis, he now is old enough to be reckoned among the adults to fill the required minyan for ceremonies in the synagogue or Temple, and he also is old enough to be held responsible for keeping the commandments that are specified in the Torah. Until this day, Eliezer would have been held liable to punishment for any misdeed that Yaaqov might have done. But from this day onward, Yaaqov is legally responsible for himself.

When Yaaqov comes to the table for breakfast, Eliezer says to his wife, "Zibrah, today another man will be seated with us at the table!"

Zibrah replies, "Yes, I can see that Yaaqov is all grown-up today! Happy birthday, Yaaqov!" And she brings Yaaqov his favorite treat, a sweet cake dripping with honey and covered with chopped nuts.

Eliezer says the customary mealtime blessing, and then he adds the blessing for special occasions, "Blessed art Thou, Lord, our God, King of the Universe, who has kept us alive and sustained us and has brought us to this special time. Amen."

During the meal, Eliezer turns to his son and says, "Yaaqov, I am going to the synagogue this afternoon to meet with my Torah study partners. Would you like to come with me and join in the discussion?"

Yaaqov replies, "Yes, Abba, I would like to do that very much."

Then Eliezer gets up from the table, goes to the side table and picks up a cloth pouch that is there, and brings it to where Yaaqov is sitting at the table, and he gives it to Yaaqov, saying, "You will need to bring these with you when we go to the synagogue."

Yaaqov opens the pouch and takes out a white wool tallit, and a set of tefillin. The tallit is a shawl that Jewish men wrap around their shoulders and sometimes over their heads while they are saying their morning prayers. Each of the four corners of the tallit has long tassels called tzitzit, that are made of specially knotted cords. Tefillin are two small black leather boxes with black straps attached to them. The boxes each contain four scriptural portions. Tefillin are worn by Jewish men on their head and on one arm for prayer on weekday mornings that aren't holidays. Special blessings are recited whenever putting on the tallit or tefillin.

Eliezer says, "This afternoon, Rabbi Yitzhak and I will teach you the correct way to put on your tallit and tefillin, and when you should do that."

Yaaqov says, "Thank you, Abba."

Eliezer says, "Today you are a man, my son."

Five days later, there is a special Shabbat Torah reading ceremony at the Hammat synagogue. Yaaqov is sitting with Eliezer, Rabbi Yitzhak, and the other men in rows along both sides of the room, facing the reading desk. The women and children are sitting in rows by the front wall, on either side of the door, and facing the reading desk and the area where the men are sitting. When it seems that everyone is in their places, with his head covered, Reuel stands and steps over to the ornately decorated Ark and he takes the Torah from the Aron Kodesh and ceremonially carries it in his arms around the room until he returns to the reading desk, then he removes the cover from the Torah, and he carefully lays the Torah scroll on the podium. Touching only the handles, he unrolls the scroll until he finds the Torah portion that is assigned to be read on this Shabbat, which is from Shemot, including the eighth, ninth, and tenth plagues, the Passover, the Exodus, the festival of unleavened bread, and the consecration of the firstborn [Exodus 10:1-13:16]. Then Reuel says, "Blessed are You, Lord our God, King of the universe, who has sanctified us with His commandments, and commanded us to engross ourselves in the words of the Torah." And the congregation responds, "Amen."

The weekly portion is divided into seven sections, called aliyot, plus a concluding section, called the maftir. One at a time, Reuel calls six men forward to read the first six aliyot. As each reader comes forward, Reuel points to the word that begins that aliyot. Then he calls Yaaqov up to read the seventh aliyot, that includes the exodus and the ordinance for the Passover. Yaaqov stands up and he goes to the podium. He is wearing his tallit. Rabbi Yitzhak comes and stands next to him, just in case he needs assistance with pronunciation. But Yaaqov does not need any help. Yaaqov is careful not to touch the scroll with his hand, instead he skillfully uses a yad made of olive wood to point to his place in the text as he is reading. He reads confidently

285

and well from the Torah, while his parents and his sister are proudly watching him. Then Yaaqov returns to his seat, and Reuel calls Eliezer to read the maftir, and a related Haftarah portion from the the Scroll of Yirmiyahu [Jeremiah 46:13-28]. After reading the portions, Eliezer returns to his seat, and Reuel invites Yaaqov to recite the blessing. Yaaqov returns to the reading desk, raises his hands and closes his eyes for a moment, and then he says, "Blessed are You, Lord our God, King of the universe, who gave us the Torah of truth and set everlasting life in our midst. Blessed are You, O Lord, Giver of the Torah." And the congregation responds, "Amen."

Then the Torah and Yirmeyahu Scrolls are ceremonially returned to their respective cabinets, and Reuel dismisses the congregation.

After the service of readings, the congregation partakes of some refreshments, and congratulates Yaaqov on attaining his religious maturity. Eliezer, Zibrah, and Miriam are proud of Yaaqov's performance of his first ritual observances as an adult. During the social gathering, Eliezer, Zibrah, and Miriam invite several of their friends to attend Miriam's and Othniel's wedding celebration in Yeriko on the twenty-fifth of Tishri.

On the morning of the following day, the eleventh day of Tammuz, Eliezer leads his donkeys, Amit and Marit, away from Hammat on his six-day, early-summer marketing tour of five Galilean towns. He is bringing lentils, peas, beans, cucumbers, onions, leeks, garlic, figs, and melons with him to sell, and he is looking forward to visiting with many of his repeat customers and friends about recent events.

While Eliezer is visiting Aharon and Bilhah in Kfar Nahum, he invites them to attend Miriam's and Othniel's wedding celebration in Yeriko on the twenty-fifth of Tishri. He also invites Marius to attend the wedding. As usual, when Eliezer arrives at the market agora in Beit Shean, he talks with Peleg. When they talk about Yeshuah's crucifixion, Peleg mentions that he had heard that Yeshuah's disciples had stolen the body so they could claim that he had risen from the dead. Eliezer tells him that Yeshuah actually had risen from the dead, and that the stolen body story was a false rumor that was spread by the chief priests as a cover-up. Peleg asks Eliezer how he is certain that Yeshuah had risen, and Eliezer tells him that his own daughter had seen Yeshuah alive again after he had died. Peleg is startled to learn that Yeshuah had risen, and he wonders what that could mean. Eliezer tells Peleg that he believes Yeshuah to be a prophet and a powerful spiritual guide, but that Yeshuah's followers are saying that Yeshuah is the Maschiah. Peleg is delighted to hear about that possibility. Eliezer invites Peleg to attend Miriam's and Othniel's wedding celebration in Yeriko on the twenty-fifth of Tishri.

~ /// ~

Meanwhile, in Yerushalayim the community of Yeshuah's followers is growing very rapidly. The apostles are preaching about repentance and forgiveness every day in the Temple at Solomon's Portico. Many people are receiving healings, and each day more people are joining the community of believers. Simeon Petros and Yohanan ben Zebedee are proclaiming thatYeshuah is the Maschiah, that he was raised from the dead after his crucifixion, and that salvation is available only through him.

So the chief priests, the Sadducees, and the Temple guards bring them before the Sanhedrin, where they are ordered not to speak publicly about Yeshuah. But they refuse to stop speaking about what they had seen and heard, and they are put into prison. But, during the night, an angel opens the prison doors and brings them out. The next day they are back at the Temple, preaching about Yeshuah and teaching the people. So the Temple guards arrest them again, and bring them back before the Sanhedrin. The apostles are beaten, ordered not to speak publicly about Yeshuah, and then they are released. But they keep preaching anyway, and the church keeps growing.

Many of the new converts sell their property and goods and donate the proceeds to the apostles. The believers are sharing everything that they have with one another. But the practical requirements of feeding and caring for ever-increasing numbers of people are stretching the resources of the apostles and the disciples to their limits. Some of the Hellenistic minority of believers thought that others were being given preferential treatment in the distribution of food, so the apostles appointed some Hellenistic believers as servers, but the need for servers continues to be outpaced by the growth in membership.

Othniel is thrilled to continue as one of Yeshuah's disciples but, despite the outpouring of the Holy Spirit, discipleship just isn't the same as when Yeshuah was with thm in Galilee. For one thing, the apostles aren't quite up to the task of administering the church's affairs. Proclaiming Yeshuah as Maschiah, and preaching about repentance and forgiveness in his name is essential, but the disciples weren't taught how to inventory or to dispose of donated property, or how to prepare and serve meals for thousands of people. Of course, Yeshuah probably could have done those things himself, but Othniel doesn't regard himself as being prepared for those tasks.

So, on the sixth day of Elul, almost five months after the disciples accompanied Yeshuah on his fateful journey to Yerushalayim, and exactly three months after the miracle of Pentekoste, Othniel returns to Yeriko to work in his father's business. But before leaving his fellow disciples in Yerushalayim, he tells them about his desire to stay in contact with them. And he invites a few of his closest fellow disciples to attend the celebration of his marriage to Miriam in Yeriko on the twenty-fifth of Tishri.

~ /// ~

On that same day, Zibrah says to her husband, "Eliezer, I have a surprise for you. . . . I am pregnant."

Eliezer responds, "How can that be? I thought that you weren't able to become pregnant."

"I thought so, too. I waited to tell you until I was certain. But, there is no mistake. I am now four months pregnant. If all goes well, our baby will be born early in the midwinter month of Shebat. Congratulations!"

Eliezer hugs her gently, and then he curiously touches her abdomen with his hand, marveling at the miracle of life growing within her womb.

After a few quiet moments, Zibrah asks, "When should we tell Miriam and Yaaqov our news?"

"Let's tell them at dinner this evening. I'm sure that they will be happy to learn that they can expect to have a new brother or sister this winter."

So Eliezer and Zibrah tell their children that they are expecting a baby in Shebat, and they are very happy to receive that good news. Now, more than ever before, the future is brimming with new possibilities!

CHAPTER 47

On the morning of the fifteenth of the late-summer month of Elul, Eliezer loads Amit and Marit with produce from his vegetable garden, and he makes his customary six-day, late-summer marketing journey through markets in five Galilean cities. Zibrah walks along with him to Tiberias, so that she can visit with her fishing crews about business, and also spend some time with her former neighbors. After spending that morning and part of the afternoon at the Tiberias main market, Eliezer walks with his donkeys to Aharon's house in Kfar Nahum.

Aharon is pleased to hear that Zibrah is pregnant, and that Yaaqov had already performed adult ritual duties. On the second day of his marketing journey, Eliezer sells his vegetables during the morning at Kfar Nahum, and during the afternoon, he travels to just outside Tzipori.

On the third day he sells in Tzipori-Sepphoris, and around midafternoon he moves on to Natzerat. On day four, he spends the morning selling in the Natzerat marketplace, and during the afternoon he walks to his campsite next to Harod Spring by Mount Gilboa.

On the fifth day he sells in Beit Shean during most of that day, and he enjoys excellent conversations with his good friend Peleg. Peleg is surprised to learn that Eliezer is preparing for fatherhood again. And on day six, Eliezer returns to his home in Hammat.

On the first day of the early-autumn month of Tishri, Rosh Hashanah, Eliezer and his family observe a day of holy rest and the sounding of the shofar. They leave Hammat on the seventh day of Tishri. Eliezer is leading his donkey, Marit, loaded down with Miram's wedding clothes, and her important possessions.

After three long days of hard walking they arrive in Yeriko just before the beginning of the tenth day of that month, Yom Kippur. They go to Obed's and Adah's house to leave Miriam's trousseau there. And Obed tells Eliezer that he will have someone care for Marit while the family is in Yerushalayim. Eliezer and his family spend Yom Kippur at the inn in Yeriko, abstaining from eating food, drinking, frivolity, personal washing, and the wearing of sandals.

Then, on the day after Yom Kippur, they walk to Yerushalayim, arriving at Yehuda's and Shira's house in the afternoon, four days before Sukkot. Arriving early for the Festival of Booths gives them extra time to construct and decorate their sukkah, and to make lulav bundles for both Eliezer and Yaaqov. They brought some etrogs with them from Hammat, but they purchase the essential freshly-cut palm fronds, willow branches, and myrtle branches at a market in Yerushalayim. The men don't actually move into their sukkah until the evening of the fifteenth of Tishri. Until then, Eliezer and his family stay inside the house with their cousins.

It has been more than four months since Miriam and Othniel have even seen each other, and the celebration of their marriage in Yeriko is only two weeks away. Miriam is looking forward to being with Othniel during at least part of Sukkot, and perhaps also before then, if he arrives in Yerushalayim before the festival. She tells herself to be patient as she waits for him.

Othniel finally arrives at Yehuda's and Shira's house at midday on the fourteenth of Tishri. He is eager to see Miriam. As soon as Miriam hears Othniel's voice, she comes running to him, and hugs him and kisses his face. Eliezer, Zibrah, and Othniel hear her squeel with delight, and they correctly guess that Othniel had arived, so they come downstairs to greet him, too.

Miriam says, "Othniel, tell me what you have been doing since we saw you at Shavuot."

Othniel responds, "Well, that is a fairly long story, so why don't we all sit down for a while/"

Othniel, Miriam, Eliezer, Zibrah, Yaaqov, Yehuda, and Shira all sit down together in the great room, and then Othniel says, "After the miraculous events at Pentekoste, the community of Yeshuah's believers started growing rapidly. The chief priests tried to stifle our activity by punishing the apostles, but that only increased the number of converts. Many of the new converts sell their property and goods and donate the proceeds to the church. The believers are sharing everything that they have with one another. But the practical requirements of feeding and caring for ever-increasing numbers of people, most of which are poor or sick, are stretching the resources of the apostles and the disciples to their limits. In spite of the outpouring of the Holy Spirit, the apostles still have much to learn about how to administer the church's affairs. For all of us, being disciples now is not at all like it was when Yeshuah was with us in Galilee. It is exciting and beautiful, but it also is a very messy situation, that none of us are really prepared to handle. Finally, after three months of trying to meet the needs of too many people, I decided to return to my father's business in Yeriko. During the past five weeks, I have been helping my older brother to produce aromatic oils and spices. My father has built a new house for Miriam and me in Yeriko. It is a beautiful home, and it is close to where I work. I am really looking forward to starting our life together! It is thrilling to me that our wedding celebration is only a week and a half away!"

Miriam says, "I also am very excited about our wedding celebration! What is our house like?"

Othniel replies, "It is a one-story house, with an enclosed portico and courtyard that includes our own private well. There is a great room, with an adjoining food preparation area that leads to the courtyard, and there are four other rooms that can be used for sleeping or any other use. I think that you will like it!"

Eliezer says, "I am certain that your father is happy, having you back with him and your older brother in the family business, but I also imagine that you are missing the companionship of your fellow disciples. Am I right?"

Othniel replies, "Yes, Eliezer, you are correct on both points: my father is very happy to have me back, and I do miss not having daily fellowship with Yeshuah and his followers. However, I still do regard myself as being one of Yeshuah's followers, and even though I am no longer serving with them in Yerushalayim, I will try to stay in contact with them occasionally. In fact, I am planning to visit with Yohanan, Simeon, and Tom later today."

Then Zibrah says, "We also have some good news to report to you: I now am five months pregnant! Eliezer and I are expecting our baby to be born during the month of Shebat."

Yehuda, Shira, and Othniel are pleasantly surprised by this unexpected announcement.

Yehuda turns to Eliezer and says, "Congratulations, cousin!"

And Shira and Othniel say, "What a great surprise! Congratulations to the both of you, Zibrah and Eliezer!"

After eating a light meal with the families, Othniel and Miriam leave to take another walk together. They both want to share some private words with their future spouses, especially since their betrothal period is rapidly approaching its end.

The following day, the fifteenth of Tishri, is Sukkot. That morning, after the final additions to his sukkah are completed, Eliezer invites his family into the sukkah, and he reads the Torah portion from Vaiyikra [Leviticus 23:39-43] to them. Then he invites Yaaqov to say the blessing for Sukkot, "Blessed art Thou, Lord, our God, King of the universe, who has sanctified us with His commandments, and commanded us to dwell in the sukkah. Amen."

During each of the seven days of Sukkot, Eliezer and Yaaqov, with their lulav and etrog in their hands, participate in the ceremonies, libations, and sacrifices at the Temple, as well as dwelling together joyfully in the sukkah outside of Yehuda's and Shira's house, while Zibrah, Miriam, Shira and Shira's daughters stay inside the house, or go out together if they desire, temporarily free from the sometimes bothersome presence of men.. Yehuda and his son occupy their own sukkah, that is next to Eliezer's. Despite the occasional rains, and the fact that the roof over each sukkah is intentionally left mostly open, everyone has an enjoyable time during Sukkot. While the men are at the Temple, many of the women also visit the Court of the Women in the Temple, to watch the festivities from special raised balconies that are constructed for that purpose. At night, huge oil lamps in the Court of the Women are lit, and they can be seen from miles away. And there also are special entertainments by musicians, acrobats, and jugglers. Sukkot truly is a festival of joy!

The morning of the fourth day of Sukkot, before Eliezer and Yaaqov leave their sukkah to go to the Temple for that day's festivities, Obed and Othniel arrive at Yehuda's and Shira's house, asking if they could visit with Eliezer. They are directed to Eliezer's and Yaaqov's sukkah, and Eliezer cautiously invites them into his sukkah. He is wondering if their appearance is an indication that some problem may have arisen concerning the upcoming marriage celebration.

Eliezer says, "Welcome, Obed and Othniel. Is everything all right?"

Obed replies, "Yes, everything is just wonderful! I came to invite your family to join ours for dinner this evening at our sukkah. Adah and I think that bringing our families together during this joyful festival, before the actual wedding celebration, would be a good way for us to continue uniting our families together. Will you come?"

Eliezer responds, "Yes, of course we will come! However, I remember having dinner at your sukkah during last year's Sukkot. Your sukkah was lovely, but it was only able to accommodate you, Adah, me, and Zibrah. How will you be able to accommodate both of our families?"

Obed laughs and says, "I am planning to temporarily expand my sukkah, as well as that table that I remember you enjoyed so much, so that all of us will fit! Don't worry! After dinner, I will put everything back the way it was, so that my neighbors won't complain."

Eliezer says, "Excellent! May I bring something for our dinner? How about some wine?"

Obed agrees, and the men hug each other warmly, and they kiss each other on the cheek. Then they all depart, to go to their respective activities.

In the final hour of that day, Eliezer and his family walk to where they remember Obed's sukkah was last year and, in its place, they find the walls of a large, uncovered, temporary pavilion, that enclose a large table whose top surface is about one cubit above the floor, and that extends around most of the inside of the pavilion, with an opening at one end. There are pillows on the floor around the outside of the table, for the members of both families to recline upon. Eliezer and Yaaqov put the wine that they had brought onto the table.

A moment later, just before sundown, Obed's daughters, Deborah and Mereth brought two trays of oil lamps out of the house, to the pavilion, and into the open space enclosed by the table. Eliezer's family watches as the girls distribute the lamps around the table, placing them on the tabletop. Then they light the lamps by touching the wick of each lamp with the wick of a already lit oil lamp..

Then Obed, Adah, Onan, Hannah, Othniel, and Micah come out of the house and join Deborah and Mereth, in greeting Eliezer, Zibrah, Miriam, and Yaaqov. Then Adah announces the order of seating, interspersing the members of both families around the table, but carefully placing Miriam and Othniel next to each other. After everyone had reclined in their assigned place, four servants started bringing plates, cups, utensils, and platters of food to the table. Then four more servants come out with two bowls of water and two towels. Working as two teams, each pair of servants help the persons seated at their half of the table to wash and dry their hands. As each person washes their hands, they say the handwashing blessing.

After everyone had washed and dried their hands, Obed stands and thanks everyone for their attendance and cooperation. Then he takes the jug of wine that Eliezer had brought, he opens it, and he pours some wine into his own cup, and then he hands the jug to a servant who quickly goes around the table pouring wine into each person's cup. After each person's cup has some wine in it, Obed lifts his cup and he says the blessing for wine. Then he puts his cup back on the table, and he picks up a platter containing bread and he says the blessing for the meal. He breaks off a piece of the bread, passes the platter to the person next to him, and he drinks from his cup, and he eats his piece of the bread. And everyone else does the same. Then Obed invites the participants to accept one another without reservation, and to enjoy the food, and each other. The meal has begun. The other platters of food are passed around, and each person ladles individual servings from the platters onto his own plate. The food is delicious, and the buzz of joy-filled conversation can be heard all around the table.

All of them had been together before, of course, but being together in this special pavilion with the oil lamps and the beautiful stars twinkling over their heads make everything seem magical! This certainly is not an ordinary meal. The enveloping walls of the oversized sukkah remind the participants of the protective presence of God. Musical sounds of instruments and singing can be heard softly in the background. For a while, at least, the members of the two families relate to each other as if they were a single family. It is a foreshadowing of the World to Come! Their special time together goes on for several hours, and it is late at night when things finally wind down and Obed invites Eliezer to give the closing blessing. Eliezer says,

> "Blessed art Thou, Lord, our God, King of the universe, who created joy and gladness, groom and bride, rejoicing, glad song, pleasure, delight, love, brotherhood, peace, nurture, and companionship. Blessed art Thou, Lord, who created all things for Thy glory, and who nourishes all. Amen,"

A magical night! And it didn't rain, either.

~ /// ~

Five days later, it is the twenty-fourth day of the early autumn month of Tishri, and Eliezer and his family are in Obed's and Adah's villa in Yeriko, getting themselves ready for the wedding. They take turns using Obed's miqveh. Eliezer and Yaaqov are putting on their best cream-colored linen tunics and slate-grey dyed woolen mantles. Zibrah discovers that she must alter her fancy embroidered maroon outfit a little, to accommodate her swelling abdomen. She is working on that alteration. Miriam is already wearing a lovely blue linen dress on which beautiful floral patterns were sewn with gold-colored thread and with shiny beads. She is wearing the necklace of colored gemstones that Zibrah gave her. Her long hair is wrapped in a piece of white linen cloth that is decorated with a design that she sewed using blue- and gold-colored threads. She is ready!

Obed and Adah are also getting dressed in fine clothes for their son's wedding. Adah is putting on a dark orange embroidered linen gown and a matching hair covering, and Obed is dressing in a white linen tunic with scarlet-colored stripes on the sleeves and at the head opening and bottom hem. Obed also is planning to wear a fancy, light-green colored hat. Deborah and Mereth are going to be wearing dresses similar in style and fabric to their mother's, but of a sandy brown color. Micah is wearing a light-blue tunic, with a woven cloth belt.

About one hour before the sun is expected to set, Obed tells everyone in the villa that guests are expected to arrive in about an hour, and that he and Micah are leaving to go to Othniel's house, in case he needs any extra help getting himself and his house ready for the celebration. He tells Adah that if the musicians come to the villa instead of to Othniel's house, to send them there to accompany Othniel's procession.

Just as the sun is setting, Reuel and Serah, Aharon and Bilhah, Marius, Joanna and Chuza, Reuben and his wife, Peleg, Marius, and Miriam's childhood friend Naomi and her husband all arrive at the villa. Most of them are staying at the nearby inn. All of them are very nicely dressed. Eliezer opens the door to greet them, and to invite them inside for some refreshments while they all wait for bridegrom and his friends to arrive. Of course, none of them know when that will happen, so they all come inside to partake of the food and drinks that are provided. When they come into the great room, Eliezer introduces them to Adah and her daughters. Zibrah has already met most of them. Miriam is staying in her room, trying not to be nervous.

About an hour and a half later, most of the people in the villa can hear the sounds of singing, instruments playing, and light-hearted merrymaking outside. Miriam comes out of her room, dazzling everyone in the great room with her beautiful appearance, and enjoying the warm greetings of her friends, relatives, and neighbors. Then Eliezer opens the door and he invites Othniel and his companions to come inside. Othniel is wearing a white tunic with purple stripes on its sleeves, and at the head opening and hem. And he is wearing a very fancy, bright magenta-colored hat. After showing reverence to the mezuzah, Othniel enters the house and is greeted personally by Eliezer, Zibrah, Adah, Yaaqov, and his sisters, and then the crowd inside pulls back to reveal Miriam seated in their midst. Othniel rushes to her and they embrace each other, and the crowd both inside and outside applauds loudly. Then Obed, Micah, Onan, Hannah, some of Othniel's boyhood friends, a few of Obed's friends, Yohanan ben Zebedee, and Mattaniah all come inside, to crowd into the entryway and great room, hoping for a glimpse of Othniel's beautiful bride. The musicians remain outside, playing their instruments and singing joyful verses from Shir Eshirim [Song of Solomon].

After a round of greetings between Othniel and his companions, and the people who had been waiting inside, the entire party moves back outside, and assembles itself into a parade, with Othniel and Miriam in the front, and everyone else behind them, in no particular order. Obed provides torches for some of the participants to carry. And then the musicians start playing their song again, and the whole group proceeds happily through the city to Othniel's house. Some of them are singing along with the musicians, and others are just laughing and talking. All along the route to Othniel's house, the people of Yeriko hear the procession, and they come outside to applaud the newly married couple.

When the party arrives at Othniel's house, Othniel opens the door, and he escorts Miriam inside, and then Othniel's family, and Miriam's family follow them inside. There are tables and chairs inside the house for the couple's families to use. Extra tables and chairs also are provided outside. And there are side tables with bowls of water and towels for washing hands both inside and outside the house. Othniel, Miriam, and many of their family members and guests wash before sitting down. Servants distribute cups of wine for everyone attending the celebration, beginning with Othniel and Miriam. Then, the servents bring out food for the wedding banquet,

Obed stands and lifts his hands, and says, "Blessed art Thou, O Lord, our God, King of the universe, who created all things for His glory."

And all of the people respond, "Amen." And Obed sits down.

Then Eliezer stands and says, "Blessed art Thou, O Lord, our God, King of the universe. Gladden the hearts of Othniel and Miriam. Bless them with joy, pleasure, delight, love, brotherhood, peace, and companionship with each other. Blessed art Thou, O Lord, our God, who makest the bridegroom and bride to rejoice."

And all of the people respond, "Amen." And Eliezer sits down.

Then Onan stands, with his cup of wine in his hand, and he says, "Blessed art Thou, O Lord, our God, King of the universe who has created the fruit of the vine."

And all of the people respond, "Amen." Onan put his cup back on the table.

Then Onan picks up a platter of bread and he says, "Blessed art Thou, Lord, our God, King of the universe, who brings forth food from the earth."

And all of the people respond, "Amen."

Then everyone watches as Othniel and Miriam drink some wine from the same cup, and when that is done, all of them shout, "Congratulations!" And the feast begins. All of the people eat, drink, and visit with one another. The musicians are making music, and some of the people are singing the songs along with them. The servants see to it that the wine cups are refilled often. From time-to-time, some of the participants stand and offer toasts to the bride and groom, and these are acknowledged and affirmed by the other participants. Occasionally, guests come to where Othniel and Miriam are sitting, to present them with gifts.

Some of the participants become tired, and they come to Othniel and Miriam to offer them their personal congratulations and good wishes before leaving the party. A few of them fall asleep in their places during the party. Othniel and Miriam have been thinking about consummating their marriage for a long time, but tonight they don't appear to be in much of a hurry to do that. They are enjoying this party in their honor with their friends, and they don't want to miss anything by absenting themselves, even for a little while. And they also are nervous. Neither of them has ever had sexual contact with another person. Each of them has some knowledge about how things are supposed to work, but that that isn't the same as personal experience. They tell themselves that they can consummate their marriage anytime. Nevertheless, sometime after midnight, after most of their guests have either left the party, or fallen asleep, or have become distracted, they quietly get up from their chairs, and Othniel brings Miriam with him to their sleeeping room. There, they explore the exciting new experience of intimacy together, with tenderness, clumsiness, patience, urgency, and abandon. And their already special relationship adds a new dimension that will help them for the rest of their lives together, just as the Creator intended that it would.

In the morning, Miriam and Othniel awaken early and they playfully make love again, and it is even better than before. Afterwards, they wash themselves, get dressed, and come out of their room to find that the party is still going on. There are a few people sleeping in their great room, including Onan and Hannah, as well as two others just outside their front door. But there still is a group of guests at a table in the great room, and they all seem to be having fun. Apparently, the musicians went home sometime during the night.

Othniel steps outside and discovers another group of invited guests at one of the outside tables, and that they are still drinking wine. Othniel realizes that he hasn't seen either his parents or Miriam's. So he goes back inside and he asks Miriam if she can remember when their parents left the party. But while she is trying to remember, Obed, Adah, Eliezer, and Zibrah walk in the door with some more platters of food.

Obed says, "Good morning, Miriam and Othniel! You both look wonderful! You must have gotten at least a couple of hours of sleep last night."

Miriam replies, "Thank you, Obed. Yes, we had a lovely night. It is so thoughtful of you to bring us some more food. Othniel and I are both very hungry." And then, turning to Adah and her parents, she says, "Good morning, Adah, Abba, and Zibrah! Did you enjoy the party last night?"

Eliezer responds, "Yes, we all had such a great time last night, we decided that we would return for some more fun!"

Miriam says, "Are you being serious?"

And Zibrah says, "No, we aren't. We just wanted to check on you and Othniel, to make sure that you both are still getting along well."

Othniel puts his arm around Miriam's waist and says, "Miriam and I are both very happy, and now, more than ever, we believe that we were made for each other!"

Eliezer smiles and says, "The one thing that every parent wants is for his or her children to be happily settled, and to be with a partner that is right for them. Evidently, we all are blessed!"

And Obed and Adah agree wholeheartedly.

Then Miriam says, "Let's all have some breakfast together!" So she clears the plates, utensils, and cups off of an empty table, and then she wipes it with a cloth.

And Zibrah fetches a bowl of water and some more towels for washing their hands.

As Miriam, Othniel, Obed, Adah, Eliezer, and Zibrah are eating and talking together, the sleeping guests awake and decide to join them. Onan and Hannah wash their hands, and then they join the family for breakfast. Onan congratulates his brother and sister-in-law, and his wife adds her congratulations, too. Marius has been sitting at the outside table, but he enters the house to sit with Eliezer's family and Othniel. Eliezer and Obed look around and discover that there still are nineteen people at the continuing party. Apparently, the only invited guests that aren't still there are Yaaqov, Micah, Deborah, Mereth, Peleg, Obed's friends, Othniel's boyhood friends, Yohanan, and Mattaniah. It turns out that many of the local Yeriko guests went home to sleep in their own beds, while most of the out-of-town guests are still at the party.

After eating their morning meal together, Othniel gives Miriam a tour of her new home. Miriam is delighted with it. Obed leaves for a little while, and when he returns, he brings two musicians, and some more wine. The party continues through that day, and part of the next day. A few of the local people that had left the party earlier return in the afternoon, looking for more free food and drinks. Obed contacts his caterers about their needing some additional provisions, and he hires two servers to clean up some messes and also to keep the party going. And it is done. A good time is had by all, and many new friendships are formed between the visitors from Galilee and the local guests from Yeriko.

Marius left Yeriko on the morning of the twenty-sixth to return to his military garrison at Capernaum.

During the afternoon of the twenty-sixth, Miriam and Othniel walk to Obed's and Adah's house, so that they could retrieve Miriam's other clothes and possessions, and also so they could thank their parents for providing such a wonderful celebration for them. Then Miriam goes to the marketplace with Zibrah and Adah, to purchase some things that they will need for their observance of Shabbat. This will be her first Shabbat apart from the family in which she grew up, her first Shabbat with her husband, and her first Shabbat in her new home. She wants it to be special for Othniel.

On the first day of the following week, the twenty-eighth of Tishri, Eliezer, Zibrah, Yaaqov and Marit join with Reuel and Serah, Aharon and Bilhah, Reuben and his wife Abigail, Naomi and her husband, and Joanna and Chuza for the journey back to Galilee. There is a tearful farewell when they leave Miriam behind in Yeriko.

CHAPTER 48

Six and one-half weeks later, on the fifteenth day of the late-autumn month of Chislev, Miriam realizes that she is pregnant. She tells Othniel, and afterwards they tell their news to Obed and Adah, and there is great rejoicing. If all goes well, their baby will be born around the end of the early-summer month of Tammuz, or early in the midsummer month of Ab. This would be the first grandchild for Obed and Adah, and also for Eliezer and Zibrah. Obed promises Miriam that he will communicate this good news to Eliezer and Zibrah, so that they also may rejoice.

About six and one-half weeks later, on the second day of the midwinter month of Shebat, a baby boy is born to Eliezer and Zibrah. Zibrah had a safe delivery, without any complications. In naming a child, it is customary to name him or her after a beloved, deceased grandparent or great-grandparent. However, eight days after the baby's birth, contrary to the customary practice, Eliezer names him Yeshuah.

Just over five months afterwards, on the twenty-ninth day of Tammuz, Miriam gives birth to her firstborn child, a daughter. Othniel names her Naavah (which means "lovely"). Naavah actually is not a family name for either Miriam or Othniel, but it is related to Miriam's birth mother's name, Ahuva (which means "beloved"). Both pairs of grandparents are present for their granddaughter's birth and naming.

~ /// ~

After Eliezer's return to Hammat following the birth and naming of his granddaughter, while working in his terraced garden, he is reflecting upon life, its uncertainty, and its lessons:

> *I was a proud Pharisee, confidently following the practices*
> *that were handed down to me. I believed that those practices were*

pleasing to God, and that other ways would not be satisfactory. I still follow most of those traditional practices that I learned, but I also have learned to be more open-minded about approaches that are different from the ones I use. I have learned tolerance. I thought that I understood God's plan for His people and the kind of solution that He would provide for the world's problems. But I learned that the solution that God has provided is very different from what I was expecting. I am skeptical and critical about things that I do not understand, and I have been shown that my logic has its limitations. I was taught a particular vocabulary for talking about God and our relationship with Him. For much of my life, that vocabulary served me very well, but when I finally encountered a truly holy person, and an authentic spiritual guide, my vocabulary was inadequate. I have seen glimpses of truth and holiness that I do not understand, but whenever I attempt to describe or explain what I perceived, my words fail me. I am a leader and a teacher, but my children have learned things that are beyond my learning.

In agriculture, sometimes a farmer has to completely turn over the soil, uprooting and destroying all of the existing vegetation, in order to prepare the soil to receive new seeds, so that he will be able to produce a more beneficial harvest later. And sometimes, the Lord uproots His people's lives in order to make possible a later harvest of changes that always prove to be beneficial. Going through this process is never easy, but it always produces good results, eventually. God's kingdom isn't a particular territory or governance structure, it is about our accepting His reign over our lives.

Struggles with faith affect us in every area of our lives and, conversely, the difficulties that we encounter in our lives also have a profound impact on what we believe. These struggles challenge everything that we thought that we knew about truth, and they force us to reconsider our priorities. We try to conduct our lives based upon what we believe to be true, but sometimes we discover that the belief systems that generated our most cherished ideas about truth can lead us to conclusions that turn out to be false. We don't know what to believe when we find that God isn't doing things the way that we think He should. We seek coherence and safety for our lives, but God offers us Himself, uncertainty, and adventure instead. Sometimes we rely on our own thinking too much. Letting go of our own ideas and following the path that God puts in front of us isn't easy. It requires that we trust God, even when doing so doesn't seem to make sense. It takes courage and perseverance, but along the way we learn humility, patience, mercy, and forgiveness. I am not as smart as I like to think that I am. But I can learn some important new things, if I pay attention. Following tradition can be a good thing, but not if doing so gets in the way of the new things that God is trying to reveal to us. I have learned to listen, both when I do not understand, and also when I think that I do. Things haven't always worked out the way that I thought that they should, but the way several important things have turned out in my life is even better than I could have imagined beforehand. Trust God and be open to all of His ways!

This is what I have come to believe. God, help me to gratefully receive everything else that you intend for me to learn! Amen!

EPILOGUE

Within a few years, the persecution of followers of the Way in Yerushalayim became so intense that many of the apostles, disciples, and other believers scattered: first to Samaria, then to Syria, Cyprus, Egypt, and eventually to Asia Minor, North Africa, Europe and Asia.

Yohanan ben Zebedee visited Othniel in Yeriko, and urged him to help with the outreach. After prayerful reflection, Othniel, Miriam, and their daughter left Yeriko, and eventually helped to establish the Christian community in Rome.

Yaaqov, using his Greco-Roman name of James, became an early Christian missionary to Gaul and Spain.

Marius served with distinction during the Roman invasion of Britannia under Emperor Claudius in 43 CE. He was meritoriously granted Roman citizenship, and eventually he rose to the rank of Tribune before his retirement from the Roman Legions. After many years of soldiering, he finally became a farmer.

But these stories are for our later consideration.

WRITER'S NOTE

This story is a work of fiction. Within its narrative there are many references to well-known historical people and events, but most of its characters emerged from my own imagination. The story is set within the context of the New Testament because it is about the transformative changes in a fictional family during the period of Jesus' public ministry, as they struggle to understand the identity and purpose of the itinerant preacher from Nazereth. In this book, I am particularly interested in my protagonist's process of becoming. Jesus is a very important character in this novel but, with the exception of one chapter, he is almost never the center of our attention. In this story, we hear about Jesus from secondhand reports of other people who tell us about what they saw and experienced. All of the places mentioned in the story really existed in first century Judaea. I have personally visited those places, and I also have examined several archaeological reports.

Readers who are familiar with the New Testament may find my use of Hebrew names for familiar persons and places to be annoying, instead of the more recognizable, anglicized versions of Greek equivalents of Hebrew names. In my story, Jesus is Yeshuah, John is Yohanan, Simon Peter is Simeon Petros, Thomas is Tom, Nazereth is Natzerat, Capernaum is Kfar Nahum, and Jerusalem is Yerushalayim, and so forth -- but those *are* the real names that first century Jews would have used. Interestingly, Greeks and Romans tended to use different names for both persons and places than native Jews -- you may have noticed that in the story. First century Judaea was a different cultural environment than our modern industrial society, and we need to be reminded of its distinctiveness, instead of tricking ourselves into thinking that those folks were just like us. If you find that you are having a difficult time keeping track of all of those Hebrew names, then ***Appendix A*** may help you to distinguish them from one another.

Many modern Christians like to assume that, if they had lived in New Testament times, they certainly would have become dedicated followers of Jesus. Maybe they would have, but perhaps not. Our current perspective is profoundly affected by more than nineteen hundred years of theological interpretation and reflection concerning Jesus' life and its meaning. It took hundreds of years for the Christian church to figure out who Jesus is, and about his relationship with the Father and the Holy Spirit. And, even today, not all who profess to have faith in Jesus are in agreement about some important details. What might it have been like to have witnessed Jesus' public ministry through the fragmented lens of first century Judaism? In those days, not everyone accepted Jesus as Messiah and Lord, and they believed that they had very good reasons for their decision. I have tried to write a sympathetic characterization of the Pharisees. Most of us are more like those guys than we would like to admit.

In my story, we observe our protagonist's growth in faith mostly through his interactions with others. We see him struggling to understand the ways of God, but we don't really get into his thoughts until the very end of the story. Even then, although he has attained a type of faith in Jesus, he still hasn't gotten everything right. And neither do we, probably. It is very difficult for us to let go of the baggage to which we have become so attached. The theological ideas concerning the Messiah, Atonement and Resurrection that are expressed by Othniel are probably more advanced than would have been typical for one of Jesus' early followers. Notice the variety of responses by Eliezer, and his friends and relatives to reports about Jesus.

Let us separate some facts from the fiction in my story. Eliezer, Miriam, Yaaqov, Zibrah, Assurbani, Marius, Othniel, and most of their friends and neighbors are fictional characters that are set within a first century Palestinian context that is overlaid with some of the familiar events that are recorded in the New Testament Gospels. The chronological outline of the story is mostly based on the Gospel of John, combined with the seasonal festivals and agricultural cycles that would have been important to a Pharisee, farmer, and traveling merchant from Galilee. The Synoptic Gospels (traditionally referred to as Matthew, Mark, and Luke) provided some of the events, especially in Galilee.

Jesus had many disciples. Twelve of the more prominent, named disciples are customarily referred to as apostles. But most of the other disciples are not named in the Gospels. The fictitious character of Othniel, and his friend Mattaniah, are envisioned by me as two of those nameless disciples.

Yohanan (John) the Baptizer, Yeshuah (Jesus), Herod Antipas, Yohanan (John) ben Zebedee, Simeon Petros (Simon Peter), Tom (Thomas), Joanna, Chuza, and Pontius Pilate are all historical characters that are mentioned in the Gospels. The Gospels of Matthew and Luke both mention a centurion at Capernaum. In my story, I have named him Gaius, and I have imagined him saying and doing a few things that almost certainly didn't actually happen. And I also confected many of the situations and words that I attributed to Herod Antipas and Joanna. I tried to name my characters appropriately: Hebrew names for Jews, Roman names for Romans, Phoenician names for Phoenicians, Assyrian names for Assyrians, and Edomite names for Edomites.

My Jewish readers may believe that my descriptions of the important Jewish practices and Festivals are incorrect, because some of the details may be different from how they were taught. However, I have tried to be faithful to what rabbinical scholars have said regarding how things probably were done during the late Second Temple period, that preceded the formation of the Talmud *[the Mishnah wasn't developed until the end of the second century or the beginning of the third century CE, the Tosefta and halakhic Midrashim in the third and early fourth century, and the Yerushalmi and amoraic Midrashim in the fourth and fifth century]*. In Judaism, many things changed after the Temple was destroyed in 70 CE.

Special thanks to my grandson, Perry Zipoy, for allowing me to use one of his photographs on the cover of this book, and also for converting my own drawing of a map of the Holy Land into a more presentable format using Adobe Illustrator software. In addition to being a wonderful grandson, Perry is an amazingly talented graphic artist!

I probably didn't get everything right. But it was very important for me to try, especially with the theology and historical background. May God bless all of us with grace, faith, hope, and joy! Amen.

Appendix A

A List of Recurring Characters in the Story

Adah - wife of Obed.

Aharon - Eliezer's deceased wife's brother, lives in Kfar Nahum.

Ahuva - the name of Eliezer's deceased wife.

Assurbani - a Herodian, profoi (magistrate) in Tiberias.

Baraket - a worker at the fish factory in Magdala, from Acco.

Bilhah - wife of Aharon.

Bodo - the owner of a large cargo-handling operation at Acco.

Eliezer - a farmer and traveling merchant from Hammat, a widower, 39-40 years of age.

Gaius - Centurion of the military garrison in Capernaum.

Herod Antipas - the Tetrarch of Galilee and Peraea, and the founder of Tiberias.

Joanna - Zibrah's friend in Tiberias, she is the wife of Chuza, who is Antipas' steward.

Kenan - one of Eliezer's friends, and a Torah study partner at the Hammat synagogue.

Marius - a Roman auxiliary soldier, tesserarius of the military garrison in Capernaum, 25-26 yrs old.

Mibzar - one of Herod Antipas' protective bodyguards, serves as a policeman in Tiberias.

Miriam - Eliezer's unmarried daughter, 20-21 years of age.

Nicanor - agoranomos (manager of markets) at Tiberias.

Obed - father of Othniel, produces aromatic oils and spices in Yeriko, knows Aharon.

Onan - Othniel's older brother, works at Obed's business in Yeriko.

Othniel - a friend of Marius, a disciple of Yeshuah, 24 years old.

Peleg - a farmer and merchant from Yizreel Valley.

Reuben - one of Eliezer's friends, a Torah study partner of his at the Hammat synagogue.

Reuel - brother of Eliezer, and a Torah study partner of his at the Hammat synagogue.

Salome - one of Zibrah's friends in Tiberias.

Serah - wife of Reuel.

Shira - wife of Yehuda.

Simeon Petros - a disciple of Yeshua, also called Peter by Romans and Greeks.

Titus - Optio (deputy commander) of the military garrison at Capernaum.

Yaaqov - Eliezer's son, 11-13 years of age.

Yehuda - Eliezer's and Reuel's cousin, lives in Yerushalayim.

Yeshuah - a preacher and healer from Natzerat, also called Jesus by Romans and Greeks.

Yitzhak - Rabbi of the synagogue in Hammat, and Eliezer's friend and neighbor.

Yohanan - a prophetic preacher and baptizer in Yarden River, also called John by Romans and Greeks.

Yohanan ben Zebedee - a disciple of Yeshuah, also called John by Romans and Greeks.

Zibrah - owner of two fishing boats at Tiberias, a widow, 37-38 years of age.

Appendix B

Hebrew Calendar of Months & Festivals

Month (#days)	(Modern Equivalent)	Festivals & Observances
Nisan (30)	(March-April)	15 - Pesach / Passover
		15-21 Unleavened Bread
		16 – Ceremonial Barley Offering
Iyyar (29)	(April-May)	
Sivan (30)	(May-June)	6 - Shavuot / Pentecost Wheat & 6 other species First Fruits Offering
Tammuz (29)	(June-July)	17 - Day of Fasting
Ab (30)	(July-August)	9 - Destruction of Temple
Elul (29)	(August-September)	
Tishri (30)	(September-October)	1 - Rosh Hashanah / Civil New Year
		10 - Yom Kippur / Day of Atonement
		15-21 - Sukkot / Booths / Tabernacles

		22 - Shemini Atzeret / Solemn Assembly
Marchesvan(29)	(October-November)	
Chislev (30)	(November-December)	25 - Rededication of Temple
		25-3rd of Tebeth - Chanukah
Tebeth (29)	(December-January)	
Shebat (30)	(January-February)	
Adar (29)	(February-March)	14 - Purim

2nd Adar *(extra days added every 2-3 years to synchronize the lunar and solar cycles)*

Suggested Readings

Bailey, Kenneth E. *Jesus Through Middle Eastern Eyes: Cultural Studies in the Gospels*. Downers Grove, IL: InterVarsity Press, 2008.

Bratcher, Dennis. *"Hebrew Calendar of the Old Testament"*.
http://www.crivoice.org/calendar.html

Brown, Raymond E. *An Introduction to the New Testament*. New York: Doubleday, 1997.

Chabad.org *"The Megillah"*
http://www.chabad.org/holidays/purim/article_cdo/aid/1473/jewish/The-Megillah.htm

Chancey, Mark A. *"The Myth of a Gentile Galilee"*. (Southern Methodist University, February 2003)
http://www.bibleinterp.com/articles/Myth_Gentile_Galilee.shtml

Coogan, Michael David (Editor). *The Oxford History of the Biblical World*. New York: Oxford University Press, 1998.

Crandall University. *"Jesus' Last Passover Meal (A First-Century Jewish Passover)"*. http://www.mycrandall.ca/courses/ntintro/lifej/LSUPCHAP1.htm

Crossan, John Dominic & Jonathan L. Reed. *Excavating Jesus: Beneath the Stones, Behind the Texts*.
San Francisco: HarperSanFrancisco, 2001.

Hezser, Catherine (Editor). *The Oxford Handbook of Jewish Daily Life in Roman Palestine*. Oxford: Oxford University Press, 2010.

Isaacs, Ronald H. *"Passover from the Bible to the Temples"*. http://www.myjewishlearning.com/holidays/Jewish_Holidays/Passover/History/Biblical_Prn.shtml

Isaacs, Ronald H. *"Reading the Megillah"*. http://www.myjewishlearning.com/holidays/Jewish_Holidays/Purim/

Isaacs, Ronald H. *"Shavuot History: From the Bible to Temple Times"*. http://www.myjewishlearning.com/holidays/Jewish_Holidays/Shavuot/History/_Biblical_Prn.shtml

Jeremias, Joachim. *Jerusalem in the Time of Jesus*, Philadelphia: Fortress Press, 1975. (Copyright 1969 by SCM Press Ltd.)

Jewish Encyclopedia. http://www.jewishencyclopedia.com

Jewish Virtual Library. http://www.jewishvirtuallibrary.org/jsource/Archaeology

Kiawans, Jonathan. *"Was Jesus' Last Supper a Seder?"* Bible Review, Oct 2001, pp 24-33, 47. http://www.biblicalarchaeology.org/daily/people-cultures-in-the-bible/jesus-historical-jesus/was-jesus-last-supper-a-seder/

Knight, George W. *The Holy Land*. Uhrichsville, Ohio: Barbour Publishing, 2011.

Korb, Scott. *Life in Year One: What the World Was Like in First-Century Palestine*. New York: Riverhead Books, 2010.

Kostenberger, Andreas J. *"Was the Last Supper a Passover Meal?"*. http://www.biblicalfoundations.org/wp-content/uploads/2013/01/Supper_6-30.pdf

Lanum, Maurice. *"The Ketubah Text"*. http://www.myjewishlearning.com/ life/Life_Events/Weddings/Liturgy_Ritual_and_Customs/ Ketubah/Details_I_Prn.shtml

Laymon, Charles M. (Editor). *The Interpreter's One-Volume Commentary on the Bible*. Nashville & New York: Abingdon Press, 1971.

May, Neal W. *Israel: A Biblical Tour of the Holy Land*. Tulsa: Albury Publishing, 2000.

Murphy-O'Connor, Jerome. *The Holy Land, Third Edition*. Oxford & New York: Oxford University Press, 1992.

Parsons, John J. *Hebrew for Christians (website)*. http://www.hebrew4christians.com

Pictorial Archive (Near Eastern History). *"Student Map 'B': Ezra-Nehemiah through Justinian"* of the Student Map Manual, as part of The Wide Screen Project: Historical Geography of the Bible Lands. Jerusalem: Pictorial Archive, 1979.

Pictorial Archive (Near Eastern History). *"Section 12, Herodian Period"* of the Student Map Manual, as part of The Wide Screen Project: Historical Geography of the Bible Lands. Jerusalem: Pictorial Archive, 1979.

Reumann, John, *Jesus in the Church's Gospels: Modern Scholarship and the Earliest Sources*. Philadelphia: Fortress Press, 1968.

Ross, Lesli Koppelman. *"Sukkot Observances Through the Second Temple Period"*. http://www.myjewishlearning.com/holidays/ Jewish_Holidays/Sukkot/History/Biblical_Prn.shtml

Rousseau, John J. & Rami Arav. *Jesus and His World: An Archaeological and Cultural Dictionary*. Minneapolis: Augsburg Fortress, 1995.

Sanders, E.P. *"Common Judaism and the Synagogue in the First Century."* http://isites.harvard.edu/fs/icb.topic1202528.files/Lesson%20 3/3b%20Sanders.pdf [also Chapter 1 of the book, Jews, Christians and Polytheists in the Ancient Synagogue, edited by Steven Fine (Abingdon & New York: Routledge, 1999)]

Sandmel, Samuel. *Judaism and Christian Beginnings*. New York: Oxford University Press, 1978.

Shanks, Hershel (Editor). *"The Galilee Jesus Knew"*. Washington, D.C.: Biblical Archaeological Society, 2008.

Steinmueller, John E. & Kathryn Sullivan. *Catholic Biblical Encyclopedia: Old and New Testaments*. NewYork City: Joseph F. Wagner Inc., 1956.

The Temple Institute *"The Festival of Passover: The Time of Our Freedom"*. https://www.templeinstitute.org/passover.htm

The Temple Institute. *"The Festival of Shavuot"*. http://www.templeinstitute.org/shavuot.htm

The Temple Institute. *"The Festival of Sukkot (Tabernacles)"*. https://www.templeinstitute.org/sukkot.htm

Unger, Merrill Frederick. *The New Unger's Bible Dictionary* (Edited by R. K. Harrison). Chicago: The Moody Bible Institute, 1988.

Vermes, Geza. *The Many Faces of Jesus*. New York: Viking Compass, 2000.

Vermes, Geza. *Jesus in His Jewish Context*. Minneapolis: Fortress Press, 2003.

Whiston, William (Translator). *The Works of Josephus: New Updated Edition.* Peabody, MA: Hendrickson Publishers Inc., 1987

Wiener, Noah (Editor). *"Life in the Ancient World: Crafts, Society, and Daily Practice"*. Washington, D.C.: Biblical Archaeology Society, 2013.

Wright, N.T. *The New Testament and the People of God* (Christian Origins and the Question of God: Volume 1), Minneapolis: Fortress Press, 1992.

Wright, N.T. *Jesus and the Victory of God* (Christian Origins and the Question of God: Volume 2), Minneapolis: Fortress Press, 1996.

Wright, N.T. *The Resurrection of the Son of God* (Christian Origins and the Question of God: Volume 3), Minneapolis: Fortress Press, 2003.

ABOUT THE AUTHOR

The author is a retired mathematician and information technologist who also is a lifelong Bible scholar. Tom is very happily married to his wife, DeAnne. They have three adult children and two grandchildren. Tom is a combat veteran of the Vietnam War as a United States Marine. He lives in Austin, Texas, and enjoys playing finger-style guitar and clawhammer banjo. Tom regularly teaches classes about the Bible at his Lutheran congregation, where he also sings and plays worship music every week. This is his first novel.